Assignment Sudan

Robert Brightwell

Published in 2024 by FeedARead.com Publishing

A CIP catalogue record for this title is available from the British
Library.

This book is dedicated to the memory of all those largely forgotten souls
whose bleached bones still lie under the rocks of the Bayuda Desert.

MEDITERRANEAN SEA

ALEXANDRIA

CAIRO

SUEZ CANAL

EGYPT

ASYUT

RED SEA

ASWAN

WADI HALFA

SUDAN

SUAKIN

DONGOLA

BAYUDA DESERT

KORTI

BERBER

ABU KLEA

MATAMMEH

KHARTOUM

WHITE NILE

BLUE NILE

The British soldier had not made a sound. One moment he was standing patiently among the ragged lines of the square, the next he was measuring his length on the sand and stones, his rifle and bayonet clattering to the rocks at his side.

"Stretcher bearers!" The sergeant's voice was hoarse through the thirst that we all suffered. I stared down at the bronzed, bearded features. He was barely twenty, half my age, but he would see no more birthdays. Months of toil through the desert, to die in an instant. Perhaps he had felt safer in the rear rank, but the bullet that had killed him had passed between two heads in front. A pair of men doubled forward and took the body away. They could see from the neat hole drilled in the front of his pith helmet that he was beyond the help of the surgeons.

The soldier in front looked over his shoulder at the new gap behind him, which glared out like the missing tooth of a child. He glanced down at the abandoned gun and then pointedly up at me. I knew that everyone else nearby already had a rifle and were in their place. I swore softly. If there was any justice, General Sir Garnet Wolseley should have been standing there to fill the breach. It was his vainglorious stubborn stupidity that had got us into this mess. Instead, the villain was two hundred miles back, probably still writing spiteful entries in his journal. If you leave your diary open when I am in your tent, don't think I will not look, for it tells a lot about a man. *I hear Lieutenant A— is good at cricket*, I had spied. *I am glad he has some talent, for soldiering is not his forte.* The condescending swine. I will not name Lieutenant A—, for he was dead from enteric fever a fortnight later. That foul disease had been the cause of most casualties in the expedition until now, but the beating of distant drums indicated that this situation was about to change.

We might all be dead in a few minutes, I thought, or facing a fate that would make us jealous of that poor rifleman. Some say you can smell fear. If you can, that square must have reeked of it, along with stale sweat and the stink of camels. But by God there was courage too; no one thought of running, not even me. We were so deep into hostile territory that there was no hope of rescue. Our only chance of survival was to use every gun we had. This was no time to wave my press pass. Bennet Burleigh of the *Telegraph* had already taken the place of a soldier further down the line. My guts tightened in dread as I stepped over the new patch of gore on the sandy rocks and bent forward to pick up the abandoned gun. The *Daily News* could also play its part.

I felt quite the martial hero for all of a moment before I realised that I had no spare ammunition. There was a Webley revolver in a holster at my belt, but the spare shells for that were back in my luggage and would not fit the rifle anyway. I turned to find the sergeant standing at my elbow, grinning as though he had been waiting for the thought to occur to me. "I think you will be needing this sir," he spoke quietly holding out a leather bandolier of cartridges, which I gratefully pulled over my shoulder.

To my right, just a quarter of a mile away, was a green oasis, the wells of Abu Klea. We had marched too far across the vast Bayuda Desert now to retreat to Jakdul, where we had last filled the water skins. We *had* to reach these wells to replenish our supplies. Only then could we march on to the Nile. There was just one small obstacle standing between me and the other fifteen hundred men of the desert column getting a drink: ten thousand bloodthirsty, murderous fanatics, intent on chopping us all to pieces.

They were all supporters of the Mahdi, the self-proclaimed prophet who now ruled much of the Sudan. Few had modern firearms as they were considered un-Islamic. Instead, they preferred to arm themselves with spears and swords as though they were still in the crusades. If I were to tell you that we have the latest breech-loading rifles and even a machine gun, you might think I was being unduly nervous. Yet just a year ago these same warriors had defeated an Egyptian army commanded by a British colonel called Hicks. His force had over eight thousand infantry, all armed with modern Remington breach-loading rifles, two thousand cavalry, fourteen artillery pieces and half a dozen Nordenfelt machine guns. I knew the numbers well as they had been accompanied by my friend O'Donovan, another *Daily News* correspondent. The Mahdists had poisoned wells until the soldiers were mad with thirst and then attacked. The Egyptian army had been slaughtered to the last man. Rumour had it that the heads of Hicks, O'Donovan and several others had ended up on pikes outside the Mahdi's tent. Now they were trying to keep us away from the water, although I doubted that they would poison the wells as they needed the precious liquid themselves. We could not wait, we had to advance into their trap. Formed into a defensive square, we edged slowly and cautiously across the desert.

If you are imagining the ruler-straight lines of a regiment of redcoats, you could not be more wrong. The British army had no units trained to fight in deserts and so Wolseley had created one. His Camel Corps was an elite force, taking the best men from over a dozen regiments, to the outrage of their commanding colonels. Only some officers of the Royal Marines sported their red coats; their men, like most of the soldiers, wore khaki. Despite being far from the sea, the Royal Navy, with their dark blue uniforms, was represented too. Yet none looked fresh. Every one of us was bearded, sunburned and covered in dust. Our clothes torn and frayed from a long and arduous journey of over a thousand miles.

As I assumed my place, I took comfort from having another line of sturdy British backs in front of me. My predecessor had been killed by snipers in the rocks to my right. They were evidence of the earlier defeat of Hicks; they were using captured Remington rifles. Yet they would not be there for long, for some of our skirmishers were already flushing them out. They were from the Royal Rifles, picked marksmen all. I watched as a man in white robes emerged from a crevice between two boulders and tried to pull back. He had barely gone a yard before a rifle cracked and he tumbled down. I gave a grunt of satisfaction. It was revenge for the poor devil I had replaced.

The man on my left nudged my arm, "Move along please, sir," he murmured as though we were queuing for a train. He had to speak above the distant thudding of drums in front of us, which was as constant as any locomotive. I realised that the square was edging forward again and so stepped two paces to my right. The front face wanted to stand closer to the top of one of the undulations in the terrain so that they could see more of what might be coming. The rank to my right was ruler straight.

6

I carefully aligned myself as it settled still once more. When I glanced left, I could see that our line wavered in and then out to the rear corner of the square. Those soldiers were from cavalry regiments, not used to fighting with their feet on the ground. The rear face of the square was even more bowed, as several men were hitting the rumps of stubborn camels to get them to join the herd carrying our supplies in its centre. Those animals inside the square were forced to kneel, so that Colonel Stewart, our commander, could see across the formation and to reduce the chance of them being shot.

More men, supplies, camels, the servants and our baggage were all in a camp a mile back where we had spent the previous night. I wondered what would happen to them if we were overrun. The soldiers, wounded or not, would be killed for certain, but what about the others? We had heard that the Mahdi's recruitment policy was rather uncompromising; you either swore your belief in him, or you were beheaded. The women had even less choice – no one cared what they thought. The pretty ones were taken as concubines while the others were used as slaves or killed. I felt a pang of sadness when I thought of Leila. She would not be a compliant concubine and the chances were that she would never discover the fate of her brother.

The continuous drumming put my nerves on edge. I tried to remind myself that I was, albeit reluctantly, in the ranks of a British square. Such formations had famously seen off all that Napoleon could throw at them at Waterloo and emerged victorious. I remembered my grandfather's tales of that day; the French had cavalry, vast batteries of artillery and some of Europe's finest infantry. There would be few guns among the men intent on coming at us and, unlike Wellington's men, we had breach-loading rifles that could get off a dozen accurate shots a minute in expert hands.

My eyes whipped round when I heard a shout to our front. The skirmishers were running back as though their lives depended on it, which they undoubtedly did. It was not hard to see why. Above some dead ground some two hundred yards ahead of us, green and white flags were now fluttering in the breeze, dozens of them. Their leaders had chosen their ground well. On a flat plain our rifles would have slaughtered most of them long before they reached our ranks. Here, however, the terrain was criss-crossed by various dry riverbeds that led down to the wells. They were able to get much closer before we could see them.

Then the chanting began. One of their unseen leaders called out something and voices replied in a full-throated roar. It sounded like the distant gullies were full of men. The air was thick with anticipation. Despite travelling hundreds of miles into their territory, most of us were yet to see a follower of the Mahdi, at least not one who would admit it to us. Now it was certain that this deficiency was about to be addressed. Although I could not understand the distant calls as they rang out again, I knew they were certain to be calling for our destruction. Well, two could play at that game. There was a disturbance to the ranks on my left. The naval brigade was pushing out the carriage of our Gardner machine gun, ready for whatever came out of the riverbeds.

"Front rank, kneel," the sergeant's voice cracked out again. The comforting line of backs in front of me duly dropped, leaving me feeling even more exposed. I hefted my gun nervously and tried to lick my lips, but there was no moisture in my mouth at all.

"When they come," the man to my right shouted over the din, "aim low for their belts," he advised, before adding with a grin, "not that any of the devils will be wearing one." The words were barely out of his mouth before a horn rang out. Then all hell broke loose. The first to appear were their leaders, mounted on horses and carrying their flags of white and green. Hot on their heels was a horde of black men wearing white robes that were unfeasibly clean. They seemed as numerous as grains of sand in the desert. While the line began opposite us, it stretched to my left as far as I could see. I was sure then that we would be overwhelmed and felt my muscles clench in terror. Certainly, our foremost skirmishers were doomed. They were running across the line of the charge and the one furthest away was speared and trampled in seconds.

"Fire!" called out a voice and the initial volley blasted out, with men then hurrying to reload. I was still frozen in shock and belatedly joined the fight, making sure to avoid the last of our retreating skirmishers. The leader opposite me had already been shot from his saddle. I heard the mechanical chatter of the Gardner gun to my left and saw a swathe of men tumble in a group. I aimed for the middle of a man opposite, who was grinning in delight as he waved a blade high above his head. I pulled the trigger, gasped at the brutal recoil into my shoulder and watched my target disappear behind the muzzle smoke. I had no idea if I had hit him; all that mattered now was to fire another bullet as fast as possible.

The man to my right was already raising his Martini–Henry rifle for a second shot as I yanked down on the lever behind the trigger guard, which opened the breach and expelled the shell case. My hand shook slightly as I fumbled a new cartridge the size of my finger from the belt and pushed it into the aperture. I was pulling the lever back into place to close the breach as I raised the gun once more. Christ, they were getting close now. I barely needed to aim, for at this range you could not miss. I fired and hurried through the reloading process again. I remember that the Gardner had stopped firing, but I had no time to look over and see what was happening.

The enemy was barely a hundred yards off now, and full of screaming fury. The front runners were tumbling down from our fire but those behind did not hesitate, bounding towards us like wild animals. My eyes stung from the gun smoke that now enveloped the square, but I picked out a target and fired. I was not as fast as the men about me, yet I had the gun open and reloaded in a few seconds. As I did so I noticed that the brass cartridge was slightly dented, but there was no time to change it. I snapped the lever back and blasted into the throng once more.

They were up to the Gardner gun now. I saw blades rising and falling as they butchered its crew. It felt only a matter of time before that was the fate of us all. My mind was suddenly filled with the memory of O'Donovan. Would my head soon be on a pike too? That image added to my terror as I tugged furiously on the lever of my rifle. The breech opened but the cartridge casing remained stubbornly inside: the thing was jammed.

"Front rank stand!" bellowed a voice. The man in front of me looked nervously over his shoulder as he rose to check that I was not about to blow his head off. He fired once more and then braced himself for the impact of the dervishes with his bayonet.

"Steady men," called the sergeant behind me, sounding as though he was strolling in Hyde Park. Could he not see that we were all about to be hacked to death? Men along my second rank were busy firing over the shoulders of their comrades in front, some jabbing bayonets in support. Throwing my useless rifle to the ground, I grabbed for the Webley. I was just in time. Tugging it out of the holster, I gazed up at a robed fiend brandishing a sword the size of a cleaver. He was swinging it back, ready to decapitate the soldier in front of me. I pointed the revolver and pulled the trigger, watching in disgust as the head was smashed like a ripe melon. The man in front of me flinched as the pistol had gone off just next to his ear, but he still managed to parry a blade and thrust his bayonet into his opponent's chest. Another of the Mahdists tried to step around the falling body I had shot, a spear raised in his arm. I pulled the trigger again and he fell back, a crimson stain on his white robe. I heard the snap of a rifle lock as the man in front hastily tried to reload. To cover him I fired three more times into the throng, almost blindly, watching as they fell back to impede those beyond.

We had bought ourselves a few yards of space. Slowly but steadily the bullets from our stretch of the line outnumbered those running towards it. The British square had done what it was supposed to and stood firm. The soldiers on either side were still firing to drive our enemies back, yet the devils were not retreating. Instead, they were pushing past the now abandoned machine gun, towards the rear of the square. As the men about me blazed away I looked down at the pistol. I only had one shot left; I did not want to waste it. I put it back in my holster and stared about for another abandoned gun, but all were in use. Even the man to my right, who had a spear wound in his arm, was still steadily firing. Just then I saw a soldier further along using the cleaning ramrod to dislodge a jammed cartridge and I hurriedly did the same in my own rifle. Soon the bent brass case was lying at my feet. I quickly reloaded, this time taking more care in inspecting the rounds.

By the time I was ready to fire again, there were no enemies within ten yards of us. The men around me had been firing faster than the

Mahdists could approach and put up a wall of lead to protect us. Those still coming out of the gullies were angling to our left, where the shooting from the cavalry troopers was more sporadic. We aimed some of our fire in that direction to cut them off. A furious fight was underway in the rear corner of the square. Glancing over my shoulder I saw that some of the rear rank of the opposite side were running across to assist. Men who were used to fighting from the saddle were out of their depth when facing an enemy on foot. Their ranks had become even more undulating than they were before.

I was distracted by a soldier to my right calling out in pain. One of the fallen warriors in front of us had found the strength to stab him in the thigh with his spear. The infantryman lunged angrily forward with his long bayonet, ramming it home with such force that the blade was bent against the rocks beneath the body when it was eventually withdrawn. A few other soldiers in the front rank leaned forward to make sure that the injured men before them would cause no further trouble. I thought that there must by now be similar ramparts of the dead in front of the cavalrymen. Soon, like us, they would have the space to drive the enemy away with their guns, especially with us firing into the flank of their foes.

I was just beginning to believe that we might see this day out after all, when I heard someone shouting behind me. For a second I paid no attention until it registered that he was not yelling in English. Whirling around, my jaw gaped open as I stared at a white-bearded Arab astride a brown horse right in the middle of our square. He was holding nothing more lethal than a green and white flag and chanting to the heavens some kind of prayer. His incantation was short-lived as almost as soon as I saw him, he was shot from the saddle. Colonel Stewart and his staff were standing just yards from the man. They were already pulling out their revolvers and blazing away at unseen enemies moving between the camels in our centre. The animals were braying in alarm, some having been hit by stray shots, and many of them lurched up onto their feet. As one rose near me, I dropped to one knee to look underneath its belly. Sure enough, there were white-robed legs moving between the herd. One was barely fifteen paces away. As the man paused behind an animal, I took careful aim and fired. I caught the villain in the calf and the bullet must have smashed the bone, for he tumbled to the ground. I hurriedly brought down the lever on the rifle and reloaded as the Mahdist tried to drag himself away. His eyes met mine as I raised the gun butt to my shoulder again. He emitted a feral snarl as he saw that the muzzle was pointing directly at him, but there was nothing he could do as I pulled the trigger.

How the hell had they got inside? I wondered. It had to be from the rear of the square where the fighting had grown even more furious. With reinforcements rushing to the area and blazing away, the clouds of gun smoke made it impossible to see what was going on. If there was a breach, they were trying to close it, which made it all the more important to kill any enemies inside the square; that was where the greatest danger was now. Men could not defend it if they were being attacked from behind. Clearly the sergeant was of the same view, for I saw him detailing a corporal and five men from the rear rank to move back into the herd behind us. The noise of battle was so loud he had to shout instructions into the man's ear. I did not fancy a spear in the back, so I reloaded my rifle once more and prepared to move cautiously amongst the camels.

"Careful where you shoot," the sergeant yelled, grabbing my arm. "Remember, you are surrounded by British backs and the colonel is in there somewhere."

Accidentally shooting our commander would not do much for my standing in the column, but I had no intention of spearheading our advance. I would let the corporal and his men lead the way. At least that was my intention, but I lost sight of them within moments as they darted amongst the living maze of standing, sitting and fallen camels. There were screams and shouts ahead, sporadic flurries of shots that I hoped meant the incursion was being driven back. Then, an ungodly gurgling groan came from just a few yards away. Crouching around the rump of one creature, I saw another camel ten yards off. Its throat had been cut by a Mahdist, whose bloodstained corpse lay nearby. The dying animal had half sprawled onto the stones, which were drenched in blood still gushing from the wicked gash. On its back, one on each side of the

12

hump, were a pair of stretchers that we used to transport the wounded. The one on my side was angled down and empty. If there had been anyone in it, they must have crawled away. Warily I advanced, poking the Mahdist with the point of my bayonet, but there was no movement. I was just about to go on when I heard someone gasped, "I say, could you help me?"

I whirled back. The voice was faint, but close enough to hear over the sound of battle. At first glance there was no one there at all. Then I noticed a blood-smeared face with sun-bleached hair poking out from behind the haunch of the dead camel. He must have toppled out of the stretcher and then had the animal collapse on top of him.

"Perhaps you could get some men to raise the leg and then pull me out," he suggested calmly, as though it were an everyday occurrence to be sat on by a camel.

"Yes, of course," I assured him, then, raising my voice, "some help here!" I glanced towards the back of the square; there was always a chance that someone other than a British soldier might respond to my call.

"Look out!" the faint voice rasped. I whipped round to find that the Mahdist 'corpse' had staged a remarkable recovery. He was back on his feet. There was no obvious wound to the way he raised his spear for a thrust in my direction. I realised the blood must have come from the camel rather than him. I dimly remembered warnings about them feigning death to get close to unsuspecting enemies. It was too late to worry about that now as I twisted round to bring my own weapon to bear. Then my right heel caught on the outstretched leg of the camel and I felt myself falling backwards. My finger was still in the trigger guard as my backside made contact with the gravel and the resulting jar must have fired the gun. The bullet went high into the air as, with a shout about Allah, my opponent sprang forward for a killing thrust. I could hear nearby soldiers coming to my aid but knew they would never make it. My right hand scrabbled in the holster at my waist. I just got a hand wrapped around the grip of the Webley as my foe stood triumphantly over me. There was no time to withdraw the pistol and so I just twisted the holster up and fired through the bottom of it. An expression of astonishment crossed his face as the slug caught him in the chest, knocking him back. A moment later, the corporal was at my side, finishing him off with a bullet to the head.

I felt nauseous with relief at my close shave, but there was no time to delay. "Please hurry," the wounded man called out. "I don't want to be trapped here if they come back. Also, I think the damned animal has pissed on me."

"He'll shit on you too when his muscles relax in death," smirked the corporal unhelpfully. He and one of his squad picked up the rear hoof and raised it to waist height while I hauled the man out. I was considerably gentler when I saw his wound. He had taken a shot to the stomach and I doubted he would make it.

"How is Bray?" he asked as I got him clear.

"Bray?" I repeated, puzzled.

"The man on the other stretcher," he explained. I went around the camel to look. The poor devil was dead, speared from below up through the canvas, which was dark with blood. As I relayed the grisly news we heard cheering from the rear corner of the square. One of the soldiers climbed up on the dead camel for a better look and announced that the Mahdists were finally pulling back. The whole battle had lasted less than fifteen minutes. I felt my shoulders sag in relief; Wolseley's desert column had survived its first encounter with the enemy, at least for now. Yet there were bound to be more traps and ambushes between here and the Nile. Then, if we made it, our illustrious general expected us to press on to Khartoum.

Christ, I thought, there had to be easier ways to make a living. War correspondents were supposed to sit safely at the rear, writing their reports over brandy and coffee in comfortable cafés. My first campaign had been fought amongst the comforts of France, for heaven's sake. I had no idea how lucky I was back then. Since that time I had been to West Africa, South Africa and now North Africa. They had all been shitholes in comparison, but this was by far the worst. Ironically, though, now I was among far more illustrious company.

When he was able to wipe the blood and muck off his face, I realised we had rescued John Leveson, the fourth Viscount St Vincent. He was

14

a cavalry officer despite being descended from a famous admiral. Despite being a supposedly select band of men, the aristocracy were overly represented. Many had seen this campaign as a splendid adventure, the chance to play their part in rescuing a hero of the age. They had imagined a grand hunt, with the primitively armed Mahdists falling back on our approach. Even if the enemy was foolish enough to face the column, our modern weaponry and well-trained soldiers would surely cut swathes through fanatics armed with only spears. The catastrophic defeats of earlier armies under the command of British officers had been blamed on their inferior Egyptian troops. Perhaps these scions of the nobility did not read the newspapers that their butlers brought with breakfast, for an army of British troops under General Graham had been landed at the Sudanese Red Sea port of Suakin earlier that year. Burleigh and other correspondents had been with them. He had reported in the *Telegraph* that the battles had been brutal affairs. Indeed, a British square had been breached then too.

While those who could be saved were carried to the surgeons and the dying comforted, I made my way to the rear corner, where the fiercest fighting had been. It was here I found many more uniformed bodies amongst the dead, several soldiers openly weeping at their losses. We had no regimental padres with us. One soldier was fervently reading from his Bible over a comrade, who was bleeding his last into the stones about him.

It was then that I came across another member of the aristocracy I knew well. In my childhood I had played cricket with the twelfth Earl of Dundonald as our grandfathers had been close friends. Douglas Cochrane had since become a cavalry captain and baggage master for the column. "Are you wounded?" I asked, noticing his jacket was torn.

He gestured at the ripped cloth, "Heaven knows how that happened but no, not a scratch. My lieutenant was hit. Poor St Vincent looks in a bad way too."

"I know, he just saved me from being skewered on a spear." I gestured to the carnage around us and asked, "Do you know what happened? How on earth did they get inside the square?"

Cochrane hesitated, "This is not to be reported to your paper, do you understand? I will not damage the reputation of brave men." When I nodded, he went on, "I don't believe that there were as many men in the left face of the square as the right. There were the same number of companies, but some of the cavalry were light in numbers. We also have the less accurate Remington rifle." It sounded like he was making excuses for his precious cavalry regiments. Then he continued, "Part of the rear face of the square swung round to support the left face, but they did not realise that there were more Mahdists in a gully opposite who tried to charge into the gap."

"Christ, they deliberately opened the square!" I repeated, astonished. Every soldier knew that maintaining the integrity of the square formation was sacrosanct, not to mention vital to survival. "Who on earth ordered that?"

"When the Gardner gun jammed it was thought the left face needed more support. Burnaby did not start it, but he continued the move." Cochrane must have seen the surprise on my face, for he held up a warning finger, "You are not to mention his name, Harrison. He realised his mistake and tried to put it right. He ordered the men to wheel back into position, while he stayed outside the square to cover them. Three troopers were nearly trapped and he charged into a throng and rescued two of them. But by then he was surrounded; he and his horse were stabbed several times and brought down. His comrades tried to rescue him, but it was too late."

"Don't worry, I will not mention the name." Besides, I thought, the cavalry officers in the column would close ranks and deny the story if I did. Burnaby was a great hero to them, a giant of a man in every sense. He had fought the Mahdists as a volunteer the previous year in the Red Sea expeditions. General Valentine Baker's wife had asked him to go to help her husband. With no official role, he went to war wearing Norfolk tweeds and armed with a shotgun. Yet while two thirds of Baker's Egyptian force had been massacred by Mahdists, Burnaby had survived. He had saved his groom from certain death and helped Baker withdraw too.

There was no time to discuss things further, for bugles were calling for the survivors of the battle to reform the square. Men had fallen out from their lines and with all the hidden gullies around us we were vulnerable should the Mahdists decide to return. I resumed my place in the ranks, while weary cavalry scouts on horseback began to slowly advance to find the wells and ensure that the enemy had really left.

We stood there for several hours as the morning sun rose high in the sky. With no shade, it was like standing in a furnace. Men shook water bottles that they knew were empty or held them upside down over their tongues for a final droplet. The distant oasis stood like a mirage before us, but however maddening our thirst, no one broke to run in its direction. We could see our scouts advancing through the tall grass and scrub to ensure that no more traps awaited us. To keep the soldiers occupied while we waited, efforts began to bury the dead. Deep graves were impossible – there was no soil, just rock and stone. The fallen were laid alone or in groups near where they fell. Their comrades helped to pile stones over them while others were granted leave to break from the ranks in small groups to pay their respects. Hoarse dry throats rasped their way through a hymn, while officers tried to recall the burial service that they must have heard dozens of times before. Out on the plain we heard cries and prayers coming from the wounded Mahdists, but few paid them any attention. The ones nearest the square had already been put out of their misery before they could do any mischief. The soldier who had been stabbed in the leg by an injured Mahdist swore that he would rather walk across a nest of vipers than go near more of their wounded. "They have to kill an infidel like us to go to their paradise," he stated firmly. "That is why, when they are dying, they are even more desperate to kill. You try offering them help and you would be dead for certain."

An exception was made for a boy of around ten who was spotted amongst a cluster of dead just beyond the square. He had been wailing in fear and pain from a bullet wound to his hip. Yet when someone tried to offer help, he lunged at them with his small spear. In the end he was disarmed and his hands tied before he was loaded on a stretcher and taken to a medic. Offered water, he spat it back and then tried to lunge for one of the surgical instruments. The surgeon thought there was little hope, but still he was tied firmly to his stretcher and bandaged.

It was well past noon when the square finally began to move once more. By then everyone was desperate for fresh water, not least the wounded, who were carried with us on camels or stretchers. A few others suffering from heatstroke were helped along by their comrades. I had feared the enemy might put up another fight around the wells or poison them in some way. Instead, our horsemen reported that they had pulled back across the desert. I was not the only one to mutter a small prayer of thanks for that. Grass huts around the springs showed that our ambushers had been resting and drinking there for a while waiting for us to arrive. They would have plenty of water with them. Our waterskins were now bone dry. No man or beast stood a chance of reaching the Nile without this precious liquid.

Perhaps they did not poison the wells as they knew that there was not much water left. The springs were in narrow clefts that you could not see until you were virtually on top of them. The water they contained was a muddy yellow. If you think that sounds unpleasant then you have not tasted or smelt the rancid filth in the bottom of my waterskin I had finished at dawn. Unlike our previous watering place, where men had bickered and argued over their place in the queues, this time soldiers stood quietly, watering in turn by company. Even those wracked with thirst were just grateful to still be alive. They could afford to wait as their mind dwelt on those comrades less fortunate. It would take only two night marches to reach the Nile from the wells, where we would find limitless water. When roll calls were done, we discovered that we had lost seventy-four men dead and ninety-four wounded, with many of those, like St Vincent, destined to travel no further.

Sentries were posted around the wells but there was no sign of the Mahdists. Colonel Stewart was worried that they would try again to stop us reaching the Nile, so wanted us to press on as soon as we could. Cochrane was concerned that they might attack our supply detachment that was now four miles back in the desert and lightly protected. They would need water too, while the soldiers required food rations and replacement ammunition. So, as soon as darkness fell, my old friend led a column of volunteers back to bring our supplies forward. As Leila was back there too, I joined him.

Chapter 2

Even after several months in Egypt, it never ceased to amaze me how cold the desert got at night. It was not actually freezing, but after the relentless heat of the day, it certainly felt like it. My coat was back in the supply column we were approaching and I was shivered as we made our way cautiously over the rocky terrain. Approaching from the wells, we passed around to the left of where the square had stood. There had been little fighting on that side and so less chance of encountering a Mahdist seeking paradise. The sky was clear and the moon and stars gave us enough light to see, but still, it was an eerie place at night. Rocks and the newly built graves threw out strange shadows and more than once I could have sworn that they moved.

There were cheers and shouts of greeting when we finally reached the supply column. Having heard the battle, they had sent forward a scouting patrol of their own to see that our square still stood and we had been victorious. Leila was one of the first to jump across the low rock wall that we had built to protect ourselves from snipers just over a day ago.

"Allah be praised, you have survived!" she gasped as she threw her arms about me and kissed me on the lips.

"I still can't believe that you have brought a woman on campaign," muttered Cochrane, shaking his head in dismay.

"General Wolseley made it very clear that the army would not support correspondents and that we would have to bring anything we needed ourselves," I replied. Grinning, I lowered my hand to squeeze her rump, causing her to gasp in surprise. "I am simply obeying orders," I added, "like any good soldier."

"But do you not care about the danger you put her in?"

"I insisted he bring me." Leila could speak for herself. "I have my own reasons for coming. How many of your men have travelled this way before? None," she answered her own question. "I have done it several times with my father. I am more useful than any man here," she gestured back at the other Arab servants now loading the camels.

"It is true," I agreed. "Without Leila I would probably have got lost in the desert and disappeared like the poor chap from the *Manchester Guardian*."

"I did not realise that you had come all this way before," said Cochrane, who was now more interested. "We will take you back to the wells tonight so you can rest up during the day. Then tomorrow night, the colonel wants to march to the Nile. Can we reach the river in one night?"

"No," replied Leila. "It will take a whole day, or two nights if you want to rest during the day."

Cochrane looked disappointed. "But I have measured the distance on my map. It is only twenty-four miles. I know the camels are tired, but surely most could cover that distance after they have been watered? It is vital that we reach the river before the Mahdists have time to gather reinforcements and block our route."

Leila smiled and spoke softly. "Does your map also show you the desert grass and the acacia trees? The camels will have been watered, but they will still be tired. The food we have carried for them has barely kept them going. They have not eaten well for weeks. If you think that they will travel through the thick grass that grows nearer the river without stopping, then you do not know camels. They will want to graze for at least an hour to fill their bellies. Then you will find a thick acacia forest in your path. The thorns are long and sharp – not something you want to encounter in the dark. Men and animals will need to spread out to find paths through the trees that will not scratch them to ribbons. If it is still night, many will get lost and then you will have to regather your army on the other side. It would be better to travel through the forest in daylight."

Cochrane nodded in understanding, but it was clearly not news he welcomed. The Nile suddenly felt a lot further away than we had first thought. While he went off to organise the rest of the supply train, I went in search of my camels. I found one dead and another wounded. It had been struck in the hump by a bullet when we had first arrived. Leila had put a salve over the wound; it had barely noticed the injury and certainly not taken much harm from it. More than fifty of the column's camels had been killed or were too badly injured to continue the journey. Piles of supplies were being prioritised for the remaining animals, the rest we would have to leave behind.

We waited until first light to make our way back to the wells. I badly needed a rest as did the men who had returned with me. We huddled under blankets in what felt like one of the coldest desert nights. At dawn I joined Leila and her servant Rafa in loading up our remaining beasts, grateful for the first rays of the morning sun to ease the chill. Soon we were saddled up and making our way back across the desert. When I had first ridden a camel, I had hated it. The lurching motion had made me nauseous. You also sat damned high above the rocky ground. A fall could be a bone-breaking experience, as a number of the newly formed Camel Corps discovered to their cost. Yet now I found the movement strangely comforting. The animal's soft feet made little noise on the gravel and rocks, and we moved almost silently through the early morning. I had only napped a little during the night and was soon dozing in the saddle. Leila rode beside me leading one of the baggage camels while Rafa followed behind with the second.

A group of soldiers rode ahead of us. I distinctly remember two of them comparing the Christian and Muslim heavens and finding their own decidedly wanting.

"I don't want us running into more of them black devils," declared one squinting into the dawn light. "They were bloody mad bastards, they kept coming at us even when they did not stand a chance."

"Aye, but they are not as bad as the Fuzzie-Wuzzies by the Red Sea," his mate replied. "I heard that they would half bury themselves in sand and rock, so you cannot see 'em until you are virtually standing on top of 'em. One minute the desert is empty and the next it is full of sword-wielding Fuzzies chargin' in on you. Brave as bleedin' lions they are. They don't stop until one of you is dead."

"According to Lieutenant Graham, this Mahdi has told his men that our bullets cannot touch them, but surely they have seen the lie of that now."

"They don't care about our bullets," the second soldier replied confidently. "They want to get to their Muslim paradise, which is all they care about. They kill one of us and they are guaranteed to get in."

"Well, they are bloody keen to see the angels," said the first man.

"Angels be damned. They get six bints apiece to pleasure them for eternity. One for every workday and Sundays off."

"Get away! How many bints do *we* get in heaven then? I have never heard the padre talk about that. All he prattles on about is what will send you to hell."

"They are never specific," replied his mate, "which probably means that officers get more."

They rode in silence for a while as they imagined heavenly delights, or perhaps considered religious conversion. Then the first soldier continued, "I wonder if they would be like those girls at the Cairo brothel. I liked them, I want some of those in heaven. Apart from the fat one that Jarvis had. She can go to the Fuzzie paradise."

It was past eight when we returned to the oasis. The wounded we had brought with us joined those from the battle in an improvised sick bay near the wells. They would stay there under a small guard while we marched on that evening. Once he knew that the wells and route to the river had been secured, it was expected that Wolseley would stir his rump and bring reinforcements.

Despite the information that Cochrane gave him about the journey ahead, Colonel Stewart decided to try and press on for the Nile that night. We had waited too long at the previous wells, he reasoned, which gave the Mahdists time to gather at Abu Klea, knowing we had to come that way. The enemy would know that we must now be heading for the river and he did not want to make the same mistake again. Stewart told me that he was sending a courier back the way we had come to update Wolseley on our progress. Along with the other correspondents, I was invited to send back a despatch. There was a telegraph line at Korti where Wolseley had his headquarters and so news would be in the London papers within a day of our reports arriving. I hurriedly sat down to write an account of the battle and our journey so far. As I had promised, I mentioned nothing of Burnaby's part in the breach, only his courageous demise. Neither did I describe how men had been wounded – there was a surprisingly high number of bullet holes for men fighting opponents armed with swords and spears. With men firing across the square, others panicked and confused, quite a few of our men had been shot by their own side. Some of our Egyptian camel drivers had also been killed, having been mistaken as Mahdists. But readers did not want to hear about that. They wanted to know that the army was gallantly advancing against its foe. The report was stirring stuff that I knew would be on the front page, for the country was obsessed with the progress of this campaign.

Once I had filed my story, Leila and I walked back to the site of the battle. There were more funerals underway for those who had succumbed to their wounds that first night, including St Vincent. The position of the square could easily be determined by the tide mark of bodies of the men that had died attacking its rear and left faces. Without the camels the centre looked vast, though the space now being filled with mounds of burial stones. As I circled warily around a cluster of white-robed bodies that had been left where they fell, I remembered the conversation of the two soldiers the night before. "They fought like furies yesterday," I admitted, "with no thought for their survival. Is it true that they believe they will go to paradise with six girls to pleasure them if they kill one of us?"

Leila laughed, "Not those men. They are Kordofanis from their province in the south. Fighting and courage is in their blood. Sometimes the young warriors will hunt lions on their own to prove their manhood. I think some of them have their own religions. They are certainly not fighting to earn six virgins for eternity."

"What about these Fuzzy-Wuzzies I have heard about near the Red Sea?" I pressed.

"They are the Beja people. They do not believe in cutting their hair, which is why it looks so wild. They have been fighting off invaders since the time of the pharaohs. Egyptians, Greeks, Romans, Turks and now you British, all have come to their lands, but none have managed to stay. They are not particularly religious either."

"So why the hell are they all fighting for the Mahdi, who wants everyone to live according to strict Islamic law?"

"He promised them freedom from Egyptian rule and their tax collectors," Leila replied. "But if he wants them to continue fighting for him, he would be a fool to try and impose his laws instead."

I found St Vincent's grave and laid a stone on the top. It was the least I could do after he had saved my life. The old square was more like a quarry now, with over a hundred men industriously piling rock. Burnaby's grave was the tallest. Virtually every cavalry trooper and most other officers had made a contribution to what now resembled a cairn of stones, which, I could not help but think, must have crushed his remains underneath. To one side, I noticed a smaller pile for the young warrior boy who had succumbed to his injury. He might not have impressed with his gratitude or manners, but none could doubt his courage.

As I passed the space I had fought from, my old sergeant stood over a mound for several men, including the one I had replaced in the ranks. He had been utterly implacable as warriors had screamed for our deaths and tried to hack us to pieces. His unwavering calm and confidence in what we were doing had given me the courage to stay in that line, as I am sure it did the others. Yet now as he looked up and saw me, his voice cracked slightly with emotion as he gestured across the square and asked, "Is it all worth it, sir, just to rescue one man?"

I shook my head, the poor souls now entombed undoubtedly deserved better, especially from their leaders. This whole affair had been mismanaged and misunderstood from the very start. "Prime Minister Gladstone would undoubtedly say it was not," I told him wearily. "Especially as the man in question does not want to be rescued."

"But we are the Gordon Relief Expedition!" cried the sergeant with indignation. "What the bloody hell have these men died for if he does not want to be rescued? Anyway, everyone knows that General Gordon has been trapped in Khartoum for nearly a year."

"We are here because the British public demanded that their hero be rescued," I reminded him. "People have been writing to the papers, to

25

their members of parliament, and marching in the streets ever since he was encircled there last March. Gladstone believes that he could have got out on a steamer or in disguise whenever he wanted, but he hasn't. He refuses to abandon the Egyptians and Sudanese who are trapped in Khartoum that he was sent to evacuate." I shrugged and added what most of the correspondents had been sure of for months. "We are really here to smash the Mahdists and save everyone in Khartoum."

The sergeant's back straightened as he considered this. Evidently, the lives of the population of an entire city were a fairer exchange for the lives we had lost than just one man, however extraordinary, but only just. "Well, they had better be worth it," he grumbled before moving off.

"Did you see Gordon Pasha when he was in London?" asked Leila.

"I did, in fact I met him a couple of times, the last one when he was travelling back here," I replied.

"What is he really like? They say in Cairo that he can see into the future."

I paused; how did one even begin to describe 'Chinese Gordon'? The first time I saw him around four years before, I thought he was cracked in the head, for anyone less like a military man was hard to imagine. He was giving a lecture in a church hall organised by a missionary society about his seven years in Sudan, first as the governor of Kordofan province and then governor general of the whole country. He stood before his audience in a dark suit and spoke to them with the passion of an evangelist preacher rather than a general or diplomat. He had the piercing light blue eyes that you normally only see in an infant. They blazed down on his audience, causing more than a few ladies' fans to flutter. On other occasions he would pause his oration and gaze skywards as though seeking divine inspiration. Indeed, throughout his lecture, he gave the impression that he had taken his orders from a far higher authority than either the Egyptian monarch, called the Khedive, or the British foreign office.

Having served with distinction in the British army during the Crimean War, Gordon had earned his 'Chinese' sobriquet by leading the 'Ever Victorious Army'. This force had been established to protect the commercial district including Shanghai from Taiping rebels then ravaging through China. With Gordon leading from the front, usually armed only with a cane, his force lived up to its presumptive title, with over thirty consecutive victories. One of the reasons for its success was Gordon's insistence on taking prisoners. Other Imperial Chinese commanders routinely beheaded everyone they found, including the families of the rebels, giving the Taiping every incentive to fight to the death. At the end of his service in China Gordon declined financial remuneration from both the emperor and Shanghai merchants. He estimated that he had saved the lives of nearly two hundred thousand prisoners and soldiers, claiming that was compensation enough.

His many military triumphs, as well as his decline of reward with such noble sentiments, was widely reported in the British press, spreading his fame throughout the nation. It was rumoured that our widowed queen's heart would beat a little faster at the mention of his name. She had declared him a fine example of an officer and approved his knighthood. Later she was to be equally strident in demanding his rescue.

But Gordon was not in that church hall to talk about his time in China. That was old news. What his audience wanted to hear was how he had achieved the Christian imperative of stopping slavery in Sudan. He described how when he had first arrived in the country, he found corruption and bribery endemic. The Turks and Egyptians ruled through bands of cavalry called *bashi-bazouks*. They brutally quelled any resistance and collected taxes, although little of what they raised found its way to Cairo. Instead, they took whatever they wanted, including women, from the towns they controlled and lived like feudal overlords. To the old Khedive's astonishment, Gordon had turned down most of his governor's salary as it was more than he needed. Unlike every other official in the country he was not there to be bought.

The largest slaver and warlord was a man called Zubaya, who had most officials in his pocket, including the governor general. Gordon explained that as a provincial governor most of his efforts to stop the slave trade had been undermined. Then he turned to the audience and gave them a prayer of thanks. Calling down on the Almighty to show his gratitude, he told those Bible-grasping old biddies that they had made the difference and helped him in his work. There was great piping of eyes and cries of hallelujah at this. Gordon looked even more an evangelist as he pounded on his lectern. Pressure from Britain to do more to stop slavery, he told them, had forced the Khedive to replace the venal governor general with Gordon himself. Finally given a free hand, he took to his task with a God-given zeal. Zubaya was driven out of the country and into exile in Egypt. When his son rose in revolt, he was captured by one of Gordon's lieutenants and executed. Before long, this new governor general had outlawed slavery across the country. Solemnly he thanked his audience on behalf of the thousands of souls that were no longer in bondage.

He did not stop there. He announced that God had guided him too as he banned public floggings and the taking of bribes and curbed the worst excesses of the *bashi-bazouks*. The Sudanese people, he concluded, were honourable, decent folk who had been much oppressed and deserved better from their masters. His audience lapped it up, one woman even affecting to swoon as he signed a pamphlet for her. If she was hoping that those sparkling blue eyes would be gazing into hers when she batted them open, she was destined to be disappointed. Gordon was a confirmed bachelor, the temptations of the flesh apparently beneath him.

Perhaps I had been a cynical newspaper man for too long, for I smelt bunkum. If Gordon really was turning the Sudan into a peaceful paradise, then what the hell was he doing here in Blighty instead of continuing his work where he was needed? Looking around the room, beyond the cheering Bible-thumpers, I spotted a dark-skinned cove leaning against the wall with a wry grin on his face. He had arrived with our speaker. His red fez gave his light linen suit an oriental flair. I made my way over to him, "Is all that true?" I asked, gesturing over my shoulder back at the stage.

"It was true wherever Gordon Pasha was," he replied. For a moment I was impressed and then I thought about those words again.

"So what happened when Gordon was *not* there?" I pressed.

The grin widened, "A leopard does not change its spots. Whenever the governor general moved on or turned his back, his officials would look to fill their pockets again. Gordon Pasha was the Sisyphus of the Sudan, which was why he left."

I nodded as though this made sense, when in fact I had no idea who the hell this Sisyphus was. My uncle enlightened me when I returned to the newspaper offices. Sisyphus was an ancient Greek condemned for eternity to push a large rock up a hill, then watch it roll back down before he started again. Gordon, it seemed, had become exhausted fighting corruption.

That meeting in the church hall had happened before a minor holy man called Mohammed Ahmad had been proclaimed an Islamic prophet called the Mahdi. While not mentioned in the Quran, it was believed that the Mahdi would rid the world of evil and lead Muslims to rule the world. Yet this prophet had a very strict idea of what constituted a Muslim. The Turco–Egyptian government of the Sudan and its soldiers might call themselves Muslims, but according to the Mahdi they were all apostates. They had taken up far too many ways of the infidel such as trains and irrigation canals. Such heresy was deserving only of death. At first few people took him seriously, but slowly his followers grew. Alliances were built with the warlike Beja and Bagara tribes and the first towns were captured. That was when the Egyptian government decided to put down the rebellion once and for all. To do this they despatched the doomed army commanded by Colonel Hicks. Their massacre in November 1883 had made everyone notice the Mahdi, even in London.

Egypt was officially part of the Ottoman Empire, ruled from Constantinople. The Khedive was appointed by the Ottoman Sultan, but Britain and France also had a strong interest in the country. The previous Khedive had borrowed a fortune from British and French banks to build the Suez Canal, thousands of miles of irrigation channels as well as, roads, railways and telegraph cables to modernise his country. Eventually his credit ran out and his son now ruled the country on a much tighter financial budget. British officers also commanded much of the Egyptian army. With Hicks' defeat, there were calls in parliament for this British officer's death to be avenged. The contagion of the

Mahdi's religious fanaticism would spread to Egypt, it was claimed, risking investments there. Concerns were expressed that the Suez Canal, which had greatly shortened journey times to India and beyond, could also be affected. Gladstone was not swayed. He had resented having to pay for British troops stationed in Egypt and he was damned if he was going to pay for a campaign to Sudan. Britain had no interest in the desolate place, and he would not risk more British blood quelling a revolt there.

The Egyptian army's attempt at putting down the Mahdi had failed catastrophically and the Ottoman Empire showed no interest in helping either. The Khedive would just have to give up the territory. The only fly in the ointment of this plan was the fate of the Egyptians and Europeans then in Khartoum, including a journalist for the *Times*, called Frank Power. They could not be abandoned to be slaughtered by these fanatics. Some effort would have to be made at their rescue. If the British government would not send an army, it did not take the British public too long to alight on the name of one man who they thought could get the job done.

Given they had a man trapped in Khartoum, perhaps it was no coincidence that the first call for Gordon's involvement came from the *Times*. It was followed by an interview with him printed in the *Pall Mall Gazette*. Gordon was just back from a tour of the Holy Land and about to leave for the Belgian Congo to eliminate slavery there. The *Daily News* supported the liberal government and my uncle had excellent connections at 10 Downing Street. We learned that Gladstone viewed Gordon as a loose cannon who would be hard to control. Yet he could not be seen to simply abandon the people in Khartoum to be slaughtered. With even the queen pressing for Gordon to be sent south, Gladstone reluctantly agreed. It was far better to risk one man than an army and Gordon was known to command great respect in the region. Perhaps he could persuade the Mahdi to hold off his advance while the Egyptians withdrew.

On the 15th of January 1884 Gordon was seen entering the War Office in the company of his friend Garnet Wolseley, Britain's senior general. Gladstone had specified that if the appointment was to proceed, Gordon must understand that their ultimate goal was the abandonment of Sudan. Four members of the cabinet briefed Gordon on his commission, which was initially to report on how the garrisons could be evacuated. Further instructions would then be issued by the government. The ministers reported to Gladstone that Gordon was keen to proceed on that basis.

I found the news from the ministers surprising as just nine days earlier in his *Pall Mall Gazette* interview, Gordon had deplored the idea of evacuating the Sudan. There were also reports in some papers that he had turned down the commission and was still proceeding to the Belgian Congo. I was just leaving the office at the end of the day when my uncle received a note from a government clerk. It advised that not only was Gordon definitely heading to Egypt, but that he was leaving that very evening. A few words from the man of the hour would make a fine headline for the morning edition. I hurriedly grabbed my coat, together with my copy of his recent interview, and headed to Charing Cross railway station.

I thought I might have missed him as one train to Folkestone and the ferry for France had already left that evening. Yet as I strolled along the platforms, I soon discovered that I was in time. The station was full of bustling clerks rushing for their trains home, yet standing by a first-class carriage was a curious group quietly chatting between two watchful detectives. The first was Granville, the Foreign Secretary, who had been one of the ministers to appoint Gordon that afternoon. To his left was Wolseley, while on his other side was the Duke of Cambridge, cousin to the queen and Commander in Chief of the army. It was well known that Cambridge and Wolseley detested each other, but they had buried their differences that evening to see off the two travellers who stood opposite them: Gordon and a man I did not know. I watched as Granville handed over train tickets and then the Commander in Chief held open the carriage door as the men boarded. As they called their farewells and the station master blew his whistle, I only just had time to scramble into another carriage further along the train.

I waited five minutes for the locomotive to pick up speed and start to carry us out to the suburbs before I made my move. As I wandered down the corridor, I was relieved to see that Gordon and his companion had not lowered the blinds of their compartment. I could make out their faces from the dim oil lamps and Gordon looked up at what must have been to him a shadowy figure in the passage. I feigned surprise and recognition, even if he could not see my features, and slid open the door.

"Excuse me, it is General Gordon, is it not, sir?" I beamed in delight at the encounter and rummaged inside my coat pocket. "I have been to one of your lectures. I wonder if you would do me the great honour of signing this interview you gave recently." I held out my copy of the *Pall Mall Gazette*. Now that they were on official government business, I had decided that a more oblique approach might be more fruitful than revealing my real identity. The companion glared at me suspiciously, clearly resenting my impertinence in interrupting them, but Gordon smiled amiably and took the paper. Encouraged, I tentatively took a seat opposite them. "Are you going to smash those Mahdist devils, sir, and bring our people home?" I asked.

"Our people?" Gordon queries. "There aren't many of those in Khartoum." Then those blue eyes bore into mine and the lips turned up into a knowing grin. As his gaze takes in my coat, I swear he can see the notepad hidden in the inside pocket. "John, what kind of man would be travelling to Folkstone at this ungodly hour with a copy of my interview?"

His companion's expression turns even sterner. I noticed his hand slip inside his jacket, where perhaps he kept a weapon. Gordon sees the move too and gestures with his palm down to show there is no danger. "Don't worry, our friend here is not after your bag of sovereigns." He turned back to me, "What paper do you work for Mr…?"

"Thomas Harrison, from the *Daily News*, sir," I admitted, returning his smile. Having been rumbled, I thought I might as well ask a question. I was not supposed to know what he had agreed to with government ministers and so instead I probed. "Do you think you can get the Egyptians out of Sudan, General? In holding back the Mahdi, the government seems to expect that you can succeed where an army has failed."

"Well, Mr Harrison, we will do God's work as best as we can." As he spoke, Gordon took a pencil from his pocket and wrote in the margin of the article. "I trust you will write favourably of our endeavours in your paper, sir," he continued as he handed the newspaper back. "Now if you will excuse us, it is late. John and I would like to sleep a little before we reach the coast."

I left them then, wishing them both well. When I got back to my own compartment, I held the newspaper up to the lamp to read the inscription. *To Thomas Harrison, Proverbs, chapter 19 verse 21, Charles Gordon.*

Not being a Bible scholar, the reference meant nothing to me. I had to wait until we reached Folkestone to understand it in full. Having watched Gordon and his companion stride away from the station to the ferry docks with a well-laden porter following in their wake, I went in search of a Bible. The first church I found was locked, but then I came across a seaman's mission, with a Bible on a lectern in the refectory. Impatiently, I leafed through the pages until I found Proverbs, chapter 19, verse 21, to read, *Many are the plans in a person's heart, but it is the Lord's purpose that prevails.*

What the devil did that mean? I wondered. I was beginning to have a strong inkling that Gordon would 'divine' his own purpose. I very much doubted it would be in accordance with the wishes of Her Majesty's Government.

Chapter 3

There are two routes to Khartoum; one involved a journey of some one
thousand five hundred miles from Cairo, along the twisting Nile and
over several stretches of rocky rapids, or cataracts. The other was much
quicker, by ship through the Suez Canal to the port of Suakin on the Red
Sea. From there it was a journey overland of just two hundred and sixty
miles to the town of Berber on the Nile. A steamer would then take you
the final two hundred and fifty miles upriver to the Sudanese capital.
There was, however, a catch to this shorter route: water supplies along
the desert stretch were few and far between. Some wells would only
have enough water for a few hundred men and animals and there were
two stretches of over fifty miles with no water at all. General Hicks had
used the Red Sea route to reach Khartoum, travelling with four hundred
and fifty soldiers. It could be done, but not with many more men as some
wells took time to refill from the rock around them.

Gordon had planned to use the Suakin route, but news came that the
Beja were already besieging Egyptian garrisons along it. Instead, he
travelled on to Cairo. Britain's newest envoy had hoped to avoid
meeting the Khedive, having referred to him as 'a little snake' in his
Pall Mall Gazette interview, but protocol demanded that he be presented
at the Ismailia Palace. Gordon apologised for his earlier indiscretion and
the Khedive was more than forgiving. He announced that in addition to
his Egyptian garrison in Khartoum, some ten to fifteen thousand of its
citizens were anxious to leave the city and escape the clutches of the
Mahdi. Then the wily Khedive played his trump card: he presented new
letters of appointment, which Gordon accepted. Gladstone must have
choked on his breakfast toast the next morning as he read through the
overnight telegrams. The man he had sent strictly to observe and report
back on Khartoum, was now once more governor general of the whole
of the Sudan.

The prime minister, for all his caution, had been outplayed. He raged
and fumed, undoubtedly calling Gordon far worse names than Gordon
had levelled at the Khedive. While Gladstone still insisted that Britain
would not be drawn into the conflict in the Sudan, events were spiralling

out of his control. As Gordon headed down the Nile in a steamer, Valentine Baker's force, with Burnaby, was landing at the Red Sea port of Suakin. Days later came news of their disastrous encounter with the Beja. Two-thirds of Baker's 3,200 men were killed, including six Englishmen. They had been defeated by an enemy less than half their number.

There was an outcry in the press, in parliament and on the streets generally. Twice now forces commanded by British officers had not just been defeated, but utterly humiliated. Even liberal-leaning papers such as the *Daily News* were demanding action. The reputation of British military power was being damaged; soon every disgruntled jackanape armed with a sharpened stick would think they could see us off. These rebels needed to be taught a lesson with reliable British troops who would show them how we really fight. Gladstone was faced with doing the one thing he had wanted to avoid from the outset: sending the British army to the Sudan.

A naval squadron protected the port of Suakin, while a force of nearly four thousand men was gathered from garrisons in Egypt and India and delivered to the port within an impressive three weeks. Now, the press confidently claimed, these Fuzzy-Wuzzies would feel the true might of the British army. Many boasted that the enemy would melt away into the desert at the sight of such a force, but to the contrary, some six to eight thousand Beja gathered around the wells at El Teb. The resulting battles over the following two weeks were brutal, hard-fought affairs that cost the British around two hundred dead and a similar number of wounded. Beja casualties were vastly higher, however, and eventually they were forced to withdraw from the coast.

Having restored honour to British arms, Gladstone withdrew this force as soon as he could. Some suggested sending the cavalry along the route to Berber and then Khartoum to support Gordon, but he would not hear of it. Memories of Hick's force being cut off from wells was still fresh in his mind. He was determined that the Sudan would be abandoned and by then was already arguing with Gordon over precisely how that would be done.

General Gordon had arrived in Khartoum on the 18th of February 1884. The *Times* carried a description of the vast cheering crowd that greeted him. Over a thousand surrounded the governor general as he slowly made his way to the palace. Women even held their children up for him to touch as they believed he had curing powers. Certainly, all were convinced that his arrival would forestall the depredations of the Mahdi and his supporters.

My uncle threw the copy of our rival paper back on his desk and looked pointedly at me. "We should have a man in Khartoum as well," he declared. "That is where this drama will be played out. The public is becoming obsessed with what is happening in the Sudan. We cannot let the *Times* dominate the telegraph wire from the city."

"Well, you can forget about sending me," I told him firmly. "Our man with Baker only just escaped with his life and you surely have not forgotten the fate of O'Donovan with Hicks. No one has any idea how many people Gordon will get out, or even if he will escape himself."

Over the next few days, much to my uncle's annoyance, the *Times* carried more reports on Gordon's activities. The old Khartoum tax records were burned as were the stocks and whips used for punishment by the *bashi-bazouks*. All prisoners except murderers were released and the city gates were opened during the day, both to allow citizens to travel freely and villagers from nearby settlements to sell their produce in the city. London then received a report that there was enough food in the government stores to feed the city for six months. That time period was significant as Gordon had ten Nile steamers available as well as a hundred and twenty local sailing barges called nuggars. Each steamer could tow two nuggars at a time. Gordon calculated that it would take six months to convey everyone who wanted to leave Khartoum the three hundred and fifty miles north to Abu Hamed, where the Nile turned south again. From there they could be transported to safety in Egypt. That, of course, assumed that the Mahdi would simply sit back and allow them to leave, which seemed unlikely.

The first steamers had already been sent, containing wounded soldiers, wives and widows, but Gordon knew that if he or the Egyptian soldiers that he was there to evacuate left, there would be unrest in the city. Fearful citizens knew that the Mahdists had raped, murdered and tortured the populace of other towns that had resisted them. It was then that we heard from our government sources that Gordon had made an extraordinary proposal.

Before he could leave, he insisted, a replacement governor general must be appointed to give the populace confidence in their safety. It must be another man well known in the region who the local chieftains would trust and respect. Someone who could hold them together to resist the Mahdi. There was, he judged, only one man suitable: Zubaya, the former slaver and warlord that he had previously thrown out of the country. The choice, he insisted, was a simple one: it was either the Mahdi or Zubaya. Neither were ideal, but Zubaya was unlikely to start a religious war which could spread into Egypt.

Cabinet members debated and argued over the issue for days. They knew that there would be outrage among many of their supporters if this notorious slaver was released and delivered back into the Sudan to continue his wicked trade. In the end they refused the request. Gordon replied that he had a duty of honour to stay in Khartoum to protect those he had come to help. He also warned that the Mahdists were moving up from the south. Once they surrounded the city he would have to curtail his evacuation efforts. A few days later the telegraph line was cut.

All papers reported that Gordon was now trapped in Khartoum, several adding that a *Times* correspondent was among the besieged – and to my uncle's satisfaction, unable to cable London. Their only means of communication now was by steamer. The vessels had to run the gauntlet of Remington rifle fire from both banks of the river.

Whipped up by the Tory papers, people demanded to know what Gladstone was doing to rescue this great hero of our age, who had only gone to the Sudan at the government's request. The opposition thought that the answer was obvious: a British army must be sent to Khartoum to rescue all those who wanted to leave. General Wolseley even let it be known that he was working on such a plan, which did not go down well with Gladstone.

The prime minister felt he had been played. Gordon had never been interested in abandoning the Sudan to the Mahdi; his *Pall Mall* interview proved that. He had lied to get the position and then done what he thought was right all along. One man was trying to manipulate the head of the elected British government and force it into a course of action that Gladstone had been determined to avoid from the outset.

Our spies in government told us that the prime minister fumed and raged about Gordon. He would not risk thousands of British lives to save one. Nor did he want the treasury to bear the cost of another campaign or administering some godforsaken desolate territory that was of no use to anyone. He would do nothing and eventually Gordon would either be forced to escape in one of his own steamers, or the fool could perish from his own folly.

Gordon had been cut off in March, the same month that General Graham sailed away from Suakin. The new governor general was then very much on his own in Sudan. If Wolseley had anticipated a campaign to rescue his friend, he had probably assumed it would take place in the summer months, when the waters of the Nile are at their highest and most navigable, especially on the Berber to Khartoum stretch, which could get dangerously low in the winter. If those were his expectations, though, then he was set to be disappointed. April and May passed without any hint that Gladstone was relenting. Then in June came news that Berber, some two hundred and fifty miles downstream, to the north of Khartoum, had fallen to the Mahdi. This made any approach from Suakin near impossible, as troops could only arrive a few hundred at a time. Wells could be poisoned and if the thirst did not kill them, any surviving British troops would be heavily outnumbered.

By then the British public had become obsessed with Gordon and his fate. Mass gatherings had taken place in Hyde Park and in Manchester demanding action. Many vicars included a plea for Gordon's rescue in their church services. Meanwhile, various crackpots came up with schemes to rescue their hero, involving balloons, disguises or bands of African game hunters. The queen was furious that her prime minister would not act. The opposition had a vote of censure passed in parliament, but still he did nothing. He was hissed at wherever he went. Finally, on the last day of July, several members of the cabinet who had interviewed Gordon for his mission threatened to resign. This action could have brought down the government and so the prime minister's hand was forced. Reluctantly, he approached parliament for £300,000 for the relief of Gordon, adding the words *should it become necessary*, to save face.

Sir Garnet Wolseley was finally given command of the expedition at the beginning of August. He knew that the level of the Nile would soon start to fall and that the garrison at Khartoum was now running out of food. Time was of the essence. But to rescue them, he first had to create an army, then transport it and all the supplies it needed by sea to Egypt. Next, he had to move them one thousand five hundred miles deep into the continent of Africa, much of the way across hostile terrain. Then he had to beat a fanatical enemy and finally rescue his friend before he starved, or the city was overrun. It was a herculean task and yet no one doubted that he would succeed…least of all Sir Garnet!

Wolseley had made his name doing what others considered impossible. After serving in India, the Crimea and China, he had first come to the attention of the British public for his exploits in Canada, where he had transported his army so quickly across the wilderness in small boats that he had taken a rebel force completely by surprise. Then he had beaten the Ashanti, capturing their capital of Kumasi. The Gordon Relief Expedition was to be the pinnacle of his career, a challenge worthy of his skills, the success of which would confirm his position as the leading general of the nation.

Such was his reputation in London that many assumed the Mahdists would simply abandon their siege at his approach. Nobody imagined that men with swords and spears would provide any serious opposition to our modern weaponry. It would be a grand procession, a victorious triumph that would bring glory to its leader and participants. Every ambitious young officer began to pull strings to be included. The situation was no different for newspaper men. Having campaigned for months to get Gordon rescued, every editor wanted a correspondent on hand for the successful conclusion of the mission. It was to be the campaign of the decade. Like a fool, I eagerly grabbed a place in the extensive press corps that would accompany the troops.

I had been with Wolseley on the Ashanti campaign. Having read my grandfather's memoirs of an earlier Ashanti war, I had been sure that it would be a disaster. The army would be pinned down by warriors in jungles until it was beaten by a force it could not shoot – virulent fevers that struck the region every summer. Instead, Wolseley's meticulous planning had seen a swift advance to capture their capital, then the withdrawal of the army again between fever seasons. The expedition had been so successful, it was used as an example of perfection in the staff college.

If a general could beat disease, then surely some hot-headed fanatics would not present that much of an obstacle. Yet for the gentlemen of the press, the situation was slightly more complicated, for Wolseley loathed war correspondents with a passion. In my case it was a feeling that was entirely mutual. He took a perverse delight in misleading us, having published in his handbook for junior officers that to do so would also confuse the enemy. That might be the case in a European war, but I doubted that there were many subscribers to the *Daily News* in Khartoum. The papers would have arrived long after they were useful, even if there were. I was pretty certain that the Mahdi did not start his day with the *Times* crossword and complaints about the cricket scores before ordering his first flogging.

On the way to the Ashanti capital of Kumasi, someone had obviously told him of my complaints and I found myself summoned to the general's tent. I had expected a dressing down, for Wolseley was notoriously prickly over those who tried to interfere with his plans. Instead, I found he was all charm and affability. I explained why I thought such deceptions were unnecessary and the frustration it caused to both my editor and readers. To my surprise, he agreed with me that his old habits were not necessary on this occasion. He thanked me for bringing the matter to his attention. By way of recompense, he offered the *Daily News* an exclusive: the army would start the final advance to the Ashanti capital in three days' time. I must have looked suspicious at this unexpected largess, while he had chuckled at my caution. The arrogant swine looked me in the eye and gave me his word that this information was true before escorting me to the telegraph tent to send it on to the paper. What could I do but transmit the report, with the general standing over me to ensure it was done.

My dark suspicions were confirmed the next morning, when I was awoken by the clatter of the camp being dismantled as the army prepared to march. Frank, my editor, was furious at yet another hurried correction. Later that day Wolseley passed me by, riding with some of his staff officers. He pointed me out and they had all roared with laughter, doubtless at the tale of me being gulled again.

I had seethed with fury and sworn revenge. My temper was not improved when he finally caught up with me when alone. Instead of apologising for his deception, he simply brushed it aside. "It was in the national interest, dear boy," he remarked with an airy wave of the hand. I fumed. Sooner or later he would fail, I thought, then the press and the public would turn on him as they had so many generals in the past. Yet for all that, I would not have wanted any other commander leading the army in the Sudan. No one else had his experience in meticulously organising a campaign. Little did I realise then, that the attributes that had won him victory over the Ashanti, would bring him close to disaster against the Mahdi.

Chapter 4

My own North African adventures began on the 1st of October 1884, when I set sail from Tilbury Docks in London to Port Said in Egypt. That might seem late given the urgency of our mission, but right up until September there was still doubt in government circles as to whether the mission would proceed at all.

While Gladstone dithered and prevaricated, Wolseley began to implement a plan that he had started work on months before. Vast amounts of equipment had to be specially manufactured, men with particular skills gathered from around the world and the cohesion of the finest regiments in the army temporarily disbanded.

British soldiers had little experience of fighting in deserts and no unit was accustomed to riding camels. Those spearheading the advance would be going deep inside enemy territory and facing a fanatical enemy far more familiar with the terrain. Wolseley decided that this was a challenge for the very best that the army could produce. He dismissed the so-called 'crack regiments' such as the Guards or Hussars; they were selected as much for their social class as for their fighting ability. Wolseley, born into no great wealth, considered the idea that these were the elite as errant bosh. Instead, he created a new Camel Corps just for this expedition. It comprised the best thirty or so men from dozens of different regiments and corps in the army.

Next, he decided that rowing boats of the same specification that he had used in Canada would be vital in conquering the Sudan. They had to be big enough to carry twelve men and their supplies, but light enough to be carried around the various cataracts in the river if necessary. Naval dockyards were inspected, but none had exactly the right craft required and certainly not in the quantities needed. The army commander in Egypt pointed out that the Nile was full of local boats of all sizes from steamers to bumboats, designed for use on the river. He was sure that fleets of them could be hired to move the army. Ministers tentatively passed on the suggestion, but Wolseley insisted that only his specification would do.

His design was sent to every boat yard in the country, who were soon feverishly producing them along with the masts, oars, sails and other rigging they would require. Initially, four hundred craft were ordered and then the amount was doubled. I doubt there was a boatyard in Britain that was not working on them through August and September. All wanted to play their part in helping the army reach Khartoum to bring Gordon home. Then the craft had to be loaded into steamers and shipped to Egypt. It had seemed an impossible challenge that summer, but astonishingly, by mid-October, eight hundred craft had been delivered to Alexandria. As soldiers would have little boating experience, to pilot these craft Wolseley also summoned four hundred experienced boatmen from Canada and even some from West Africa, where he had used similar craft against the Ashanti.

The papers were full of letters from furious colonels, apoplectic at this riding roughshod over regimental tradition. Businessmen too were appalled at the cost, while old Egypt hands told all who would listen that they knew better. The Duke of Cambridge, Commander in Chief of the army, was so appalled when he saw the scheme that he collapsed with an attack of gout and had to be carried home. Despite this wave of protest, Wolseley refused to compromise on any aspect of the mission.

While I had waited to depart, London merchants had not been slow to spot the business opportunity in hundreds of officers, not to mention newspaper correspondents, needing to equip themselves for the coming journey. 'Purveyors of Desert Travel Equipment' and similar such businesses sprang up and were soon doing a roaring trade. I was assured that I could not sleep on the ground, for my body would draw up moisture from the rocks and guarantee I suffered from fever. More importantly, prone figures on the ground would attract snakes, scorpions and venomous insects that crawled in your ears. I was soon persuaded to buy a collapsible bed and chair along with a large bell tent. I drew the line at a desk for my trade, choosing a writing slope instead to contain ink and paper.

As well as a steamer trunk for my clothes and other possessions, the largest pieces of my luggage were a pair of rectangular galvanised metal tanks. These were supposed to hang on either side of a camel or donkey.

Assurances were made that these would keep me supplied with water whatever the distance between wells or an oasis. I discovered that each of Wolseley's boats would be supplied with a water filtration device that promised to remove all impurities from the Nile water. It was essentially three large bucket filters containing lint, charcoal and other chemicals that fitted on top of each other. You poured river water in the top and into the bottom bucket drained something perfectly drinkable. That at least is what the salesman told me and so I bought a smaller version of one of those too.

I had been a correspondent for too long now not to prepare for the worst. I also carried a medical chest with bandages, a reel of thread for stitches, forceps with bullet grip ends, quinine for fever and laudanum for pain. To this was added Pargeter's Camphorated Cholera Belt. Worn around the waist, it guaranteed to ensure you avoided dysentery and cholera. I bought the latest Webley pistol for my personal protection along with a sealed box of cartridges. An almost identical sealed box of Webley ammunition disguised a stash of silver coins. Gold was too valuable to be of use haggling in the desert. Maria Theresa silver dollars were well regarded in the region for their size and purity. There would be no banks in the Sudan and so I needed to take money with me, as well as disguise it from thieves.

As I watched my luggage loaded aboard, I thought I was reasonably well prepared. At least half of the boxes I had brought contained food. There were tins of meats such as bully beef, ham and mutton. There were also tins of jam and butter along with boxes of biscuits, tea, powdered milk and a few bottles of madeira and brandy to counter the chill of the desert nights. Wolseley had made it very clear to all members of the fourth estate that the army would provide no support for the press. We would have to shift for ourselves.

A week later, halfway through our voyage, I began to wonder if the whole expedition would be over far quicker than I had first thought. Most of my fellow passengers were army officers and almost universally of the view that there would be no fighting at all. Colonel Fortescue's views were typical. "The bloody wogs would be mad to charge our guns," he barked. "We did for their army two years ago and they were dug in with artillery."

"But that was the Egyptian army," I pointed out. "From what I heard, the tribesmen our army fought near Suakin were quite formidable."

"Formidable?" he scoffed. "What the hell do you damned ink monkeys know about formidable?" Before I could answer, he went on, "I'll tell you what is formidable. The Gardner machine gun will fire over eight hundred bullets a minute, what do you think of that, eh? The Martini–Henry can easily fire twelve shots a minute that will travel nearly two thousand yards and is deadly accurate to a range of four hundred yards. Those facts are formidable, and you worry about some hairy tribesman armed with a spear?"

"It does seem unlikely that they will make a stand against us," added Fortescue's aide, a Captain Jennings. "It certainly would not last long if they did." I had to agree that put like that, it did seem that any conflict would be a very one-sided affair. The fighting at the Red Sea had been a bloody business, but enemy casualties had been estimated at around ten times our own. They could not put up with that level of slaughter for long.

"This so-called Mahdi is just some jumped up chancer," insisted Fortescue. "He will melt back into the desert where he came from once he sees that the game is up." The colonel leaned forward and lowered his voice conspiratorially. "Wolseley knows they won't stand and I would bet the gamekeeper's cottage that Gordon knows it too. Those two are as thick as thieves. They were pups together fighting at Sebastopol."

"What do you mean?" I asked, intrigued.

"Wolseley talked Gordon into going to Sudan. He must have known that Charlie Gordon of all people, would not cut and run, leaving all those poor souls to get butchered. Our Sir Garnet is a wily fellow. He probably guessed that Gordon would get trapped and that sooner or later a rescue would have to be mounted. That is why he began working on his plan so early." He barked with laughter, "Old Gladstone made him sweat, though, for we are going far later than he would have wanted."

"But would Wolseley take such a risk with the life of his friend?" I queried.

"He wants to be C in C when old Cambridge retires," confided Fortescue. "He knows the old man won't recommend him and he is not well regarded in court, so he needs another successful campaign that will make him popular with the public. Once there are pictures of him in the papers shaking hands with Charlie Gordon at the gates of Khartoum, he will be unassailable, you chaps will see to that."

"But surely he does not have any serious rivals now?" I pointed out. The logistics of the campaign made such a strategy seem highly risky to me.

"Bob Roberts is popular," Fortescue replied. "He is not as naked with his ambition, and people like that. He also does not surround himself with toadies and lackies like Wolseley. Half of the so-called Ashanti Ring that our commander has on his staff have been promoted beyond their abilities. Look at Buller. He made a fine captain and has the courage of an ox; the trouble is he has the brains of one as well. Damn near pickled too most of the time."

I put that comment down to the envy of the colonel, who was clearly not among Wolseley's favoured few. "Do you think Gordon knows he is a pawn in Wolseley's plans?"

The colonel thought seriously about that for a moment. "If he does, he probably does not care. He is a strange bird, with no interest in money. I hear he could have been a mandarin in China, and he gave up the governorship of Sudan before. Power does not seem to attract him and some damn fine women have tried, but to no avail. When I last met him, he was talking about setting up an orphanage in the Holy Land." Fortescue frowned and shook his head slightly at a memory. "I tried to interest him in a new command, but he only smiled at me as though he was privy to some joke. Deuced odd behaviour. I can't see what makes him tick. The fellow is more of a damned mystic than this Mahdi."

We arrived in Port Said on the 14th of October but stayed aboard. The harbour was a chaos of ships and launches weaving around each other to reach the wharves. After the peaceful trip across the Mediterranean, it was an assault on the senses. There was a constant din of steam whistles from ships, trains and cranes. The fresh sea air was replaced with a malodorous stink as the city sewers emptied into the bay. I looked down at one point to find the swollen corpse of a dead dog entangled with our anchor chain. We waited while the ship tied up, took on coal and dropped off cargo. Then we cast off again to join a queue of ships waiting to pass down the first stage of the Suez Canal. To a landlubber like me there was no order to the affair at all, with captains yelling at each other from their bridges and trying to manoeuvre each other out of the way. It was a wonder there were no collisions, but at last we were travelling down the narrow channel. Not for long, though, for another steamer became grounded ahead of us. We had to wait there a day for tugs to work their way through the throng of shipping and pull it clear. Eventually, we reached the inland port of Ismailia where I disembarked with relief and caught a train to Cairo.

If I had thought the harbour disorganised, it was nothing to the port railway station. Soldiers armed with sticks kept back a crowd of grubby Egyptian men and boys, who glared with undisguised avarice at the nets of stores being lowered down onto the quay. I knew I had twenty assorted boxes. The trouble was that virtually all the passengers had the same. There were dozens of almost identical cases of bully beef and other stores, with porters eagerly gathering them up and loading them on to trollies. At one point I counted twenty-one boxes on my carts, but by the time they were loaded onto the train there were just nineteen.

The Cairo terminus was even worse. Without soldiers keeping the locals back, I doubt I would have left with more than the clothes on my back. Stepping down from the train, I was immediately surrounded by several uniformed porters, each insisting that they would give me the best service. Two were grizzled ancients, who probably knew every trick in the book about parting a newly arrived traveller from money and possessions. I chose the youngest; at least his back looked strong enough to load a cart.

As I watched my stores being piled on the platform, I found myself wondering how much of it I was likely to use. The first half of my journey would be via train and steamer and would take less than a month. If my fellow passengers were right, by the time I reached the

Egyptian border with Sudan, the siege of Khartoum might already be over. Still, I doubted I could simply turn around. Wolseley would surely bring Gordon back to Egypt, if not all the way to London for them both to be lionised in the streets. My editor would demand an interview with the great man to justify the expense of the journey. With every other correspondent having the same goal, I would need to keep my wits about me to be one of the first to secure such a prize.

My porter introduced himself as Hassan, speaking excellent English. He took an interest in my water containers, which he assured me would be most useful in the desert. As there was far too much for one man to carry, he organised the ancients to help and arranged a cart for my possessions as well as a carriage for me. I was impressed, he was a very capable man, who had earned a generous tip.

The obvious place to stay in Cairo was Shepheard's Hotel. It was in the European enclave of the city, where police kept beggars and other street traders to a minimum. Everyone would try to stay at Shepheard's, it being by far the most popular hotel with British travellers. Fearing it might be full, I was relieved to learn that Wolseley had already travelled upriver to Wadi Halfa on the Egyptian–Sudanese border. Many of his officers were already on their way to join him. Some of the correspondents had gone too, but I found a handful of familiar faces on the famous balcony in front of the building. Burleigh was there, as was John Cameron of the *Evening Standard* and MacDonald, who was syndicated to several papers. On the next table were a couple of foreign correspondents who nodded in greeting. I recognised Chambois from *Le Temps*, a haughty bastard who had sold out the French army for an exclusive. Banks and businesses in France had invested heavily in Egypt and their readers were keen to follow what was happening. There was an Italian too, as they had a small colony in the Horn of Africa.

"What took you so long?" called Cameron, while gesturing for the waiter to bring me a drink.

"I know I am not too late," I replied, grinning as I joined them. "My ship was full of officers and men joining the expedition."

"I rather fear we might *all* be too late," countered Burleigh grimly. "Have you heard the latest news from Khartoum?" I shook my head and he continued, "Gordon managed to get a message out at the beginning of September. It took several weeks to get to Wadi Halfa, but he says he can hold out until the middle of November at the latest."

"But that is only a month from now," I exclaimed. "Everyone on my ship thought that the Mahdi would lift the siege once he heard we were coming."

"Well, according to Gordon, they are still around the city in strength," replied Burleigh, "and you can be sure they know we are coming now. The Mahdi is bound to have people here in Cairo who keep him informed."

"But we will never be able to travel one and a half thousand miles up a river in a month." This put a whole different light on things. The British army might be able to defeat the Mahdi's men, but if they only reached them after Khartoum had fallen and Gordon was dead, then Wolseley's great gamble would have failed spectacularly.

"The local Cairo commander warned Wolseley back in August that his plan to go up the Nile would take too long," continued Cameron. "He said the Suakin to Berber route offered the only chance, despite the Mahdists occupying Berber. But the general would not hear of any alternatives to his scheme."

"He is damn right to avoid Suakin," countered Burleigh and I sensed that they had already argued this point. "I would not go there again. Sending a force piecemeal, five hundred at a time into a desert full of Fuzzies who would defend or poison the wells is a recipe for disaster."

"At least the Nile guarantees water all the way," I agreed, "and the river can be used to transport men and supplies." Privately, I thought that if Khartoum fell when we were only halfway there, I would not be too disappointed. It would be tough on Gordon, but he had chosen to make his stand there. I had no wish to end up like my friend O'Donovan with my head on a pike. But would the army retrace its steps and return home? It certainly would if Gladstone had anything to do with it. He would be anxious to curtail the costs in gold and blood of the campaign. It was also likely his ministers would keep Wolseley close to the telegraph and under control. Having had one general go rogue on them, they would not want another. Yet many in the army would want to go on to Khartoum and avenge Gordon anyway, especially those in the new Camel Corps.

"You will need to get yourself an English-speaking guide and some servants to manage your camp," said Cameron, interrupting my thoughts. "Though it will not be easy as most of those willing to go up country have already been taken."

"A good number are reluctant to come," added Burleigh. "They think that our expedition will go the same way as Hicks'."

"I think I have solved that particular problem already," I told them confidently. "I met an extremely capable porter this morning at the station. He spoke excellent English and says he has some knowledge of travelling up the Nile. I have asked him to become my guide and he can sort out the servants too."

"Well, do not delay," advised Cameron. "The army will be moving soon. I am catching a train south this afternoon."

My optimism, it turned out, proved unfounded. Later that day Hassan called to see me at the hotel. He told me that his wife was ill and did not want him away for a long time. I was sure he was lying. His wife had probably reminded him that life as a railway porter was far safer than coming with me into a hostile desert. I even offered to increase his fee, but he was adamant that he could not go. Nor did he know of anyone else who could serve in his stead.

Burleigh told me that he had been obliged to pay his man fifteen pounds a month compared to the five he had paid for the Suakin expedition. The fellow in question, a Turk, warned me not to hire an Egyptian. They would, he insisted, rob me blind and abandon me long before we reached our destination. Over the next three days I interviewed one man whose English was so poor he was barely coherent. A second man recommended by the hotel concierge had perfect English yet was so ancient I was sure he would not survive the rigours of the trip. Then I met a Syrian who initially wanted twenty pounds a month, but was adamant that he would travel no further south than Dongola, a town halfway between the Egyptian border and Khartoum. That was no use either. By then Burleigh had gone too and I was getting desperate. I had booked a train ticket for the following day to take me on the next stage of my journey. I was contemplating going up alone and trying to find someone on the way.

I was coming back from meeting another translator reluctant to travel out of Egypt when I was accosted in the street by a man called Faisal. I had been muttering in frustration at the crowds of people I was pushing through in the street and how not one of the lazy wretches would come with me, when my prayers were answered.

"Are you looking for a guide, sir?" he enquired in good English. I stopped in surprise. He was a wiry middle-aged man who looked capable. His left eyelid drooped a little, but that would not stop him organising the loading of camels. The encounter seemed remarkable good fortune...almost too convenient. Something about him made me feel uneasy. Perhaps sensing this, he suggested that we retire from the surrounding throng to a nearby café where he could show me his references. I readily agreed, for I was in no position to be picky. He had only travelled as far as Wadi Halfa on the border, but he assured me that he would be willing to go further. His two letters of recommendation were excellent and yet there was something I still did not trust. I wondered if it was only his eye deformity that had made him seem shifty and so, not wanting to judge too quickly, asked him more about his travels.

As he began to talk, however, I found it increasingly difficult to concentrate on what he was saying. An Egyptian woman had sat down at a table just beyond his left shoulder. She stood out from the crowd for a number of reasons. Firstly, few Egyptian women appeared on the streets, certainly in the European quarter. Those that did generally wore black and scurried about with heads bowed. Invariably, they were old, ugly and sporting a moustache. This one, though, wore a loose robe of white and a headscarf but no veil. Sitting amongst the other merchants and businessmen in the café, she looked perfectly at ease. The final reason she held my attention was that she was an absolute corker. A flawless beauty whose eyes met mine with a glance of mutual interest. There was a spark between us, I was sure of it, and I lost interest in Faisal's conversation and suggestions for our journey. I glanced across at her companion, a burly Arab who could have been a bodyguard. He certainly did not seem to mind that she was continually glancing in our direction. She was paying more attention to Faisal's explanations than I was, leaning in slightly to overhear.

My new man was just making his pitch for twenty pounds a month when she stood to come over. The lithe body moving under the loose robes made me wonder if I could put my train ticket back a day or two after all. I stood to introduce myself, but to my surprise it was not me she spoke too. She bent down to angrily whisper in Arabic into Faisal's ear. Then I noticed a small dagger in her hand, which had nicked his neck; blood was trickling down on to his collar. Finally, she looked up at me, a smile driving the anger from her features. "You should not trust this man," she warned. "He will rob you and then abandon you as he did my father."

Faisal had turned ashen. Muttering his apologies, he wriggled out from the chair and bolted back out into the street like a scorched cat. I was back where I had started, but perhaps with a lucky escape. "I must thank you for your assistance," I began. "In a city this size you would think it would be easy to find someone reliable to act as a guide, but I am finding it remarkably difficult."

"I assume you are a government official as you are not in uniform?" Without waiting to be asked, she sat down on the recently vacated seat opposite and appraised me cooly. Her English was excellent and there was an unnerving confidence to her. I glanced back at the man sitting at her former table, who nodded back companionably, clearly unperturbed at being abandoned.

"I am a newspaper correspondent," I explained, handing her my card.

"The *Daily News*," she read, "Is that a big paper in London?"

"Pretty large," I admitted. "You read and speak English very well."

"You should see me add up a ledger," she countered and held out her hand in greeting. "I am Leila Ibrahim; I have helped my father run his business for many years."

I took the hand; it was warm and soft. Her thumb ran over the back of mine in more of a caress than a grasp. She was close enough now for me to smell her scent. It was an exotic musk that left me picturing her rubbing expensive oils into her skin. My mouth had gone dry with

52

desire. It was only with a considerable struggle that I managed to turn the conversation back to the issue that hitherto had been at the forefront of my mind.

"I don't suppose you know anyone reliable who could act as a guide, to help me follow the army to Khartoum, do you?"

She paused, considering, and then decided. "As a matter of fact, I do. I can be your guide."

My jaw must have gaped. I suspect my face was a riot of desire and confusion. The thought of being alone with her in the desert was enough to send an electric charge through my body. Then, with the greatest reluctance, my mind began to consider the practicalities and I saw it was impossible. "But...but I cannot take a woman. I mean I am a war correspondent, there is a good chance that we will be in battles. You would be alone in an army of men. By heavens I would welcome your companionship, but I really don't think that I can bring you. It would be too dangerous."

"Tell me," she replied calmly, "how many of the guides you have interviewed have actually travelled all the way to Khartoum and back?" When I admitted it was none, she continued, "I have done the journey twice with father. We took trading caravans there. My father's name is known in many of the settlements we will pass. There will also be other women travelling with your army so I will not be alone. Many of the camel herders will bring their wives." She smiled, holding my gaze and added, "And I suspect that you have no idea which type of camel would be best for the journey."

"I did not know that there were different types," I admitted. By God, bringing her with me was a tempting prospect. "But surely your father would not want you travelling all that way, especially if he relies on you for the business."

For the first time her confidence wavered. "A year ago, my brother took a caravan south into the Sudan. He was not with it when it returned. The others insisted that he had become a follower of the Mahdi. My father refuses to accept that his son has abandoned him. He will allow me to go if I can find out what has happened to my brother." She gestured over her shoulder to her companion, "Especially if I take Rafa for protection."

I looked at the big man and wondered how 'protective' he would be. But the prospect of a long journey into the desert was now much more appealing. So it was that I chose my guide. I had no idea at that moment how useful she would turn out to be.

Chapter 5

We started our journey to Khartoum the next morning. The concierge at Shepheard's had organised two carriages to take us and our luggage to Boulac railway station in the city. Leila's baggage consisted of a large cloth bag. She looked on in amusement as my various possessions were carried out of the hotel, particularly the big metal water carriers. The first stage of the trip, while we followed the Nile, was by train. We were going two hundred and thirty miles south to the town of Asyut. It would take around twelve hours, far faster than we could cover by boat.

The station was as crowded as any part of Cairo, but Rafa quickly found some porters to carry my possessions onto the southbound train. Leila ordered him to watch over them on the journey, while I led her to the first-class carriages. We entered one marked 'Europeans Only'. Leila, still in white robes with a matching headscarf wrapped around her shoulders, neck and over the top of her head did not look remotely European, yet nobody challenged her as my companion. Her skin was light enough to be taken for a Greek. I had seen some English ladies at Shepheard's wearing far more ostentatious robes for comfort in the heat. Most of the compartments were occupied by officers hurrying after the army, but I found a vacant one so that we could be alone.

For all its first-class pretentions, the carriage was old. Its floor timbers had shrunk with the heat, and you could make out the track beneath through the cracks. Everything was covered in a fine yellow dust. Yet for all that, I suspected that this would be the most comfortable part of the trip as I sat down on well-used horsehair stuffed seats. The line ran on the west bank of the Nile, which was occasionally just five hundred yards away. At other times it was over a mile distant, as engineers had tried to keep the track straight, while the river undulated through the countryside. Soon it was as though the view had not changed for millennia. There was a broad strip of irrigated land on either bank. Donkeys were powering water wheels to fill irrigation channels that were shaded with lines of date and palm trees. Then the greenery stuttered to a halt and the land beyond became desert. It seemed timeless to me and just as I had imagined, but when I said this to Leila, she disagreed.

"Thirty years ago, we would not have been on a train. We would have been riding camels or on a boat to make this journey over many days. Look there," she pointed out of the window at a large canal running parallel with the river. "That is new and feeds many other irrigation channels that have greatly increased the land under cultivation. There, you see telegraph poles. They are new and they stretch all the way to Khartoum and beyond. And you came to Cairo on part of the Suez Canal. All of this was built by the old Khedive. He wanted to make Egypt a great country again, but you British forced him to abdicate. Everyone knows that his son is a puppet of your prime minister."

I had inadvertently made her angry. She was clearly proud of her country, but I thought she only told part of the story. "The old Khedive did build many things," I agreed. "But he did it on borrowed money. Under his rule the national debt of Egypt grew from three million to ninety million. I know this because we covered it in my paper. No one would lend him any more funds. The country was bankrupt. That was why Britain and France intervened."

"And who had lent him that money?" she spat back before answering her own question. "Companies in Britain and France; you were just protecting your investments. Now we have Britain and France running the country. Your people even have your own law courts so that you are not treated like Egyptians. Two years ago, some of our soldiers rose up in revolt. They wanted Egypt for the Egyptians, not the Turks, the French or the British. What happened? Your British navy bombarded Alexandria and then your army under this General Wolseley defeated the Egyptian army that your officers now command. The new Khedive does whatever you want."

What she said was true enough, although she had omitted that the rebels had massacred many Europeans during rioting in Alexandria. I was surprised at her patriotic passion. I had not intended to antagonise and searched for something to say that would placate her. "I am not sure about the Khedive doing what he is told," I countered. "He made Gordon governor general of Sudan again and I know that was absolutely the last thing that Gladstone wanted. He did not want an army going to Sudan at all, but his hand has been forced as Gordon will not leave."

"Perhaps the Khedive does have some backbone," she agreed. "He does not want to give up the territory of Sudan and certainly not the garrisons stationed there." A mischievous smile crossed her features as she added, "Perhaps the tables have turned. Now we have you British fighting Egypt's war."

It was good to see her happy again, yet I was not convinced that the Khedive's problems were solved. "Everyone in London is convinced we will have an easy victory, but I am not so sure. We have better weapons, yet they cannot fight thirst if our men are trapped away from water." Without thinking I added, "They should put up a better fight than those soldiers who fought with Valentine Baker, though."

Her reply was sharp and angry again. "They were not soldiers; most of them were from the Cairo police." When I looked surprised at this revelation she went on, "How would your London policemen feel if they were rounded up, forced on a boat and taken a thousand miles away to fight fanatical warriors in another country? Would *they* put up a better fight?"

"I had no idea they were policemen. Why did they not send soldiers?"

"Because the army has British officers and your Mr Gladstone refused permission to send them. The Khedive wanted to rescue his Red Sea garrisons and still commanded the men in the police. They had been trained with their rifles and Baker Pasha was commissioned by the Khedive. Few Egyptians want to go to Sudan. Everyone has heard stories about what the Mahdists did to prisoners. There were many desertions among Hicks' soldiers and even more among the police. I heard stories of men cutting off their trigger finger or blinding an eye with lime to escape the draft. Many were loaded on the ship in chains to stop them escaping, their women wailing on the docks, convinced that they would never see their husbands again."

I tried to picture the scene and gave a shudder of disquiet. "As it turns out, most of them were right," I agreed sympathetically. "Many must hate the Khedive now and probably the British as well. Do some actually support the Mahdi?"

Her voice softened; the anger gone. "Some would like a powerful Arab leader to stand up for them against the Europeans. But they are fools who would swap a weak tyrant for a strong one. Only the most fervent Muslims would choose the Mahdi. He has declared that we Egyptians should all be put to death. He believes we have taken on too many Christian ways, like this train. From what I hear only a third of the Sudanese really support him. The rest follow him through fear. Those who do not swear allegiance are put to death and the wealthy are often tortured until they hand over their riches. We used to sell wine in Sudan, but now anyone caught with it is given eighty lashes, smokers of tobacco even more. No woman is allowed to visit the marketplaces and any man speaking to a woman not of his family is given a hundred lashes. His rule would be far more oppressive than the Khedive's."

"Yet you think your brother might have joined him?" I prompted.

She looked sadly out of the window at the passing countryside before continuing. "My father doted on Ishmael and wanted him to take over the business. When my brother did not return, he felt betrayed, as though his son now looks on the prophet as a father. He told me it would hurt him less if his son was dead, but I know he would do anything to get Ishmael back. I want my brother back too. He was always easily led. Perhaps he now realises that he has made a mistake."

"So what do you plan to do?"

"You British will have to fight the Mahdi's men if you are to free Gordon. I will ask the prisoners if my brother still lives and if he does, I will bring him home."

"He may not want to come," I pointed out.

She laughed, "He is still my little brother. I will box his ears as I did when he was a child." She paused then, thinking more seriously about the many obstacles that she faced. "If I have to," she added grimly, "I will bring him home in chains."

We talked about her life in Egypt. As a merchant she had more status than most women, for her father delegated much of the business to her. "If men refuse to trade with me," she laughed, "I tell them that I will

58

deal with their wives in the market and soon all their secrets will be known around the bazaars."

"Given the twenty-five pounds a month you are charging me for your services," I grinned, "I suspect that you drive a hard bargain."

"I usually get what I want," she replied, holding my gaze. "Now, tell me about the other places you have been."

As the train rattled on, it disturbed the desert dust that lay on the tracks. Clouds of it drifted into the carriage through the gaps in the floorboards until we were coated in a fine layer. Every three or four hours the train stopped at a station for the locomotive to take on fuel and water. We too needed refreshments. Station workers were on hand to sell cups of tea, figs, breads and other sustenance and there was water to wash our hands and faces. Other station attendants approached the first-class passengers with brushes to sweep the dust off our clothes, although they hesitated to touch a woman. When all the men were spotless and Leila still a dusty orange, I borrowed one of the brushes and gently dusted the sand off her shoulders. There was more on her clothes, particularly areas that were horizontal when she was sitting. Her lower arms and thighs were covered with the dust and there was more than an ochre tinge to her chest too. I was about to give the brush back when her hand closed my fingers around it. "Keep that," she whispered. "You can brush me down properly later."

Back in the carriage, never have I swept more diligently. I swished those bristles over every curve until her robes were pristine. There was a tension of desire in the air of that small compartment, we both felt it, I am sure. Not that we could do anything about it then; the corridor was well used and the blinds at the windows were broken. We pulled into Asyut station well after dark, but the train was expected, and the platform was lit by lanterns carried by railway officials. Most of the passengers were heading down to the steamer landing, a quarter of a mile away. Rafa managed to commandeer a cart for our luggage, which he took down to the quay. There was no room for us and so Leila and I walked the short distance down to the Nile. She pointed out the bats flying overhead. Judging from the noise of the crickets all around us,

59

they ate well. We were hungry too, but not for food. I ran my hand down her back and felt her tremble with desire under her robe.

Wolseley had banned all correspondents from using boats flying the red flag that showed that they had been commissioned by the army, even if there was room on them. It was another example of his petty behaviour towards newspapermen. I knew that there was a civilian steamer also waiting to meet this train. It was called the *Fiod* and I had booked our passage with a cabin for five pounds. By the time we climbed aboard, the evening had turned pleasantly cool after the heat of the day. As Rafa stowed the baggage in the hold, I took Leila off to find our retreat. Despite the louvred slats in the door, the cabin was like a furnace, but by then we were so close to the boil ourselves that we did not care. In no time at all our naked, sweating bodies were entwined on the sheets, satisfying a lust that had been building since we had first met.

The steamer was already moving when we rose the next morning, the paddle wheels on either beam pushing us against the current of the river to progress at little more than walking speed. We had three hundred and thirty miles to cover to reach Aswan, which would take around five days. Another reason for our slow progress lay astern of the ship. In tow behind were a dozen freshly built wooden boats, a batch of Wolseley's cutters that were being brought upriver to be introduced to their crews.

That journey felt very much like the calm before the storm. There was nothing we could do but enjoy the voyage and some spectacular scenery along the way. We passed the vast temple at Karnak and even stopped at the smaller but completely intact temple of Edfu. Leila and I had time to wander among the columns and marvel at the crispness of carving that had only recently been uncovered after thousands of years. When the ship moored up each evening the crew provided a reasonable repast, usually mutton or goat. It was no Shepheard's, but it was far better than we were to enjoy in the desert. At night we would retire to the cabin to enjoy the carnal pleasures of each other's bodies, yet often we would leave again to escape the heat. Lying on the top deck, staring up at the eternity of stars with a sated woman in your arms was as timeless a pleasure as they come. The ripple of the river, a gentle breeze to keep us cool and sometimes the distant silhouette of columns and sphinx. It would have been a moment of true heavenly perfection if you could ignore the snoring of a dozen fellows who lay around us.

As we approached Aswan, however, we were reminded of our earthlier purpose in the region: the distant call of bugles, cavalry exercising their horses along the riverbank, more boats unloading stores along the new temporary wharfs and a hundred of Wolseley's new craft, which were now being hauled out of the river. The first cataracts were just beyond Aswan, but one of the many things that the old Khedive had invested in was another length of railway line around them. The boats were being loaded onto railway carriages to take them safely onto the next stretch of calm river. As we walked off the jetties and through the shoreline palm trees, we found that we had finally caught up with the main army. Hundreds of white tents were laid out before us as far as the eye could see on either side of the railway tracks. I thought it would be time to unpack our own canvas, but Leila had a better idea. She knew one of the merchants selling meat, vegetables and fodder to the army and so took me along to greet him. He was delighted to host us in the Nile equivalent of a private yacht. It was called a dahabeah – the back half resembled a houseboat, while the front had the sails and masts of a dhow.

The man certainly lived well. He opened our first dinner with a couple of bottles of Veuve Clicquot, which he later admitted had been liberated from private supplies sent upriver by General Buller. He laughed as he told us that Buller had organised for dozens of cases of champagne to be sent to the camp and camels to carry them all the way to Sudan. The general certainly planned to campaign in style. We dined on roast lamb from the merchant's flock, but the tea, biscuits, butter and jam served for breakfast the following morning all came from packaging marked for the army. It was clear that a fair amount of pilfering was going on. I made a point of checking that Rafa was guarding our own possessions carefully and discreetly retrieved the fake box of Webley ammunition that contained the silver coins.

I needed the cash, for Leila informed me that Aswan would be the best place to purchase the camels we needed. Hundreds of the animals were arriving each day as word had got out that the British were paying good prices for the beasts. She wanted to go outside the town to intercept the best ones before the army buyers could acquire them. I went with some trepidation. From what little I had seen of the creatures, they had a vicious streak, biting, kicking and spitting at the unwary. Give me a horse any day, but everyone insisted that we would need camels in the desert. Leila selected six animals, each of them white. Three for us to ride and three for carrying the baggage and supplies. They certainly were not cheap, but she told me that they were Bishari camels, which were apparently some of the best. Then we had to buy saddles, harnesses and baggage racks. My Webley tin was more than half depleted by the time we had finished, although I don't doubt that it would have been completely empty without Leila's guidance. The Egyptians haggle with the same commitment that an Englishman might show for cricket. It is a sport with them. You mention a price and they all throw up their hands and insist that they might as well cut the throats of their children, for they are bound to starve at such a rate. Then as you stand in the baking sun, they will insist on an astronomic sum and gradually come down with glacial slowness an ounce of silver at a time. Having agreed a price for one saddle, don't think that they will simply settle on the same price for a second one. Hands will shoot up at the very suggestion and the whole saga must begin again.

I was gasping for some chilled stolen champagne when our bargaining was completed, but it was then I discovered that we would be riding our purchases back. The animals were all fitted with their saddles and tack, then tied together in two strings of three. I was to ride one of the lead animals. There was an air of anticipation amongst the surrounding Arabs. The crowd around us had grown larger in expectation of some entertainment. Coins exchanged hands as men gambled on the outcome, while laughing children did impressions of how they thought I would fall. It did little to instil confidence. The animal was made to sit on the ground, and I was summoned forward for my debut. There was no stirrup. You were expected to vault onto the animal's back and hope it did not try to rise as you did so. Leila urged me to mount quickly. "Camels sometimes bite if you stand too long beside them," she warned. I scrambled aboard and to my relief the creature stayed still on the ground. Arabs do not ride with their legs astride, but half crossed so that they wrap their calves around the hump. I picked up the reins and hit the animal's haunch with the whip to make it stand as I had been taught. Instead of ascending, however, I watched as its head turned and surveyed me with a look of withering contempt from under those long eyelashes.

Leila gave a yell and I guessed she must have hit the beast too, for suddenly I was lurching into the air. I had been warned to lean back as camels get up on their rear knees first but caught by surprise I did not lean far enough. Then as I stretched out, the front started to rise too and I nearly tumbled over the creature's arse, my hat falling to the ground. There were roars of laughter from the watching crowd as I teetered on the edge of disaster. Then as I finally settled in the saddle, I had the satisfaction of watching those who had gambled on my fall paying up. It was bloody high on the back of that camel and the stone and rocks beneath looked particularly unyielding if I had fallen. As Leila handed me back my pith helmet, I loosened the chin strap from the peak and secured the hat to my head. It would protect my skull if I came off.

Leila mounted with the ease of someone who had ridden camels all her life. Soon we were leading our charges away along the track. The saddle rocked in a circular motion as we progressed. You had to forget everything you had learned about sitting straight on a horse. On a camel you slouched and relaxed your limbs, swaying with the movement of the beast beneath. Not for nothing are they known as the ship of the desert, for I was feeling decidedly seasick by the time we reached our destination.

Chapter 6

In the cool of the late afternoon, I went for a stroll along the railway line that led through the centre of the camp. There were stockpiles of supplies all along the tracks. Noting the half-dozing sentries lying about, it was not hard to see how some items had been stolen. A train passed as I walked, most of its carriages laden with Wolseley's boats, but a few carrying blackened sacks of coal.

I easily identified my fellow correspondents. While all the military tents were in ruler-straight lines, identical in design and a uniform white, to one side was a cluster of canvas shelters in varied colours and shapes. One had a large awning in front of it and sprawled in chairs underneath were several familiar figures.

"Harrison, you made it at last," called out Cameron. "Did you find a guide, or do you need to borrow some of our servants to bring up your tent and gear?"

"That is kind of you, but I have a guide and I am staying at one of the houseboats on the river."

MacDonald confirmed that I was the last to arrive. Some of the others had already gone on to Wadi Halfa.

"We should celebrate," announced Cameron, "and I have just the thing. Prepare yourself for a surprise; it is just a shame we have no ice." A moment later and he was proudly presenting a bottle of Veuve Clicquot.

Burleigh laughed as I exclaimed, "Not champagne again! I have been drinking that morning, noon and night on the houseboat. I am surprised General Buller has any left with you pilfering his stocks too."

"I bought it from an Arab trader," replied a crestfallen Cameron. "I did not know it belonged to Buller." He glanced quickly around to ensure that no one was nearby to see him with the illicit plunder. "Hell, I am not sorry though," he continued. "Those generals issued orders to keep me off two army ships, even though there was loads of room. Now, who has some cups?"

As Cameron poured the drinks Burleigh added, "Buller has had so many cases sent upriver, I doubt he will miss one or two. It would be a lot easier on the camels if his tipple was brandy." We laughed at that and then toasted the rescue of Gordon. As I drained my cup Burleigh continued, "I suppose you have heard about Frank Power?"

I wondered if the *Times* man had got another story out of Khartoum. I could easily imagine my uncle's annoyance if he had. He had wanted a *Daily News* journalist in the city, but it was far too late to send one. "No, what has he done now?"

"He got himself cut to pieces, along with the colonel that accompanied Gordon to Khartoum." Registering my shocked expression, Burleigh went on. "Gordon sent the pair of them downriver with his journals in one of his steamers. They managed to get through the fire from the besieging lines and well past Berber before they ran aground, holing the boat. From what we hear, they went ashore to try and buy some camels, but were betrayed and slaughtered in the village."

My mind was suddenly filled with an image of the dour colonel sitting with Gordon on the train. He must have been roped into the trip on the day that Gordon was appointed. I had not met Power. He was only in his mid-twenties and had travelled to the Sudan with O'Donovan. Their deaths brought home the urgency of the mission we were on. Yet sipping champagne as we surveyed a neatly ordered camp, there was little sign of haste. "But if the river is becoming impassable already," I began, "shouldn't we have men rowing up it now hell for leather? Those small boats will offer little protection if the Mahdists can get close with Remington rifles."

"Those bloody craft have already wasted months we don't have," agreed Cameron. "The Nile is full of boats; we should have used them."

"Well, the boats are here now, so what else is causing the delay?" I pressed.

"There is a shortage of coal for the steamers on the next stretch of the river," Burleigh explained. "It is getting through now and some of the faster steamers will set off tomorrow. The army won't let us travel on those, but I am told that we can use an older craft that will embark the following day. According to my man, it will travel barely faster than walking pace."

"Another steamer?" I queried. "But I have just bought some camels. I think I will be travelling on those."

"You could, but— My God, what a vision." Cameron was distracted by something over my shoulder and even Burleigh's pipe was half hanging from a slackened jaw. Turning, I found myself grinning with more than a touch of pride. The white camel and white-robed rider moved as one. She swayed in the saddle in an effortless, undulating motion that made me imagine the naked body beneath. Clearly others were thinking along similar lines, for the sentries followed her every move. Soldiers were calling their mates out of their tents to see this vision of beauty, so that soon there was a line of khaki along her route. She rewarded them with a beaming smile before gently guiding the animal away, leading a second white camel on a rein behind

"She is coming this way!" Cameron straightened his hair, then glanced back into the tent. "Damn, we have finished the champagne."

"Don't worry, she's already had some." I kept my voice as casual as possible as I added, "Gentlemen, allow me to introduce my guide."

There were exclamations aplenty then, but eventually Burleigh uttered some coherent thoughts. "You cannot take a woman to war, Harrison. While I am sure she is a pleasure to follow into the desert, you need someone who knows where they are going."

"I'd follow her into the gates of hell itself," muttered Cameron, clearly quite taken.

"She has been all the way to Khartoum twice," I told them proudly, "and she has her own reasons for wanting to accompany us." By then the camel was falling to its knees and Leila dropped lightly to the ground. I introduced her to my friends. She watched in amusement as Cameron rushed around getting her the best chair and some clean water to drink. "We have just been talking about the next stage of our journey," I told her. "There is a slow old steamer in a couple of days, but now we have camels, I thought we would be better to travel on those."

"No," she disagreed quietly. "While there is a steamer, you should use it to carry your baggage. The camels will stay fresh walking along the river; there is plenty of grass for them and they can drink whenever they want. You need to save their strength for later." She looked around the circle of assembled men. "I know you think that you have travelled a long way, but the journey has not even started yet."

It was a sobering reminder of the challenges ahead. She instantly earned the respect of my colleagues as plans were hastily changed. The next day we watched as some of the tents were struck down and packed onto a train to take men and equipment beyond the cataracts to where their steamers awaited. Then it was our turn. Leila and I enjoyed a fond farewell in the merchant's houseboat before she and Rafa led away my six camels up the riverbank. My fellow members of the press corps rearguard shared a baggage car with all our possessions, watching through the open door as the locomotive pulled us past the turbulent stretch of the Nile. We saw Leila and the other servants leading our caravan of camels at a slow walking pace and waved as we swept past. It seemed likely that we would reach Wadi Halfa, our next destination, well before them. That is until we saw our steamer, the *Fayum*. It was a floating wreck that should have been condemned years ago. No wonder Wolseley was content for the press corps to use it; he was probably hoping that it would sink with us aboard. Its master announced that the engine was being repaired and so we could not leave until the following morning. Fortunately, there was a welcome distraction: the Ancient Egyptian temple of Philae was on an island opposite the mooring so we spent the cool of the evening exploring. Chambois had joined us and declared the site *"Très magnifique,"* before insisting that his great-grandfather had been there with Napoleon Bonaparte's Egyptian invasion.

Returning to the ship, we found it had more wildlife aboard than Noah's ark and was probably just as ancient. It certainly had not been designed originally for steam, for its fuel bunkers were far too small. A coal delivery had been received while we were away and there was now a pile of it across the main deck that you had to scramble over to get from the bow to the stern. The single cabin we shared turned out to be home for the most vicious mosquitoes I was ever to encounter. Cameron was bitten through corduroy breeches. To defend ourselves we draped mosquito nets and did our best to fill the room with cigar smoke to keep the blood-sucking fiends at bay. It did not work. Somehow one or two still found their way inside the nets to feast. If it was not the buzzing of insects keeping us awake or the heat, it was the rats. You could hear them in the night gnawing on our pile of luggage in search of food. I woke up once to find one the size of a kitten staring at me from a few inches away on the mattress.

The *Fayum* was never going to be a fast ship, but before we embarked the following morning, we found no fewer than twenty-four of Wolseley's boats tied to the stern. Their drag in the current meant we could not exceed walking pace. We also had to tie up each night to avoid running aground in the dark. Every day we saw sailing barges crawl slowly past us; some were transporting soldiers, but most were full of supplies, particularly fodder for the huge herd of camels waiting ahead. Leila and my beasts of burden arrived days before us. Our voyage took a week to cover the 210 miles to Wadi Halfa. So far, we had travelled 230 miles in the first train: 330 miles in the first steamer, ten miles on the second train around the cataracts and now this last distance, a total of seven hundred and eighty miles. Yet as we stood wearily covered in coal dust and insect bites, we knew that we had but reached the Egypt–Sudan border. We were only halfway.

The trip had taken less than a month, but now things would get much harder. There was a series of cataracts in the river ahead of us which stopped the steamers going any further. The old Khedive had started a railway line around them but had run out of money before it had gone thirty miles. It would help get the cutters over the first stretch, but then the crews would be on their own to navigate the rest. A train was waiting in a siding near the river to take the boats on the next stage of their journey, but there was no great sense of urgency about the place.

As we stepped ashore, we found another vast army camp with rows of neatly ordered tents. A space had been allocated for correspondents, but Leila was not in it. I was sure that she must have arrived earlier and so went in search of her. It was then that I saw a company of British infantry, who were to be part of the new Camel Corps, being introduced to their mounts.

Camels were a completely unknown entity to almost everyone in the British army. Burleigh told me that ignorance of the creatures was such that a company of farriers had been sent upriver to keep them supplied with shoes. It had been assumed that they had hard hooves that would need to be shod, rather than the soft pads that spread out in contact with the ground. Thousands of camel saddles had been made and shipped from Britain. Heaven knows how they had been designed, but they came with stirrups, which camels were not used to. As soon as they felt a weight on the iron they would often try to rise, with tumultuous consequences. Soldiers soon learned to throw themselves into the saddle in the traditional manner, but the saddle also had bucket holsters for rifles, which got in the way. Eventually, they learned to wear their guns on the sling over their backs until they were safely proceeding.

This, of course, came with experience, and the men I saw had none of that. Perhaps the creatures sensed they were in the presence of novices, or maybe they had been standing in the sun too long and were fed up. I was to learn from my own riding that there is no more cantankerous an animal than an irritated camel. These poor troops found that if they approached their mount from the front, they were invariably spat at with vile-smelling vomit. Coming from the other end could see them kicked or assailed with pellet-like droppings; while from the side, long necks and snapping teeth would try to keep them at bay. It often took two soldiers working together just to get a hold of the head rope. Even then, the animals would bellow angrily like lions.

Arab camel herders, who had rudely been sent away by sergeants, confident that the finest soldiers in the British army could master any task, were sheepishly summoned back. Only then was progress made in saddling and getting soldiers mounted, but it was far from an impressive display. No training had been given in how to control the animals and soon they were whirling about in columns of dust, roaring in indignation as soldiers beat or kicked them in an effort to comply with orders. Yet the sergeants and officers giving the commands, often could not get their animals to comply either. Riders swiftly discovered that irritated camels can bend their necks to bite their rider's knees or butt them with the backs of their heads and even drop and roll to throw riders off their backs. After an hour, of the thirty men I was watching, six had been sent to the sick bay suffering bite and kick wounds while the remainder, with a lot of Arab help, had finally managed to get their beasts walking a wide circle.

Just as I was about to leave, the ambitious officer in charge of these pioneers decided it was time to attempt a canter across the plain. I had not tried that yet myself and quickly saw the challenge. The back of the animal rolled as it broke into a run, making it even harder to stay aboard. Three more men fell heavily to the ground, while a fourth discovered the hard way that the saddle girth was not tight enough. He and his saddle slipped off the animal's rump. To add injury to insult, he got a hoof kick in the face as his ride went on without him. After witnessing the chaotic display, I felt even more apprehensive about the journey ahead on my own mounts.

My next challenge was to find those animals and Leila. She was nowhere to be seen, but my guide was a memorable figure. When I asked some of the soldiers if they had seen a pretty woman in white robes, they all pointed to the west and told me she had a camp on the edge of the desert. A quarter mile stroll, just beyond the alluvial plain of the Nile, I found a tent pitched in the shade of a grove of palms with a familiar collapsible chair outside. Any irritation I felt at having to walk such a distance in the midday heat melted when I saw her. With no one else about she had removed her headscarf. The top of her robe was also unfastened, a breeze rippling it against her curves. If my mouth was not already dry, it would have been with desire. She smiled as she saw me and offered me some water, but I took her in my arms instead, a need far stronger than thirst to quench.

My camp bed was only designed for one, yet that was all the room we needed, first one on top and then the other. Afterwards we found room to lie on our sides, naked and sated. She had her back to me and I idly draped an arm around her waist, stroking her stomach. Even her skin smelt dusky and exotic. As her round buttocks pressed into me, I felt the stirrings of desire again.

"It was clever of you to put the camp here so we could have some privacy," I said, nibbling her ear as I glanced through the still open door

70

of the tent. "We certainly could not have done this in a camp full of soldiers."

"That was not the only reason. It is not healthy to camp on the plain. The river and animals have left disease in the soil. Your soldiers have become ill."

"It is probably just the heat that is affecting them," I replied, moving a hand up to her breast. "I am sure that our officers know what they are doing."

To my disappointment she swung her legs off the bed and sat up. "There are already over a hundred men in the tents they use for the sick and some of them die and are buried every day. Would you like some water?" She stood and walked over to the purification device I had brought from London.

"I had no idea things were that bad," I told her as I got up to open a trunk carrying my clothes. "It is time I started to take precautions."

"What foolishness is that?" she asked as she turned round holding out a cup.

"This," I announced as I tightened it around my middle, "is a Pargeter's Camphorated Cholera Belt. It is guaranteed to stop me catching cholera."

"A belt cannot stop you catching a disease," she retorted. Her nose wrinkled, "And it smells. You are not coming near me wearing that."

I laughed. "You do not understand modern science. Medicine is far more advanced in London than Cairo. If cholera belts did not work, then the army would not have issued them to every soldier in Egypt."

"These same soldiers that are now dying of disease in the camp?" she shot back as she shrugged her robe back over her head. "It sounds to me that medicine makers in London are much like those in Cairo. They sell oils, powders, amulets and now belts, but very few of them make any difference at all."

"Perhaps those that died were not wearing their belts," I muttered, pulling on my trousers. We finished getting dressed, for Rafa would soon be back from the Nile where he'd taken the camels to drink and graze. That evening we walked back through the camp to join the other correspondents for dinner. In the cooler part of the day, men were loading more of the cutters onto the train to take them past the next cataracts. Their crews, however, remained in the camp. Some strolled about between the tents, smoking and chatting among themselves as another day came to an end.

There was a timelessness about the desert somehow. Everything was as it had been for thousands of years. Perhaps it was this and the heat that discouraged men from rushing. We all knew that seven hundred miles to the south a city was starving and relying on us for its rescue, but there was no greater sense of haste than at the renewals desk at my local library. The chaotic training I had seen that morning was not uncommon among the Camel Corps. Standing orders had been issued that they would advance their camels at walking pace and dismount to engage the enemy. We had several squadrons of the horse-mounted Nineteenth Hussars who would act as scouts. They could gallop safely and fight from the saddle if required.

Chambois, who had visited the French Foreign Legion garrisons in North Africa, was scornful. "Your whole Camel Corps is absurd," he scoffed. "The French army knows that a man can walk as fast as a camel and so they march through the desert on foot. Camels are only used to carry supplies and guns. What is the point of these animals for riding?" he demanded. "They just slow you down as you have to find food and supplies for them as well. The Legion would be in Khartoum by now and Gordon would be safe," he insisted.

"A camel can walk for much longer than a man," Leila replied calmly. "But their strength must be saved for when it is needed, such as to cross a desert. Then they will need several days to rest and recover."

"And what about your little boats, pah!" Chambois threw up his arms in a gallic gesture of disgust. "What a waste of time. You British want to bring your own navy with you, but as you know, the river is already full of boats."

It was scathing criticism by the Frenchman, but it was hard to argue against. We had all heard of a report from Colonel Kitchener, who advised that there were native craft for four thousand men already waiting ahead at Dongola. Wolseley's insistence on manufacturing, transporting and using eight hundred boats of our own, was an enormous waste of men, resources and most importantly, time. Yet we knew our general considered his carefully calculated plans inviolate. He had not listened when other generals and even ministers had tried to talk him out of ordering the boats. He certainly would not take advice from one of the despised correspondents. He had staked his reputation on his scheme and we were stuck with it now for better or worse.

Dongola was not quite halfway to Khartoum from where we were at Wadi Halfa on the border. We already had a small advance guard there. Cameron was still sure that the Mahdists would start to fall back as our men got within striking distance. "They must know they cannot beat us," he insisted.

Burleigh was not so sure. "Like every soldier in every war," he warned, "they believe that God is on their side. In this case they have God's prophet giving them orders. Having declared a holy war on the infidel, the Mahdi can hardly change his mind and slink back off into the desert. I think they will stand."

We tucked into a dinner of tinned mutton and rice, with some fresh dates to go with our coffee. Leila was treated like an honoured guest, particularly by Cameron, who was clearly quite smitten. He readily agreed with her that the land next to the river did not seem a healthy place to camp. Chambois also concurred, pointing out that the soldiers' clothes were damp in the morning from where they drew up moisture from the ground. Burleigh's reasons for moving were even more prosaic. "The camp is too bloody noisy," he complained. "One bugler could blow the *reveille* for the whole assembly, but no. Every bloody regiment must have its own bugler sound off. Then there are more calls for boots, breakfast, caring for the mounts… If that was not bad enough, several times a day we have volleys crashing out for the dead. They are planting them just a hundred yards from the sick bay tents. These regular reminders of mortality cannot be helping the poor devils struggling to pull through their fever."

In the end, much to my consternation, they all decided to up sticks and join Leila and I on the edge of the desert. They gave us a few yards of space, but the days of lounging together naked in the tent, with a breeze coming through the open flap, was over.

Chapter 7

Over the next few days, we did very little. Some of the newly mounted infantry went out on patrols to get used to their animals. They went past us one morning trying to keep in a column four men wide. Unfortunately for them, camels can be choosy about which of their fellows they will ride alongside. One in the fourth rank was determined to ride in the third. The sergeant was bellowing at the hapless trooper to get his mount back, but with little success. When they came back four hours later I noticed that the third rank was still five men wide. For all their stubbornness, though, camels were in many ways easier to control than horses. They all kept a steady walking pace and would trudge calmly on for hours.

I needed practice in the saddle so I sometimes joined Rafa in his ride down to the river to water our animals. There was a telegraph office in Wadi Halfa and we had all filed reports to our editors on the journey so far. Frank had cabled back to ask when I would be moving on and when we would arrive in Khartoum. It was a good question. We were all anxious to continue our journey, but it would be dangerous for a few lightly armed journalists to travel alone. Some disgruntled *bashi-bazouks* or other bandits would see us as a rich and vulnerable prize. We had to wait for a column of the Camel Corps to leave so that we could join them in the next stage of the advance. When I asked a colonel when that was likely to be, he rounded on me furiously. "You bloody hacks have no idea of the complexities in managing a campaign. You fill papers with nonsense suggesting that we are going too slowly. It won't do Gordon any good if half the army or its animals die of thirst or starvation through lack of supplies on the way, will it?" With that he stormed off.

We, of course, had not seen the London papers for weeks, but clearly the army were getting reports of the contents, and they were not happy. Judging from Frank's questions, there was impatience in London. After all, the last we had heard from Gordon was that his food supplies would be running out around now. We were still weeks from Khartoum. I remembered well all the protest marches, petitions and preaching to get this relief mission agreed. Everyone who had taken part felt it was *their* mission and they wanted, no, demanded, that it succeed. The papers would be reflecting their readers' wishes.

I had not replied to Frank's questions, but the following day I received another telegram from him. *Received Gordon's latest message [stop] Urgent [stop] Give best estimate of when in Khartoum.* I stared at the paper in surprise and then at the soldier in the telegraph office. "Do you know about a new message from Gordon?" I asked.

"No sir," he replied woodenly, but he glanced over at his officer watching us closely from the corner of the tent. I was sure he was lying.

"I want to send a reply," I told the soldier and picked up a new telegraph form. *What was Gordon's latest message?* I wrote and handed the paper back. I had a strong suspicion that I would not receive any response until the army was ready for the information to be released. Well, there is more than one way to skin a cat and I went off to look for another source. I found Cochrane talking to some of his troopers and waited for him to notice me standing to one side. Instead of greeting me, he turned on his heel and wandered among a herd of sitting camels where he crouched beside one to check on its girth.

"I thought you would be along," he grunted as he tugged on the strap.

"Do you know what is going on?" I asked as I dropped down beside him. "Frank tells me that Gordon has got another message out, which is widely known in London but not here."

"No, I don't, but something is afoot," Cochrane whispered. "Wolseley is expected back here tomorrow for a meeting with his senior commanders. Now sheer off. If I am seen talking to you, he will have me sent back to Cairo."

I hurried back to the camp with my news. Burleigh and Cameron were sure they could find out more from their sources, but all they could learn was that there was increased urgency to move men up the line.

Wolseley arrived on the train from the south the following morning. There was no point in trying to speak to him; he would never give a correspondent useful information. In fact, if the London papers were being critical, it would be best not to remind him of our presence in the camp at all. He would probably send us all back to Cairo. In the end, the information found us. Late that afternoon an earnest young man in civilian clothes was seen weaving through the nearest army lines and making his way over the stretch of open ground towards our cluster of tents.

"What ho, you fellows," he called out cheerily. "What are you doing hiding all the way out here?"

"St Leger!" I replied in delight, for here was a man who might be able to shed some light. St Leger Herbert held a unique position amongst the press corps in that he was a special correspondent for the *Morning Post*, but he had also been private secretary to several senior men, including Wolseley. He was thus the only journalist that our general was likely to trust. "Can you tell us what the hell is going on?"

"I suppose that there is no harm in you knowing, as your editors already have the information," replied St Leger. "I say, any chance of a drink? I am parched." He walked with a limp as he had been wounded in the fighting at the Red Sea the year before. Swiftly, a chair was provided in the shade of the awning. Burleigh poured him a stiff scotch, probably in the hope that it would help loosen his tongue. "Ahh that is better," he gasped after taking a deep pull on the glass. "It has been a long day." He looked around to see us all staring expectantly at him and finally blurted out the news. "Gordon got another message out. The courier must have got to Suakin, for the news reached London before it got to Wolseley, which he is not happy about."

"We know that much," interrupted Cameron impatiently. "What did it say?"

"It was dated the fourth of November. Gordon thought then that he could hold out in Khartoum for another forty days. He also warned that there were twenty thousand Mahdists around the city. Their numbers were if anything growing, even though they knew the British army was on its way."

"But that means that he will run out of food in roughly a month," I pointed out. "We will never get to the city in time, certainly not in numbers to defeat twenty thousand."

"Several of the staff feel that Gordon can hold out for even longer," stated St Leger. "I was in the meeting, representing Colonel Stewart who commands the advance guard at Dongola. They think that when the alternative is being butchered, the good citizens of Khartoum will eke out every last scrap they have."

"But his original deadline was around now," countered Cameron. "Perhaps this extra forty days is the 'eking'. There must be a limit to how much they can stretch things out."

"When does Wolseley think the army will arrive?" Burleigh cut in with the more pertinent question.

"I can't tell you that," said St Leger quietly, "but you can judge as well as me that we are unlikely to get there in time." We all silently pondered what state Khartoum would be in when we did finally reach it. I pictured those bright blue eyes staring out from sunken sockets as Gordon looked up the river in vain for the relief column. Would the Mahdists fall back as we got closer? There were ten thousand men in the Gordon Relief Expedition; we would be outnumbered two to one. Yet surely the advantage in weaponry would more than make up for that.

"Is there no way we can get there sooner?" pressed Burleigh.

"The Nile goes south past Dongola to the town of Korti," explained St Leger. "You will have seen on the map that it then bends around to make a big loop to the north, taking us four hundred miles out of our way. Wolseley plans to stick to the river with his boats, for that will give us fresh water. Our soldiers can deal with garrisons such as Berber as we pass them."

"You British are mad!" interrupted Chambois, slapping his knee in frustration. "You persist with these ridiculous boats, even when you know that they will arrive far too late. Then you try to fool yourselves that General Gordon can hold out for months until you arrive. If Gordon was French, he would be on his way back to Paris by now. Our Foreign Legion would have marched on foot, needing far fewer supplies, so they would not be waiting weeks in camps like this for them to catch up." We all glared in irritation at the boastful man from *Le Temps*. He had been banging this same drum for some time. Our annoyance at his manner was compounded by the fact that we thought he was probably right.

"Our Gallic friend here might have a point," agreed St Leger amiably. "General Buller has suggested that the army leaves the river at Korti then marches across the neck of the loop to re-join the Nile just a hundred and fifty miles north of Khartoum. It would save several weeks. If Gordon knew we were coming, he could arrange for his steamers to take us the final stretch into the city."

"Then surely we must go that route," insisted Cameron. "It is our best chance of reaching Gordon in time."

"I doubt it will be that straightforward," I interjected, while looking around for Leila. She had been sitting slightly outside our circle as we had gathered to meet our guest, but she had been listening quietly. "Do you know this area?" I asked. "How easy would it be to cross?"

"It is the route that the caravans take," she replied.

"There you are then," cried Cameron triumphantly, but she held up a finger to cut him off.

"It is an area called the Bayuda Desert," she continued. "You would have to walk a hundred and eighty miles across sand and rock. There are only two places to find sufficient water on the way and you would need to stop at both to keep the camels alive."

"I am sure we could do it," insisted Cameron.

"You have not crossed any desert yet," Leila gently reminded him, smiling.

"Would there be water for ten thousand men to cross?" I asked.

She paused, considering, "Certainly enough for several thousand and their camels."

"We don't have enough camels for the full force," Burleigh reminded us, before glaring at Chambois. "We would certainly need them for that desert, as would your precious Foreign Legion. Most of our men are expected to arrive by water and boats do not need fodder to keep moving. It would take an age to get thousands more camels for men and their supplies, as well as food upriver to feed them all." He turned to St Leger, "There are what, two thousand men here? Where is the rest of the relief force?"

"That I can tell you," replied the journalist, grinning, and taking a notebook from his pocket. "It was a question that Wolseley asked at our

78

meeting. I made a note of the numbers for Colonel Stewart when I get back to him. Now, where was it..." He flicked through his pages of notes, "...ah yes here we are. You are right, there are two thousand men here and another thirteen hundred with Stewart at our forward base in Dongola. There are also two thousand nine hundred travelling between here and Dongola, most of whom are in the boats. Two hundred of the craft have already been despatched but there are a similar number of boats here still awaiting crews. Another fourteen hundred are travelling on the river between Aswan and here. Beyond them eighteen hundred are still camped at Aswan and six hundred are still travelling between Asyut and Aswan."

"Some of them will never get here in time," concluded Burleigh.

"Strictly between ourselves," confided St Leger, "our general is immensely frustrated with the pace of the advance. His staff officers blame each other, but all are now trying to get as many men up as quickly as possible. There will be a column of the Camel Corps leaving tomorrow if you want to join it. I am taking the train back as far as it goes and have an escort waiting for me."

We began to make our preparations to leave for the next stage of the journey. Leila told me that it would take around two weeks to travel between Wadi Halfa and Dongola. We would have no access to a telegraph then and so, before we left, I wanted to find an answer to Frank's question. Thanks to St Leger, I had an idea of who might tell me, but he would require delicate handling.

General Redvers Buller was a huge man with no obvious neck. His head just grew from his shoulders. He was undoubtedly brave – he had earned the Victoria Cross fighting the Zulus – yet no one would claim that he was particularly shrewd. His approach to most problems was to charge straight at them; perhaps that was why he favoured the Bayuda route. Why waste weeks rowing in the wrong direction when you can march straight to the Nile just above Khartoum? Yet as Wolseley's right-hand man, he was bound to know his chief's view on correspondents and would not want to tell me anything. I deliberately waited until late in the afternoon to make my move. By then he was likely to be well oiled with liquor and less guarded. On the other hand, his temper had a famously short fuse. He might kick me out before I had uttered a word.

"General Buller," I stood in his tent entrance with my best cheery grin, a gesture that was not returned, "I have been wondering if we were considering crossing the Bayuda Desert to reach Gordon in time. If we were, my guide has crossed it a couple of times before and I would be happy to share the information they have given me about the route."

Glassy eyes regarded me blankly as though still registering what I had told him. A half-drunk bottle of champagne stood on the table before him and another was upturned and empty in a bucket. "Who the devil are you?" he barked at last.

"Thomas Harrison of the *Daily News*," I replied genially. I continued to favour him with my best smile, but it was still not reciprocated. If anything, his look grew even more sour.

"Then you should know that I do not give interviews to correspondents," he snapped. "If you want information, you should write to General Wolseley." His expression turned into a sneer at this, as he clearly knew what a pointless exercise that would be.

"I do know that, sir," I explained patiently. "And I appreciate that we journalists are normally asking for news to report, but on this occasion, we might have information that you would find useful."

"I very much doubt that." He began to raise his hand as he glanced through the tent flap, looking, I suspected, for his sentry to throw me back out. I needed something else quickly to show that I was on his side.

"I see you drink the same brand of champagne as Monsieur Chambois," I said gesturing to the bottle on the table.

"Eh, what's that?" The hand stilled in the air. Buller was in charge of supplies for the whole army. I was sure that he would know that quantities were being pilfered. He was likely to take a particular interest in his precious champagne.

I looked the general firmly in the eye as I sold out my irritating French colleague. "Yes, Monsieur Chambois of the *Le Temps* newspaper in Paris, he greatly enjoys Veuve Clicquot. He must have his own supplies," I added innocently, "but I am sure the other evening he was drinking the same brand."

80

"Was he now," muttered Buller, leaning forward now to write Chambois' name on a slip of paper.

I suppressed a grin of satisfaction. That would pay the devil back for nearly getting me killed at Sedan. His tent was bound to be searched although I doubted that they would find any champagne. It was Cameron who sourced the occasional bottle and we drank it as soon as he 'found' it. Having earned a small reprieve, I hurried on, "About the Bayuda Desert sir…"

"What about it?" Buller was on guard again. "Has St Leger been talking to you?"

"Heavens no, sir. His lips are tighter than the neck of a Scotsman's purse." The general gave a short bark of amusement as I went on. "It is just that when you look at the map, it is the obvious route to take. Why waste weeks by going four hundred miles out of our way following the Nile, when we can just march across the desert. I have heard that Gordon has got out another message. While I don't know what it contained, I imagine he cannot hold out much longer, every day must count now."

"General Wolseley has given his orders," Buller countered, his voice, clipped. I could tell it was a decision that he did not believe in. "The army is to follow the course of the Nile in accordance with his plan."

I grinned conspiratorially. "With the greatest respect, General, we both know that General Wolseley often says one thing to correspondents and then does another. I was thinking that this might be another of his attempts to deceive the enemy."

"Let us both hope that you are right," Buller confided, "otherwise Gordon might have to wait until the end of January for the army to reach him. But the Bayuda route is not without risk."

I hid a smile of triumph. The end of January was a full six weeks beyond when Gordon thought Khartoum would fall. Surely his estimate of how long supplies could last would not be out by that much. The river route would be too late; Wolseley would have to cross the desert to stand any chance of rescuing his friend. "My guide says that there is water at a place called Jakdul, and springs at an oasis called Abu Klea. She thinks there will be enough water in both places for several thousand men and camels."

"She?" repeated Buller frowning and then his brow cleared. "Ah yes, I have heard of your guide – she has made quite an impression among the men." He gave me a warning stare. "I cannot say I approve of women in the camp, but in this case I dare say she is right. The water in Jakdul is in tanks naturally formed in the rock. Levels depend on winter rainfall and how much has been used by passing caravans, or indeed armies. Wolseley is concerned that such a supply would be vulnerable to poisoning. He thinks an army could be trapped there without enough water to return or press on."

It was a reasonable concern, I thought. After all, the Mahdists had poisoned wells to trap Hicks. Yet given the nature of our mission I did not really see that he had a choice. He had to try the Bayuda route, perhaps with an advance guard and then send the rest of the army on when the water supply was secure. Of course, we did not have camels for the whole army, most of the men were in those damned boats. But if Chambois was right, they could march into the desert as fast as they could ride.

I left Buller's tent then, and made my way down to the Nile, where several irrigation water wheels lay redundant, after their owners were paid to stop their awful creaking racket. A few crops had gone yellow in the fields but on the other side of the river there was a broad band of verdant green before the desert began again. A few women from the nearby town were washing clothes on the bank. Much of it was khaki as they were making a good living washing for the soldiers. I carefully watched over my shoulder to ensure that I had not been followed. You could not be too careful with Wolseley; he might have detailed a few officers to keep an eye on us correspondents. When I was satisfied that no one had followed me from Buller's tent I made my way to the telegraph office. It would have to be an innocuous message, but it helped that my editor was also my uncle. I sent him a telegram to his home address. *To Uncle Frank, stop. Re your last stop. Aunt Agatha's birthday is 30 January TH.* The clerk barely gave it a second glance before it was placed on the transmit pile.

By the time I reached my tent, a furious Chambois was being marched down to the quay where he was ordered to take a boat back in the direction of Cairo. His tent had been searched and while no champagne had been found, a vast stock of other stolen army supplies had.

Chapter 8

Camels can sense when bad weather is coming. They had been even more bad tempered than usual that day, growling from the back of their throats whenever they were asked to do anything. I had not detected the cause of their intransigence, but Leila unexpectedly announced that there was a storm coming.

"I doubt it, there is not a cloud in the sky," I pointed out.

"Soon you will not be able to see the sky," she replied. Gesturing out into the desert she added, "A sandstorm is coming, we must organise shelter."

"Captain," I shouted to the officer riding ahead of us. "We need to stop. My guide tells me that there is a sandstorm coming." The officer turned in the saddle and glared petulantly at Leila, as though she had arranged the storm personally, just to annoy him. Then with a heavy sigh he called his column to a halt. They were the company of infantry that I had seen introduced to their camels some three weeks before. Their commander certainly did not approve of women on the campaign, and he vehemently resented taking advice from them. Yet over the previous ten days he had learned that Leila was invariably right.

The distance between Wadi Halfa and Dongola, our next destination, was two hundred and forty-five miles. The horse-mounted cavalry planned to cover it riding fifteen miles a day. Leila had suggested that he set a similar pace for his camels. "What is the point of a camel if it cannot cross the desert faster than a horse?" the man had grumbled.

Leila had patiently explained that in a desert a camel could ride for sixteen hours a day with little food or water for a week. Then it would need a least a week of rest with water and fodder before it could be used again. "You will need the strength of your animals later in your journey," she had warned. "You should save it until then."

The officer had seen the sense in what she said. We were travelling frequently along the banks of the Nile where there was ample water and grazing. At other times we used the railway cutting which had been partially blasted out of the rock for the line that had not been completed. These infantry soldiers had little idea of how to look after their animals.

The pack saddles supplied by the army were roughly made and initially the officer had refused advice on how to pad them. Yet after several animals were left with bleeding callouses, he changed his mind.

The soldiers destined for Wolseley's cutters were also learning new skills. We watched them being introduced to their craft; it was obvious that many had not held an oar before. Our general had changed one part of his precious plan with regard to his boats. Formerly, they were to carry twelve men, being ten soldiers and two boatmen, such as the Canadians or Ashanti. Now they would carry just the soldiers. The expert boatmen would only be on hand for the start of the journey to show them how to manage their craft. Others were stationed at the cataracts. There, they would build experience of how best to beat the eddies and rocks. The spare space in the cutters was now taken up by more supplies, so that in addition to their own rations, they were now carrying some for the rest of the army.

The soldiers had all been issued goggles in preparation for sandstorms, something that I had not thought to bring myself. They now got them from their kits and hung them loose around their necks until required. They had long since learned how to hobble their camels to stop them getting up. Leila made sure that the animals were sitting facing towards the river, away from the coming wind. Then a rope was tied around their foreleg and thigh to stop them straightening the knee. Once they were secure, the tents were unloaded. They were bell tents with a central pole that came in two sections, but Leila shouted that we should only use one pole to keep the tent lower. The canvas on the windward side was to be spread out and anchored down with rocks. The captain heard her instructions and wisely ordered his men to follow suit.

I still felt no great urgency. There was barely a puff of wind, and the sky was benignly clear. As tents were pitched, we started to gather lumps of stone to weigh down the sides; there was no shortage of those in this part of the desert. Soon there was a line of low canvas humps that were barely any higher than the row of sitting camels beside them. I thought we had finished our task, but Leila had Rafa and I collect yet more rocks so that there was a small rampart anchoring the edge. Some soldiers nearest us had stopped work and were larking about. Leila shouted at them, but they bristled at that. "We don't take orders from bloody *houris*," one replied before another added that it was all a waste of time as there was no damn storm at all.

"Look!" Leila pointed out into the desert. I stared back over my shoulder to see that the horizon between the clear blue sky and the ground was no longer distinct. There was a foggy orange blur where it had been. "It will be here in just a few minutes," she warned anyone who would listen. It had to be at least ten miles away over the flat terrain, I thought, yet I had long since learned not to argue with her over matters involving the desert. The soldiers too quietly redoubled their efforts at gathering rock. Sure enough, when I looked again a minute or so later, the blur was much closer. There was a height to it now, a wall of orange hundreds of feet high with a growing whistling noise. "Get inside!" Leila yelled along the line and this time no one was slow in obeying. We had to crawl in on our hands and knees. Rafa was already inside, bracing his back against the central pole. We had put extra guy ropes on the windward side, making sure the pegs were well hammered in and covered in rock. The noise was louder now, competing with a rising growl from the hobbled camels as the storm approached. It sounded as though a horde of banshees was bearing down on us. Then the storm hit.

The whole tent rocked. I saw now why Rafa had put his body against the pole, he was grunting in the effort of keeping it vertical. I went around the other side and pulled it to take some of the strain. For a moment I thought the tent would be snatched away and we would be left exposed. The canvas walls rippled like the sea and there was a loud hissing as millions of grains of sand were hurled against them. I heard shrieking and shouting outside as others were less fortunate, but you would have been mad to even try and look, never mind help. I doubted it was possible to see a single yard ahead, and that was if you had the goggles the soldiers had, which I did not. All we could do was hunker down and wait for the tempest to pass. Given the speed of its approach, I thought it would only last a few minutes, yet we remained in that tent for half an hour. The windward sides were soon sagging with the weight of sand piled against them, but Leila told me not to try and push it off. She had to shout in my ear over the noise of the storm to tell me that the weight of the sand would help keep our tent grounded. I sat there wondering how the poor oarsmen in Wolseley's cutters would survive when the tempest hit them. Hopefully they would see it coming and have the sense to haul down their sails. They would surely be blown to the far side of the river and then have little choice but to crouch down beneath the gunnels of their boats.

Then, as suddenly as the storm arrived, it moved on. The noise died away in an instant, leaving an eery silence. Cautiously, we pushed open the canvas flap to find everything covered in several inches of sand. It had formed drifts around the rump of every camel and was banked a foot high on the windward side of our shelter. Looking along the line, two of the tents had collapsed but their occupants had stayed under the canvas and like us were now emerging. One tent, though, had vanished entirely. It had been snatched away and those inside forced to fend for themselves. One had managed to find another tent, two had blundered blindly into camels and crouched against their sides, but the last was found curled into a ball in the desert. His goggles had been scratched by sand until they were almost opaque, while his exposed hands were red raw and bleeding. He had managed to pull his shirt up over his mouth and nose but was coughing and spluttering from the dust he had inhaled. It was a grim reminder of the power of the desert.

By the time we had dismantled the tents and were ready to march again, the trail we had been following had disappeared. Instead of a rocky path, the ground was covered in low dunes of fresh sand. The captain and I both looked hopefully at Leila. She did not let us down. "Do you see that rock which looks like a nose?" she asked, pointing south. "The path goes to the right of that."

We were never far from the river that whole journey. Often, we could look to our left and see the distant strip of trees and crops that grew around it, if not the precious water itself. The trail was straighter and shorter but as the railway bed ran out it became more precarious. At one point we had to walk in single file on a path across a cliff face with a sheer drop down the other side. On an uneasy horse I would have been nervous, but the calm plodding camels took it in their stride, as though they had been there a dozen times before. I never saw a skittish camel;

they would just keep going until abruptly they would decide to stop. Then only food or water was likely to shift them. We had water skins and buckets to give them a drink each day and bundles of Egyptian corn called *dhura* to eat. But every second day we led them down to the river to drink and graze. It gave us time to replenish our own supplies and rest in the shade during the heat of the day, before setting off again in the cool of the evening.

One of our rest stops was the cataracts at Ambigol. It was a rocky corner of the river and judging from the sun-bleached timbers of many old craft scattered among the rocks, it had foundered many boats in its time. Wolseley's cutters were unloaded at the bottom of the rapids and their stores carried along the shore. Lightened and with the aid of one of the Canadian boatmen and ropes from the shore, its crew could then haul their vessel against the current along a channel near the bank. Even then it took two hours to cover three hundred yards, and a day to cover the mile and a half of the cataract. Many of the boats had freshly painted names on their prows, most after wives or sweethearts, although I did see one called *Gordon's Revenge*. Reloaded, they looked low in the water with their crews aboard but were soon pulling strongly away against the current.

By then these new sailors had rowed some two hundred miles and looked proficient with their oars. With no shade from the sun, though, their skin was brown or burnt, some peeling badly and their hands were calloused, but they showed no lack of determination. Beyond their helmets, they were hardly recognisable as soldiers, for their uniforms were filthy with river mud, they had not shaved for weeks and their webbing belts and rifles were all piled in the bottom of their craft. Not that they needed to fear reprimands on their appearance, for their sergeants and officers looked exactly the same. I was glad to be on a camel, for at least we could usually find some shade to avoid the worst heat of the day.

If there were no trees, the company we were with would use groundsheets and tent poles to give some shelter from the noonday sun. We would mount up again late afternoon and ride through the evening. The temperature dropped sharply as the sun went down and in contrast

88

to the day it felt almost freezing. We would soon be recovering jackets from our saddlebags to keep warm.

The desert was an eerie place in the moonlight. Half dozing in the saddle, you would swear that the shadow of a rock had just moved. More than once I drew my Webley in alarm. Twice I was jerked awake by the sound of rifle fire from the soldiers ahead. The second time there was a fusillade of shots at a suspected Mahdist moving in the gloom. When the men cautiously advanced with bayonets fixed into the night, our assailant was found to be a now dead goat, who at least provided a good dinner. Visibility could be deceptive in the daytime too. In the heat haze a line of trees might only look a few hundred yards off, but when we turned towards it, often we would find it was a couple of miles away.

The villages we passed were welcoming, although I noticed that most of their women had been hidden away from this sudden influx of foreign soldiers. But they were more than happy to sell us eggs, goats' milk and other supplies. Leila told me that they believed we were there to crush the Mahdi and spare them from his draconian rule. Occasionally we met some of the locals as they travelled along the trail we were using. Invariably, the man, unburdened, would be leading the way astride the family donkey. In his wake, on foot, would be the wife carrying on her head and under her arms their possessions, including the large palm leaf mats they slept on.

As we got closer to Korti, we found several villages that had been abandoned after Mahdist raids earlier in the year. As we rode past the burnt-out huts it felt like we were entering more hostile territory. I was glad to have our armed escort. The captain insisted now that the men wore their ammunition belts to be ready for any unexpected action. Any anxiety was quelled, however, as we arrived at the army camp in Korti. There must have been some two thousand men already there and more arriving every day in boats and on the trail we were using.

The camp was in a very pleasant setting near the river with groves of acacia and palm trees to provide plenty of shade. It was the size of a small town, with a main thoroughfare through the middle. All the regiments had their own avenues of tents off it. Wolseley and his headquarters were at one end of this 'high street', while space had been allocated to the correspondents right at the opposite end. We were hardly made to feel welcome and while officers had generously shared supplies with us on the journey, now we were back under Wolseley's vindictive gaze, any support was swiftly withdrawn. We had to provide our own shelter, food and even fodder for our animals. While many of my colleagues were back down the trail behind me, Burleigh was there as well as Cameron, St Leger and Piggot, the man from Reuters.

We had arrived on Christmas Eve and the army was doing its best to give the camp a festive air. The next day we put all our efforts into creating a seasonal dinner. There were no birds to be had, at least not for us, but a strange concoction involving dates was boiled in a clean handkerchief to make a barely recognisable Christmas pudding. It made a change from the usual biscuits and jam to liven up the inevitable tins of bully beef. The last of our spirits had been hoarded for this moment and so we enjoyed brandy and madeira, while gazing enviously at the distant officers' mess. That was bound to be better supplied, especially if Buller had anything to do with it. Despite Cameron's best efforts, not a bottle of champagne could be found as the general now jealously guarded his hoard.

That afternoon we sat in the shade of some acacia bushes and listened to a regimental band playing Christmas carols to the enthusiastic singing of the troops. We joined in, singing songs about deep snow in the baking heat of the Egyptian desert. No one could begrudge the men their celebration after the arduous journey getting here.

That evening after a Christmas concert attended by Wolseley and his staff, we gathered in our tents to discuss what would happen next. There were rumours that the relief force might cross the Bayuda, while others insisted that they would stay with the cutters. The boat crews were certainly expecting to press on up the river. Gordon's aid and Power from the *Times* had been killed by tribesmen at the top of the northern bend of the Nile. Many soldiers talked enthusiastically of exacting revenge for those murders before pressing on to subdue Berber. The officer in command of the boats had confided to Burleigh that he thought it would take a further forty days of rowing to reach Khartoum.

"But that would take until mid-February, when Gordon's supplies will have already run out," Piggot fumed.

"This is ridiculous!" I exploded. "Wolseley is obsessed with those wretched boats, but they are no damn use. Even if they make it to Khartoum, it will be too late. The only hope is to march across the Bayuda. The whole army should go, leaving the boats behind."

"We don't have enough camels for the whole army," Cameron pointed out. "Buller could have bought more if he had known Wolseley was considering crossing the Bayuda, but our commander had flatly ruled it out. There are few spare animals around Korti."

"We could go on foot and leave the camels we have to carry supplies," I insisted, thinking back to the claims Chambois had made. "If the bloody French can march in the desert, then surely we can too." I turned to Leila, "Do you think it can be done?"

She considered for a moment. "It would take longer on foot and so you would need to carry more water. It is also easier to get lost without being able to see over the top of the bushes that grow in the desert." She shrugged and concluded, "If you were not attacked, I suppose that most of the soldiers would make it."

That was hardly the ringing endorsement I was hoping for. Yet to get nearly all of the army at the Nile within striking distance of Gordon in a couple of weeks was still better than using the boats. Fuelled by the last of my brandy, I retired to my tent and wrote an article for the paper. It was a vitriolic piece that praised Buller's suggestion and roundly condemned Wolseley for his inflexibility and incompetence. Unless plans changed, the bulk of the army, I predicted, would arrive far too late to do Gordon any good. At best they might provide men to avenge his death.

In the cool of the next morning, as I awoke with Leila asleep in my arms, I wondered if I had been a little intemperate. To launch men into the desert as I had described, would be a hell of a gamble. Wolseley's reputation would be ruined if his army was killed by thirst or ambush by poorly armed tribesmen. On the other hand, the public were unlikely to forgive him if he allowed their precious Gordon to be butchered. I wondered if the talk of the boats travelling four hundred miles around the bend in the Nile was another one of his deceptions to keep us in the dark. I decided to give him the benefit of the doubt for a few days. In the meantime, I suggested to Leila that it might be time to start filling up the camel-borne water tanks. Until now the beast carrying them had enjoyed an easy life, for we had never been far from the river and our water skins had sufficed. But it would take a while to fill the tanks as water had to be passed through the filtration buckets first.

The Nile at Korti was as clear as I had seen it. The river was wide and as the current slowed, I suppose the sediment dropped down to the riverbed. Burleigh thought that it might be clear enough to drink straight from the bank at a pinch, although I noticed he did not try it himself. Rafa and I spent much of the day pouring river water into the top bucket of the filtration column and then emptying the bottom one when it was full into the camel tanks. If there was going to be an expedition across the Bayuda, then I and most of the other correspondents had determined to go with it. There was no point in joining the boats if they did sail. You stood as much chance of witnessing the relief of Gordon with them as on a fourpenny trip around Morecambe Bay.

My worst fears were confirmed the next day, the 28th of December, when the river force was finally given orders to advance. It was not to abandon its craft; instead, some eight of the ten thousand strong Gordon expedition was to be sent around the loop of the Nile. We correspondents were invited to witness this military lunacy, as a flotilla of fifty-five boats set off to join others upstream. Wolseley was standing proudly on the bank to take their salute, while the regimental band of the Royal Sussex regiment played. More boats still to arrive at Korti were to follow them in due course. This left the two thousand men of the Camel Corps standing with their animals on the bank. Rumours were that some of them might also accompany the boats.

It was the end for Gordon, I was sure of that. There was no way that these two thousand men could march across a desert, then a hundred and fifty miles along the Nile, probably being attacked and ambushed along the way, only to defeat an army of fanatics ten times their size. For all the talk of their greater weaponry, much of that too had gone with the boats. The land-based force was left with one Gardner machine gun and a battery of small seven-pounder cannon that could be dismantled and carried on camels.

I thought back to my meeting with Gordon on the train. He had certainly exceeded his brief, but he was trying to protect the people of Khartoum from murder, rape and enslavement. Instead of being offered assistance, let alone the promised rescue, he had been hung out to dry. First by Gladstone's prevarications and now by Wolseley's refusal to abandon a plan that had not evolved with the times. I was so angry that I went back to my tent, got my letter and took it to the camp post office. It would take weeks to travel back down the Nile and then on to London – Gordon would almost certainly be dead when it arrived – but at least it would give some explanation of how it had happened.

Chapter 9

The next morning Wolseley summoned Piggot, the Reuters correspondent, for a brief interview. The general insisted that the Camel Corps would be marching along the Nile to support the boats and invited the correspondent to use the telegraph to pass this information on. Piggot was a wily devil, who had heard me talk about my experiences, and to Wolseley's great annoyance, he declined the offer. It was our first clue that the Camel Corps were preparing to move, and we were now sure that they would not be riding along the riverbank. There were other signs too that day. Great piles of stores were placed out in the camel park in long lines, each bundle big enough for one animal; saddles and harnesses were being repaired and troughs of Egyptian corn were piled high so the animals could eat their fill.

Yet as we wandered through the camp, it was soon apparent that only half of the Camel Corps was filling water containers and preparing to leave. Most of the light and heavy cavalry camel regiments sat idle, gazing on enviously at their comrades in the mounted infantry and Guards regiments. One such cavalryman who was checking his camel was fed was my friend Cochrane. Having made sure I was not being watched, I picked up a large sheaf of corn and, holding it partly in front of my face, sidled over to him. "Do you know what is going on?" I whispered.

"We ride for Jakdul Wells tomorrow afternoon," he replied quietly while studiously examining some saddle bindings.

"So why are most of your cavalry regiment staying here?"

"We don't have enough camels, so our beasts will be used to carry supplies to the wells and then they will come back here for the rest. Wolseley also does not want to risk the entire force if the wells have been poisoned. I am one of the few from my regiment going with the first wave to help handle the camels. Then I am to come straight back to report if the wells have been secured."

"Thanks," I whispered, dropping some of the corn stems in front of his animal and turning away. The creature would need all the food it could get if it was to trek the hundred miles from Korti to Jakdul, come straight back again and then head out on the crossing a third time. I would never be allowed to send a telegram with this news and so I shared it with the others when I got back. Piggot decided to go with this advanced guard as he was concerned that Wolseley might have him sent back for refusing to cooperate with his own deception. The rest of us resolved to wait to join the cavalry regiments and the second crossing. I still had O'Donovan on my mind. The army Hicks commanded had been trapped by poisoned wells and if I had been the Mahdi, I would have polluted the wells at Jakdul. It would block the Bayuda route and force the British to stick to the Nile. Our enemy probably knew from spies better than we did that this would be far too late for Khartoum.

The first desert column finally left Korti at three the following afternoon. Once more the military band was on hand to lend a celebratory air, although this time their tunes were almost drowned out by the roaring of camels. As nearly three thousand beasts were forced up onto their feet, they growled their disapproval as though they knew what ordeals were to come. If anyone was foolish enough to stand in front or behind, they risked being spat at or covered in dung. I had already discovered to my cost that camels can fire dung pellets some distance when annoyed. Soon they were twisting around, biting and kicking at each other or at anyone who got in their way. Gradually, they settled on who they would walk with and which animals they most stubbornly would not.

Wolseley ignored the resulting chaos and rode forward on his horse to join Colonel Stewart in covering the first few miles south. In their wake came the Guards Camel Regiment, which made up the advance guard. They had to carry their own possessions while in their wake came the main supply column. Dozens of angry, sweating troopers tried to organise two thousand baggage camels while communicating with the local camel drivers. The Sudanese knew far more about handling the animals than the soldiers but could not speak a word of English. Some of their loads fell off before the animals had gone more than a few feet and they were hurriedly forced to kneel again while the cargo was re-secured. If there was ever any order to the vast herd, I did not see it. Soldiers and camel herders rushed about trying to keep the creatures moving in the right direction, but it was not long before they disappeared into a cloud of their own dust. The column must have already stretched out a mile before the Mounted Infantry Camel Regiment, which formed the rear-guard, was finally able to set off themselves.

By the time Wolseley rode back to camp, we could see that the front of the column had already stopped to allow the rear to catch up, but it was moving again before nightfall. Leila had passed a critical eye over the departing herd and thought that some were unlikely to make the journey between Korti and Jakdul once, never mind three times without rest. We had already resisted attempts to requisition our camels by an over-eager quartermaster. He had pointed out that they looked some of the strongest animals in Korti and wanted me to loan them, but I refused. "Your general has insisted that the army provide no support for correspondents. I am not now helping the army," I told him. "Anyway, I need these camels to follow the column and do my job." He went off muttering something about treasonous behaviour, but I did not care. Leila and Rafa had done an excellent job in keeping our mounts in capital trim. I had no idea what challenges awaited us, but I strongly suspected we might need every ounce of strength they could muster. As things turned out, we needed it rather sooner than I thought.

"Knock-knock, sir. If that is Mr Harrison, I would like a word with you in private." The voice, from just beyond the closed tent flap, came as I was going to bed.

"Who is it?" I called, pulling on my trousers while Leila reached for her robe.

I did not recognise the voice; it had an upper-class drawl and I guessed it was one of the well-connected aristocrats who had joined the column. I was even more mystified when the man replied, "I would rather not say, sir."

I crouched through the flap to find a young army lieutenant standing outside. "What the devil is this about?" I asked as he led me a few yards away from the tents.

"I have been sent to tell you that General Wolseley has read your letter to London," the officer began quietly.

"What? The impertinence. He has no right to read our private correspondence." I was furious. It was impossible to avoid the army reading our telegrams. Governments often censored them as the information they carried was immediate and could be damaging. But private letters were another thing entirely, at least to me. It would be weeks before they reached their destination and by then would have no value to the enemy. "I will make a formal complaint," I began to bluster, but the lieutenant reached out and put a hand on my arm.

"That would be a very bad idea, sir. You don't understand, I am trying to help you."

"How is waking me up in the middle of the night helping me?" I demanded, my voice rising. Leila was peering out from the canvas flap now. I did not doubt that some of the other nearby tents contained curious ears listening in.

"Because at nine o'clock tomorrow morning," he replied, "I will be obeying General Wolseley's orders to come back here to arrest you. Then I must personally escort you all the way back to Cairo, ensuring you send no telegrams or letters on the way." I must have stood and gaped at him in surprise, for I don't recall saying anything. Meanwhile I remember hearing a muttered 'bloody hell' from one of the nearby tents. Now that he could see that he had my full attention the lieutenant went on. "I don't want to travel to Cairo and miss the rest of the campaign. When I mentioned this to General Buller, he suggested that if I were to speak to you now, well, you might not be here when I came to arrest you in the morning."

Now things began to fall into place. This privileged young man had tried to get himself out of an onerous duty by complaining to Buller. Perhaps he hoped someone else would be sent in his stead. I wondered if Buller had read my letter too, for in it I had given him the credit for suggesting the Bayuda route back in November, when additional camels could have been obtained. Perhaps he remembered our earlier conversation, but whatever the reason, he was inclined to do me a favour now. But where to go? I turned to Leila, "If we follow the column into the desert," I asked, "will we have enough water in the tanks to get back if the wells turn out to be undrinkable?"

"Yes, if we are careful," she replied. She looked up at the three-quarter moon and added, "There is enough light to travel at night, it will be more comfortable then too." In a moment she was off to collect Rafa and the camels while Burleigh, who had been eavesdropping on my conversation, emerged from his tent to wish me well.

"We will see you at Jakdul," he whispered.

In a moment I had been joined by several other correspondents, who helped me collapse the tent, dismantle the bed and pile my possessions ready to leave. We had all become quite proficient at breaking camp on the long journey so far. There were far fewer boxes of supplies now after two months of travelling through Egypt and Sudan, which was just as well with the extra weight in the water tanks. In just half an hour the animals were saddled and loaded up and we were ready to leave. The lieutenant had stayed nearby and now walked with us as we led the camels quietly through the camp to the southern perimeter. His presence ensured that the sentries did not bother us.

"Good luck, sir." The officer wished us well, shaking my hand. "Don't take this the wrong way," he added, grinning, "but I hope I don't see you again any time soon."

In less than an hour after I had been so rudely disturbed, I was in the saddle, rocking gently with the movement of the creature beneath me as we made our way under the stars across the Bayuda Desert. If you are imagining huge endless sand dunes, you would be mistaken. There were some low ripples of sand that had been shaped by the wind to look like giant fish scales. There were also grey plains of cracked clay, pockmarked with tufts of desert grass, which proved the land was not always arid. Water from these infrequent rains would gather in what were now dry riverbeds. These gullies were easy to spot as often they were filled with stunted thorn bushes that made the most of the moisture underneath. Across the desert ran great formations of black rock, sometimes protruding through sand or clay like low lines of polished coal, elsewhere rising up from the ground like black cliffs. It was a strange and eery landscape at night. We found ourselves whispering to each other, even though there was no one near to listen.

At first we followed the trail of the column, which was easy as it was a hundred yards wide, the mud and sand having been churned by thousands of hooves. There were regular drops of dung, trampled plants and occasionally broken boxes from spilled loads. From one I could make out the side of tins glinting in the moonlight. After a while I suggested to Leila that we move off the track and follow a parallel route. In the morning, when Wolseley learned I had absconded, it would not be hard for him to guess the direction I had taken. I would not put it past the vindictive swine to send that lieutenant with some men after the column to bring me back. We angled slightly east and then continued pressing forward.

There are tales of flying carpets in Arabia, and I think that they are based on riding a camel at night. The creature's soft feet make no sound as they tread the stones and rock beneath you. Its head is well below your eyeline as you sit half crossed legged around the pommel of the Egyptian saddle. You could easily feel you are sitting on an undulating carpet as the desert and stunted trees pass by beneath you. Having had little sleep, I began to doze in my saddle. That was a risky business as it was a long drop if I fell. I was awoken by the harsh intrusion of the sun's rays over the horizon. Dawn and dusk come quickly in Sudan. One moment the sky is dark, and the next blood-red streaks are reflecting off the slim clouds which develop a fringe of gold. In minutes most of the sky is a vivid blue and the first warmth of the day can be felt on your cheek. The shadowy desert of the night quickly becomes a bizarre checkerboard of colour. Random patches of black rock and light grey clay are mixed in with golden sand and green tufts of desert grass and stunted acacia. I turned to my right to look for the column, but there were several ridges of rock and clumps of trees between us now. I heard it, though. In the still dawn air, as the sun blazed across the sky, two buglers found it necessary to blow the *reveille*.

Like us, the column had been making the most of the cool of the night to progress across the terrain. I suspected that rather than announcing the start of the day, the bugle call was instead signalling a rest. After hours in the saddle, that was an excellent idea. I pointed to a large black rock that would provide some shade and suggested that we stop for a while. We soon had a kettle of water boiling for tea, with biscuits and jam for breakfast.

"How long do you think it will take us to get to Jakdul?" I asked Leila.

"Three days," she replied without hesitation. "But if you are worried about the Mahdists, it might be wise to be with your soldiers when we arrive." She had a point and so I suggested that we continue to travel parallel with the column that day but try to re-join them in the morning. We would be past halfway then. Even if Wolseley had sent out a man to bring me back, we would have to go on to the springs first for water. We were using our own tanks sparingly, but Leila gave water to each of the camels and then we were on our way again.

There was a surprising amount of wildlife in the desert. When we stopped again to avoid the midday sun, crickets the size of small birds appeared, jumping from the coarse grass to make their calls from the canvas awning we had rigged up for shade. On a nearby rock I saw a large monitor lizard, preying on them for food. Speaking of fresh meat, I also spotted a small group of antelope. They were safe, though, for I couldn't hit one with the Webley, the only firearm I had with me. Besides, I worried that the sound of gunfire might attract unwelcome visitors.

We set off again at three in the afternoon. We had been riding for only a few minutes when I had a sudden thought. "Have you heard any bugles since dawn this morning?" I asked Leila. She shook her head, as did Rafa. It gave me a chill of disquiet. Even though we did not plan on rejoining the column until dawn, I wanted the comfort of knowing where it was. I decided to change course so that we angled slightly more in their direction. Two hours later and there was still no sign of them. We stopped to climb one of the black rocks that gave us a view over the terrain for miles, but there was nothing. No scouts, no soldiers, not a single camel or even a dust cloud to show where they were. Two regiments of men and nearly three thousand camels had just vanished.

"They have to be out there somewhere," I insisted. The dipping sun showed that we were moving in a southerly direction. "Are you sure we

100

are still heading towards Jakdul?" To my alarm Leila hesitated in giving a reply.

When you are lost in a pitiless desert, you want certainty and reassurance from your guide. The last thing you want to hear is the more honest response I received of, "I am not sure." She stared about to the west, her brow furrowed as she searched out a familiar landmark. "When I travelled this way before I came on the main trail, which is the one your army is using. When we struck east, I thought I would find it again when we came back west, but I cannot see it."

There was no sign of any trail, just rock and sand with patches of grass and trees, scattered about in a random pattern for as far as the eye could see. Foot or hoofprints would not show on the rock. The desert wind would soon cover them on the sand too. Yet we were not looking for some itinerant pedlar, we were searching for an army. They had to have left some sign of their passing, be it dung, dropped baggage or even an empty food tin glistening in the setting sun. It would be dark soon; already the shadows were lengthening to distort the landscape even further. I was sure that if they were level with us we would see them, which meant they had either passed this way or were behind us. I pulled out the Webley, cocked it and fired the gun into the air.

"Aren't you worried that the soldiers will find you and send us back to Cairo?" asked Leila.

"Right now, I am far more worried about being lost in the desert," I replied, as I pulled on the trigger again. We both listened and for a few seconds there was nothing. Then at last, faintly on the wind, came the sound of two answering shots. "That is from the northwest," I announced. "The army is behind us, that is why we cannot see their trail." I felt an immense sense of relief coupled with a desire for the security of the column.

"They will probably have rested during the day and will be marching during the night," predicted Leila. "If you want them to find us, we could light a fire on this rock." We did as she suggested and used the beacon to also brew more tea. Two hours later we could see some scouts riding towards us in the moonlight. They were horsemen of the Nineteenth Hussars.

"Major French," the cavalry officer introduced himself. "I have seen you before in the camp. You are one of the correspondents, aren't you?"

"Harrison of the *Daily News*," I confirmed, noting with relief his lack of reaction to the name. He clearly did not have orders for my arrest.

"We have seen a couple of Arabs travelling through the desert, but they both made off at the sight of us. We are going on; if you want to join the column, I suggest you ride a mile to the west and wait for it to catch up."

With that he led his party off and we took his advice. An hour later we were riding in the ranks of the Guards Camel Regiment that still led the force crossing the Bayuda. Colonel Stewart was at the front, clearly identifiable in a steel cavalry helmet with an orange scarf tied around it, compared to the others in their khaki pith helmets. We had been joined by Piggot, who was comparing experiences of the journey when St Leger rode up.

"Have you seen the time?" he asked. I looked up, the moon was still high. St Leger laughed. "No, on your watch, Harrison. Happy New Year to you all, for it has just turned 1885." I had forgotten completely that it was the last day of the year. We had been measuring days only in terms of Gordon's survival.

Soon men all around were congratulating each other and comparing their trek in a chilly desert that night with what they were doing the year before. Someone began to sing *Auld Lang Syne*. We all joined in, as we had at every New Year's Day I could remember. Leila laughed at our raucous rendition, which spread down the column. She found it even funnier when she asked what the song was about. Not one of us had the first idea.

"We sing that song because we always have at midnight on New Years Eve," explained Piggot, grinning. Soon the soldiers expanded their repertoire to other tunes of the day. *My Grandfather's Clock* was popular at the time, although not perhaps the ruder version sung enthusiastically by the soldiers. If Leila understood the English slang, she chose not to show it. The songs cleaned up a bit as Colonel Stewart passed down the line to wish his command a happy and victorious New Year.

There was still the hope that the Mahdists would withdraw as we got closer to Khartoum, but everyone in that column must have wondered how much of 1885 they would see. I know I did. As things turned out, a good number were to enjoy very little of it. If we were in any doubt about the vagaries of fate, Stewart described how exactly a year before, he was about to play in a New Year's Day cricket match with no prospect of military action. St Leger had been with him then as now and they reminisced that just weeks later he was with General Graham fighting the Mahdists around Suakin. Now he was leading the only force with a realistic prospect of rescuing Gordon.

The column came to halt around a small oasis an hour later. Leila knew the place from her earlier journeys and had got her bearings back. Engineers put a pump down an old well, but it produced just a few gallons of a muddy soup that was only good for camels. It was still dark when we began to set up our bivouac, but well past dawn before the last of the camels from the rear of the column arrived. Some of them looked in a bad way, with bleeding callouses from the sharp edges of crates, or other wounds. Several had already been shot or abandoned behind us and we were only halfway to Jakdul. The soldiers too were already complaining that their water was leaking away. The skins they were using to carry it had to be treated carefully or the leather would dry out and crack. I knew to slosh the water inside regularly, so the top of the skin was kept moist. Leila used a paste made from crushed wild melon seeds to plug leaks. She had to caution soldiers from leaving their skins resting on the ground, explaining that water could seep through them into the earth.

Perhaps mindful of diminishing water supplies, Stewart picked up the pace on the first day of the New Year. Then came the news we'd been hoping for; Colonel Kitchener, ahead of us with more scouts, reported that the wells were unoccupied by Mahdists and the water was good. Everyone now had an incentive to press on without delay. The march resumed at eight in the morning, with the two regiments reversed in the roles of advance and rear guard. We kept going until around midday and then rested in what little shade could be found or made with tents until mid-afternoon. Then we went on again until sundown for a brief rest, before starting another long night march. I had to concede that it was not a pace I could have kept up on foot, but once the camels got moving, they just plodded steadily on until the next camp. By midnight, the thirst of some of the soldiers was becoming acute. They could hear the water slapping around in my camel tanks and were soon imploring us for a drink. They were getting desperate, and as Leila was sure that we would reach Jakdul around dawn the next day, there was no point in hoarding water if men were suffering from thirst. So we were soon pouring water into cups to give them enough to make the wells.

Of course, Leila was right, and we found the wells at Jakdul as promised the next morning. The column had travelled a hundred miles in just sixty-four hours. Of the approximately three thousand camels that started that stage of the journey, we had lost around thirty. Half were dead and the rest had been turned loose to die or recover. It did not bode well for the next two trips over the same ground.

The wells were easy to spot – a vast monolith of black stone rising up from a hollow. Water for miles around drained in its direction and had cut channels through the boulders to reach three large pools. The surrounding rock provided shade for the stored water, reducing evaporation. The bottom pond was partly covered with green slime and only good for the camels, who supped from it greedily. A short climb up a slope revealed a second pool of clear cool water and a yet more precarious scramble unveiled a third. Leila confided that once, on a previous visit, she had swum naked in the top pool. It was so deep in the centre, she could barely see the bottom. There were far too many prying eyes to try that this time, more's the pity.

The pools were like a different world to the hot desert outside. In permanent shade, the air felt cool, almost too cold. Grasses and plants grew around the perimeter of the water and scarlet dragonflies flitted about in the shade. It was like an enchanted grotto. The first soldiers to follow us up to the top pool stared in reverence and wonder for a moment, perhaps trying to remember when they had last seen so much crystal-clear water. Their thirst soon overcame them. They rushed forward to fill their water bottles, one of them even plunging his head beneath the surface for a drink. Our engineers calculated that there were at least half a million gallons across the three reservoirs, more than enough to bring up the rest of the Camel Corps. They got to work pumping water into troughs made from tin-lined chests to water more camels and horses. By noon every living creature had drunk their fill and the camels had all been unloaded.

But they could not rest for long. After a final drink and some *dhura*, the column set off on their return journey that evening, led by Colonel Stewart. It was hoped that as the camels were unburdened for the return, they would make good time. St Leger and the Mounted Infantry Camel Regiment went too, along with Piggot, who hoped to file a report on the journey so far, though I doubted that Wolseley would let him. I stayed behind at the wells with Leila, Rafa and our camels. Also remaining were the Guards Camel Regiment and Colonel Kitchener and his scouts. I was happy to rest and wait for the others to return. It was perfectly safe. The soldiers set up defences against any intruders and Kitchener's men kept an eye out for anyone approaching. They captured a handful of locals crossing the plain with dates and grain bound for the town of Metemma on the Nile, near where we would reach the river again. They told us that the Mahdists had a garrison there of at least two thousand men. Officers chuckled with delight; it was clear that they did not know how close the British army was. They looked forward to taking them by surprise.

While we sat around by the pools recuperating and occasionally venturing out of the shade to feel the sun's warmth, there were scenes of suffering and despair to the north of us. Having made the first leg in under three days, it took Stewart ten days to get back to Korti and then return to the wells. He brought with him the rest of the Camel Corps along with the men of the first Royal Sussex Regiment, who had been added to our force. He had rested the exhausted camels for three days in Wolseley's camp, but it was not nearly enough for the beasts to recover their strength. By all accounts the journey back to the wells had been a brutal affair. Many camels, now loaded up again, were on their last legs. Tied together in strings of two or three, suddenly one would just drop with exhaustion, often tugging at the halter of its fellows and dislodging their loads. If the camel was unloaded it might get up again, but a few gave a pitiable groan and just expired on the spot. As the journey was taking longer than before, the water supplies were more stretched. Holes in leaking skins had widened and the intermediate wells were even dryer. Some of the camel drivers became so desperate for a drink, they abandoned their charges and went off in search of their own supply. All the remaining press corps were in this march. Some recounted how they had been forced to sleep with their waterskins under their blanket to stop others stealing the precious liquid. Kitchener's scouts reported their approach. To ease their thirst, a couple of camels with full water tanks were led out to greet this new column. We could mark their progress even before they came into view between the hills, as vultures could be seen circling above, feasting on the line of camel corpses left in their wake.

Soon I was joined by St Leger, Burleigh, Cameron, MacDonald and several others. They pitched their tents near mine in a small correspondent's canyon. The newcomers had just finished watering their animals when we realised that one of our number was missing: the man from the *Manchester Guardian* had not arrived. Asking around, we learned that he had got himself lost, but had been seen by an officer and given water and directions. Somehow, though, he had missed the trail now trampled by thousands of animals in both directions. It sounded absurd, but I remembered how easily we had got lost, and Leila knew the desert. Perhaps he had seen a group ahead and tried to ride directly towards them. The heat haze could make far off figures look closer, until they abruptly disappeared entirely. We waited for him that evening and all of the next day. Scouts searched for him on their patrols, but he was never seen or heard from again. He was the first of our number to be lost, perhaps to thirst or a bandit. Sadly, he would not be the last.

Chapter 10

While scanning the horizon with field glasses for our Manchester colleague to no avail, we did spot another caravan of camels arriving, with a much-needed cargo of *dhura*. Along with it came an extraordinary, larger than life character, Fred Burnaby. Most correspondents had met him following his earlier exploits; I had interviewed him when he had made a solo balloon crossing over the English Channel. He had laughed that the Duke of Cambridge had rebuked him for leaving the country without permission.

Burnaby was well over six feet tall, barrel-chested and strong. He had once carried two Shetland ponies, one under each arm, down a flight of stairs. A loud cheery fellow, he was a colonel in the household cavalry, the queen's official bodyguard. I had heard his jocularity was not popular with its snobbish officers, but the troopers adored him. He was only required to guard the monarch for five months of the year and so he used his long periods of leave to go on expeditions of his own. He had visited Gordon in Khartoum during Gordon's earlier spell as governor, using the Suakin route. He had also travelled extensively in Central Asia, publishing popular books of his adventures. He did things his own way. As he dropped lightly from the saddle and enquired cheerily if he was still in time for the fighting, I was not surprised to see that he had spurned Wolseley's uniform. There was no khaki on Burnaby; he still wore his dark blue uniform with red striped trousers.

Many of the cavalry troopers cheered his arrival. He had been wounded fighting with Baker and then with the subsequent British attacks around Suakin. Sent home to recover, he had returned to Egypt and the Sudan while officially on leave. Wolseley was delighted to have him and made him second in command of the Camel Corps. If Burnaby was most welcome among us, the fodder he had brought to the wells was even more so. Even my animals were thinner than usual, but the camels who had already traversed the desert three times were on their last legs. Ribs were clearly showing, humps were sagging, many carried wounds from rubbing saddles and yet we would have to rely on them for the next stage of our journey.

Colonel Stewart announced that we would leave again at three the following afternoon, so the *dhura* was hurriedly distributed, a small pile for each animal. At least there was still plenty of water for them and for us to refill tanks and water skins. We knew that the Mahdists had a presence on the bank of the Nile and Stewart did not want to give them too long to build defences. Burnaby was more concerned that they might run off before we got there. He told his troopers that he would be extremely disappointed if they did not account for at least half a dozen of the enemy each. I thought that Leila would want us to stay at Jakdul for a little while longer to rest the camels – she had been appalled at how badly the British army had treated them – but to my surprise, she was all for pressing on too.

"We have been here too long," she murmured that evening, gazing up at the rock that surrounded the wells. "Word will have reached your enemies that the British are at Jakdul. They will know that you must now be heading to the wells at Abu Klea for your next water."

"Most of the soldiers would welcome a fight and be pleased if they did try to stop us." I retorted. There were around two and a half thousand men at the wells then. Three hundred would stay to protect the water but the rest would move on. I guessed that eighteen hundred of them were soldiers, with artillery, the Gardner machine gun and some cavalry on horses. The rest were mostly drivers for the baggage camels we were taking and other miscellaneous characters, such as war correspondents and their guides.

The soldiers were the finest men from our best regiments. I fully expected them to be able to deal with any spear-wielding warriors. They certainly would not break and run. This far out into the desert there was nowhere to retreat to. Stewart issued orders that if the column was to be attacked, the soldiers would form four squares around the herd of camels in the middle. The squares would be arranged so as to provide covering fire for each other. The artillery and the Gardner gun would face the main threat. We scribblers of the press were detailed to remain with the camels, which suited me fine.

We set off on the 14th of January, twelve days after I had first arrived in Jakdul. The march was to begin at three in the afternoon to make the most of the cool of the evening. We spent the day dismantling tents, topping up water containers and loading the camels. Just after two o'clock we set out to an assembly point in the desert. As the camels strode out from the shade into the heat of the afternoon, I realised how much I would miss the more temperate climate of the wells. Still, I could not stay in the middle of the Bayuda forever; we had to press on, for, God willing, Gordon was still waiting for us.

We took our places in the forming column: the Camel Corps, around a thousand baggage camels and half of the Royal Sussex regiment. They were originally intended to protect the wells while we were away, but as we had seen no Mahdists there, Stewart had divided them up. Half would remain at the wells, and the remaining two hundred and fifty men would come with us. Unfortunately, we had no camel saddles for them. They had been perched on baggage camels to get to Jakdul and so they were to again, adding extra weight to the already exhausted beasts.

There was no military band to see us off this time as we rode once more into the desert. Just the collective groans and growls of thousands of weary camels as they were forced up onto their feet, with the accompanying cracks of whips and shouts of men. Burnaby was riding with a black umbrella to protect him from the glare of the sun. I cursed myself for not bringing one myself. Still, the cork pith helmets the rest of us wore kept our heads cool and our eyes shaded. We had barely gone a quarter of a mile when there was a clatter beside me. One of the camels gave a deep grunt and then collapsed as though it had been shot. The South Essex man it had been carrying on top of two large crates, tumbled to the ground while the two other camels tied to it stopped and waited patiently.

"Come on, you daft bugger, up you get," shouted the soldier, dusting himself down. The camel's long neck and head was sprawled out on the rocks like a hairy snake. The man tried to raise it by pulling on the rein only for it to drop lifeless back on the ground. "Gawd, look at that," he exclaimed. "One minute he is walking fine and the next he is dead as a doornail." He looked up at our notably stronger baggage camels and asked hopefully, "Could I cadge a lift on one of your animals, sir?" Rafa helped him up onto one of our beasts, while three of the baggage handlers started a heated debate over what to do with the dead animal's load. It was all in Egyptian and so I could not understand a word, though I guessed each was insisting that their animals could not take the extra weight. We moved on, so I have no idea what happened to it. Yet when we eventually came back the other way, the route was marked with piles of white camel bones and more than a few abandoned crates.

The column gradually stretched out that afternoon. While my mount plodded on in its usual quiet manner, when I looked over my shoulder, I could see that the stragglers were already half a mile back with at least two more collapsed camels. We stopped at sunset to allow them to catch up. Only a few days from a new moon, there was little light to see and so we settled for the night. Camels were unloaded, watered and fed with *dhura* to stop their stomachs rumbling. By the time we attended to our own needs, it was nearly pitch dark. There was little vegetation in the desert, but Rafa had been gathering dry sticks and soon we had a small campfire and a kettle eventually boiling over it. A cup of hot tea, biscuits and jam in our bellies, then we settled down to sleep, for it was too late to pitch a tent. I lay there under a blanket with Leila in my arms and stared up at the night sky. On such a dark night, I could see thousands of stars. Particularly in the Milky Way. I remembered going to a lecture where an astronomer explained that each one was a sun like our own and could have planets with living creatures on it. The scale of it boggled the mind and made everything we were involved in seem rather trivial.

We always had a breakfast of bully beef and biscuits, with another steaming cup of tea. The mornings were cold, and we had learned that this was the best time to eat bully as it was firm then and could be sliced. Later in the day if the tin had been left in the sun, it would be a warm, red, stringy mess floating in a slurry of fat.

Reveille had sounded at twenty minutes past three in the morning and we fumbled about in the gloom getting ready to leave at first light, which came at five. There were patches of sand dunes across the desert now and some of the camels slipped and fell trying to traverse them. We had our man from the South Essex riding with us again and he was already in need of water. He showed me the waterskin he had been given, which was riddled with leaks. Not expecting them to cross the desert, the regiment had been given the last of the spares used by the Camel Corps, probably containers that they had already rejected. Several of the Mounted Infantry Regiment camels from the Corps dropped dead that afternoon. They had been better looked after than the pack animals and were not carrying extra stores as well as men. I was beginning to wonder if any of the animals would still be alive when we reached the Nile.

When we camped once more that evening, St Leger came down the line to find our little correspondent camp. He told us that we had now travelled around thirty-five miles from Jakdul in a day and a half, which was a slower pace than the first stage of the journey. I mentioned the South Essex struggling with their water, but he assured us we were expected to reach the wells at Abu Klea by the end of the following day. Leila was still doubtful. "They are bound to have heard by now that we were at Jakdul. They know we must come to Abu Klea next. They will not let us simply walk up to the wells."

Fred Burnaby happened to be sitting by our fire at the time and chuckled with amusement. "My dear lady," he grinned at her, "we should be delighted if they tried, for then we could deal with them once and for all." He gave a weary sigh and added, "I rather fear that we will come all this way and they will melt before us to rise up again when we have left." Several others nodded in agreement.

Even Cameron tentatively demurred from the woman he privately called his 'Cleopatra'. "They must know that they would be slaughtered if they made a stand against us." I kept quiet, for I had long since learned that my 'pharaoh' was invariably right.

We set off again early the next morning. After an hour Leila pointed out some hills in the distance. Abu Klea was just beside them, she told me. We were in a shallow valley and the hills on either side converged on that point. The ground in between was mostly sand and loose rock with gentle undulations for dry stream beds, which criss-crossed the ground. They would carry any rain down the valley towards the wells. I stared at the destination through my field-glasses; there was little heat haze at that time of the morning but there was no sign of armies standing before it. We pressed on, but I noticed increased numbers of the

Nineteenth Hussars on their horses riding out ahead of us and on our flanks. Stewart knew the reputation of the Mahdists and he was not going to be taken by surprise. We stopped again at mid-morning, having covered around twelve miles since dawn. Our commander established his headquarters in the shade of a mimosa tree and looked relaxed as he sat on a rock waiting for his tea to brew. Taking our commander's lead, we found a place in the shade to rest ourselves. I stretched out on the rocks and pulled my hat over my eyes as the fast-forming camp bustled about me. There was just the clack of boot nails on rock, a murmur of voices and the relieved groan of camels as they were finally allowed to rest to disturb the peace of the morning. I was content to doze and so I did for nearly an hour.

"Eyes up, Harrison," called Burleigh quietly. I sat up to see what had disturbed my slumber. My fellow correspondents were all staring south, like hounds that had just caught a scent. There were several hills blocking our view of the oasis at Abu Klea. Down the slope of one of them came three of the hussars, galloping full tilt. We had seen scouts riding back and forth all day, but they moved mostly at the trot to conserve the strength of the animals. "It looks like we have flushed out some game," the newspaper man continued. While the rest of the camp was oblivious to the new arrivals, my colleagues grinned wolfishly. Years on countless campaigns with various armies had given them a sixth sense for imminent action. I knew they were right; something was afoot. We got to our feet and headed towards Stewart's mimosa tree to find out what.

The colonel did not seem surprised to see us as we joined his gathering staff. "Well, gentlemen," he grinned, "the enemy is ahead of us. Our scouts have exchanged a few shots with their outposts. I intend to engage at once."

"How many are there?" Burleigh asked.

"At least a thousand we think." Stewart gestured up the slope in front of us, "I am riding up there to see for myself in a few minutes, you are welcome to join me." He started to draw on the sand with his swagger stick to show his commanders that he wanted them to advance on a broad front. The nearby soldiers now realised that something was happening. By the time a bugle summoned them to stand to, many were already running for their camels. The camp of hot dozing men was transformed into an ant's nest of activity within seconds of the last note of the horn's call. Cheers went up as they understood what it signified. They had been travelling and suffering discomfort in the desert for months. Now at last they were to get to grips with the devils who had dared challenge Egypt, and by association, the forces of the queen.

While his soldiers prepared their weapons and checked ammunition levels, a group of mounted camels headed off to the nearest high point of land. Stewart led most of his staff, who were chattering excitedly about the prospect of action, along with every correspondent in the camp. Unlike Wolseley, he was not shy in sharing his plans as he knew our lives were on the line too. Even though she had been reluctant to join such a gathering, I had brought Leila with me. She was the only one among us who had seen the springs at Abu Klea before and I thought her experience would be useful. We still had a squadron of the Nineteenth Hussars ahead of us as we climbed that final slope, so we knew the enemy were still some distance off. We could hear the occasional shot as the horsemen kept them at bay. Yet as we crested the rise, we all stared ahead eagerly.

Most of the oasis around the wells was still hidden behind another rise in the ground, but we could see there was a large tent. Even without field-glasses you could make out the Mahdists, their white robes contrasting starkly with the green foliage and the rocks of the desert. There were hundreds of them running for the high ground on either side of the trail down to the wells. As I raised my glasses my suspicions were confirmed: we could forget the tales about swords and spears: most of the men I could see had rifles in their hands.

One of the staff officers, a Major Wilson, who had been making a map of our route was studying the terrain. "It looks like they plan to snipe at us as we make our approach," he muttered.

"We will send our own skirmishers ahead of us through those rocks," replied Stewart, dismissing the concern. "They will be able to pick them off at a longer range and our artillery can provide support against any strongpoints. There are only around a thousand of them we can see. Our scouts reported a few in hidden ground, perhaps two thousand at most and they won't all have rifles."

"They might not show you all their forces if they want you to attack." Leila's voice came from the back of the group and Stewart frowned in irritation. He was not used to having his views challenged and certainly not by a woman.

"What else would we do but attack?" he snapped. "We certainly cannot go back even if we wanted to, we need water." Then, as others standing near her stepped away, he demanded, "Who the devil are you anyway?"

"She is my guide, sir," I intervened. "And I think alone amongst us, she has actually been to the wells at Abu Klea before." I turned to Leila, keen that she demonstrate her value to the gathering. "Could you describe to the colonel the ground we cannot see?"

"The oasis stretches back a half a mile along the valley floor, but is a little less in width," she replied. Then she looked Stewart cooly in the eye and added, "Plenty of room to hide many thousands of men."

"I did wonder why they are letting us see their forces," Wilson, the intelligence officer intervened. "They knew we were coming. Our scouts have found fresh trails of hoofprints and glimpsed horsemen in the distance. If they were planning to ambush us, it makes no sense to give up the element of surprise."

Stewart looked slightly mollified by this reasoning and glanced briefly between Leila and Wilson. "You may both have a point," he conceded, "but it does not change the fact that we need that water." He stared back down the trail we had come where eighteen hundred soldiers were mounting up and forming into their regimental columns. Ahead of them, galloping up the hill towards us was a familiar figure in a dark navy uniform. "Burnaby," Stewart called out. "You are my second in command, what is your opinion? Should we attack now or not?"

The cavalryman reined in beside us, kicking up a cloud of dust and scattering small stones down the slope. He was notoriously a man of action and so perhaps Stewart assumed that he would be in support of his plan. The colonel was destined to be disappointed. Burnaby did not reply at once. He studied the ground ahead carefully, noting the enemy positions that were building on either side of the oasis and then glanced up at the sky. "By the time we get the columns down there," he explained, "there will be little daylight left. Precious little cover too on that open ground. They could easily shoot at us in the dark from those rocks and we will struggle to drive them off. It would be better to stay up here on the high ground overnight. We can build some rock walls to give us some shelter and attack in the morning."

I thought he had finished, but then he pointed at the track that led down the middle of the valley to the wells. "When we do advance," he counselled, "we should avoid that trail, it is the route they expect us to take. Baker made that mistake when I was with him. They showed themselves and we marched straight towards them." He shrugged and added, "Well, you know what happened then."

There was a moment of sobering silence as we all recalled accounts of that massacre. Many of those present, including Colonel Stewart, St Leger and Burleigh, had been there a few weeks later with General Graham. They had fought over the same ground and seen the remains from that encounter. The recollection settled the debate.

"You are right, Burnaby, the prudent course of action is to stay here tonight," Stewart concluded. "With luck they will attack us over this open ground in the morning and we will cut them to pieces." He stared down the trail that led directly to the oasis and then gave a little chuckle. "If some of the swine have buried themselves on either side of that path to pounce out on us, they are in for an uncomfortable night."

Soldiers riding up the hill behind us to launch their attack looked puzzled as they were ordered to dismount again after only half a mile. Instead of charging their enemies, they were instructed to build a rock wall around the hill we were on and a larger but lower one to our right. The local word for such a defence was a *zariba*, which the Sudanese would make from thornbushes to keep goats in and predators and thieves out. In this case, thorns would not stop bullets and so we built ours out of stone. We correspondents joined most of the army on the lower hill, where there was certainly no shortage of building material. The perimeter was soon marked out and then we set to industriously piling rocks. If there was any doubt as to the importance of the task, we had only to look south.

When the Mahdists had seen that we were not blindly marching into whatever reception they had planned, their riflemen began to swarm in our direction, their white robes working their way towards us over the higher ground on either flank. It would not be long before they were sniping at our positions, when we would need all the cover we could get.

The camels had been hobbled at the rear of our hill and unloaded. Boxes of food, camel saddles, collapsible chairs, tent poles, anything that might help stop a bullet was piled into the stone wall. Only the little water we had left and the ammunition was kept inside. The Gardner gun and most of the artillery were placed on the slightly higher hill where they had a clearer field of fire.

While we worked, Wilson, the intelligence officer, had ridden to join the forward scouts and then beyond them to see more of the oasis for himself. What he found confirmed Leila's suspicions. There were many more Mahdists in the part of the camp we could not see. They had spears and swords instead of rifles. While he had a limited view across their camp, he could see dozens of their leaders' green and white flags fluttering in the light breeze. Wilson estimated that there were at least another two thousand in the camp and possibly more. This meant that we were outnumbered by over two to one. He reported back to Stewart, who had the good grace to ask him to let Leila know that she had been right.

Wilson was a studious man, a cartographer by trade, who freely admitted that he had not seen action before. He showed no sign of nerves, though, as he chatted amiably to Leila to improve his understanding of the lie of the land beyond what he could see. By now the first Mahdist bullets were buzzing over our heads like metal hornets. They were fired at extreme range so many spent bullets just 'clacked' off nearby rocks and fell harmlessly onto the ground. The Martini–Henry rifle was accurate at twice the distance of the Remingtons used by the Mahdists. Any sniper who got too close in daylight soon found himself facing a flurry of much more lethal return fire. Yet there was not a lot of cover for us if they were to get closer at night. Our rock surround was still only waist high, and in some places barely above the knee. It was a long perimeter to build – one hundred and fifty yards wide facing the oasis – but the sides stretched four hundred yards to make room for the camels and the horses, which had now returned from their scouting and were in a hollow at the rear.

We had not been the only ones busy. Our enemy had been building a *zariba* of their own on a nearby hilltop. It too was waist high and clearly intended to protect their riflemen as they fired across to our encampment during the night. Just before night fell, our artillery finally came into action. The small guns that screwed together did not at first look impressive: the breach was carried on one camel, the barrel on another while a third took the wheels. Yet their gunners were the best in the army. Without any ranging shots, they quietly took aim at the enemy *zariba* around a mile away. The first shell landed plumb in the centre of the position; we witnessed bodies and rocks being thrown through the air in the explosion. Two more shells followed and by then the position was totally destroyed. It was a powerful demonstration that what we lacked in numbers, we made up for in firepower.

By nightfall I was looking forward to some food and a mug of tea. Instead, I had to make do with a few swigs from a waterskin accompanied by biscuits and jam. Orders were given that there were to be no fires, smoking or talking to avoid guiding the enemy to our position. We were sure that under the cover of darkness they would try to get closer and perhaps even launch an attack. Soldiers slept in their greatcoats, with their rifles, bayonets fixed, at their sides. Along the front face of the *zariba* they were lying shoulder to shoulder, ready to spring up and fire volleys over the wall at a moment's notice.

The water situation with the South Essex men was now desperate. We had donated all the water in the camel-borne tanks to be distributed amongst them. It was an easy decision; we had some in waterskins for our use, while our lives might depend on those soldiers being fit and able to fight in the morning. We would all only survive by driving the Mahdists away from the wells at Abu Klea. I was increasingly convinced that to do that, we would need every man we could get.

In the darkness, the sound of drumming carried on the wind from the oasis; there were a hell of a lot of drums. We heard chanting too. I imagined thousands of men dancing around fires calling for our deaths. It was damned unnerving. Their snipers were getting closer. When bullets hit the walls, there was a much sharper crack on the stone as they carried more force. Yet still none of our number was hit. We kept our heads down and waited for the dawn. I even managed to sleep a little, but not for long as every so often there was a flurry of shots from our sentries. The noise of the drumming slowly rose and fell, perhaps to give the impression they were coming closer. With wary fingers curled around triggers, it only took a lizard to dislodge a stone for several guns to blaze in that direction. Half-asleep men would jump up and add their fire to the mix, their muzzle flashes illuminating a cloud of gun smoke that obscured the view. Alert enemy snipers then returned fire and more bullets buzzed about our heads until the sergeants determined that there was nobody there and called for a cease fire.

I well remember one furious voice yelling at men on a section of the wall who had woken us up twice with false alarms. "You are worse than old ladies with the vapours!" he roared. "Unless some hairy-arsed bandit has got his hands on your balls, you keep your fingers off the trigger!" An ironic cheer from tired men greeted this admonishment, but they did not wake us up again. Surrounded by so many armed and possibly overly alert men, I felt safe that evening. If the enemy charged us in the night, we would certainly hear them stumbling over the loose stones and there was no cover on the surrounding slopes. With crossfire between the two hilltops we occupied, I was sure we would give a good account of ourselves. But what would happen in the morning? We would have to advance towards the wells and into whatever traps they had laid.

I felt I had barely closed my eyes before bugles calling for the men to stand to, brought me awake. Stewart wanted his men ready to face a dawn attack. Tired, cold men crouched in readiness behind their parapets, while a handful of officers with field-glasses jumped up like jack-in-the-boxes to check on the enemy position. Sitting further back, we gentlemen of the press thought that an attack was unlikely. "If they won't come at us under the cover of darkness," grunted a weary

Burleigh, "they certainly won't in daylight. They don't need to; they have water and we don't. They can sit back and wait for us to come to them." It was a pithy summary of our situation and as I felt the few cups of liquid in my water skin, I knew he was right. The edge of the oasis was in sight, a bare four miles down the valley, and we would have to be there by the end of the day.

The Mahdists had used the night to bring their snipers in closer and we began to lose some horses and camels herded in the rear of the *zariba*. More boxes and stores were piled up to give them protection while Stewart sent out some of our own skirmishers to drive the riflemen back. He and Burnaby strolled around the position with the casual disregard to risk expected of a British officer. They attracted bullets as jam does wasps. I crouched lower whenever they came our way, usually to exchange a cheery reassurance that all was under control. It was a miracle that neither was hit. Their bugler, obliged to follow the commander to transmit orders, was not so fortunate. He was struck in the side and swiftly carried away.

The next few hours saw both sides play a game of bluff as they tried to entice the other to launch an assault. The artillery was given orders to pick off choice targets, but they had little more than a hundred shells left. One of the camels carrying their ammunition had died and been abandoned by its herder on the journey. They fired sparingly but to great effect. A group of forty Mahdist horsemen, including several of their sheiks, judging from the flags, was hit by a single explosive shell. Only half of them rode away. A few limped off but the ground was left bloody with human and equine corpses. Another round destroyed a new sniper fortress constructed overnight.

At first it seemed the strategy was working. We watched with interest as some three thousand of the enemy appeared and began to advance in loose order to within a mile of us. Stewart ordered his artillery to hold its fire, hoping they would continue to come. Instead, they stopped and began a new round of drumming, some of them leaping about to the beat. Stewart then tried a tactic that had been used in the Zulu Wars. He sent another line of skirmishers forward until they were just within range of this new force. They were to open fire and provoke the enemy to shoot back. Then, on a given signal, they were to retreat as though in panic, hoping to draw the Mahdists after them. This pantomime was duly performed, but our assailants were far too canny to fall for the trick. In exasperation, Stewart ordered his artillery to send a few rounds among the massed ranks. Beyond three more patches of bloody sand and rock, the effect was to cause the enemy to withdraw back out of sight. By nine o'clock Stewart had reluctantly concluded what we had suspected all along. "Well, if they won't come to us," he grumbled, "we must go to them."

Chapter 11

Cameron had been past the area designated as the hospital. He reported that so far despite a night and early morning of sniping from the hills, while there were some wounded, only seven bodies lay covered with blankets. From the boots, or absence of them, he had determined that four were soldiers and three were camel drivers. We had lost considerably more animals, who did not have the sense to duck. The Mahdist snipers evidently had a loathing for any Sudanese with us, who had been condemned as apostates by their leader. They had shot at any they could see and as the herders stayed with the animals, they were more exposed as the walls were lower. Now, though, the army was to emerge from those walls and march into the valley with no cover at all.

For us correspondents there was a decision to be made. We could stay in the *zariba*, which would be protected by a detachment of the Royal Sussex Regiment, or advance with the rest of the army inside the square. Many decided to stay, which would afford a good view of proceedings. I watched Burleigh, determined to stick to him like glue. There was a strong camaraderie in our correspondents' camp; we had to help each other, especially when, thanks to Wolseley, the army offered little support. Yet at bottom, we never forgot that we were competing to get incisive copy back to our papers first. Burleigh was the most ruthless and would do whatever it took to get a story. When he announced that he was going with the army, I knew that I would have to go too. He grinned when he saw me pick up the satchel that held my notebook. "Are you sure that you want a close look at what might be the final act of this campaign?"

He was trying to put me off coming, but it would not work. "The prospects for those left here are not much better if the square is overrun," I muttered, out of earshot of those who were staying.

He shrugged in acceptance, but his grin softened when he saw the taught lines of my features. "Don't look so worried. We are lucky – we have both been in tighter spots before." I wasn't so sure about my own career, but Burleigh had certainly led a charmed life.

He had confided once that he had left England after getting a servant girl pregnant. He had fled to the United States at the outbreak of the Civil War with the design of a torpedo device he was trying to sell. The Confederates had thought him a spy and locked him up, but he had convinced them he was loyal to their cause by volunteering to fight. For the next year he fought in their navy as a virtual pirate, disrupting union shipping. He was captured cutting telegraph lines in Union territory, but managed to escape prison by prising up the floorboards and entering a sewer. Later, he was involved in a scheme to free Confederate prisoners held on Lake Erie. Again, he was arrested. A second escape followed and by the time the war ended he was back south in Texas. That was where he started his newspaper career. After his war exploits, it was perhaps not surprising that civilian life bored him. He returned to London to become a war correspondent and since then, wherever there was action, he could be found. It was no surprise that he was determined to go with the square.

It took some time to organise the formation. Men first had to retrieve the artillery and Gardner gun from the other hill to go in the centre. Most of the camels were left behind, but over a hundred were taken and herded into the middle too. They carried some water, ammunition and half of them bore cacolets: a pair of stretchers, one on each side of the hump. Our best skirmishers had been sent out to suppress the snipers while the double rank square formed, but we lost our first man before we had even set off. He gave a cry and collapsed with a bad wound to the chest. He was bleeding heavily by the time the stretcher bearers doubled over from the *zariba*. They carried him back to the makeshift hospital. Burleigh glanced at the blood-stained rocks and then looked at me, shaking his head. We both suspected that another blanket-covered body was about to be added to the row.

Having reported on the Franco–Prussian War, where armies advanced in loose formations, it was strange to see men fighting in a tightly packed square. It was a scene my grandfather, who had fought Napoleon, would have been more familiar with. As we advanced over ground with hidden gullies, we had no idea from which direction an attack might come. We were also likely to be greatly outnumbered and so needed to be able to deliver massed volley fire while defending our flanks. As General Graham had discovered at Suakin, the square was the best formation to defend against a Mahdist attack.

"Well, Thomas," Burleigh said as we stood in the middle of the square, "it seems the rest of our band is staying in the *zariba*. You, like me, have weighed the odds."

"Weighed the odds?" I repeated and then laughed. "I have done nothing of the sort. I simply imagined Frank's reaction if he read your report from the heart of the action and mine describing seeing some puffs of muzzle smoke from a few miles away." Naturally, I would have preferred to stay in the *zariba* too, but it was professional pride that had driven my decision. Burleigh was a good friend, but he was also a ruthless bastard, who relished having an exclusive. He was the best of us, widely regarded as such because he stayed close to the action. If I wanted to continue building my reputation in this bizarre occupation, then I would have to do the same. I was not joking about my editor's reaction either. The fact I was his nephew would not reduce his rage if I did not deliver the story, it would probably enhance it.

"If there is a big story today," Burleigh continued, "we will not be writing it."

"What do you mean?" I queried.

"If we win, it will be nothing more than the British public expects. A mere stepping-stone on the journey to rescue Gordon. They will not care that those throbbing drums are making our guts churn, or that we imagine hordes of fanatics in every fold of the ground. It is what they expect their soldiers and newspaper correspondents to endure. This is going to be a bloody business and if I am a judge, a close call. Yet if we lose, if the cream of the British army is beaten by spear-wielding savages, why that story will be shouted from Land's End to the tip of Scotland. We will be dead, of course, as will everyone in the *zariba*. Some lucky devil in Cairo will write the tale from fragments of news coming down the telegraph."

"You are a ray of sunshine this morning," I grumbled. Feeling unnerved, I found myself glancing longingly at the zariba. Leila and the others would be crouched down between the lines of camels, safe enough for now. I could not help but wonder if I would ever see her again. Their fate if we were beaten did not bear thinking about and I felt a wave of self-pity before I tried to pull myself together. "We won't lose," I insisted. "These men will not break. We are a mobile fort of human flesh. When they finally show themselves, we will cut them to pieces." I was trying to convince myself, yet as I looked around that 'mobile fort', it looked horribly vulnerable to being whittled away.

"I am glad we have Burnaby with us," my friend continued. "He has persuaded Stewart to keep away from the main path. That is the route they would have expected us to take. I will wager a fortune that it harbours traps and ambushes aplenty." Instead, we were walking across the undulating hill to the right of the track. He was right that they must have been waiting along the trail, for that was where the drumming was coming from. Folds in the ground hid all but the occasional sniper. Around five hundred yards away, along the crest of a ridge on our right were more gunmen, who would pop up from behind a rock and fire wildly in our direction. If they were lucky, they could duck back before our skirmishers returned fire, but not many of them made it, for our riflemen could shoot the eyebrows off a wasp.

Burleigh and I walked in the centre of the square near the front. While we were on foot, most of the officers were mounted to give them a better vantage point over the folds of ground in front. We did not doubt that the enemy were now working their way across to our new path, yet there was no rush, for we were making pitiful progress. Every few hundred yards a halt was called to stop the camels bulging out of the back of the square. Only when they had been driven forward to its centre would we set off again. I hated being stationary as Burnaby in his cavalry blues and Stewart, who still insisted on wearing his metal helmet unlike our cork ones, stood out as our leaders. Bullets buzzed around them as they stood their horses uncomfortably close to us.

"No shotgun today, Colonel?" my companion called out to Burnaby, before turning to me. "Our friend here used a shotgun at both battles at El Teb, near Suakin, and must have potted at least a score of the enemy with it."

"I did," Burnaby agreed. "But when I got home the Liberals kicked up a fuss about it in the press. They claimed it was unsporting to use such a weapon in war. *Unsporting!*" he repeated indignantly. "I would like to see some of those wet milksops with us here now. Then we would see how their noble principles survive the first charge. I'll wager they would be shooting with anything they could get their hands on."

"You should ignore the fools, sir," called out a cavalry captain. To demonstrate that he followed his own advice he brandished his own shotgun and waved it in the air. Trotting beside his horse was a fox terrier that we knew by now was called Smoke. The animal was not the only dog with us; the Grenadier Guards had adopted an Egyptian hound that was now trotting calmly beside them.

Further conversation was interrupted by a crackle of gunfire to our left, near the trail. Some of the Hussars were scouting there. They had just dismounted and opened fire on some two hundred Mahdist horsemen and three hundred spearmen, who were approaching from the other side of the valley. None of the enemy had rifles and the cavalry used their carbines to pick them off at extreme range. At least fifty men in white robes must have been hit before they finally had the sense to stop and seek cover. The scouts had also spotted a couple of other groups crossing the valley ahead, beyond the range of our rifles. It was clear that a reception was being planned for us, but from which direction was anyone's guess. Wilson, the intelligence officer, first noticed the green and white flags gathering in front of the oasis. We could not see the flag bearers, just the flapping scraps of cloth as they caught the breeze above one of the dunes. "Is that where they really are?" he wondered aloud. "Or are they attracting our attention away from an ambush somewhere else?"

"They are crafty blighters," muttered Burnaby. "I would not put anything past them."

"It does not matter," Stewart sounded irritable. "We will have to pass near those flags anyway if we are to reach the water. There is no choice but to face whatever they have planned for us." He glanced over his shoulder at the back of the square, where the camels had now been moved forward again and commanded, "Bugler, sound the advance."

125

The instrument had barely touched the man's lips when there was the crack of another gun to our right and a soldier fell to the ground. The body twitched horribly; he had been shot through the neck causing spinal damage. A surgeon ran over, but it only took a cursory glance for him to look up at Stewart and shake his head.

The bugle call rang out and the square began to move once more. The body was still now and had been dragged a yard outside the square, the fallen helmet now covering his face. His comrades grimly marched over the dark bloodstain in the sand, some doffing their own helmets as they passed in a mark of respect. There was nothing more that could be done for him, at least for now. I glanced back the way we had come and was reminded that it would be the second body we had left in our wake.

More bullets buzzed about us, but they were hurried shots, for our own riflemen were constantly scanning the rocks on our right. Yet we were such a big target, we knew every so often they would get lucky. A quarter of a mile further on there was another shout of pain and a body tumbled from a saddle to the ground. It was St Vincent, clutching a bleeding belly. Again, the surgeon rushed over. This patient was at least alive, but there was little he could do then other than press a bandage to the wound. The square moved on; we could not afford to keep stopping or our losses would be even greater. I lost sight of St Vincent as the herd of camels stepped around him but glimpsed him again a quarter of an hour later. By then he had been loaded into one of the cacolets stretchers and was aloft on a camel. Suspended above the heads of the rest of the square, he was perhaps more exposed to enemy fire than the rest of us. Indeed, the man on the opposite side was complaining, having just been shot in the wrist. As we now know, he was to suffer a worse wound that day. By then there were four patients being carried and we had travelled just over a mile. Given there were around fourteen hundred men, one hundred and fifty camels and two dogs in a tightly packed square that was shuffling slowly across the desert, that was perhaps good going.

We took another half an hour edging across that rocky terrain, and I venture that an athletic tortoise could have gone faster. More men were hit by snipers, but most were able to return to their position in the ranks after being bandaged as many bullets were near spent by the time they

126

reached us. I remember one of our own skirmishers being hit while outside of the square and a surgeon running out to attend to him. The sawbones was hit in the leg as he crouched over his patient and also fell to the ground. We had to stop and send a squad of men to bring them both back, but neither was seriously injured.

The chaos in the centre of the square grew steadily worse. Most of the camel drivers could not speak English, but they understood that there were more shots coming from our right and naturally they edged to the left to avoid them. They were soon pressing into the left rear corner of the square, invoking furious Anglo-Saxon oaths as men shouted and pushed at them to move back into the centre. More salty language came from the score of sailors who were pulling the Gardener gun. Unlike the rest of our artillery, it could not be dismantled and loaded onto camels. The Royal Navy contingent had pulled that heavy carriage hundreds of miles over rock, sand and gravel. They wanted to pull together at a steady rhythm but were continually impeded when nervous camel drivers crossed their path. Eventually, they got the chance to put their burden into action.

A squadron of enemy cavalry, perhaps fifty strong, emerged from a gulley to our right rear. If they charged they could have run down the skirmishers we had out on that side. Beresford, the naval commander, had been desperate to try out his weapon and virtually begged Stewart for permission to engage. The colonel agreed; it would do no harm to demonstrate our superior firepower. Shouts went out to our riflemen to get out of the field of fire while the sailors grunted and pushed to get the carriage pointing out of the corner of the square. The Mahdists must have seen the activity but continued trotting forward, oblivious to the danger. The noise of the machine gun was deafening: it fired volleys of five bullets in quick succession and they were soon blasting through and around the horsemen. It only took a few bursts to see them routed and the survivors galloping out of sight to a cheer from the rest of the square.

It was a small victory, but things were getting tougher now. We caught sight of flags flapping over hidden gullies that we imagined full of men and the closer we got to the wells the more the enemy moved in around us. We had covered two miles by then and the water was only another mile or so away, to our left, but we could tell by the increasingly loud drumming, which came from that direction, that their main body stood between us and the precious liquid we would need before the day was done. A couple of times large groups of men rose out of hollows in the ground. Beresford shouted to be allowed to use his Gardner gun but Stewart did not want to delay the advance. So the facing ranks of the square were ordered to fire volleys at the enemy. Each time when the muzzle smoke cleared, the enemy had gone. Their snipers, though, were an ever-present menace. The number of men sporting bandages or being carried on camels was steadily growing. Several times we had ducked as bullets whizzed close over our heads. More men suddenly appeared on our right. When a soldier facing in that direction gave out a cry and tumbled to the ground, Burleigh stepped forward. "I am going to get those villains the next time we fire some volleys!" he shouted to me over his shoulder as he bent down to pick up the fallen rifle.

I was left standing alone in the middle of the square. Stewart and his staff were towards the front, staring out at the terrain ahead. Most of the camels had once more drifted towards the rear, where soldiers were none too gently driving them on. As the Mahdists we had seen on the right opened fire, I edged to the left. It was then that a shot rang out from that direction and a soldier fell dead at my feet. Here is where my tale began, with men rushing forward to take away the body while his sergeant looked expectantly at me and then at the gun now lying on the sand.

You already know what happened next; the terror as that screaming horde of white-robed figures erupted from the earth just a few hundred yards away. The Gardner being overrun, and panicked firing with both rifle and Webley to keep them at bay. The relief I felt when we had driven them back and then the shock of finding some inside our square. It was a desperate action as I have already described. I am not sure how that square held together and closed up the breach. If it had not, we would all be dead for certain. The poet Sir Henry John Newbolt wrote his work *Vitaï Lampada* about it thus:

> The sand of the desert is sodden red,—
> Red with the wreck of a square that broke;—

The Gatling's jammed and the Colonel dead,
And the regiment blind with dust and smoke.
The river of death has brimmed his banks,
And England's far, and Honour a name,
But the voice of a schoolboy rallies the ranks:
"Play up! play up! and play the game!"

I don't recall a schoolboy's voice and it was a Gardner and not a Gatling. The poet implied that the values of sportsmanship and honour ingrained in every English public schoolboy won the victory, but that was nonsense. Most of the men there had not been to such a school and take it from one who has, I was certainly not thinking of cricket then. My mind was only on survival and as some of the cavalry boys to my left discovered, you cannot keep firing a rifle to your front if someone is sticking a spear in your back. That was why I stood in that square, for we all knew that we fought together as a single unit or we died together, overwhelmed in a hopeless melee. For the men about me there was more at stake: regimental pride. They knew that they had been handpicked from their battalions; they would not allow their company to be the weak link in our defence.

My fellow correspondents interrogated me at length for details of the battle when I returned with the party to bring them up to the wells. They told me that from the distance they were watching from, the square stood like a rock as waves of enemy troops washed about it. They had no idea it had been breached as the incursion had been veiled by a wall of gun smoke. Cameron said he could not think of another instance where a broken square had managed to reform while under such an attack. Wearily I answered their questions, for by then I had not slept in two nights. Mindful of my promise to Cochrane, I did not tell them of Burnaby's involvement in breaking the square. I am sure that Burleigh had discovered this too, but he also kept the news of his friend's action to himself. The truth only came out years later in the memoirs of officers who had fought that day.

Column inches were scribbled into notebooks as the rest of the *zariba* occupants prepared to move on towards the wells. A quiet reverence fell over the party as we crossed the battlefield, where many of the memorial cairns already stood. Nearby, rows of bodies, like tidemarks of seaweed on the beach, showed where our enemies had perished.

Chapter 12

I had hugged Leila with the gratitude of a drowning man finding a lifebuoy when we had been re-united. Just hours before it had seemed certain we would both perish. I still struggled to understand precisely how we had withstood that fanatical onslaught. Yet we were far from out of the woods yet. My guide was not wrong about the difficulties of the next stage of our journey. After those from the *zariba* had spent the day replenishing their water bottles and, if they were able, surveying the battlefield, preparations were made for another night march. There had been more deaths among the wounded and a couple of hurried burials before we departed. The seriously injured were to be left at the wells with a guard of a hundred men and one of the surgeons. It would be a precarious existence if the enemy returned in number. Wounded soldiers capable of riding a camel preferred the safety in numbers of the column. More than a few who marched on, were sporting bandages from the earlier battle.

While the men and horses had been watered, only some of the two and a half thousand camels still with the column had been able to drink. The wells were deep holes in the sand with gravel bottoms that gradually refilled from the surrounding ground. There was not time for them to replenish to give all the creatures water before we were due to march again. They would be five days without a drink if we reached the Nile on the morrow and had been in poor condition to start with. There was no more *dhura* to eat and the desert grasses around the wells were poor fodder. As well as the hard riding and lack of food, a number also suffered bullet wounds, particularly to the hump which, fortunately, contained no major organs. One of my beasts had been shot in the neck and killed during the sniping around the *zariba*. We redistributed the baggage among the remaining beasts, leaving the water tank behind as there was no time or water to fill it. It was a two day journey to the Nile, where our water problems would be over. The approach to Khartoum would then take us on or along the river. There were rumours that some of the Mahdist besiegers of Khartoum would now be marching north to reinforce those who had attacked us. If it was true, our commander wanted our backs to be against the river with a limitless supply of water before we faced them.

If the animals were suffering, there was a distinct change in the mood of the humans in the column too. The herders were close to mutiny as several of their number had been shot in the confusion of battle. Others had been attacked inside the square by Mahdists, who were particularly incensed at Muslims helping their enemy. Soldiers were in a state of post-battle shock, particularly some of the more aristocratic officers. They had used their influence to get included in the column, which they imaged to be a jolly jaunt with little actual danger. Back in London, no one had thought that the Mahdists would be foolish enough to pitch spears against men with rifles and machine guns. Now we knew that they would. They had come within an ace of victory too. With the deaths of the likes of Colonel Burnaby and Viscount St Vincent, it was clear that the grim reaper was no respecter of station in life. I sensed that they were now regretting those pulled strings that had got them here, not that they would admit it.

Even among the correspondents there was heightened apprehension. The light-hearted banter of days before had been replaced with a grim realisation that we were now in a serious fight. We also knew that despite our recent victory, the war was far from over. We were an isolated force of just over a thousand men deep in a hostile desert, surrounded by enemies perhaps ten times our number. It would be weeks before the river column in their boats would be able to join us. It was hoped that Wolseley himself would lead reinforcements across the Bayuda once he was advised that the wells were secure. However, that too would take time and it promised to be a torrid wait. Yet we were not just expected to survive. Somehow, we were to help Gordon lift the siege at Khartoum too. I had been in tight spots before and there were more to come in my career, but I confess that that was a gut-wrenching moment. I could not see any prospect of success. Instead, my mind lingered over scenes of a beleaguered force trapped against the Nile, being gradually whittled away by sniping Mahdists until it was completely overrun. That afternoon I would have given everything I owned to be safely back in London.

We were ready to leave at two in the afternoon, but it was gone four when we finally set off, with just two hours of daylight left. We were formed up in a column some thirty camels wide and around eighty long, but inevitably it was the baggage animals that caused the problems. The drivers were having a furious argument and were on the point of refusing to move at all, but Rafa stepped in, pointing south and yelling at them, following which they grudgingly began to form their animals up. Leila explained that the men were reluctant to continue. Many were bitter that soldiers had shot at them during the confusion of battle. In response, Rafa had suggested that they go south and see if the Mahdists would treat them any better. They knew as well as he did that they would be butchered, and this time not by accident. Edicts had been issued by the Mahdi that the British were to be killed as were the apostate Egyptians. Any Sudanese supporting them were to suffer the same fate.

Bugles sounded and slowly we lumbered forward. Leila had ensured that our own mounts had fared better than many. They had been given a little water, but it was clear that others around us were on their last legs. They were still tethered to each other in groups of three or four. We had barely been going an hour before the first of them started to go down. As their paced slowed, they were pulled forward by the animal in front until their necks were stretched at an unnatural angle. Sometimes they stumbled forward to catch up, but more often they were held back by an equally exhausted creature behind. Eventually, one of a group would give a pitiful groan and simply collapse to the ground, falling onto its side and spilling its load, invariably pulling on the animal in front causing another cargo to tumble.

Cochrane was still the baggage master. Some of his men, with the aid of the herder, would try to get the animals back on their feet but if they could not, the animal would be abandoned and its load redistributed. We had fifty spare animals at the start of the march, mostly from the Heavy Cavalry Regiment contingent. Their men had borne the brunt of the battle, and following casualties, had many more camels now than riders. By dusk nearly all of those replacements had been used. We were to lose around two hundred and fifty of the creatures before we reached the Nile. Soon Cochrane and his men were forced to abandon supplies as well as animals, for there was no means to bring them with us.

As animals fell and were reloaded, we frequently had to halt the column to avoid it becoming too extended. By dusk we had only travelled around three and a half miles of the twenty-five to the Nile. It was now obvious to all that we would not get to the river by dawn the next day. At least in daylight it had been easy to make out the broad caravan trail that led from the wells to the river. At night we had to rely on a local guide and on the column staying together. That was easier said than done, for we were all exhausted from at least three nights with little sleep.

As I stared at the men riding around me, it was hard to believe that they were the cream of the British army. None of us had been able to wash since we were last at the river. We were dirty, our skins rough from the dust of the desert. I dare say we smelt as bad as our mounts, although we had got used to the stench. Clothes that had been fresh in Cairo were now all tattered and torn, and in many cases adorned with bloodstains or bandages. No one had shaved for a fortnight. While many had sported beards for months, even those who had maintained fashionable moustaches such as Stewart and Wilson the Intelligence officer now resembled bristly vagrants. Only our commander's still-gleaming metal cavalryman's helmet set him apart from the rest.

Inevitably, the column began to fall into disarray. Men dozed in their saddles and chins rested on chests. Some camels plodded on regardless, while others sensed their somnolent rider and came to a rest themselves. Several times I heard a wail in the darkness followed by the thud of a body hitting the ground. Then a cry of pain and shouts for someone to grab their mount before it made its way off through the herd. I nearly fell off myself once. Leila had seen me slipping from the saddle and grabbed my shoulder. I woke suddenly to find her looking at me, fatigue showing in her features. It took my tired mind several seconds to realise I was still on a camel and that I could not reach out to kiss her without falling off for certain.

As we progressed the ground became more fertile and we noticed more desert grasses. Hungry animals with dozing riders moved out of the line to find a patch to graze. Other grumbling creatures insisted on stopping whether their rider was awake or not. Gradually, the front of the column stretched out to several times its original width. As a result, that night several men vanished, and at least two were later captured. What's more, Cochrane later estimated that by the following day at least a hundred more camels were missing, either accidentally or by being cut loose by resentful drivers.

As Leila had predicted, by around ten that night the dispersed column found itself entering an acacia forest that grew in a shallow that crossed our route. We had managed to stay in the centre of the column, where a narrow gap had been cut for the trail. Even then I could hear the sharp thorns scraping against the cargo netting on the baggage camels. Rafa had to unhook one animal that had been caught up in the foliage, getting badly scratched in the process. We escaped lightly. The air was full of curses and ruminant growls as men and animals found themselves entangled in vicious barbs that had appeared all around them in the darkness.

By one in the morning most of the column was finally through, although Cochrane and his men were still bustling about trying to track down missing beasts. We finally dismounted to rest ourselves and our animals. MacDonald estimated that we had covered fifteen miles from the wells, which meant we had ten to go. The sun rose at five-thirty and it made sense to rest up as we would now not reach the river before then. The town of Matammeh was at the end of the trail and would almost certainly have a Mahdist garrison, reinforced by the survivors of the men we faced at Jakdul. To continue would see exhausted men and animals, who had not slept properly for three nights, facing a large, unknown host who would surely know of our approach and have prepared traps and ambushes. Stewart held a brief conference with his officers. To our dismay he decided to press on; he still hoped to find the river before the enemy. Leila thought it was the right decision, as if the baggage animals did not get water soon, they would start dying in droves. They were our only means to move the vast supplies that an army needed on the march in a desert.

135

With groans from men and beasts, the column lurched back up onto its feet again and plodded on. I watched the eastern horizon for a glimmer of light and wondered if the distant Nile would be visible in the dawn glow. By the time the sun's rays lit up the ground ahead we had covered another two miles, but all we could see was a flat featureless plain stretching into the distance. The disappointment was palpable and men started to glare suspiciously at our guide. We had been angling to reach the Nile a few miles from Matammeh so that we had time to take on water before the enemy found us. Now Stewart ordered a slight change in direction; we were to head to the nearest stretch of river. Cavalry scouts were sent on ahead to confirm that our calculations of distance covered and remaining were correct. We stumbled on, many animals now barely able to keep putting one foot in front of the other.

There was an air of expectation among the men. In the next few hours we would find the Nile again, but it was likely that we would have to fight to secure a place on the bank. What would be waiting for us on the distant horizon? And if we survived that how would we reach Gordon? We should have been feeling nervous or apprehensive, but most of us were just bone tired. There was less than a pint left in my water skin and my throat was dry with the dust of the desert. I was just imagining scooping up hatsful of the Nile and the sensation of cool water cascading over my head, when we heard the distant crackle of rifle fire ahead. Not many guns, just a dozen or so. Perhaps our scouts had encountered an enemy patrol. We waited and in front of the dust cloud they were throwing up we saw our horsemen coming back. They were at the trot rather than the gallop, which might have signified a lack of urgency or perhaps their mounts were too spent to go any faster. A frisson of anticipation spread down the column, which due to the exhaustion of its animals now stretched back nearly half a mile. No one had the strength to chase up the stragglers.

In the past we would have kicked our animals up to overhear the scouts' report to Stewart, but this time we did not bother. We would find out for ourselves soon enough. So wearily we trudged on until we crested a gravel ridge and saw our first signs of civilisation in weeks. It had to be the town of Matammeh at the end of the caravan trail. A wall surrounded a vast huddle of mud brick buildings. Perhaps it was the heat haze, but it was far bigger than I had expected, a fortress-like structure in the middle. My eyes searched for the Nile, but its many floods had pushed up a bank of stones and mud that obscured our view of the water. After spending the last miles imagining my first sight of the river, it was a bitter disappointment. Not that I had long to dwell on that, for trumpets and drums came to us on the breeze, proving that the Mahdists were all too aware of our approach. Horsemen and riflemen were already pouring out of Matammeh and heading in our direction.

We were on a flat featureless plain, where patches of desert grass interspersed with wide swathes of gravel. The folly of Stewart's insistence on pressing on was now apparent. His men were exhausted, hungry and disorganised, in no state to fight a battle. They needed to rest and regroup before they could consider forcing an advance, yet there was damn all cover to do that. Stewart pointed to a gravel ridge that was barely twenty feet at its peak over the surrounding country, then announced that we would form a new *zariba* there. Several officers grumbled in dismay; they wanted to push on. I could see why, as there were no large rocks to build walls and already some of the Mahdists were opening fire on us at an impossible range. We would soon be peppered with shot. Cochrane began organising the baggage camels so that they would make a square rampart around the top of the hill. They were forced to kneel in rows three deep to form a perimeter, while some of the crates of boxes and tins that they carried were unloaded beside them to offer some protection. Unfortunately, the top of the hill was not flat, the crown rose up above this animal rampart, and so offered little protection there. By the time we had added our animals to the middle row at the rear of the *zariba*, the nearest Mahdists were no more than half a mile away. They were spreading out into the clumps of grass, no doubt with the intention of coming closer, but could not resist shooting at the growing target of our new camp. They must have been aiming high, for we heard the 'tink' noises as bullets bounced off the gravel around us. I remember a soldier crying out as he was struck on the shoulder. It was more in surprise than pain; he suffered nothing more than a bruise as the slug had long since lost any harmful velocity. This benign period was not to last long.

As the last of the rearguard drew up to the *zariba*, enemy skirmishers had closed to a more lethal range. More animals had been driven into the centre of the space to give additional cover. Hungry men were crouched around them trying to unpack stores to find food and the small amount of remaining water. A few of our soldiers manned the perimeter, firing into patches of grass where puffs of smoke gave away the positions of snipers. It was a near hopeless task, for if the devils had any sense, they would roll away after taking their shot. We had to hit individual men, while they had a whole camp of soldiers and animals to aim at.

I saw the first man killed half an hour later. A soldier was exclaiming over a bullet hole in his kettle. When his companion leaned over the back of a camel to look, he fell back, shot clean through the head. Inevitably, lots of shots were hitting the animals, but they were remarkably resilient to gunfire. If they were hit fatally then their neck would drop, and they would die very quickly. Otherwise they would give a groan, much as when you got them to rise up, and then continue to stare placidly about. I saw one struck on the top of the head; he just shook his noggin for a moment and then calmly went on chewing the cud.

Leila, Rafa and I found Burleigh, Cameron and others of the press corps wedged between two lines of camels. The immediate priority was food, and it did not matter what. We ate the first tins we could find as it was too dangerous to rummage around looking for more. Breakfast was thus tinned bully beef and peaches. Rafa even managed to get a stove going for some tea. Conversation quickly turned to what would happen next.

"We are waiting for them to attack us," opined Burleigh. "There is at least two hundred yards of clear ground around every side of the *zariba*. They will never survive the crossing of it."

"What if they don't attack?" countered Cameron. "They must know we are short of water; they can afford to wait us out." It was a grim thought, with no obvious argument against it. There had to be at least a

138

thousand Mahdists scattered in the plain sniping at us, while the continuous thunder of drums from Matammeh indicated that there were probably several times that number without rifles waiting between us and the river.

If they had stormed the *zariba* in the first couple of hours of us getting there, they might have succeeded anyway. While a few soldiers guarded the perimeter, the rest of the exhausted army snatched a few hours' sleep. They slumped down in the shelter between dozing camels and were soon snoring. It was almost impossible to move around without disturbing them and getting a stream of invective for your trouble. Not that I bothered, for like them, I was almost dead on my feet and having got some food in my belly I needed to rest too.

I awoke to a sharp pain in my ankle. It felt like it had been struck with a small hammer and on inspection, I found a spent bullet half embedded in the leather of my boot. I must have been asleep for a couple of hours, for the sun was bearing down and the sound of gunfire all around me was considerably louder. The camel I had been resting against was dead, shot through the top of the neck. It had not even stirred enough in its death throes to wake me. I could hear orders being shouted to direct our fire into patches of grass and the distinctive clipped bursts of the Gardner gun to keep the enemy at bay. Leila and the others had gone, perhaps to look after their own animals or see what was happening around the *zariba*. We might all be called to help in the defence and so I picked up the Martini–Henry rifle I had kept with me since Jakdul. I had a bandolier of fifty cartridges over my left shoulder and this time I had checked every one for dents before loading them in. My right shoulder held the strap for my now nearly empty water bottle while my right pocket carried the comforting weight of the loaded Webley. With spare shells for that in my left pocket, I felt ready to cautiously emerge.

There were fewer soldiers resting in the centre of the camp now. I squeezed past several before I noticed Cameron sitting and staring fixedly at a tin of sardines. "What is the matter?" I called to him. "Is that your last one?" He did not reply and I had a sudden sense of foreboding. There did not seem to be a scratch on him but when I shook his shoulder, he fell forward. That was when I saw that the back of his head had been smashed in by a bullet. I reeled for a moment from the shock. Heaven knows I had seen enough death in my time and even on that journey, but of soldiers, not war correspondents. I knew Power from the *Times* and O'Donovan from my own paper had been murdered, but this was the first time I had seen one of our band killed. So far in my career we had led a charmed life, observing, being shot at certainly – I had barely escaped with my life at Sedan – but we were treated as non-combatants. The Mahdists made no such distinction; we were all infidels, deserving of nothing but death. The bullets whining over our heads and through our position, were often fired blindly from men hidden in the long grass a few hundred yards away. They also made no distinction for rank, as I was to discover a few minutes later.

I had no idea what to do about Cameron's body. I could not move it on my own, but it felt wrong to leave him pitched face down in the dirt. I made my way to the hospital area in the centre of the *zariba*. They would have stretcher bearers, I thought, and could place my friend with the other dead. I had to crouch down as I got close, for the centre was the highest point of the hill and got little protection from the surrounding animals and men. Extra ramparts of packing cases and camel saddles had been piled up to give the surgeons some shelter as they worked. The first thing I saw was a line of six blanket-covered bodies lying just outside the rampart, one was probably the soldier I had seen shot earlier. Then I saw a man inside wearing a red army uniform coat, which was unusual. It was St Leger, crouched down, writing a letter. He was weeping, which surprised me, for he had always struck me as a man who could maintain a stiff upper lip whatever the circumstances. It was only when I looked at the ground beside him that I understood. Lying on the stones was his close friend Colonel Stewart. Part of the column commander's uniform had been cut away and there were blood-soaked bandages around his groin and lower stomach. His face was ashen and I saw now that he was gasping some dictation to St Leger.

"Shot through the spine while he was looking at the enemy," muttered one of the orderlies when he saw me staring. "He won't last long."

"Who is in command now?" I asked.

"No idea," the man replied. "Burnaby was second in command, but he has already bought it."

There are times when you wonder if things can get any worse. We were tired, thirsty, outnumbered, penned in, gradually being whittled away by a fanatical enemy several times our size and now our two most experienced leaders were dead or dying. I stared back at Stewart and saw beside him the shiny metal cavalry helmet that he had insisted on wearing. I wondered if that small vanity to help him stand out among his men had also attracted the fire of the enemy snipers. St Leger was getting a grip on himself as he took down the colonel's final words to his friends and family back home. Of course, unless things took a considerable turn for the better, it was very unlikely that anyone would read them. Instead, they looked destined to be scattered to the desert winds when we were overrun.

When I caught up with Burleigh a few minutes later, I discovered that there was both good and bad news. On the positive side we did have a new commander. While Beresford, the naval officer, was technically the most senior in terms of rank, as the bulk of the column was army, its command had devolved to the Intelligence man, Colonel Wilson. The bad news was that Wilson was a quiet, bookish fellow, who did not have anything like the force of personality of Stewart or Burnaby. Nor had he any prior experience of being in action. His first active command was destined to be a baptism of fire. Our new chief certainly did not want for advice. While Stewart, from his death bed, urged him to wait in the *zariba* for the enemy to attack, other leaders such as Beresford and the Guard's Colonel, Boscawen, were equally adamant that he should launch an attack of his own before we all died of thirst. In the event he did neither.

Colonel Sir Charles Wilson has been roundly condemned for his actions in Sudan, often by those trying to deflect attention from their own deficiencies. I will own that initially I was not impressed with him either, but now I am sure that we all owe him our lives.

By midday bullets were raining down on us like metal hail. Many had little force to them as they were fired at extreme range, yet by then more than a few Mahdists had crawled through the desert grass to get

141

close enough to kill. A steady stream of men were being helped to the now crowded hospital area and the row of blanket-covered bodies was slowly growing. It was clear that something had to be done. The Mahdists were showing no intention of storming our position. They did not need to; they only had to wait until we dropped from sniper fire or thirst, for by then there was barely a cupful of water left between us – the wounded were left to wail piteously for a drink. Yet instead of listening to those calling for action, Wilson ordered that gravel high points a hundred yards on either side of the *zariba* be captured and fortified. The Mahdists were using the dead ground on the other side of them to creep up closer to our position.

Many officers were furious at the waste of time and effort. Beresford immediately sent a messenger urging that the column should advance at once. He cannot have been mollified when he learned that his courier had been killed by a sniper. Yet Wilson was not swayed by these appeals, even though the only items we could fortify these positions with were boxes that formed the defence of the main position. Men had to run across open ground carrying these burdens as bullets whipped about them from all directions. Once on the high ground they would crouch behind their box and open fire on Mahdists from that vantage point to start pushing them back, before returning for another crate.

Things were getting desperate. Burleigh decided that he would have a go at running boxes himself. He went three times before coming back shaken and covered in blood; a man had been shot just in front of him. He told of another officer who had had a miraculous escape when merely winded after a bullet struck a brass button on his tunic. Cochrane was busy too, taking the remaining boxes and saddles to build a new rampart around the hospital. As a result of their efforts, the poor camels on the perimeter were now entirely exposed to enemy fire, although many of those in the outer line were already dead.

By one o'clock the new bastions had been built and while the enemy fire was just as frequent, some of it was now from a greater distance away. The press contingent and servants gathered in a small hollow between two lines of camels to discuss what was likely to happen next. In a matter of minutes, despite our shelter, we had all been hit by bullets fired high into the air. I was struck on the arm by a slug that cut through my shirt and drew blood. Another man had the heel shot off his boot and Burleigh thought he had been badly wounded in the neck. "Pull it out!" he almost screamed as he half slumped to the floor. "It is near my spine. Oh Christ, don't let me be a cripple." I leaned over him expecting to see a bloody mess, but instead there was just a vivid red mark deepening on his neck.

"It's all right," I assured him. "It has not even broken the skin."

"You bloody fool," he groaned, "look again, I can feel the blood going down my neck."

I reached down his collar, pulled out the still hot bullet and dropped it in his hand. "There it is. You really are fine."

He sat up and stared around at us, barely able to believe his reprieve. Bennet Burleigh was a courageous man, he had proved that many times in the past, from his fighting in the American Civil War, to running the boxes to the outer bastions that morning. He was to be mentioned in despatches for that, the first official recognition of bravery ever given to a war correspondent. Yet now before our eyes, his nerve broke. Perhaps it was the man who had been killed in front of him just an hour before, his most recent escape from injury or the cumulative effect of recent days, for we had been through a lot. I noticed his hand had started to shake as he looked around us and announced, "We are all done for if we stay here. Wilson has no idea what he is doing and will get us all killed. Our only hope is to make a run for it back to Jakdul. We need to take some ponies rather than camels and ride for our lives."

"You will never make it." Leila's voice was calm and logical. "Their pickets surround us and they will have cavalry around us too. Anyway, you do not have water for you or your ponies to reach the wells."

"We just need to get to the other side of that acacia forest," Burleigh insisted. "There are dozens of lost camels there; surely we will find some with water skins on them."

It was desperate long odds to me, but such was Burleigh's reputation among the press corps that two others chose to join him. They swore that they would not leave each other behind and went off in a search for ponies. Leila watched them go with a fatalistic sigh. "If I have to die,"

143

she murmured to those of us left, "I would rather it be by a quick bullet than by inches of thirst in the desert."

"You don't think there is any hope, then?" I asked glumly.

"The emirs will not be foolish enough to order their men to storm the *zariba* as your Colonel Stewart hopes," she replied. "But I think your Colonel Wilson knows what he is doing. If he were to march his men off to the Nile, then the *zariba* would be overrun by those that surround us. These new bastions will help keep them further back, so that they have more open ground to cover. A few will try to charge us, but when they are shot down, the rest will just wait. They know we cannot go back."

"So, Wilson *will* order an advance," I concluded.

"Of course," Leila looked puzzled that the matter was in doubt. "It is our only chance."

I wondered how many men would be left fit to fight. Certainly less than a thousand, especially as some would have to be left to defend the *zariba*. They would have to march two miles across open land infested with enemy snipers. Those that survived that ordeal would then have to climb up a steep bank defended by thousands of sword-wielding fanatics. I looked up into the sky; we had perhaps four or five hours of daylight left. If we did not beat them today we would be overrun at night or too wracked with thirst to fight them tomorrow. Our chances looked so slim, I almost wished I had joined Burleigh.

Chapter 13

Orders were given for the square to form up at two in the afternoon. The men were to gather at the rear of the *zariba* where there were fewer snipers. Even then they were to lie flat on the ground until the formation was ready to advance. There were inevitable delays as men argued over who should stay and defend the *zariba*. This turned out to be the hussars, as their horses were blown. Some of the heavy cavalry companies that had been badly mauled at Jakdul also remained. There was a last-minute decision to double the amount of ammunition the men carried with them too. Normally, they had seventy rounds, fifty of them in their bandoliers, but now they had to carry another seventy in their packs too. Each round weighed two ounces so that was 17 pounds per man just for ammunition. There was precious little room for food and very few had any weight of water left to carry, although water bottles and skins were to be taken in the hope some might reach the Nile.

The question for me was, should I go with the square as before, or stay in the *zariba*? Burleigh had left with the others for his mad pony ride. The remaining correspondents were divided. Some, like MacDonald, were staying as they had at Jakdul. St Leger, though, was determined to advance with the square. He wanted to avenge Stewart, who was still alive in the hospital. For me, my decision was driven by a mixture of logic and despair. The logical argument was that if the square was beaten, then the *zariba* would be overrun or forced to surrender anyway. The end result would be the same: every white man would be killed, and Leila and Rafa might be taken captive, but as slaves. My only hope to live was if the square was to succeed. So it made sense to join it, for they would need every man they could get.

I could pretend to you that this was my reasoning, and it was in part. Yet by then I was in a barely restrained funk. Our position seemed utterly hopeless. I was convinced that I would be dead in hours either way. I felt light-headed and reckless. Perhaps it was the sun and lack of water, but I did not want to sit passively waiting for death to find me. At least I could go down fighting. A bullet through the head like Cameron would be a lot more merciful than I could expect if taken

145

prisoner. Leila wanted to come too, but I insisted she stay behind. I made it sound noble, insisting that slavery was probably better than death. That may have been the truth, but the real reason was that I could not bear to see her die too.

I was not alone in my anguish. With good reason, men acted as though they were about to march to their doom. Comrades shook hands and wished each other well. A few shed manly tears. I crawled around between the kneeling camels to make my own farewells, embracing MacDonald and the others who were staying. There were murmurs of "Good luck," for we all knew our fates were inextricably linked. The *zariba* could be overrun before the square was defeated, but it certainly could not survive if the army was beaten. Even St Leger shook my hand, his eyes close to tears again.

"I thought you were coming with me?" I queried, wondering if he had changed his mind.

"I am," he reassured me, but then he lowered his voice. "Sir Herbert," he whispered referring to his friend Colonel Stewart, "thinks only a few of us are likely to see the Nile." He paused and gulped back his emotion before holding out a small, stoppered morphine bottle. At first, I thought he was offering me an easy way out if I was wounded. Then as I took the glass phial, I realised from the weight that it was empty of liquid. "It contains a note of what has happened here so far, some words from Sir Herbert to his wife and from me to my family, that sort of thing." He patted his own pocket and added, "I have one too." Slightly embarrassed he added, "I don't want to croak, Harrison, but if you make it to the river and I do not, I would be obliged if you would throw it in the water. There is a chance it will float downstream and be found."

Of course I agreed, although with the various cataracts, the chances of it remaining intact *and* being found by someone who understood English looked slimmer than our own of surviving the day. "Should you not be getting ready?" I asked, gesturing at his attire. He was still in his red uniform jacket and was only armed with his pistol. "Are you not bringing a long arm?" I asked patting my own Martini–Henry.

"I usually stand among the staff," he replied, "and my revolver has not let me down yet." We got ready to run down the slope to where a

146

rough square of men could be seen lying among the stones. The snipers had noticed what was going on and, whenever someone tried to move, were sending a hail of shot into the gap between the *zariba* and the gathering point. There were a score of men moving, often running twenty yards and falling to the ground for a moment in the hope that the enemy did not have time to line sights up on them. One man was coming back the other way, a bloody hole in the arm of his tunic. Staying in the zariba was rapidly getting much more appealing option. This was only the start of the ordeal to come, but I knew we had to go on. I reminded myself that fighting through to the Nile was our only chance of survival.

"Come on then!" I shouted to St Leger as we stepped around a dead camel that marked the perimeter of our shelter and started to sprint down the slope. The level of fire increased markedly. There was almost a continuous crackle, drowned out only by the buzz of several bullets that must have gone just above my head. I am sure my helmet was knocked by one of them. After thirty yards St Leger dropped to a shallow hollow in the ground and, gratefully, I went down beside him.

"Take off that damned red coat," I told him as I peered forward to gauge how much further we had to run. "I am sure that it is drawing their fire." He did not reply and when I turned to face him, I gave a gasp of horror. A bullet had hit St Leger just behind the left eye socket. His skull had been smashed and his remaining eye stared back at me lifelessly. "Oh Christ, first Cameron and now this," I remember muttering. I thought Burleigh and those with him would soon be dead too. At that moment I was certain that none of the press corps would see the Nile again. I was in a daze and cannot have been thinking straight as when I got up, I tried to bring St Leger's body with me, holding it under the arms and dragging it along. I had barely gone a few yards when another soldier running for the square pulled me back down again.

"We can't take corpses with us, sir." He spoke gently, seeing that I was a civilian and in a state of shock. "Best leave him here and they will come from the *zariba* to collect him to bury with the others." With that, he grabbed my arm and we were running again.

Having risked life and limb to get there, my welcome into the square was hardly effusive. Colonel Wilson, our new commander, frowned at me. "I trust you have come here to fight and not write," he muttered.

"This gentleman fought with my company at Jakdul, sir," called out a new voice. I turned to see my old sergeant watching from the rows of prone men that formed the front of the square. "We have a space in our ranks if you want it," he added, as though he was offering a spare slice of cake instead of a near certain death sentence. Yet with Wilson watching suspiciously, I could hardly turn him down. I accepted gratefully and crawled across to take my place in the line.

I must have waited there fifteen minutes while the final preparations were made. Wilson had learned from our earlier experience. There was a small reserve of men in each of the corners. Each face had around two hundred men, and the total must have been well below a thousand. The Gardner and artillery had been left in the *zariba* where they could give us covering fire. There were just sixty camels with us, sitting calmly in the middle of the square as the battle raged about them, despite one of their number already lying dead in their midst. While some carried empty water tanks should we reach the Nile, and others medical supplies and ammunition, at least half were carrying empty pairs of cacolet stretchers. It was a grim reminder that heavy casualties were expected during the next phase of our journey. The soldier lying beside me noticed me glance back at the camels and must have guessed at the thoughts whirling through my head. Every man there must have had the same, but you would never know from the whispered conversations. "Never mind them, sir," he said quietly, jerking his thumb back to the animals. "We will all be drinking from the Nile in an hour or so."

"We bloody well better be," grunted the man on the other side. "My mouth is so dry I could not lick a stamp." He ducked as another bullet whined low over our heads and added, "Christ, the way they are guarding it, you would think it was a river of champagne."

"It'll bloody taste like champagne when we get to it," insisted the first man.

"I will have to take your word for it," his mate replied. "I have never drunk champagne. Anything better than camel piss will do me right now."

Further conversation was stilled by the shout behind. "The square will rise!" The command had come from Colonel Boscawen, who had risen to stand beside Colonel Wilson. The latter, not a regimental man, had evidently decided that someone more experienced commanding a square would be better at giving the orders.

"Now we are for it," muttered the man beside me as I reluctantly got to my feet. I have never stood in front of a firing squad – I came close in France once, but I imagine that the experience is very similar. Death felt almost a certainty as the volume of fire from the desert increased ten-fold when they saw us emerge from the ground. You could hear the bullets hitting the stones all around us. At least two struck my helmet, one half burying itself in the cork it was made from. Several men gave cries of pain as they were struck, but at least along the front face of the square, no one fell out. I saw now the wisdom of Wilson's extra ramparts either side of the *zariba*, for they had forced most of the snipers back to extreme range. Our sentries left behind and the Gardner were picking off any that tried to get too close.

"The square will advance by the left, slow march," Boscawen continued once he had checked that we were all standing. I was glad we were not waiting about, although the slow pace that the men about me began was almost tortuous. I had been apprehensive about joining the front face, which would lead any assault, but now I realised that it was certainly safer than the sides. The gunfire was all coming in from our flanks. I heard a shout for a surgeon behind me and saw a man stagger back from the left face with a wound to the shoulder that left blood running down his arm. He could still walk, though, and so stayed with the square. Two more men dropped to the ground but still we did not stop. As their comrades stepped around them to leave them abandoned on the ground, men ran down from the *zariba* to carry them to shelter. There was a lull in the fire as we moved towards one of the outer bastions, which blocked the aim of our enemies, and then we were into open ground again. Instead of marching directly to the river, though, our route angled towards the broadest patches of bare gravel on the way. Captain Verner, who had scouted to the river before, was sent out ahead to select the clearest line of march. No sniper could survive exposed on bare ground and so they were forced to keep their distance. I could hear the distinctive rattle of the Gardner as it sent volleys over our heads into the grass around us wherever it saw puffs of muzzle smoke. One of the swivel guns cracked out and there was an explosion to our left, with at least one body flying through the air.

With a sense of grim determination, we pressed on. There was no more cover now, just the flat plain to cross. The square was a hundred yards wide, a huge target to aim at and there was a constant rattle of bullets hitting the ground and grunts as men were struck. Fortunately for us, most of the Mahdists fired from extreme range, more in hope than expectation, and their bullets barely broke the skin. However, we knew there were others, patiently wriggling through the grass. They were the ones to worry about.

We made our first stop after just two minutes. The Guards' colour sergeant had been hit in the leg. We all stood there waiting, like coconuts in a fairground stall, while he was bandaged and loaded into a cacolet. This gave the enemy time to get in position. Setting off once more, we had barely covered a hundred yards when there was a volley of fire from a nearby patch of grass. A dozen men fell from the left rear corner of the square, at least two I could see were dead and several more were badly wounded. Once more we came to a halt and the surgeons scurried forward for the wounded, while reserves in the corner filled the vacant places in our line. We had only been marching for five minutes. I was certain then that we would be whittled down to nothing, long before we saw the river.

Another swivel gun shell landed where enemy shots had come from, and with it more screams to match those of our wounded. The puffs of smoke from the grass kept coming, though, and another man went down in our ranks. "The square will lie down again," roared Boscawen and I gratefully dropped down to lie on the stones. I thought we would just wait there while the wounded were loaded onto camels, but instead Captain Verner was recalled into the square. Once he was safely inside our ranks, the front and side faces were ordered to fire three rounds into the surrounding grass. We were firing blind and who knows if we hit anything. If we did, their screams were lost in the sound of gunfire. Yet it felt good to be firing back after being so long on the receiving end. Hundreds of bullets scything through the grass would also have given the Mahdists notice not to come too close.

It might have been my imagination, but when we finally got to our feet again the sniping seemed diminished. Perhaps we had killed some of those nearby after all. Verner was sent forward once more, and we resumed our march. It was to take a further hour and a half to cross that plain. There were no more close-range volleys as before; they kept some distance now. While we could not see men gathering to attack us, those on the higher *zariba* and bastions could. The Gardner continued to crackle out its volleys, while occasionally the screw guns fired where they could see groups of men gathering. Fortunately, the range of these guns meant that they could destroy ambush parties long before we reached them. We dropped to the ground and fired volleys into the grass twice more as we crossed the plain. The sun was sinking in the sky behind us and so most of our enemies would have been squinting into its glare to take a shot. By then around half of the cacolets were full and we had a fair few walking wounded. Yet we were making steady progress. With the slow pace of march and frequent stops we had only covered one and a half miles, but now the steep embankment between us and the river was just half a mile off.

The drumming from men hiding on top of the slope ahead grew louder. Those of us in the front face of the square had fared rather better from snipers than those in the sides, but now we would be leading any assault up the bank. I had not cared about this when we had set off, for I thought there was little chance of making it across the plain alive, but now this new risk was very much apparent. "They will cut us to pieces when we reach the top," muttered the man next to me.

"Quiet in the ranks!" barked the sergeant behind us. The army is not keen on men thinking for themselves, but I struggled to see a way out of our predicament. Our artillery could not see or hit men waiting on top of the embankment. They would only have a few yards to charge us when our first ranks – my ranks – breasted the slope. We could fire a volley, but there would be no time to reload before we were bayonet to spear point and hopelessly outnumbered. It would take just one break in our line and they would pour inside our formation. Then we would be done for.

I could see no way to beat them and glanced back at Colonel Wilson, to see if he bore the confidence of a man with a plan. He was as inscrutable as the sphinx, but from the way he kept glancing around the desert, I sensed he was still seeking some inspiration. Then, when we were eight hundred yards from the slope, he ordered a halt. He had turned to discuss something with Boscawen, perhaps what the hell we were to do next, when a miracle occurred.

The Mahdists must have been watching us and they saw our formation stop beneath them. Maybe they thought our men were refusing to advance, or possibly they had whipped their warriors up into such a fervour, they could not be restrained. Dozens of flags appeared on the top of the slope in front of us. Then their army showed itself around the banners. With a wild roar, they launched themselves down the slope like cream being poured down the side of a pudding. Five thousand fanatical, murderous warriors charging towards you might not sound like a miracle, but it was a hell of a lot better than us attacking them. There was not a stick of cover to protect them as they closed in on us and every soldier in those ranks knew what an opportunity had just been presented. Some began to cheer but Boscawen shouted for them to be quiet, as he did not want to alert the enemy commanders to their folly. "Front rank, volley fire!" he bellowed. We gratefully raised our rifles to our shoulders and sent bullets into the distant throng. I and the men about me hurriedly reloaded and fired again. Smoke was already obscuring our view so it was impossible to aim beyond pointing the muzzle at the top of the slope, in anticipation of your bullet dropping a little over that distance and hitting this swarm of humanity.

"Cease fire!"

I thought I had misheard, but a bugle call echoed the command, and all around me muzzles were raised as the guns fell silent. The order had come from Wilson, a man who had never commanded in battle before.

He must have seen the puzzled faces turning in his direction. Even Boscawen looked surprised, if not a little alarmed at this unexpected pacifism as a horde of our enemy charged to hack us to pieces. Yet, as our square fell silent, our new commander showed no concern. I glanced over his shoulder at the setting sun behind him. Red and gold streaks were rippled across the sky, as if foretelling the blood on the sand that would result from this evening's work. The question was: whose blood would it be? When I looked back the leading Mahdists were closer, their emirs on horseback, holding their banners and racing through the throng to the front. They were no more than six hundred yards away now. The Martini–Henry was lethal at that distance, not in my hands perhaps, but in many of those about me. Admittedly, the marksmen would have laid prone rather than standing to shoot, but we had a much bigger target to aim at. I could make out the individual running figures. There were black warriors in white robes and Arabs wearing something akin to a nightshirt with large patches of clashing colours, which showed their devotion to their humble leader. They were certainly taking our silence for encouragement. They had picked up speed as they ran down the slope and now sprinted towards us. Their distant yells and calls for their god to smite us came on the wind. Through the dust they kicked up, we could make out the glitter of spear points and the longer sword blades. A few had guns with them and there was a crackle of shots, but on the run, they were wildly inaccurate.

Five hundred yards now. When I looked back over my shoulder, Wilson was not even watching them, instead he was shouting something to Boscawen over the rising din. Turning again to my front, I saw that the Mahdist horde were dividing, some to launch themselves at our left face, but the vast majority were still coming straight at me. I stared along our ranks, my heart racing faster than the enemy, but the men stood implacably still. I was the only one stealing looks over his shoulder. I glanced at my watch, just to give myself something to do. I learned later that we waited silently for forty-five seconds while the enemy charged towards us, but I can promise you it felt more like forty-five minutes. It was half past four and the second hand crawled like a snail around the face of the instrument.

Four hundred yards and you could see the colour of their beards now. "Come on, you buggers!" muttered the man next to me. Whether he was referring to the enemy or imploring his officers to give the order he craved, it was impossible to say.

"Steady, boys," called the sergeant behind us, but I noticed that this time even his voice was hoarse, betraying the tension within. Three hundred yards; my aged Aunt Agatha could hit a Mahdist at this distance. I turned once more to Wilson, wondering if I dare fire without an order, for if we did not start shooting soon it would be too late. This time he was watching the enemy. He waited several more seconds and then nodded at Boscawen, who at last snapped the order to the bugler, "Commence firing!" Guns were up at shoulders before the lad had his instrument to his lips. Only the first note of the call was heard, the rest drowned out by a roar of fire. I had my next cartridge in the breech as the signal was repeated. I did not need the sergeant yelling, "Independent fire!" to exhort me to shoot as fast as possible. I glimpsed one of the emirs tumbling from his saddle from the first volley, then squeezed the trigger again. The smoke was now obscuring my view as I loaded once more and fired. My fingers started to work automatically; there was no time to think and no clear view to aim. Just keep firing bullets, one after another, at chest height into the desert ahead.

Third, fourth, fifth...by the sixth shot I realised that we must be stopping them. By now they should have been lunging towards us through the surrounding acrid smoke. The gunfire was an almost continuous roar, but occasionally there were gaps and through them I could now hear the screams of men ahead. I knew that we had put up a wall of lead and that it had stopped the Mahdist attack in its tracks. Not that we could afford to relent, for we were out-numbered at least five to one and isolated deep in a hostile desert. If the enemy were foolish enough to attack over open ground, we had to kill as many as we could. I heard the left face open fire as the warriors swarmed around our position, and I think some in the rear face fired too. I paid no attention to what was happening elsewhere, I just kept firing until the smoke around me was so thick, I could barely see the man alongside. Then the bugle sounded again. I had no idea what the signals meant, but the soldier to my right put out his arm to push my muzzle up. It was the order to cease fire.

I stood still for a moment, breathing heavily, and relishing the thought that we were still alive. Just hours before, I had been certain that I would not live to see the sunset that now blazed a triumphant gold above our heads. We had made it across the desert and destroyed the last force that stood between us and the Nile. Counting the cartridges in my bandolier, I found that there were only six left. We had fired a few rounds crossing the desert and so I estimated that we had used thirty-five repelling that final attack. With five seconds to reload each time, we had been shooting for less than three minutes.

The smoke cleared to reveal a scene of devastation before our eyes. The pile of bodies began a hundred and fifty yards in front of us and went back a hundred paces. No more than a dozen had got closer than that and none had reached our line. Our heavy high-calibre bullets must have passed through more than one torso in that tightly packed throng, with those falling holding up men following behind, until they too were hit. In some places they were piled two or three deep. I could make out moving limbs and the groans of those still alive, but no one would be foolish enough to go and help the wounded. We had learnt that lesson at Jakdul. Unlike that earlier encounter, there were no suicidal sudden rushes on our line from among the wounded either. They were further away and must have realised that such an attempt was pointless. Beyond this bloody boundary of destruction, we could see the survivors of the attack. Most were running as fast as their legs could carry them back in the direction of Metemma, although they left a trail of wounded stragglers in their wake.

A hoarse cheer rose up from the ranks and this time no one tried to silence it. I glanced back at Wilson, who was looking calmly satisfied with the result of his first action in command. He had taken a huge risk in giving the order to cease fire, gambling that waiting until we could not miss would knock the stuffing out of their attack. He shook Boscawen's hand and the two men started to discuss what to do next. From the pointing, I gathered that Boscawen wanted to use the cover of darkness to go back to the *zariba* and bring up the wounded. I was

155

relieved when I saw Wilson shake his head. Much as I wanted to help Leila and the others, I could barely talk now due to thirst and to leave the river without refilling our bottles was insane. I was no expert, but it seemed to me that it would also give enemy snipers the opportunity to get far closer under cover of darkness. We might lose more men on the return journey than we had already. Instead, men began to put spare ammunition from their pouches into their bandoliers for ready use. I was just taking a handful of cartridges for my own when the order was given to ascend the ridge.

I searched eagerly for water as we crested the top, anticipating the cooling liquid soothing my throat within minutes. I was to be disappointed, though, for there was another mile of plain ahead of us. But now at least in the fading evening light we could see the silhouettes of palms and other trees growing along the distant bank. Tired men found an extra spring in their step as dry throats urged them on.

Soon the desert gave way to clumps of desert grass, which got steadily thicker as we approached. Grazing goats bleated at our intrusion. They belonged to an abandoned village on the shore ahead of us. It was dark now, but there was enough starlight to reflect off the water ahead and we hurried on. Then, finally, after twenty-one days in the desert, two battles and countless deaths, I stood on the shore of the Nile again.

Even then the square kept formation and order was maintained; who knew what lurked in the darkness this far into enemy territory. As part of the front face, we were allowed to water first. I well remember us all walking into the river, some cavorting like children at the seaside. I bent forward to fill my helmet with water to tip over my head, grinning with delight as it washed down my back. Another man plunged in entirely and was shouted at for stirring up the riverbed mud as men filled up their water bottles. I submerged the neck of mine and was soon gulping down the contents. It was the colour of tea. My water filter salesman back in London had assured me that it would be full of typhoid and cholera but right then I did not care. My lips were cracked and my tongue swollen with thirst. I would take my chances as, pestilent or not, I desperately needed the liquid. With the other sides of the square shouting at us to hurry up, I filled the bottle again and hooked it onto my belt before dipping my hat once more and taking my place back in the ranks. We rotated round so that the next face could take their turn. I stepped out of line and wandered up to the wounded with my helmet full of water, intending to offer them a drink too. The first pair of cacolets I came to carried the Guards colour sergeant, who had been hit in the leg early in our march. I quickly saw that he was beyond thirst now. His body had been suspended high in the air on the back of the camel, above the men around him. He had taken at least two further bullets while on his stretcher, including a fatal one to the head. His mount, though, despite sporting several injuries of its own, gazed down at me with a camel's habitual look of condescension.

I found some surviving wounded to share my water and was embarrassed when one man wept in gratitude or relief that we had made it this far. They were being unloaded from the camels now, who were grumbling loudly that they had to wait their turn for a drink. One animal had broken free with its passengers aboard and waded so deeply into the river to avoid recapture that the wounded could reach down and get handfuls of water for themselves.

As one need was satisfied, another came to the fore. We had been driven, that last mile particularly, through thirst. Now we had drunk, we remembered that we were also hungry, but there was precious little food to be had. One camel carrying food supplies had been killed and abandoned on the march. Most of all, though, we were tired. We had not had a decent night's sleep in five days and that last march and battle had used every last reserve of strength. Captain Verner, who had led the square across the desert to the Nile, collapsed with exhaustion among his men. When they were moved to a new place in our defences, despite shaking him and even slapping his face, he could not be roused.

Wilson had us form three sides of a square, our backs toward the river, and sent some pickets forward to warn of an enemy approach. It sounds overly prudent, but unless the Mahdists brought a marching band with them, I suspect that they could have got inside our formation with ease. I would wager that within an hour every one of us was abandoned to Morpheus. My last thoughts were of Leila and the others we had left

157

behind. There had been no sound of further attacks on the *zariba*, but they were horribly vulnerable with their depleted number of defenders. And what about us? What would we do next? Less than a thousand fighting men, trapped deep inside enemy territory. Could we really fight our way to Khartoum and rescue Gordon? I was soon past caring. The man next to me lay his head on his pack and was soon snoring. I was not far behind.

Chapter 14

I am not sure if it was cold or hunger that woke me. Perhaps I sensed men stirring nearby. It was nearly dawn and the soldiers were being roused to stand to in case the Mahdists launched a dawn attack. There was no sound coming from Matammeh. The desert was as quiet as the grave it had become for many, so that the bugle call for *reveille* made me jump. As light spread across the sky, there was not an enemy to be seen. The only movement was our camels grazing on the crops of an absent farmer. The abandoned village was just eight hundred yards away on some high ground that covered the shore we were on. My stomach did not feel right, but I put that down to the sudden influx of water the night before. It would settle, I thought, once I had something to eat. A detachment was sent forward to occupy and fortify the village buildings and, with little else to do, I went with them. Other men were preparing for a march back to the *zariba*. In time, I thought, I would return with them to bring Leila and Rafa water. Mother Nature, however, had other ideas.

As I strolled forward, I looked at the crop the camels were devouring; it was a field of peas. The pods were small and not yet fully formed, but my hunger was such that I reached down and grabbed a bunch and ate them, shoots and all. But instead of being settled by this nourishment, my guts groaned in protest and the earlier twinge of discomfort I had felt became a sharp pain. I was nearly at the village when it happened: the strong sensation that my bowels were turning to liquid. I barely had time to drop my trousers and perch on a low wall before I became very *very* ill. I will spare you the details, but there was now no question of me accompanying the army, or indeed straying more than a few yards from a latrine or vacant piece of desert. I doubt it was the pea shoots. That water filter salesman had probably been right about the Nile and what it contained…

Some passing soldiers offered me a drink, but I declined, fearful that it might make things worse. So while part of the army marched off to the *zariba*, I remained slumped on the shaded side of the wall, trousers still around my ankles and a feverish sweat on my brow.

During the afternoon part of the village was turned into a hospital. The wounded were carried past me to the houses that offered shade. One of the surgeons grinned when he saw my plight. He had worked through the night and was still caring for his patients, but he promised to send help. A short while later an orderly came by with a bottle containing foul-tasting water, which the man assured me would do me good. It contained salts, he insisted, and I should go back to the hospital for more in the morning.

I remember slumping back against the wall, feeling like death. I could not help but wonder if I would end up under a cairn of rocks in this godforsaken country, like Burnaby and others before me. I must have fallen asleep and was awoken by Leila shaking my shoulder, a look of concern etched on her features. It had taken all day to evacuate the *zariba*. Even then, some had been left behind to guard supplies for a second run with camels on the morrow. I could hear the rumbling growl of the huge herd of creatures behind me as they pushed their way into the river for their first drink in days.

"What is the matter?" Leila asked. "Have you been wounded?"

"No, it's my guts," I gasped, clutching my midriff, amazed that she could not smell the cause, for there was a mess just the other side of the wall. Yet I was not the only one suffering; several soldiers were similarly affected. Some had staggered to the hospital, from which a stench of sickness already emanated, not to mention a gathering swarm of flies. Rafa helped me to my feet and together we made it some distance away, where a camp of my possessions was already being set up. The water filter was soon working. As an added precaution, Leila boiled the clean water before she added tea and a powder from her own small medicine chest. I drank it down gratefully while they told me of their time in the *zariba*. Most of the enemy had followed the square as they knew that if it was beaten the remaining camp would have to fall. Yet after that final charge had been driven off, all of the Mahdists had retreated to Matammeh. Over a hundred camels had been killed in the fighting and several hundred more wounded. Leila thought they would struggle to find two hundred animals fit enough to travel the short distance to the *zariba* and back in the morning for the remaining supplies.

We sat around the fire wrapped in blankets against the evening chill and I began to feel a little better. I was hungry now and the tempting smell of roast lamb drifted across the camp – a small flock in a nearby farm had been found by our scouts. It left my mouth watering. I had not eaten properly for days, but Leila insisted I wait until the morning. "You must drink only clean water for a whole day," she insisted. Rafa fetched some meat, though, and she promised to cook it with some rice for my breakfast.

On the wind now came the sound of the enemy's drumming from the direction of Matammeh. I was just wondering how long we might enjoy the sanctuary of this new camp, when a familiar face appeared in the glow of the campfire. "It is good to see you survived, Harrison," he said.

"What the hell are you doing here?" I gasped. "I thought you would be halfway to Jakdul by now."

"We were forced to turn back by a Mahdist cavalry patrol," Bennet Burleigh admitted. He had the grace to look somewhat embarrassed at the admission. When I had last seen him, he and his companions were loudly insisting that those in the *zariba* were doomed and vowing that they would make it to Jakdul or die in the attempt.

"Did you all make it back?" I asked, wondering if our little band of correspondents had been whittled down any further.

"Yes, and we made sure that Cameron and St Leger were buried. There are over a dozen bodies in a small cemetery on the *zariba*."

"There were at least as many killed in the square on the march here," I told him, "and several times that number wounded. But if they had not charged us when they did, I doubt any of us would have made it." We lapsed into silence for a while as we considered this good fortune. Although, with the continued drumming in the background, I cannot have been the only one wondering if we had merely delayed the inevitable. "What do you think will happen next?" I asked. My colleague's reply was far from encouraging.

161

"Colonel Wilson has had some prisoners interrogated. He thinks that a force is likely to march on us from those besieging Khartoum, while another Mahdist army could be approaching from Berber in the north. Who knows when they set off, for they have known we were crossing the desert for over a week. They will do whatever they can to stop us reaching Gordon."

"Then we need to get on the move again," I insisted. "We cannot just sit here and wait to be slaughtered. Perhaps we can ambush one of these forces if we catch them by surprise."

"You can't move this army for at least a week," Leila interjected. "Unless you want to travel on foot and carry over a hundred wounded men and all your supplies with you." She saw my questioning expression and went on, "Even the camels that are not wounded are on their last legs; one collapsed and died just as it reached the river. They will need a week of regular water and grazing on the crops growing on the riverbank, before they are in any condition to travel again."

I did not argue, for she knew far more about the beasts than the rest of us. Anyone could see that they would need some time to recover. Burleigh only added to the gloom. "When we do march, some will be on foot anyway, for we will not have enough fit camels to carry everything."

"So are we just going to sit here then and wait to be overwhelmed?" I muttered. Reaching the river had felt like a triumph. Yet now we seemed little better off than we had been in the *zariba*. We had an endless supply of water to be sure, but we were still hopelessly outnumbered, and surrounded deep in a hostile terrain with no prospect of reinforcement. The idea that we could lift the siege of Khartoum and rescue Gordon was patently absurd. I swore softly and added, "Wolseley's whole bloody plan was flawed from the word go. We will all be long dead before his wretched boats get here."

To my surprise Burleigh was more upbeat. "I have spoken to Wilson. He plans to drive the enemy out of Matammeh tomorrow. Once we are behind its walls, we will be much harder to dislodge. We will have some shade and comfort of the buildings too."

162

I was annoyed at his optimism. "But even if we have enough supplies with us for the month it will take the boats to arrive, I doubt Gordon can hold out that long. We are already well past his deadline."

"Wilson is getting word to Wolseley that a route to the Nile is now open. He is bound to send more reinforcements through the desert, although unless they have found more camels, they will have to come on foot. Perhaps some of ours will be sent back down the trail when they are able to move. We will soon have more men up and then we can advance on Khartoum."

"And then, if Allah wills it," added Leila, "we will find my brother and bring him home."

She gave me a firm glare as she said it, for we had already argued over this matter at Jakdul. I had been astonished to discover that even if the British did not reach Khartoum, she was still determined to go to the enemy camp in search of her sibling. It had been so long since we had set out on this journey that I had almost forgotten her reason for becoming my guide. I had tried to persuade her to at least wait for the rest of the relief column to arrive in their boats, but she knew as well as I did that they would never arrive in time. We might have been driven back by then or they may not arrive at all. Even she admitted that advancing alone into enemy territory was a desperate move, which was why she had forbidden Rafa from accompanying her. She was placing her faith in her brother, convinced that if she told any captors who she was, he would come to her rescue.

I could not follow her into the depths of a Mahdist camp as she carried out her search, but the thought of leaving her behind made me realise how much I would miss her. It was not just as a lover, although she was enthusiastic and passionate. She was just as ardent in her discussions around the campfire when we were alone. She resented the way the Europeans had taken over her country and thought we had benefitted enough from the old Khedive's efforts to modernise Egypt. We were like cruel moneylenders, she claimed, who encouraged people into debt and then seized their goods as surety. But what I admired most of all was her calm confidence, whatever the desert threw at us. She and Rafa had ensured that our camels were the best looked after and were among the few still capable of making the return journey to the *zariba* in the morning. She may even have saved my life with the medicinal powders she gave me. Plenty of soldiers had died of dysentery or other such diseases on our march. Yet after the administration of her medicine, I felt my stomach strengthening to the point where I rather resented having to wait for breakfast before I could eat.

I was tucking into a small bowl of rice with a little roast lamb just after dawn, with more promised for lunch if I kept it inside me. The pair of us sat alone by the campfire. Rafa had left with our camels to join the group going to the *zariba*. Burleigh meanwhile had joined the seven hundred men Colonel Wilson was leading to attack Matammeh. Despite the fact that there were still three thousand Mahdists inside, they felt that the two artillery guns they brought with them would soon reduce its walls and drive the enemy away. The assault would certainly stop the enemy interfering with the collection of the last of our supplies from the *zariba*.

As the sun rose, we found a spot in the shade from where we could watch the attack. Leila had given me a piece of root to chew on which she claimed would help clean my teeth and freshen my mouth. It had an aniseed flavour. We made an odd couple: a newspaper man and a pretty Egyptian trader. I relied heavily on her knowledge, as had groups of soldiers and the other correspondents on the march. But equally she needed my support to be allowed to travel with the army. More than a few thought it no place for a woman. I had grown very fond of her; indeed it was an effort to stop my feelings growing deeper. We had never talked about a future together, for we knew it was impossible. Leila would never want to live in London, which would be totally alien to her. I on the other hand, once this assignment was over, would be happy never to set foot in a desert again.

While we often enjoyed an argument, there was no disagreement that morning as we watched the assault begin. We were both convinced it would fail. I could not see the Mahdists being stupid enough to charge across the open desert towards lines of our rifles a second time. We only had the advantage while we could keep the enemy at a distance, but in street fighting we would lose that. A man with a spear on a rooftop could easily kill a soldier in an alley beneath him and probably get away too. Leila was unsure our explosive artillery shells would even penetrate the walls. They were made of two layers of mud bricks, with rock and sand piled in between.

We watched the soldiers march and counter march, the guns fire and some cavalry dart about, but beyond a stream of women and children leaving by a side gate, their efforts had no effect at all. There was a steady beat of drums from inside the city as though they were daring us to make an assault. Fortunately, Colonel Wilson was not that foolhardy. I thought that they were about to give up when Leila spotted a big red banner that had appeared over a hill near the river. For a worrying moment I feared that the Mahdists had launched a surprise attack on the army's flank. Then as the flag moved, I saw it was attached to the mast of a ship. The steamer moved into full view, the guns pointed at the shore, staying silent. It was not alone – three more vessels followed on behind. From the halyards of one flapped a large familiar flag. They were Egyptian colours, which meant that these boats must have been sent by Gordon. Soldiers ran down to the riverbank, waving their hats in the air and cheering.

In a matter of minutes our situation was transformed. As well as their crews, the boats carried five hundred Egyptian and Sudanese soldiers to reinforce our dwindling band. As I watched them streaming ashore, I briefly entertained the idea that Gordon himself might be among them. If so, our mission would be complete and we could return in triumph, but that hope was soon dashed. The steamers had been patrolling the river for several weeks now, looking for our relief force, which they had expected much earlier. They carried letters from their besieged governor who, as far as they knew, still held out in Khartoum.

Now that we had river transport to reach the Sudanese capital, plans changed quickly. Wilson wanted to use the steamers to make contact with Gordon as soon as possible, but they needed wood for fuel and our position at the Nile also had to be secured. The following day our camp was a hive of activity. Wooden buildings in nearby abandoned villages were demolished for firewood. Two steamers patrolled downstream for any sign of approaching Mahdist forces, but none were found. A cavalry patrol rode south in the opposite direction to see if the Mahdi had sent men from his own camp to attack us, but again sighted nothing. Taking no chances, Wilson had most of the remaining men start the construction of earthworks and defences that would secure our foothold on the Nile. Finally, he planned to send a force of four hundred men and nearly a thousand of our fittest camels on a march back to Jakdul. These men would provide protection from enemy cavalry patrols for a courier, who would ride on to update Wolseley on recent events.

As men all around the camp scurried about their duties, we correspondents were not idle. We had been invited to add our own despatches to the package going back to Korti. The last reports we had sent covered the battle at Jakdul; now we hurriedly scribbled our accounts of reaching the Nile. MacDonald read us his copy, which was scathing of Stewart and blamed him for not resting the army and camels before the final push on to Matammeh. He was bitter over the deaths of Cameron and St Leger, but it was easy to be clever with hindsight.

"You won't get any credit for speaking ill of the dead," I warned him. "Stewart was one of Wolseley's favourites."

"Stewart is not dead," he replied. Seeing my surprise, he went on, "He is still alive in the hospital, although I hear his back is broken. Wilson has gone to discuss the way forward with him as he was given instructions from Wolseley for when we reached the Nile."

I finished my next feature for the *Daily News*, which was bound to be the lead article when received. London readers would be desperate for news of our progress. I had described a heroic advance across the hostile desert and a victory against overwhelming enemy numbers, before finally making contact with Gordon's forces on the Nile. With any luck, I thought, my next submission would include an account of the beleaguered governor general of the Sudan welcoming Colonel Wilson to his capital. As far as we knew, the Mahdists had no ships that could oppose our fleet and once we had established contact, we could provide reinforcements and food to help them withstand the siege.

It all felt straightforward. I remember feeling quite upbeat as I strolled afterwards down to the riverbank. After our arduous journey, the Sudanese capital was now no more than a few days of steaming away. I speculated on what Wolseley's plans were for the next stage of our mission. I doubted that the pompous prig had anticipated the new allies that had joined us. Around half were Egyptian soldiers in their grubby white tunics and red fez hats. The rest were Sudanese, many the feared *bashi-bazouks*, warlords who had lived off the local villages. The rest were black troops from the south, who I learned were called *bazingers*. They were if anything even more warlike. They were soon enthusiastically beating their drums to counter the rhythms still emanating from Matammeh and looked disappointed that the attack on the town had been postponed.

The steamers were all ancient, but apart from the smallest were well prepared for war. The three largest each had two gun emplacements surrounded by heavy timber to protect them from enemy fire. One was in the bow and the other was behind the bridge, high enough to shoot over the paddle wheels to either side and possibly the rear. Pieces of armour plate had been found from somewhere and fixed around the bridge to protect the captain and helmsman. Along the main deck on either side of the paddle wheels, the bulwarks had been extended upwards to chest height with more timber. Loopholes had been cut into this so that soldiers could crouch behind them and fire on the shore with relative impunity. They looked like floating fortresses and had been steaming up and down the river for months now, proof, I thought that their defences were effective. It was all very reassuring.

There was certainly a spring in my step as I made my way back to where Leila had set up our camp. My guts had been sound all day. Keeping down breakfast and lunch, I was looking forward to a hearty dinner. Even the predictable bully beef did not dishearten me. The tin had been kept cool during the day by being buried under the Nile riverbed, a stick marking its position. Burleigh and MacDonald joined us, the latter bringing a small bottle of whisky that he had been saving. "I was going to share it when we met Gordon," he confided, "but I think we are close enough now and deserve a dram." I savoured the spirit and felt content.

In the morning Rafa would join the party taking the strongest camels back to Jakdul. Leila and I would not need them, for we would be going

167

on by boat. With astonishing naivety, it felt to me then that we had made it through the worst of our trip.

Chapter 15

My mood soured the next morning. Leila and I were packing up our camp when Burleigh came jogging up the slope, his face red and sweating. "We cannot go on the boats," he announced abruptly. "Wilson says the correspondents are to stay ashore."

"What the hell do you mean?" I demanded. "We have travelled thousands of miles to see Gordon rescued. We have suffered losses and fought battles with the army. They cannot deny us witnessing and reporting on the conclusion of this campaign."

Burleigh shrugged. "They are strict orders passed down by Wolseley, nothing can be done. I am going to get my servant to put my tent back up." As I watched him walk back down the hill, I was surprised. The Burleigh of old would have moved heaven and earth to get on those ships. Now he was meekly accepting the situation. Perhaps his nerve had not recovered from recent events. He had twice ridden through the Mahdist lines during his abortive run to Jakdul and it was little short of a miracle that no man had been hit as the bullets had whistled around their ears. Well, he might be willing to obey orders, but I wasn't. As Leila spoke up, I realised that I was not alone in that conviction.

"I must get to Khartoum to find my brother," she whispered. "We have to get on those boats."

"Don't worry, we will," I assured her. I could easily imagine my editor's fury when, having spent a fortune of the paper's money equipping me for this trip, he discovered that when Gordon was rescued, his war correspondent was sitting in the desert over a hundred miles away.

We went down to the river and found a scene of chaos. Just about all the ships' crews were involved in a furious argument with each other. I found Verner, who explained that Gordon had left instructions for the return of the ships to his capital. He did not want any Egyptian troops to be left on the vessels. They were to be marched home. The crews were to comprise only Sudanese, many of whom had family in the city or surrounding towns. The problem was that the two groups had been living in close confinement on the steamers for months. Ownership of sleeping mats, cooking pots, weapons, goats, possibly even some of the women on board, had become confused. Additionally, some of the Egyptians did not want to leave, while a number of the Sudanese did. Nobody was in charge and clearly Gordon had not shared his orders in advance. Any thought that the ships might sail that morning were instantly abandoned. I thought we might take advantage of the situation to slip aboard, but the wily Colonel Wilson was one step ahead of me. He had placed British sentries at each of the gangplanks, who politely, but firmly, informed me that correspondents were not allowed on the vessels.

It took the rest of that day for new crews to be sorted for the three largest steamers. Wilson used the time to send detachments of soldiers to nearby abandoned farms. They were to gather up every sack of Egyptian wheat that had been harvested, which were to be loaded aboard a barge towed by one of the steamers as well as the holds of the vessels. The food supplies would be vital if the garrison at Khartoum was on the verge of collapse.

Beresford, the senior naval officer, was supposed to take command of the fleet, but was injured. This time it was not through combat; he had boils on his buttocks from riding camels, which had become infected. Desperate not to miss his moment of action, he had hobbled to the surgeon that morning demanding that they lance them and get him back on duty. They treated him but insisted he stay in the hospital for a couple of days.

While sailors and Sudanese soldiers were allotted to ships, other men set to chopping up the huge pile of wood that had been gathered into shorter lengths that would fit into the boiler. While I watched this fuel being carried aboard I saw my opportunity. The sentries were hot and tired now, paying less attention as dozens of men walked past them with stacks of wood on their shoulder. I could not go dressed as a European, but Rafa had left some baggage and I borrowed one of his dirtiest robes and a headscarf to cover my hair and part of my face. I had wanted to take my rifle to help deal with any challenges ahead, but that was impossible. I rolled up my trousers and wore my normal clothes underneath with the Webley pistol and some ammunition in the pockets.

The Sudanese went barefoot and so Leila carried my boots and socks hidden in a bundle of her possessions. She too was well known in the camp in her white robes. If she was seen going aboard, they would be bound to look for me. She arranged to trade some garments with a Sudanese woman. Soon two disreputable looking characters were making their way to the shore.

I had my scarf covering much of the left of my face and was careful to balance some wood on my right shoulder to obscure that side. Then I put my head down and shuffled into the line towards the leading ship, the *Bordein*. I did not dare look over my shoulder but trusted that Leila would follow on behind. I was right on the riverbank when I felt my right trouser leg start to slide down. I had rolled it up and the cloth had been tight against my calf when we had set off, but walking had caused it to slightly unfurl and slip down. With every step it felt like it was unrolling further, until I was sure it was below the level of the robe. The sentries were bound to notice, but I did not dare stop, for that would only have drawn attention. The gangplank was just in front of me when, as I feared, I attracted the glare of the soldiers.

"Look at this lazy bastard," called out the man beside me. "He's only got one bundle. You've got two arms, mate," he added, pushing me forward and not expecting me to understand. "Jesus, we will be here all day at this rate."

I scurried gratefully forward and dropped my paltry contribution to the fuel supply on a pile with the rest. I looked around to find that Leila was already at my shoulder. Without a word she grabbed my elbow and led me forward in the ship. We went into the shade on the eastern side of the vessel. Beneath the overhang of the bridge above us, and with the high sides of the bulwarks, it was dark and gloomy. My skin was tanned now from weeks in the desert and few people would notice that I was a European. I ducked down to pull my trouser leg back up. Then we went on to the forward gun position, where the extra ramparts hid us from prying eyes.

I was surprised at the number of women on board for the journey; there were even some children running about, not to mention a handful of goats, chickens and a cat. This was as much a home as it was a vessel of war. Few people took any notice of us as we settled into a corner. However, I was soon less concerned about being discovered than about their cooking arrangements. Barely two feet away from a pile of shells for the forward gun, an old crone had laid out some stones on the deck and was in the process of building a small cooking fire. Glowing embers from the kindling drifted away on the evening breeze; we would be fortunate not to be blown to kingdom come by exploding ammunition before dawn, I thought, but it was clear from the relaxed air of those around us that this was an entirely normal occurrence. I tried to remind myself that the *Bordein* had been plying its trade up and down the Nile now for decades, although not as long in its armoured state.

"Is it an easy run on the river to reach Khartoum?" I asked Leila quietly.

"I have no idea," she replied. "When I came before we took the camels on the trail running along the edge of the desert. The river was out of sight behind trees and ridges thrown up by the floods for most of the way. But if these ships have sailed from Gordon, they must be able to make their way back to him."

I hoped she was right. Now I was aboard, I could not fail to notice that the *Bordein* was bloody huge compared to the open cutters that most of our force were using to travel upriver. These ships were heavy too, with extra armour, bulwarks, guns and over a hundred people aboard each vessel. With the dropping river levels, there had been concerns that the cutters would not make it all the way to Khartoum. Our depth in the water had to be at least treble theirs, but I reasoned that the captain must know what he was doing. He probably knew the deep-water channels like the back of his hand. At least I hoped he did. The idea of being shipwrecked deep in enemy territory, did not bear thinking about.

A group of *bashi-bazouks* and *bazingers* came forward and settled down with their families. One of the imposing black men stared at me and grinned. I was sure he had seen through my disguise. He must have assumed I was some eager white soldier and, like him, keen to get to grips with the enemy. Leila overheard their conversations and told me that we were set to cast off at first light in the morning. She had brought a blanket in her bundle of possessions. We wrapped it around ourselves

172

and leant up against the gun emplacement. Sleep would not come. I tried again to persuade Leila not to set off on her own. Yet despite me spelling out the dangers, she was still determined to try. I just hoped that the faith she had in her brother for her protection was justified.

Eventually, we lapsed into silence, lost in our own thoughts. I must have dozed, for I was awoken at daybreak by the clanging of metal. The boiler was being lit, and soon I could smell woodsmoke from the funnel as a dawn glow spread across the eastern horizon. We were given some freshly cooked flatbread for breakfast by the old biddy, who was now using one of the six-pounder shells as a rolling pin. I was just wondering what the day held in store, when a young boy tugged on my shoulder and, holding out his hand, asked me something in Arabic.

"He says will you give him a silver coin, like the other white man hiding on the boat," translated Leila.

"What other white man?" I asked, frowning. I was soon informed that another white man was disguised as an Arab on the side deck. Curious now, I crept to the corner of the deckhouse and, keeping my head low behind a barrel, peered around. There, ten yards off, were the familiar features of Melton Prior of the *Illustrated London News*. I quickly ducked back before he saw me. You might think I would be pleased with Melton's company, and in many circumstances I would be. But during the night I had been imagining being re-united with Gordon again. I had assumed that I was the only journalist aboard and had the exclusive on the governor general's rescue. My mind had soared to flights of fancy, the story syndicated around the world, fame similar to that of Stanley of the *New York Herald* when he had found the British explorer Livingstone. Why, now Stanley was as famous as Livingstone. I had already been thinking of some memorable quip I could say and boast of when I finally shook Gordon's hand again. To resolve the story that had gripped the nation for nearly a year would be the pinnacle of any journalist's career. It would all be ruined if I did not have an exclusive. I did not want to share the glory, or worse, risk my rival getting his story back before me.

I am not proud of what I did next. Creeping back to the boy, I rummaged in my pocket for one of the big Maria Theresa silver dollars.

I had to ensure I bought his loyalty. I promised him the coin if I was the only Englishman in disguise on the boat when it sailed. I told him that if he pointed Prior out to the soldiers when they came aboard, my rival would be removed, but he was not to say anything about me. Even Leila looked shocked at this treachery as she gave the translation. "We are newspapermen," I explained. "We are here competing for stories and exclusives, He would probably do the same to me given half a chance," I insisted, although I was not entirely sure about that.

With the sun now up, I watched Colonel Wilson and around a dozen soldiers approach the *Bordein*. A similar number were headed towards one of our sister ships, the *Talahawiyeh*, which was coming with us. I held my breath, hoping the lad could be trusted. He did not let me down. Within two minutes of Wilson's boots clattering up the gangplank, I heard shouting. It was Melton Prior's distinctive tones. I stole a glance to see him being pushed none to kindly back to the shore and briefly wondered if Wilson would send someone to check that no other correspondents were missing from our camp. Perhaps he did not have time, for the captain of the vessel seemed determined to make the most of the daylight. In no time at all several sailors were at the capstan winding in the anchor, while I kept my face well covered from any more prying eyes.

With a toot of the whistle and the grinding of gears, the great paddle wheels started to turn. For a moment we did not seem to be moving at all, but then slowly the bow began to swing out into the river. We were travelling against the current, but making progress and gradually the tents of the camp began to fall behind.

According to my watch, it was seven forty-five on the morning of Saturday the 24th of January 1885. We were finally on the last leg of our journey of some four and a half thousand miles from London to rescue General Gordon. The boy was back now asking for his coin, I hoped to God it was money well spent.

Chapter 16

"You disobeyed my express order, and that of the British government!" Wilson shouted at me. He was furious, and this was a man who had stared at three thousand charging warriors with apparent unconcern. "I would have you put ashore to find your own way back to the camp were it not for the fact that you have also brought a female guide, and I dare say you were warned not to bring a woman on campaign too."

"You cannot seriously expect any correspondent to come all this way and then not see the conclusion of the campaign," I retorted. "My publisher has paid a fortune to have me report on Gordon's rescue. He would be livid to find I had stayed back at the camp and missed it. Anyway," I continued, "why is the British government worried about the press reporting on us reaching Khartoum? It has been the talk of London for months now."

Wilson took a deep breath to calm himself and then looked about the crowded bridge of the steamer. It had gone noon when I was discovered and frogmarched to his presence. By then we must have travelled at least a dozen miles upstream. We were deep into enemy country, and I was fairly certain he would not put me ashore. He would be roasted in Fleet Street by the press if he did, but he could still lock me in some stifling cabin below decks. The dozen men of the Royal Sussex Regiment aboard were eavesdropping on our conversation with obvious interest, as was his aide, Lieutenant Wortley. "Come this way," he muttered before leading me aft to the stern of the craft. A couple of *bashi-bazouks* trailed fishing lines over the rail, but only gave us a curious glance and, speaking no English, paid no attention as Wilson spoke again. "If you give me your word that you will allow me to approve any copy you send, I will permit you to stay at liberty," he said at last.

I did not really see that I had a choice and so I agreed. But I was still curious as to his concern. "Can you tell me what it is that you do not want me to report?"

He twitched irritably and then admitted, "Her Majesty's Government is concerned that General Gordon may be less than grateful for his rescue, given how long it has taken to be effected. Ministers are concerned that he could express his displeasure to the press."

I laughed. "I don't doubt that he is bloody furious at Gladstone for his prevarication, but you need not worry. I report for the *Daily News*, which you will recall is supportive of the Liberals. My editor wants copy describing the rescue; the gratitude of the governor general for his deliverance will be taken for granted. I doubt they would publish a critique of government policy even if I was to send one."

Wilson nodded, satisfied. He knew the political leanings of all the leading papers and what I had told him made sense. "Well, Mr Harrison," he concluded, "I hope your casual assumption of Gordon's rescue comes to pass. It may not be as straightforward as you seem to think…" With that he turned on his heel and strode back to the bridge of the vessel.

Perhaps he was trying to unnerve me, but I felt a twinge of apprehension all the same. Wilson did not seem the sort prone to panic. While talking to him, I had taken the opportunity to look about. In addition to the British soldiers and boat crew, there had been around a hundred *bashi-bazouks* and *bazingers* on the vessel, as well as some of their families. I could see that we were towing a small sailing vessel called a felucca and noted half a dozen men resting in the shade of the furled sail. Beyond them the *Talahawiyeh* steamed in our wake. She was towing a barge or nuggar that contained most of the sacks of wheat from nearby farms. The river was wide here, several hundred yards, with us in the middle. There were small islands between us and the shore, some with vegetation, but most looked as though they were under water for parts of the year. They reminded me that river levels were falling, and I wondered if that was what Wilson had been referring to as there was no danger from the shore. All I could see were lines of date palms along the bank and small patches of cultivated fields. The only movement was the occasional donkey turning one of the old wheel pumps that irrigated the crops from the river. It was a benign setting, but I had a growing fear that it would not remain so for long.

With no more need for deception, I went forward to find Leila. She beamed with relief when she saw me still at liberty and put her arms around me. "I was so worried they would put us ashore," she admitted.

"They might have done but for you," I told her. "Now, where are my boots? I don't want splinters from this deck." I shrugged off Rafa's robe and had soon resumed my European appearance.

"So they will still take us to Khartoum?" she pressed, clearly thinking about her brother.

"They will," I assured her. Then I added, "You don't know about anything in the river between here and the city that might stop us, do you?"

"No. I told you before we came by the caravan trail and only saw the river a few evenings when we watered the animals."

I stared over the bow; all was calm. I decided to make enquiries of the vessel's captain and so made my way back towards the bridge. I saw him as I climbed the steps up to the little platform, but Wilson and his aide were at his side, the latter shooting me a chilly glare to indicate that I was not welcome. Stepping back a few paces I found myself on the midship gun platform, with a big brass cannon in the middle of it. Thick waist-high timbers protected the crew, who had draped a canvas between the cannon and the timbers and were dozing in the shade from the fierce afternoon sun. Only one man stood resting his elbows on the bulwark and surveying the shore. From the braid on his uniform, he was certainly not a gunner. I thought if he was one of Gordon's officers, there was a good chance that he spoke English and so went over to introduce myself. "Thomas Harrison," I said, holding out my hand, "from the *Daily News* in London."

The grizzled face turned in my direction, dark eyes twinkling in amusement above a grey beard. "Ah, our stowaway." He spoke English with an Arabic accent. Then he took my hand and added, "I am Colonel Khashm al-Mus Bey of Khartoum."

"Then you must know this stretch of river well," I replied.

"Of course, my family live in the city, and this," he raised an arm and gestured to both banks of the river, "is my ancestral homeland. I am of the Sha'iqia people, we have lived here since the beginning of time."

"So tell me, Colonel, will it be easy to reach Khartoum, now we are aboard the steamers?"

I did not like the way Khashm chuckled again before he answered. "It will not be as you English say, 'smooth sailing'. The river levels are so low now that normally I would not attempt it. But," he gestured over his shoulder at the vessel following on astern, "we have Captain Gibril with us and he is the best pilot on this stretch of the Nile. He knows every rock and he says it can be done."

"So it is just the shallows we have to worry about?" I pressed.

This time he gave a roar of laughter. "There is also the little matter of the sixth cataract and then the Sabaloka Gorge, where cliffs rise up on either side of the Nile and it narrows to less than a hundred and fifty yards wide. Our enemies will be able to shoot down on us, so these," he patted the thick bulwarks, "will offer little shelter." I must have looked appalled, but he went on. "Then as we approach Khartoum, we will have to pass the Mahdist camp at Omdurman. They will undoubtedly know we are coming and will have their artillery ranged against us. But if we keep close to Tutti Island, which is held by our people, we might get through."

My imagination had barely got beyond the word 'cataract'. I had seen several of these stretches of rapids now on our journey and the difficulties that small rowing boats containing just ten men had endured getting through them. Often they were part dragged through by men with ropes on the shore. Even then, some were wrecked on the rocks. "How on earth are we going to get these steamers through the cataracts?" I demanded. "There are well over a hundred people on each one, not to mention the vessels we are towing. Surely it cannot be done."

"These steamers have done it many times," Khashm assured me, before adding, "but usually when the river is higher." Seeing that I was far from reassured, he went on, "It is much easier going this way, against the current of the river. We pass through slower and so have more time to avoid rocks in the rapids."

"Do you believe we can make it, then?"

"We must," he replied simply. He stared towards the bow, perhaps imagining his family waiting many miles beyond and then he fixed those dark eyes back on me. "It is not just the food that the *Talahawiyeh* is towing that the city desperately needs. We are bringing something perhaps even more important: hope." I nodded and he went on, "The wheat will make bread to stave hunger, but the sight of your soldiers, few though they are, will show the people that they have not been forgotten. Everyone knows that Britain has sent an army to save them."

That will be news to Gladstone, I thought, who believed our mission was to extract Gordon. Yet Khashm was just getting into his stride. "My men and the city garrison have kept those Mahdist devils at bay for nearly a year, but it is your army that will break the spirit of these fanatics. They will all know now at Omdurman that just a thousand of your soldiers have twice beaten much larger foes. They have also heard how the fearsome Beja were eventually defeated at the Red Sea. The Mahdi will be aware that ten thousand of your men are marching and rowing towards him. He must know that his days are numbered. He will slink back into the desert like a beaten dog and leave my people alone." He laughed and added, "I have heard tell of a prophesy by a holy man. He foretold that if Gordon was killed the Mahdi would be dead within the year. There are rumours that orders have been given for Gordon to be taken alive, to be kept in a cage in the Mahdi's tent."

The colonel certainly appeared confident of victory despite the dangers ahead. I was very glad to be in a convoy of two steamers; if something happened to one then at least the second was there to carry out a rescue. Yet that afternoon there was barely a hint of danger. A group of horsemen was spotted on the western bank, who opened fire on us with their rifles. The range was extreme, however, and I doubt either steamer was hit. Certainly no one was wounded on the *Bordein*. Wilson would not let the men waste ammunition in responding. A little later we saw a man setting out from an island near the eastern bank ahead of us, waving a cloth over his head to attract our attention. We slowed the engines to approach and soon he was coming alongside. I stared down at him, wearing just a loin cloth and expertly handling a craft he must have made himself with bound bundles of reeds. It was a scene that must have been unchanged from the times of the pharaohs.

The fellow asked to speak to Khashm, who was clearly well known among these people, and warned that around the next bend the Mahdists had established an artillery position to cover the river. Wilson ordered the felucca we were towing to be filled with our soldiers and some of the Sudanese fighters and sailed to the shore. They would then take the battery by surprise from the rear. The plan was executed, but when they got to the place on the riverbank, they found the Mahdist guns had gone. Tracks in the sand showed where they had been and there were other signs that men had been living there until very recently. It was odd, for surely word must have spread that the British were coming and with steamers available, we would obviously be making for Khartoum.

By the time soldiers reported back on what they had found, the sun was starting to set. We moved slowly round the next bend, but it was getting hard to spot the rocks and sandbanks ahead. Instead of recovering our soldiers, we dropped anchor by the abandoned emplacements. A village had been deserted there, perhaps because of the Mahdist soldiers, but Wilson did not waste the opportunity of gathering more wood. He had men tear down the abandoned buildings and bring the larger timbers on board, while a few *bazingers* slaughtered a camel they found for meat. As the engineer let the fire in his boiler go down and topped it up with water, Leila and I sat with some of the others on the foredeck, eating roasted camel meat and watching the last gold of the sunset disappear to the west. It had been a pleasant day's steaming, but I doubted that this cruise would continue for much longer in such a calm manner.

Wilson had the boilers lit before dawn to ensure that we were ready to start steaming as soon as it was safe to navigate. As we set off again, a cool breeze came over the bow, in what was usually the best part of the day, before the sun got too hot. There was still no sign of enemy activity, although we had got word of another gun emplacement at a place called Wad Habeshi, that we would pass late that afternoon. Soldiers and gunners checked their ammunition in readiness, but by lunchtime were being detailed for another fuel gathering expedition to the shore. More abandoned buildings were torn down and lumber recovered before we were on our way again. By four in the afternoon, we were easing around the bend in the river at Wad Habeshi. Our wooden ramparts were lined with men pointing rifles at the shore, but once again we found the position abandoned. Khashm recounted that when they were last there, three cannon had fired shells at them and the trenches we could see on the shore had been packed with men firing rifles. Now, though, the place was as quiet as a tomb. We furrowed our brows in puzzlement. If they were not trying to stop us, where were they? Wilson was worried that they were all marching north to attack our camp at Matammeh. If we lost that bastion on the Nile, then we would be cut off. Even if we could persuade Gordon to leave, we would struggle to get him to safety. But there was nothing we could do about that now.

We were approaching the cataracts. With evening drawing on, the captain wanted to anchor for the night. The ships' masters knew these dangerous waters better than any, but Wilson, whose nautical experience probably did not extend further than the Isle of Wight ferry, would not hear of it. There were ninety minutes of daylight left and he insisted that they could not be wasted. To be fair to him, it was hard to see how bad the cataracts were from the northern end. Khashm told me later that there were ninety-nine islands in this stretch of the Nile, which obscured the view of the channels between them. Captain Gibril in the *Talahawiyeh* was ordered to take the lead with the *Bordein* following some five hundred yards in its wake. Water swirled around mud banks and rocks. As the sky began to turn red, we carefully watched the lead steamer as it made progress ahead. Perhaps our helmsman was watching the sister ship a little too closely, instead of making sure that we followed exactly in its wake. Suddenly, there was the creak of steel plates beneath us and as we staggered to keep our footing, the vessel came to a sudden halt.

In an instant our serenely calm cruise turned to pandemonium. Wilson demanded to know what had happened, although it was obvious to everyone but him that we had run aground. His aide was shouting for the women and children to be loaded into the felucca as though we might sink in an instant. Fortunately, few could understand him and so he was ignored. Much of the yelling was drowned out by the whistle, as our captain signalled to Gibril that we were stuck. I did what any sensible person would and went to look over the side. As far as I could tell the bow of the vessel was undamaged, but we were stuck fast. The paddle wheels came to a stop as I watched.

"Will we sink?" asked Leila.

"No, I think we are resting on sand or mud," I told her. I remembered running aground on a boat in the Ashanti campaign. It had been the devil to get off, as the mud created a suction on the hull. The paddle wheels started to move again, this time in reverse, but even at 'full astern' they did not move us an inch. "We will probably have to be towed off," I predicted to Leila, "but not until morning. If he has any sense the other captain will not risk these treacherous channels again in the dark."

Indeed Captain Gibril was too wise for such folly. As darkness fell, he dropped anchor in the lee of a large island in the middle of the river to await the dawn. Yet if I thought I was bound for a restful night, I had not reckoned on Colonel Wilson. Perhaps he felt a muff for giving the orders that had caused our impasse, but he was determined that we would be ready to proceed again at first light. I watched as men inspected the hold for leaks and then orders were given to lighten the ship. As much weight as possible had to be removed from the bow to help it come off the sand and it was a job for all hands.

"You wanted to come with us," Wilson's aide, Wortley sneered. "You will now have to pitch in with everyone else."

"I have no problem with that," I told him cheerily. "My life is on the line here as well. That is why I have twice now taken my place in the ranks of your squares." I meant it too for we were all literally in the same boat; we would live or die together. Leila and I were soon helping to unbolt and lift the heavy timbers that made up the rampart around the forward cannon. We could carry one between us to the rear of the ship. A chain of Sudanese were passing supplies out of the forward hold, while our soldiers set to work removing the gun barrel from its limber and eventually hauling both aloft. It was pitch dark when we had finished, with lanterns illuminating the now bare foredeck. The vessel

182

was still stubbornly stuck fast. Sailors dropped long poles over the side to try and push us off, but all they succeeded in doing was burying the ends of their sticks. By now the boilers had been allowed to cool to save fuel. So as there was nothing more we could do that night and we were all tired and hungry, finally, Wilson admitted defeat and allowed us to rest.

It was just as well that I had some stale flatbread for a supper, for there was no time for breakfast. At first light our commander was in a fever to get going again. This time the plan was to land all but essential crew on to a mudbank astern of us, then use a cable to pull the ship free. Wilson wanted to employ the felucca to disembark his passengers, but with no wind and a strong current, the captain warned it could be swept away. This time the colonel listened to the expert and two smaller rowing boats were used instead. They too were attached to cables so that they could be hauled back to the ship when they had disgorged their passengers. Even so, it took over and hour to get us all on the mud. I felt even more exposed standing on that bare bank. There was not a shred of cover and if a Mahdist boat had hoven into view between the other islands, we could have been cut to pieces. It also stank. Our boots were sinking down to the ankle in some places and green slime oozed at the water's edge. A heavy hawser was run out to us and we all took hold, even the children. Soon we were slipping, sliding and straining, but for all the good we did, we might have been trying to tow a pyramid. By then, when we were covered head to toe in mud, the order was shouted to stop. I thought that the *Talahawiyeh* might be summoned back, but there was one more trick to try first. The *Bordein's* boilers had been lit and were now finally producing steam. Again, we were ordered to haul on the cable and this time the ship's engines were working full astern to assist. I watched as the great wheels threw up gallons of water against the hull and then slowly but surely the vessel began to move, hailed by a cheer from the mudlarks around us.

An hour later and we were all back on board, dousing ourselves with buckets of Nile water to wash off the mud. It was already so hot that our clothes would be no more than damp within a few minutes. Slowly the *Bordein* edged itself forward, the engines only going fast enough to slightly outweigh the current against us. More men with poles stood at the bow to test the depth and try to stay within the channel that the *Talahawiyeh* had used the previous day.

It was nearly noon when we finally drew alongside our sister ship. Both vessels were now at the northern tip of a large island in the middle of the river. The usual channel to take was around the eastern side but Wilson did not want to take any more chances. We had already wasted half a day. Every day, every hour even, might make a difference to Gordon's rescue. Wilson had Gibril rowed over from his vessel to pilot the *Bordein* around the island. The captain would then be rowed back to guide the *Talahawiyeh* – that at least was the plan. Gibril was a wizened old cove, but spritely as he climbed the rope ladder up the side of the *Bordein*. Soon we were moving again, weaving between the rocks and smaller islands, often using the stronger currents where they had carved out deeper channels. It was obvious to any landlubber that the river was dangerously low. Twice we were forced to run through ridiculously narrow gaps between rocks, our engines at full speed to counter the rapids heading in the opposite direction. The fact that we were moving slowly against the current gave us more time to avoid obstacles. Khashm had already told me that it would be impossible for these vessels to make the return journey before the waters rose again. Fortunately, Gordon had several smaller steamers in Khartoum, that could be used to take me, and perhaps him, north again.

We were nearly at the southern tip of the island when disaster struck once more. This time we all knew instantly what had happened: the jolt, the lifting of the bow and the foaming paddle wheels making no progress at all. I was near the bridge at the time and the old pilot acted quickly to shut down the engines, before staring with a furrowed brow at the swirling currents. Wilson slammed his fist down on the bridge rail in frustration, knowing that further delays were now unavoidable.

Gibril had himself rowed across the channel ahead of us in a small boat. Every few yards he would lower the tip of a long pole until it touched the bottom. We all watched his progress and could see that the tip of his stick did not drop by more than four or five feet at any point. The sandbanks must have shifted in the current. The eastern channel was clearly impassable for boats our size now. This only left the possibility of the western side of the island. If we could not get through there, Gordon was done for, as, in all probability, were the rest of us. I watched anxiously as Gibril had his boat rowed back to his own vessel. The little craft looked to be tossed like a cork in a drain over some of the rougher stretches, but eventually he made it back to the *Talahawiyeh*.

For a while it did not move. Then I saw through my glass that nearly all of its crew and passengers were being put ashore on the island. Whether this was to reduce weight or save lives if the vessel foundered it was hard to say. As the *Talahawiyeh* disappeared out of sight around the other side of the foliage-covered island, Wilson gave orders for our own vessel to be lightened. The forward turret and gun were still in the rear of the vessel from the last grounding, but we soon discovered that the water on the island side of the ship was so shallow we could wade ashore. I jumped in; it came up to my chest. Helping Leila against the current, we staggered on until we were standing on a small beach with date and palm trees beyond. A crowd of us moved inland until we could make out the western channel, where the *Talahawiyeh* was slowly making progress. A man in the bow holding a long pole was feeling his way ahead like a blind man with a cane, and steadily they came level with us. With a final toot of their whistle, they dropped anchor on the southern end of the island.

Now all we had to do was get the *Bordein* off the sandbank again. More cables were run out to the island and this time attached to pulleys tied to trees to the north of the stuck vessel. The engines were thrown into reverse, we all pulled and at the first attempt the ship came free. By the time we were all back on board, Gibril had rejoined us via his dinghy. We were soon retracing our steps to follow the new channel up the western side. Reunited, the ships moved on, but the light was fading fast. Ahead we could see the rising hills that formed the Sabaloka Gorge. That was certainly not a channel to attempt in darkness and we anchored again in the lee of another small island. Later, when I looked at the chart, I saw that during the whole day we had travelled precisely three miles upriver.

Chapter 17

It was just as Kashm had said; if we were to be ambushed by the Mahdists, then Sabaloka Gorge was the most likely place it would happen. In some places the river narrowed to just a hundred and fifty yards, well within the range of riflemen on either bank. Steeply sloping hills gave them the ideal elevation to shoot down on us. We wondered if this was where they had moved their captured artillery pieces from the emplacements downriver. They could rain shells down on us and from so far below, it would be difficult for us to return fire. I stared across at the *Talahawiyeh* and began to regret my decision to join this voyage. The steamers had been sailing the Nile for months and I had naively assumed that the run to Khartoum would be relatively smooth. Now I doubted if either vessel would reach its destination. It would only take a single direct hit to the paddle wheels, engine or waterline of the hull and we would be done for. Then the Mahdists could finish off the survivors at their leisure.

At least we did not have to worry so much about running aground in the gorge. Hemmed in by the cliffs, the water would be deeper and faster flowing. After a hurried breakfast, orders were given to rebuild the forward gun position. Soon we were grunting with the effort as we carried the heavy timbers back to the bow. Wilson had wanted to sail at first light although he had now learned to listen to the advice of his captains. They were worried that the enemy might have laid chains or some other obstacle across the waterway. Orders were given to weigh anchor as soon as the sun was over the eastern hills to illuminate the channel.

I was in no rush to enter this lion's den and sat quietly for a while holding Leila's hand. We did not speak but I am sure we were both wondering if we would survive the morning. Around us soldiers prepared themselves by their loopholes in the bulwarks with a ready supply of ammunition. In no time at all the boilers were up to pressure and the wheels began to churn the water about us.

Everyone scanned the riverbanks for movement, those of us with field-glasses concentrating on the western bank. We were just sixty miles north of Khartoum now and fifty miles north of the main Mahdist camp at Omdurman on the western side of the river. We watched the river become narrower and narrower, expecting at any moment a hail of shells and bullets to rain down on us. Wilson asked the captain to hug the eastern shore where he could and often the boat would be in the shade of the cliffs. A morning breeze whistled through the gorge. For the first time in ages I felt cool during the day, or perhaps it was the chill of fear. The engines were going at full speed to make headway against the current, but we were still moving ponderously slowly. I remember jumping at a loud clang, but it was just the engineer dropping a spanner. The only sound was the clank of pistons and the hiss of steam. Emboldened, I stepped up onto the exposed bridge and scanned every inch of cliff I could see, yet all I saw moving was a grazing goat.

"This makes no sense at all," I muttered, before adding hastily, "not that I am complaining."

"They definitely knew we were coming," agreed Wilson, still staring up at the cliffs. "Those horsemen we saw on the first day were bound to have reported steamers heading to Khartoum."

"Perhaps they did not think we could get through the cataracts," suggested Wortley.

"Possibly," replied Wilson, not taking his eyes off the shore. "But you would think that they would have some guns here as a precaution. Hello, what is that?" About a mile ahead of us was a small group of figures standing on the shore. Through my field-glasses, I could see that they had goats with them, a few drinking from the river. They would hardly be there if they expected to find themselves in a crossfire, but perhaps they could tell us where the enemy was. We drew closer, all the while searching the area in vain for a sign of ambush. The boys stayed by the shore and Khashm had himself rowed across to question them. When he came back, he was surprisingly nonchalant about the disastrous news he carried.

"They say the men have been summoned to Omdurman and that they have captured Khartoum."

"Good God!" gasped Wilson, "we are too late."

"Not necessarily," Khashm replied. "They have been boasting that the city has been overrun for the last two months. Dozens of times men have called this news out from the shore as we have passed. Yet we know Gordon was still resisting them two weeks ago."

"But that would explain why they have not attacked us," countered Wortley. "Their men have to be somewhere."

"We have to go on to be sure, one way or the other," insisted Wilson. No one disagreed, for it would be madness to turn back now. If the city still held out, then our appearance would boost the morale of the defenders and give the besiegers a warning of what was to come. The barge of food being towed by the *Talahawiyeh* would also be vital. Checking the charts, I saw that there were no more cataracts and gorges, it was just a smooth run to the city; or at least it would be at high water. Now the level of the Nile was dropping by the day. At least we had Gibril with us, who, I was assured was the best pilot. If there was a way through, he would find it.

First, though, the priority was fuel, for we had burned most of ours going against the current in the gorge. A few miles upstream we found another abandoned village. There we found grain stores in this one and Wilson marked it on the chart in case they could be recovered later to help sustain the siege. The wooden supports from the buildings were taken, as were the timbers in the big donkey-powered water wheels that irrigated the fields. Without them no crops could be grown, but unless we succeeded, they would only feed the Mahdists. Soon the engines were clanking away again as we made our way upriver.

We were fired on that afternoon. Half a dozen men with rifles sniped at us from the western bank. We were well within range and a shot clanged off some armour plate while thuds rang out as several hit our wooden bulwarks. We could see where they were from the puffs of smoke above the rocks, but Wilson, judging they would be hard to hit, ordered our soldiers to hold their fire. The Sudanese were less restrained and blazed away with abandon. Judging from the splashes as bullets aimed short went into the river, their aim was as wild as their enthusiasm. We were soon past, with no one aboard hurt, nor twice later when a fusillade of shots came from men hidden on the bank. The river was wide again now and interspersed with islands and mudbanks that we had to weave between. A rifleman would have to be a good shot to hit another man at that distance.

By evening we had to refuel again. We wanted enough timber to reach Khartoum the following day, and, if necessary, to get away from there as well. Both ships dropped anchor opposite another abandoned village on the east bank. We saw no one at all on that side of the river; whether they had fled from us or the Mahdists it was hard to say. Soon boats were going back and forth loaded with wood, but the Sudanese did not pass up the opportunity to loot a few goats, two of which were slaughtered and cooked on the shore, using wood intended for the boilers. Wilson fumed at the waste of time and fuel, but Khashm did little to control his men. He just shrugged and explained that they needed to eat and had found some food. I had seen the Sudanese colonel inspect some bully beef our soldiers had been eating the previous day. He had poked the slippery mess with the point of his knife and wrinkled his nose in disgust, declining the offer to taste it.

Leila and I had gone ashore too and we did not pass up the opportunity for some roasted meat and flatbread. As the grease ran down my chin, I wondered when I was likely to eat this well again.

"Do you think Gordon is still holding out?" Leila asked quietly.

"Khashm thinks so," I told her. "He says there are boats in the city and if it looked likely to fall then refugees would be using them to come downriver. We would be passing them, or at the very least see wreckage from them if they had been destroyed."

This made sense to me. There were thousands of people in the city; surely some would get away. Tomorrow, I thought, we would reach Khartoum, the culmination of an ordeal that had taken around five months. It was the most arduous journey of my life, and I could not help but imagine how it might end. There were sure to be crowds of cheering people on the wharves as we pulled in. I pictured myself following Wilson down the gangplank and there in front of us would be Gordon. He would be thinner now, gaunt even, but I thought those piercing blue eyes would be the same. I pictured them twinkling in amusement as he recognised me, one of the last people he spoke to in England, there with

189

the first of the British relief force. He was bound to give me an interview and even with Wilson's censorship, it would be an extraordinary coup. Only the *Daily News* would have the words that everyone wanted to read, and my name would become famous. Of course, there was the matter of getting that copy to a telegraph first, but the smaller steamers in the city would be able to navigate the shallows much more easily. I would worry about that challenge later.

While I was daydreaming about professional glory, I noticed that Leila had gone quiet. She too must have been thinking about the future. For her, though, the challenges were more arduous. "You don't have to cross the siege lines," I assured her, not for the first time. "Gordon will have spies that can find out what has happened to your brother. They can get messages to him from you and pass on any reply." With luck, I thought, the ungrateful sibling would be dead. Then she could return with me in good conscience. Her company would make the journey back to Cairo far more enjoyable.

"I will need to see him myself to persuade him to return with me," she insisted. "He will not trust a messenger."

"If that is necessary," I conceded, "the spies can guide you to him. It won't be safe for you to travel alone."

She smiled and put her hand on my cheek. "Nothing is safe out here, but if Allah wills it, I will find him and persuade him to return." I put my arm around her and gave her a hug.

Looking around at those of us gathered on the shore, Leila was not the only one to have feelings of trepidation for the morrow. There was an air of calm before the storm: a few were getting drunk; others took wives or concubines into the darkness for some privacy. There was a burst of female curses from the gloom, which caused much merriment amongst the men left around the fire. I gathered that the young lady was criticising the stamina of her partner. The closest we came to bloodshed that night was when one of his comrades offered to finish off the job the man had started.

I imagined Wilson pacing the deck of the *Bordein*, impatiently waiting for us all to re-embark, but there was nothing we could do now until daybreak. I was in no rush to get back on board. That was especially the case when Leila tugged on my sleeve and gestured into the darkness.

There was an air of desperation and sadness to our lovemaking that night. We both knew that it could well be the last time. Our futures hung in the balance. Afterwards, I remember lying in the rough desert grass and staring up at the myriad of stars in the sky. Those twinkling lights had shone down on this land since biblical times, even before the great temples and pyramids had been built. It always made me feel small and insignificant when I considered the constellations, for they would still be shining long after we were all gone. What trace would we leave? I doubted that the Mahdi would be allowed the time to build any great mosque. Newspapers would rot and grave markers blown over and scattered to the wind. I guessed that in a thousand years the pyramids would still stand, but of our presence in this land there would be no sign at all. I was still in a maudlin state of mind when shouts went up from the shore. The last boats were leaving for the ship.

My mood lightened with the dawn. We were nearly at Khartoum and our journey's end. Whatever awaited us there would have to be dealt with and then I could go home. After that I would be happy never to see the Nile again. There was a feeling of grim determination amongst my shipmates too. Soldiers again checked on their ammunition as they settled themselves against the bulwarks. This time we were sure to be fired upon, as we had to pass first the main camp of the Mahdi at Omdurman. Among the Sudanese, those who did not have families on board, would see them in Khartoum. They grinned and chatted amongst themselves at the prospect of a reunion.

The *Talahawiyeh* led the way, its big paddle wheels churning up the muddy water near the shore before it pulled slowly upstream. There was a cheer as our anchor cable came up and then, with much clanking from the engine, the *Bordein* followed in the wake of its sister ship. According to my watch, it was six o'clock when we set off and for the rest of the morning barely a soul ashore was seen. Occasionally, there would be a puff of smoke amongst the rocks and we knew that a rifle had been fired in our direction. Only once did I hear a thud, which may have been a bullet hitting the planking. Here we were, heading into the heart of the enemy position, and it felt barely more dangerous than a Baptist tea party.

Wortley had evidently forgiven me for stowing away and came up to ask my opinion. "Do you think that they have already lifted the siege?" he wondered out loud. "They must have had word of our earlier battles and know that there is no hope for them when the rest of the column gets here."

I wanted to believe him, I really did, but long experience has taught me that life is rarely that convenient. "It would be difficult for the Mahdi to sell that to his followers," I replied, "when he has told them that God will help them sweep us infidels away. They would string him up if he admitted that God had changed sides." I stared upstream and concluded, "I think they are still up there somewhere. We should probably enjoy the peaceful stage of this journey while it lasts."

By noon, through the heat haze, we could just make out the green foliage of Tutti Island. The Nile was shaped like a Y at Khartoum, with us coming up the shaft at the bottom. The city was built in the cleft at the top, where the White Nile flowing in from the southwest joined the Blue Nile from the southeast. At the confluence of the rivers, where the currents swirled and eddied, great quantities of silt had been deposited and this had formed Tutti Island just to the north of the city.

A short while later we came under artillery fire for the first time. The shells dropped at least half a mile short, but we saw the splashes in the river at around the same time we heard the distant boom of guns. They had to have come from the cannon that the Mahdi's men had captured from Hicks' army. Whoever was firing them had no idea of their range, or perhaps they struggled to see us in through the haze. To them we were two shimmering dark dots against the background of the river. For us it was even harder to see the source of this new attack. We guessed it had come from Omdurman, the Mahdists' camp on the western bank of the Nile. We knew it was just north of Khartoum and so trained our glasses in that direction.

For a while we could see nothing at all beyond a shimmering mass of desert and a dark line of trees by the riverbank. Then, as we pressed on closer, what I had taken to be desert resolved into a vast camp. The canvas, covered in desert dust, was the same colour as the land around, but we could see shadows of walls and roads that ran through in all directions. It stretched for miles along the bank and had to house tens of thousands of men. As I studied it, I picked out several more puffs of smoke and a second later more water plumes appeared, this time much closer. The quiet phase of our voyage was at an end.

The *Bordein* was now close behind the *Talahawiyeh*. As well as the artillery, we had to avoid the mudbanks and small islands that littered this stretch of the Nile. For either vessel to be holed from a rock or a shell now would be a disaster. The redoubtable Captain Gibril picked out a careful course through the obstacles and we stayed doggedly in his wake. It was still too far to see any details of Khartoum beyond a smudge of white buildings on the distant riverbank. Yet we could now see boats moored against Tutti Island. Khashm told us that Gordon's men held that position. The boats were proof; if the island had been overrun then the boats would have been used to escape. Gibril evidently thought so too, for we changed course to hug the eastern bank and keep as far away as possible from the guns at Omdurman.

Thank God the Mahdists had no idea how to use their artillery or we would have been blown apart. We were now well within range, but I guessed that they had slaughtered any of Hicks' gunners when they had captured the guns. They were now trying to work out how to use the modern artillery as they went along. Yet as a shell landed dangerously close, covering me with water, I knew that even a blind man had to get lucky sooner or later. I strained my eyes ahead looking for any sign that the Khartoum garrison were able to give us covering fire. Their ramparts were silent. Surely they had seen us? I imagined a lookout reporting to Gordon that at long last British forces were approaching. Perhaps even then those blue eyes were watching the two shimmering dots of the steamers through a glass. I smiled at the thought and then ducked involuntarily as another shell buzzed over the top of us to explode on the muddy northern tip of Tutti Island off our port beam.

"Your brother's friends are giving us a hot welcome," I shouted to Leila as we both crouched down below the wooden ramparts that surrounded the bridge.

193

"Can you see Gordon Pasha's flag?" she shouted back, gesturing at my field-glasses.

"No, I can barely make out the buildings on the waterfront through the haze," I replied as another shell exploded, this time two hundred yards to starboard. "But unless they get lucky with those guns, we should be there in an hour or so." My confidence survived for barely another second before all hell broke loose.

A Sudanese soldier shouted a warning in his own language, which I did not understand. The meaning was clear a moment later as a barrage of rifle fire came at us from Tutti Island, now little more than two hundred yards off our port beam. The sudden noise was deafening. I instinctively flinched low, glancing up at the man who had given the warning. He had already been hit by several bullets to his head, neck and chest. He was still being struck and pirouetted like a ballet dancer as he fell back onto the deck. I could feel bullets hitting the other side of the thick wooden bulwark that my back rested against. Above the roar of gunfire, there was a ripple of thuds all the way down the deck, with the frequency of rain on a tin roof. I stared around in astonishment, for it made no sense. I was not the only one slow on the uptake.

Wilson stood staring open-mouthed at the shore, and by some miracle he remained unscathed. "We are on your side!" he bellowed, pointing at the huge red flag of Egypt, with its white stars and crescents hanging over our stern. By way of reply, his cork helmet was shot off his head and a splinter gouged out of the rail by his hand. Only then did he drop down into cover. Soldiers by the loopholes had recognised our changing circumstances rather quicker than their commander and were already returning fire, one cursing as he was struck in the shoulder through the embrasure. Wilson caught my eye as the din of battle continued around us. As we stared at each other, we realised that the men on Tutti Island could see our flag all too clearly, as they could the one flying from the *Talahawiyeh*. They had waited until we were right alongside before launching their attack. The fact that they were shooting at us meant that they were not Gordon's troops. They were the Mahdi's, but how had they managed to hold a position on the island under the guns of the city?

"Khartoum has fallen," wailed Khashm, stating what we were struggling to contemplate. "My wife, my children," he continued and then he buried his face in his hands and began to sob.

"The *Talahawiyeh* is turning, sir," shouted Wortley at Wilson as he peered out through one of the loopholes.

"No, we must press on," Wilson gestured to our pilot and pointed due south. Bullets were clanging off the engine plates and splinters off the paddle wheels. The man nodded, keen to get his vessel away from the barrage of fire. "We must know for certain," Wilson went on. He glanced at the weeping Khashm and added hopefully, "Gordon may be holding out in the city. We might be able to carry him and some of his people off."

I confess that I was not thinking that far ahead. My mind was still reeling from the possibility that we might be too late. Ten thousand men marching, riding and rowing for month after month, battles fought, hundreds dead from wounds and disease, yet all for nothing. No, it couldn't be. Gordon *had* to be still there. I crawled across to a loophole facing forward. Through it I could now make out the white of buildings in the city's river frontage. Perhaps Gordon had moved any guns facing in this direction to cover the south, the only part of Khartoum not protected by the Nile. It was the only explanation for him not to be giving us covering fire, yet even I began to think that I was clutching at straws.

The great paddle wheels churned the water faster as the engines went to full speed ahead, and I felt us turning towards the middle of the river. Over the bulwark I could see the masts of the *Talahawiyeh* which was now reverting back on course to follow us onwards. Still we were being peppered by bullets, yet the gunners in the midship turret were now hauling their piece round to give our ambushers a taste of their own medicine. Rifles on the *Bordein* were cracking out steadily; I heard a British corporal calling out to his men to concentrate on gunners around their artillery. Alarmed, I risked a quick look through a loophole facing the island. One of their captured Krupps guns could fire a shell right through the ship at that range. I saw two of their cannons in a mud embrasure, but they were surrounded by a score of corpses that must

195

have made up their crews. Two more men fell to our rifles in the second or so that I was watching. Our turret gun boomed over my shoulder and my view was obscured by smoke. I turned to see Leila with her arm around Khashm. She was talking to him in Arabic, evidently trying to assure him that there was still hope.

I ducked back from my loophole as a bullet slammed into the wood just the other side of the bulwark. It was another close call, but then so was this whole voyage. As more waterspouts splashed up nearby from the Omdurman guns, the chances of us getting back to the rest of the column looked slimmer than a cigarette paper. My guts tightened as I imagined a more likely fate: being butchered by these fanatics like poor O'Donovan before me. I was distracted from any thoughts of self-pity when I was suddenly showered with sparks. Looking up, I saw that one of the wires that held the funnel had been shot through. The stack was now tipped back and cinders were showering the deck. Reaching down I used my hand to beat out a spark that had landed on an ammunition box and then knocked off another small piece of burning wood. "We need to get that chimney secured again," I shouted, "or we will be ablaze or blown up in a minute."

I doubt the *bazinger*, who had been part of the gun crew, understood me, but it was plain as day what was needed, if not how it would be achieved. He now picked up a coil of rope and ran forward. The base of the funnel was above and behind the wheelhouse and well beyond the protection of the bulwarks. To go there seemed suicidal, but the man did not hesitate. Bounding up, he was soon on the platform above the engine. He cursed as he reached out to try and pull the stack down and got burned for his trouble. Those on Tutti Island had seen him too and there was a clang as a bullet hit the funnel near his head. Conscious that he only had seconds before he was hit, he uncoiled the rope and pulled one end through the metal loop that the old wire stay had been tied to. As I watched in horrified fascination, a volley of shots was fired from the shore. Two more holes were punched through the side of the funnel, but one struck the soldier in the side. He gave a grunt of pain but still had the strength to throw the ends of the rope down to me. I bent down to grab them and when I looked up again the man had disappeared.

There was no time to waste; I looped them through a ring on the deck and hauled hard. The funnel was secured. A sailor came to tie the rope off, while I went forward to find out what had happened to our saviour.

"That man deserves a Victoria Cross for what he just did," declared Wilson when he saw me.

"Where is he?" I asked, staring about.

"Overboard." Seeing my surprise, he went on. "Did you not see him take the second bullet? He staggered, fell over the rail, bounced on top of the wheel cover and was gone."

"Was he dead?" It was an instinctive question on my part, but as soon as the words were out of my mouth, I realised that it was absurd. There was no way that we could possibly turn round and look for the poor devil while we were still under such fire. That point was emphasised by a bullet shattering one of the remaining shards of glass in the wheelhouse windows above our head.

Wilson put a hand on my shoulder in understanding. "He fell in front of the wheel. If he was not already dead, the paddles would certainly have killed him." Then he gestured over my shoulder, where a plank had somehow been shot out of the front of the wheelhouse leaving a gap facing forward. "Now, let's go and find Gordon."

There was still hope, for as we moved out of range of the rifles on Tutti Island, we were only under fire from the artillery at Omdurman and their aim had not improved. Without us to pin down their gunners, a cannon on Tutti opened up on us too, but to little effect. There was no need now to hide behind the bulwarks. Most of us crowded forward for a clearer view of the city. The Sudanese soldiers chattered excitedly amongst themselves – most of them had family in the city. Some were already weeping in despair, while others banged on the rail and shouted at the bridge for us to go faster. They pointed at landmarks as became clearer through the heat haze.

"Government House is that large white building in the centre of the riverfront," said a voice behind me. I turned to see Khashm at my elbow with Leila, who must have persuaded him to come forward to see things for himself. "If Gordon is holding out, he will be there and he will be flying the Egyptian Flag," he continued. We were too far away to make

197

out a flag, but some thought they could hear gunfire coming from the city. We pressed on, getting drenched in spray as one shell exploded in the river just ten yards off our bow. Perhaps their gunners were getting better after all. There was no thought of turning back now, though; we had come much too far for that. Within a couple of hundred yards the heat haze diminished and swiftly we were rewarded with a better view. We could now make out windows and, more importantly, a flagpole. It was bare… If there was any further doubt of Gordon's presence, the crowd in front of the building opened fire on us with rifles. Evidently, the ships were now clearer to them too and we watched the puffs of muzzle smoke in dismay before the rattle of musketry reached us across the water. The implication was clear and there were howls of grief from many of the Sudanese. One had to be stopped from jumping overboard in front of the paddles and others tore at their hair and sank to their knees as the reality of the situation sank in.

"Perhaps Gordon is holding out somewhere else in the city," suggested Wortley, weakly.

"No," Khashm was quiet but firm. "He would have made his stand at Government House. They are dead." His voice broke slightly "They are all dead, perhaps some of my daughters live, but they will wish they are dead to spare them their shame." He turned, sobbing, and pushed his way back through the crowd.

"We don't know for certain that Gordon is dead," insisted Wortley stubbornly.

"What the hell do you want us to do?" I snapped at him. "Land at the wharf under fire and then send our twenty-five soldiers to conduct a street by street search? None of us would get off the jetty alive."

Wilson had not uttered a word. It was obvious now that the city had fallen; we were too late. The full might of the British Empire had been sent to rescue just one man and it had failed. After months of delay, prevarication and our long, arduous journey across the desert, Khartoum had fallen no more than two weeks before we reached it. There would be an uproar when the news reached London. Gladstone would be blamed for certain, and Wolseley too, with his mad scheme to use the boats. Our ambitious general would try to find his own scapegoat and

198

Wilson was the obvious candidate. "Don't worry," I told him. "They cannot blame you for this. I will vouch for you. We could not have done any more to get here sooner."

To my surprise he just laughed. "Harrison, right now I would be delighted to accept any blame, for it would mean that I have lived long enough to return to the rest of the army. They know for certain we are here now, and they will know where we are going. I very much doubt that our trip downriver will be as peaceful as the one up it. They are bound to have men waiting for us at the Sabaloka Gorge and if we run aground again..." He let the sentence tail off then took a deep breath and continued, "But we have no choice." Turning to the helmsman he gave the order, "Put the wheel over and head north. Signal for Gibril in the *Talahawiyeh* to lead the way."

Chapter 18

There were more howls of despair from the Sudanese as the *Bordein* slowly put about. Even though we were under fire from three different directions, many put their heads above the parapet for what they must have suspected would be the last glimpse of their home. I saw one woman holding her young son up so that he could see over the bulwarks, while she whispered in his ear, tears streaming down her face. It was a poignant scene, or at least it would have been if bullets were not whipping above our heads and shells bursting all around. The kid was lucky not to have his head blown off. I kept my noggin well under cover. Most of the rifle fire was at extreme range, but I heard a mitrailleuse firing from the city and knew all too well that the big slugs from that beast could easily reach us and cause damage. We were fortunate in that, with all the smoke and haze, the devil firing it clearly had no idea where his bullets were going, for I saw no sign of a regular patten of splashes in the water about us.

The *Talahawiyeh* was now heading into the middle of the river to take us further away from the guns on Tutti Island. Inevitably, this brought us closer to the batteries at Omdurman, but that could not be helped. We had been under fire for over two hours and it was little short of a miracle that neither vessel had been sunk already. My stomach tightened with fear as we began to run the gauntlet again, not that I could show it. Wilson studied the shore through his field-glasses with the calm, studious air of someone birdwatching on a peaceful marsh. He did not even flinch when a bullet shattered the few shards of glass still stuck in the wheelhouse windows. He merely brushed the broken pieces off his sleeve and then stared aft at the unmanned six-pounder in irritation. "Wortley, why have the gunners not recommenced firing?"

The young officer ducked as the whine of a shell passed low overhead. "Many of them are still too upset, sir." He pointedly looked to the other corner of the wheelhouse. Wilson and I followed his gaze. Hunched against the side was a figure who had pulled a reed mat over his head to be alone with his thoughts in this cauldron of battle. The polished boots and a colonel's epaulettes on his shoulder confirmed it was Khashm. He was clearly in no state to get his soldiers fighting again and so Wilson turned to Ibrahim, his interpreter.

"Tell them that if they want to avenge their families, they have to fight," he insisted. The Egyptian nodded. Even though this was not his homeland, he would have had some sympathy with the poor devils who were now wondering what had happened to their wives and children. Plumes of smoke still rose up from the streets of Khartoum where buildings had been burned by the Mahdi's supporters, perhaps to quell the last of the resistance. While Ibrahim did his best to get the Sudanese soldiers back to their stations, it was a bullet from Tutti that finally did the job. A man howled in pain as he was struck in the arm. Luckily it was just a flesh-wound – he could still wave the limb angrily at the marksmen and hurl insults at them – but it spurred on his comrades to finally pick up their own weapons and join the British soldiers in returning fire. They were all shooting blindly into the smoke surrounding the island and heaven knows how many of the enemy were hit. But it did not matter, it just felt good to still be putting up a fight. I missed my own Martini–Henry or I would have been shooting too. My pistol was worse than useless at anything more than around twenty feet.

To my astonishment we kept extending the range to our enemies without taking any significant damage. The funnel had stayed secure and even though a scoop in one of the paddle wheels had been smashed, we were still making good progress. Slowly but surely the rate of fire diminished, until we were beyond the range of even their largest guns. As soon as it was safe, the *Talahawiyeh* stopped in the middle of the channel so that we could come alongside. If I had thought that our escape was a marvel, that of our sister ship was little short of miraculous. She had been struck by a shell just above the waterline. It should have blown the bow off the craft, killing or drowning its occupants, but by some lucky chance the shell had failed to detonate. A boat was lowered alongside the hole and a net pushed inside to try and get it out. As men in the dinghy tugged and pulled, to my horror there came the sound of a hammer hitting metal from inside the ship. I prayed it was widening the hole, otherwise the fuse was being given every encouragement to detonate. Eventually the wretched ordinance was hauled out and dropped into the river. By then we had ascertained that between the two steamers, despite being under fire for four hours, we had lost just two men killed and fifteen wounded.

There was no great air of celebration to our deliverance from the very heart of the enemy position. Amongst the Sudanese there was no more than a sullen acceptance that we were still alive, with a number still appearing not to care either way. The British contingent too thought it was far too premature to celebrate. "They will not let us back through that gorge as easily as we came through it to get here," grumbled one, and I was sure he was right. The river levels were still dropping as well, which meant that the cataracts would be an even more challenging obstacle to our return. Not only that, but this time we would be travelling with the current. We had been steaming markedly faster away from Khartoum. While we might be making quicker progress, it also gave us less time to spot obstacles ahead and avoid them.

With the *Talahawiyeh* made safe, we got underway once more until by nightfall we were some twenty miles north of Khartoum. Only then did Wilson allow us to stop again, although he had little choice, for we were nearly out of fuel. Both steamers anchored off an island near the eastern shore. Two of the Sudanese were sent off for information on what had happened in the city. Most of the rest were sent ashore to gather as much wood as they could find. Leila suggested we go onto the island too. I was reluctant and she guessed the reason why.

"Don't worry, I am not going to leave tonight." She sighed, staring out into the darkness. "I thought it would be easier if Gordon still held Khartoum. There would be spies who could help me get into Omdurman to find my brother. If the Mahdi was retreating, then I might have been able to persuade him to come with me. But now…" She let the sentence hang, biting her bottom lip as she considered her options. I could tell she was afraid and for good reason. I had always thought that her mission was optimistic at best, but now it was near impossible.

"You cannot hope to bring him if he is not willing," I pointed out. "Now Khartoum has fallen, he will be even more convinced that the Mahdi is the chosen one. You have done your best to get this far, but it would be madness to go back."

"I must try," she insisted. "I have promised my father."

"He would want one of his children back," I told her, "rather than lose you both. You cannot do this alone, surely you see that. Perhaps when the rest of the British army comes up things will be different."

As I said the words, I wondered what would happen in London when they received news of Khartoum's fall. Gladstone, who had never wanted to send an army here, would probably see the *casus belli* as lost. He might well order Wolseley to march us all home. Yet the public would be furious at the demise of their hero and much of the blame would go to the prevarications of their prime minister. He might be forced to take action to restore the prestige of British arms. No one would countenance the cream of the British army being baulked by some religious fanatic. I wondered if the entire relief force might be marched up the western bank of the river, destroying the army at Omdurman and restoring order in Sudan just to prove a point. Perhaps I had not seen the last of Khartoum after all.

As I dropped down into a boat with Leila to be rowed ashore, I realised that I was getting ahead of myself. We were not back at Matammeh yet and our chances did not look good. It was more likely that I would see Khartoum as a prisoner, perhaps facing execution if the British force did not withdraw. We walked across the island. It was good to feel solid ground under my feet again. There were a few small fields of abandoned crops and some huts that were now being torn down for their supports. The truncated bleat of a goat nearby indicated that an animal was being prepared for the pot. It could be cooked over a pile of the thatch. The reeds that surrounded the island would hopefully hide the flames from any prying eyes, although I swiftly deduced that our location would not stay secret for long. Many of the Sudanese were gathered in small groups, whispering furtively in the darkness. They looked suspiciously at me and stopped talking when we were close, clearly worried what Leila might overhear.

"They are up to mischief," I told her.

"Some are planning on going over to the Mahdi's forces," she replied. "I heard them discussing it on the *Bordein*."

I was shocked. "Why on earth would they do that?" I demanded. "Those murdering fanatics will have stormed through the city killing their families."

"Some hope their wives and children are prisoners. Changing sides is the only way they will see them again. For many of them this is their tribal homeland, they have nowhere else to go. They have been here for generations."

"But surely they do not want to live under that tyrant?"

"This is their home, whoever rules it." She held my arm to get my attention as I glared around at my treacherous shipmates. "Tell me honestly, if for example France conquered England, would most of the English leave for another country, or would they stay in their homes and try to get by with their new rulers?"

"That would never happen," I insisted.

"But if it did," she pressed, "what would they do? What would *you* do?"

I stopped to give the matter some serious thought. "I might well stay, but I have the means to leave if I wanted. I suppose, though, that most people could not afford to go somewhere else and set up a new life. They would have to stay and make things work."

"Exactly, especially if the French were holding their families prisoner. Now do you see why some of them are leaving? It will not do us any harm, for the enemy knows roughly where we are already."

"Yes, but can we get back without them?" I countered. "If Gibril abandons us, we will never get through the cataracts again." By now we had pushed our way through the reeds to the other side of the narrow island. I had followed the sound of splashing and as I pulled the last stems aside, I glimpsed in the darkness at least a dozen men wading through the shallow water to the far shore. One glanced over his shoulder and saw me. He scurried on with the guilty air of one who was not planning to return. "We should go back to warn Wilson," I concluded. "We have to make sure that Gibril and the engineers stay with us."

By the time we got back to the *Bordein*, I was relieved to see that the pilot was also aboard. He had been shot in the arm on the run to Khartoum, but the injury was now bandaged and he was talking to Wilson over a map. While I waited, I went down to look in the engine room. The chief engineer was there, oil can in hand, although there was no sign of his assistant. When I returned to the shattered wheelhouse there was a new visitor there, one of the Sudanese sent to find out what had happened in Khartoum.

"Come on in, Harrison," called the colonel when he saw me. "You might as well listen to this too." The man was babbling in his local tongue to Ibrahim, who eventually held up his hand to allow him time to translate.

"If this is still Wednesday," he said, glancing at a clock on the wall that was stopped with two bullet holes through it, "then they attacked the city two days ago on Monday. He says that the Mahdi heard we were coming and ordered an assault to take the capital before we could reach it."

"But what about Gordon?" I asked. "Does he know what has happened to him?"

"This man has spoken to a chief in the local village. He says riders have come from the city to say that it has fallen. Thousands of its citizens have been slaughtered and more taken as slaves. The governor general is dead. He had heard that the Mahdi wanted Gordon Pasha taken alive and was angry when his head was brought to him on a spear."

I wondered if the Mahdi was worried about the holy man's prophecy. There was a moment's silence before anyone spoke again, as we all reflected on the futility of the last few months.

"What a waste," Wilson breathed at last. "Now all that is left for us to do is bring back our men and the tragic news."

"About that," I interjected, "we may be bringing back rather fewer people than you thought." I explained what Leila had told me and he shared my initial reaction of anger. Khashm was summoned, who wearily advised that even if he ordered men to stay, they would ignore him.

"Well," announced Wilson, "I will speak to the men as soon as they are back aboard with the wood to remind them of their duty." Ibrahim looked as if he was about to suggest something, but then changed his mind and held his counsel.

Three hours later, after roasted meat had been distributed, and the wood chopped and loaded aboard by those who had not deserted, Wilson had the hands summoned aft so that he could talk to them. Everyone was tired and wanted to sleep. They glared sullenly up at the colonel, who stood at the wheelhouse rail like a headmaster about to reprimand the school for farting in prayers. I have no idea what he said quietly to Ibrahim, but I am pretty sure that it bore little relation to what the translator imparted. The Arabic version was at least three times as long as the terse statements that the Colonel instructed.

Leila gave me an accurate translation. "He says that the murder of Gordon is a great insult to the British queen. She sent her soldiers off many months ago to make their way here. He is reminding them that just a small part of the army has beaten much larger forces of the Mahdi's twice. He says we will go back to rejoin the other ships at the camp near Matammeh and await the rest of the British army. Then we will march on Khartoum and avenge your families. Not a single Mahdist throat will be left uncut. The Nile will be red with their blood. Any of the curs that survive will be driven deep into the desert. He insists to them that if they remain loyal and we find their women and children among the slaves, they will be returned to them. In conclusion, Ibrahim stated that the Mahdi offered only death and bondage. The British are our friends, Gordon Pasha treated us fairly, we must stay loyal."

It was an impressive speech and I saw a few tired backs straighten as a result. This benevolent impression of the British was countered slightly when Wilson posted sentries to ensure that no more of the Sudanese made a run for it. Perhaps more in line with the colonel's actual words, they had orders to shoot to deter desertion. One shot was fired over the heads of a couple of men seen swimming to shore, but Wilson forbade a fatal shot. "We probably should not alert the enemy to our location with gunfire," he muttered irritably. The strain of our predicament was telling on him. He had not slept for twenty-four hours and paced up and down, impatiently waiting for the dawn.

As the light crept over the eastern horizon, we were once more stirred into life. Carpenters completed the repairs on the damaged paddle wheel, while efforts were made to lighten the ship. The water level was still dropping. If we could reduce the draft of the vessels by even an inch, it might make all the difference. The holds were full of sacks of wheat intended to feed Khartoum and these were no longer required. Chains of men passed them up and dropped them over the side. The nuggar, towed behind the *Talahawiyeh*, was similarly filled with food and that too was emptied into the Nile. One of the junior Sudanese officers even suggested that now might be the time to abandon the guns and ammunition. They along with the soldiers were now the heaviest things aboard, but Wilson just glared at the man with suspicion. Evidently, our own comrades were no longer to be trusted.

By seven the boilers had been lit and optimum steam pressure achieved. We were ready to get underway. The aim was to make as much progress as possible. Gibril hoped we might make it through the Sabaloka Gorge before nightfall, which gave us a chance of outrunning any planned ambush. The *Talahawiyeh* would once again take the lead with her skilful pilot, but this time Wortley was sent aboard too, to keep an eye on the crew for Wilson. I'd had a feeling of foreboding as those paddle wheels had started to turn once more, but as the morning progressed my nerves began to ease. We made good progress down the middle of the river; the repair on the paddle wheel held up well, the fresh timber visible every thirty seconds or so as it rotated round. We saw a few men riding up and down the riverbank on horses, but only one group bothered to fire rifle shots at us and they were well out of range. A few even waved at us, whether in friendship or to encourage us to stop we could not tell. We certainly were not going to heave to if we could help it; we aimed to steam all the way to the camp near Matammeh without interruption.

Lunchtime came and went and still we pressed strongly ahead. We were on track to make the gorge by five, which Wilson estimated would give us just enough light to get through. Our vessel's captain, though, was not so sure. He muttered darkly about the current and hidden rocks and suggested it would be better to wait for dawn. In the end it all became irrelevant. I was on deck when it happened at around four in the afternoon. We had been steaming steadily for nine hours and perhaps eyes were getting tired. Given what followed I must admit that I had been staring ahead too and had seen no disturbance in the water. Without any warning the *Talahawiyeh* suddenly rose up out of the Nile, her bow twisting around to port. There was the awful sound of grinding metal and steam hissed from her boilers. Clearly something catastrophic had happened and we immediately stopped our own engines, but we were level with the ship long before we lost headway.

"We have struck a rock!" shouted Wortley as we drifted past. "The ship is lost." It was obvious he was right; having slipped off the underwater obstruction, the *Talahawiyeh* was already listing to one side. As we anchored nearby, the nuggar that the *Talahawiyeh* had been towing was pulled alongside. The crew and passengers were already tumbling down into her.

"Send the felucca back to help," ordered Wilson. "They will not all fit into that barge." I was shocked at how quickly the disaster had happened. With two ships, one could always help the other, as we had shown in the cataracts. Now we were very much on our own. If anything happened to the *Bordein*, we would be done for and the hardest part of the journey, the gorge and the cataracts, lay ahead.

By the time the bedraggled survivors had been brought alongside, it was clear that we would not have enough light left to make the gorge. Instead, Wilson ordered his little flotilla to remain anchored in the middle of the river. Most of the *Talahawiyeh*'s crew remained in the nuggar and felucca, as there was not room for them all in the *Bordein*. We would have to tow them the rest of the way. Wortley came aboard with Gibril, both insisting that they must have hit an underwater rock, with not even a ripple to betray its presence. You could not help but stare out at the vast expanse of muddy brown water that surrounded us and wonder what more surprises the Nile had in store.

There was a grim silence amongst the company now as everyone reassessed their chances of survival and found few grounds for hope.

Soldiers quietly polished their weapons, while the Sudanese gathered in groups speaking only in whispers to avoid being overheard.

"Do you think we stand *any* chance of making it back to Matammeh?" I muttered to Leila.

"Perhaps the Mahdi will choose to be merciful," she answered, revealing that she had already lost hope of that goal. "He may have regretted Gordon's death and he knows that the British have a powerful army approaching. We may be more useful to him alive, as hostages, to dissuade your army from attacking."

That prospect did not sound at all appealing. Even if we were shown such 'mercy' I doubted the Mahdists would treat their hostages little better than dogs. We were infidels after all and they would take triumph from our subjugation. Not only that, I doubted that such hostages would stop Wolseley from attacking; he certainly would not spare a thought for a war correspondent. He had gambled on increasing his reputation with the rescue of Gordon. When he learned his friend was dead, he would want to salvage what he could from the disaster that this expedition had become. That would mean the destruction of his enemy, whatever the cost. As things turned out the Mahdi was not inclined to mercy at all. We learned that when a single rider reined in on the riverbank bearing a white flag of truce.

In hindsight we should have left him to kick his heels on the shore, but a boat was lowered to hear what he had to say. He was an old white-bearded fellow, one of their emirs or leaders. He strolled calmly aboard as though he fully expected to receive our surrender. Gazing imperiously around the *Bordein* and noting the crowded nuggar and felucca, he *salaamed* Wilson and then quietly began to set out his terms.

Ibrahim recounted that the fellow carried a letter from the Mahdi addressed to the commander of our company. It called on us to immediately lay down our arms. Then all the Christians amongst us were to convert to Islam. Following that, with the Muslims aboard, we were all to pledge our loyalty to the Mahdi and become his followers. Our emissary went on to explain that the Sudan was just the start of his leader's ambitions. Soon he would move on to Cairo and then Istanbul, before sweeping through Europe to drive out or convert the infidels. He made it sound as though we might as well join now and perhaps become the emir of Chingford in due course, rather than wait until they were on our family's doorstep in London.

As he sat waiting expectantly for our inevitable acceptance, Wilson quietly asked what would happen if we refused. Somewhat surprised, he informed us through Ibrahim that such a decision could only result in our complete destruction. Our vessels would be sunk and any survivors slaughtered. The colonel gave a wry smile before turning to his interpreter and instructing our visitor to go to the devil. Ibrahim had not even opened his mouth when Khashm interrupted, "Perhaps I could have a word with you, sir, before you give your final response on this matter."

"You are surely not suggesting we should accept?" demanded Wilson angrily. "These villains probably butchered your family not three days ago. I would not give two pins for our chances once we have laid down our guns. They would kill us even if we were foolish enough to convert to their prophet." I was sure he was right. If there was a chance of preserving my precious skin, I would be all for it. I have no great Christian faith. To save my life I would pledge allegiance to Mohammed, Buddha or some jungle tree god. But Wilson was right; even if we did convert, the Mahdi would not trust us. He would know we were playing him false and plotting escape. Almost certainly he would put our heads on spikes as another triumph to show his followers. At best we would be kept in cages, curiosities to be poked and spat at, which was little better. No, all things considered, I would take the slim chance of continuing downriver. Perhaps I would find some wreckage to hold on to until the current took me past the British camp.

"Please, sir, it won't take a moment," repeated Khashm as he led the way aft a few yards away from our visitor so that he could not overhear the discussion.

Wilson stared first at Wortley and then at me, as though he could not imagine what there could possibly be to discuss. "It would not do any harm to hear what he has to say," I suggested.

"Well, what is it?" demanded Wilson when we rejoined the Sudanese colonel. "If you are going to suggest that we allow your people to surrender, I cannot agree. We need Gibril, the crew and engineers to get us downriver and your soldiers to man the guns. We are not beaten yet."

"I agree, sir," Khashm spoke calmly. "I want to make it back to Matammeh too, but a flat refusal will not help our cause."

"Surrendering certainly won't either," snapped Wilson.

"Sir, I would like your permission to try something a little more subtle," began Khashm. "You can refuse the offer as you intended, but as we show him to the boat, I will have a quiet word with the emissary. I will tell him that I have tried to make you surrender but you are too obstinate to accept you are beaten. Then I will ask for a written pardon from the Mahdi and in return I will offer to sabotage the *Bordein* in front of the guns at Wad Habeshi. This would leave you with no choice but to surrender. If the Mahdi thinks you will be handed to him on a plate there, he may hold off attacking us as we go through the Sabaloka Gorge."

"I have never heard such a disreputable scheme in all my life!" Wilson looked disgusted at the suggested subterfuge. "That may be how you do things in Sudan, sir, but British officers behave with more honour."

"We may all be dead already," persisted Khashm, "but is it not wise to give your command every chance to escape the enemy? In addition, you can give your honest answer to the Mahdi. Any such dishonour will belong to me, and I am past caring about such matters."

Unexpectedly, I saw a glimmer of hope. "It is our duty to get the news of the fall of Khartoum back to the British camp," I intervened. "We should do all we can to get through, even if some of it is a little unpalatable. Otherwise more men may be sent upriver and suffer a similar fate." Wortley too nodded in agreement.

Wilson ran his fingers over his moustache as he gave the matter further thought. "If you would excuse us, Colonel," he said to Khashm, "I would like a word with my officers in private." With that he led us further aft. Strictly speaking I was not one of his officers, but I went too. I wanted to make sure that this straw of hope, slim though it was, would be grasped. "I don't like it," Wilson started when we were alone. "Treachery begets treachery. How do we know he will not really wreck us in front of the guns to earn his pardon? The fact that he could even think of such a villainous scheme astonishes me."

"If he was going to betray us," I started, "he could have just spoken to the emissary, and we would have been none the wiser. That he has shared his plan speaks to the fact he is trying to be straight with us." I glanced back to where Khashm waited patiently for our judgement. "You saw how cut up he was when he learned the city had fallen. My guide Leila has spent some time talking with him and she thinks he is a good man. She is usually a good judge of character."

"So I should base our strategy on the opinion of your guide?" Wilson almost sneered. "I don't like it – these Sudanese do things differently to us. Some have already tried to change sides."

Wortley coughed discreetly and then added his own opinion. "Khashm will understand better than us, sir, how the Mahdi and his officers think. I imagine that the prospect of capturing us and parading us before his followers would have greater appeal than our bodies being washed down river as wreckage. He may be right that they would leave us alone in the gorge. If they don't, with lowering water levels and a faster downstream current, I very much doubt we will make it at all. We did not see the rock that sank the *Talahawiyeh* and she went down in a little over a minute."

"For what it is worth," I concluded, "I too believe Khashm can be trusted and if we are to have any chance of survival, I don't think we really have any choice but to accept his offer."

Chapter 19

It was left to me to give Khashm the go ahead for his scheme. Wilson wanted nothing to do with it, but reluctantly agreed that we should take every chance at survival. Instead, he took his frustration out on the envoy, warning that the British army would take terrible revenge on anyone who interfered with our return. When our visitor calmly repeated his ultimatum, the colonel really lost his temper. He accused the emir of being an idolater and the Mahdi of being a charlatan. I thought he was going to have the man thrown into the Nile before he finally got a grip on himself. With icy disdain he turned to Khashm and asked him to show the envoy back to the shore. The two men sat in the back of a rowing boat with a couple of the Sudanese crew at the oars. It was dusk when they set off and must have taken them five minutes to reach the far shore. Their heads were soon leaning closer so that they could whisper in private. I felt a twinge of uncertainty as I watched. Was the envoy being gulled, or was it us who were really being tricked? We would only know for certain if we managed to steam safely past the guns at Wad Habeshi.

When the Sudanese officer returned, he recounted that the emissary had agreed to take his offer to the Mahdi. "The old man is a local chieftain," Khashm explained. "But whether he has any authority to stop us being attacked in the gorge I cannot say."

Wilson listened to the report in the little cabin underneath the wheelhouse. There were a dozen bullet holes in the walls and the windows were all shattered, but we did not care about revealing our location now. A lantern was lit and the tired eyes of all present glistened in the light. Wilson had aged a year in a day. Perhaps it was the flickering flame, but his cheeks were drawn and his shoulders slumped. "Please sit down, Colonel," he gestured Khashm to the spare chair between Wortley and myself. "Whatever happens tomorrow," he continued, "I want you to know that I am grateful for your intervention. As you know, it is not the sort of thing I would normally consider, but on reflection, you are right, we should give ourselves every chance."

"God willing, we will get through," Wortley added brightly, staring in concern at his commander's haggard features.

"Inshallah," Khashm repeated, 'God willing' in Arabic, and then gave a wry smile. "I struggle to believe in a god that wills the death of my wife and children. I will put my faith in your Mr Martini and Mr Henry instead." He laughed bitterly at his own joke, yet that was the moment when I felt more confident that he was being straight with us. Would a man thinking of aligning himself with a religious prophet make such a blasphemous remark? I doubted it.

"Well, we will know tomorrow," concluded Wilson. He pulled a battered hip flask from his pocket. "I borrowed some brandy from the surgeons before we set off and had planned to share this with General Gordon, but it was not to be." He pulled four battered tin cups towards him and began to pour. "I have thought on what you said about our value as prisoners," he continued, glancing at Khashm. "I think you are right. I am resolved not to be taken alive." He passed out the cups and then raised his own, "To death or glory, gentlemen."

We all drank that toast and I think we all meant it too, for to be taken would certainly be a longer lingering death.

One thing is for sure, we would never have got the *Bordein* through the gorge if we had been under fire. We saw men watching us from the rocks above, but not one shot was fired in our direction. Perhaps it was Khashm's subterfuge that stopped any attack. On the other hand, they may have thought that they did not need to bother. From the heights they had a clear view of the foaming torrent. The destructive power of the Nile was clear. As we entered Sabaloka, I felt sure they were right.

The cataract began in the gorge where the steep sides constricted the river. The normally lazy current was pushed forward by the water behind until waves boiled around obstacles, with eddies and flows to smash the unwary into ledges of rock. Coming upstream we had barely made any progress with the engines on full power, but now we risked being dashed to pieces before we had a chance to take evasive action. I remember staring ahead where rockfalls had narrowed the main channel to a gap that was only inches wider than the beam of the ship. Torrents of muddy water churned through the space. I did not need reminding that there was another large rock just a hundred yards beyond. It had been precarious coming the other way, but now it seemed certain that the vulnerable paddle wheels would be destroyed, if not the hull holed as we passed through.

As we approached the narrowest part, Gibril had the anchor dropped. Immediately the *Bordein* swung round as the hook bit into the mud from the hawser in the bow, to leave us pointing stern first. Next, he ordered men into rowing boats to take ropes to the shore on either side, to hold the ship steady in the centre of the channel. This set off some debate among the remaining crew; from the waving and wailing, I gathered they were adamant that the small craft would be pulverised on the rocks. Eventually, they were persuaded to set off, making landfall well upstream of the gap. Four men in each craft then rowed furiously against the current to return, for we needed more men on the rocks to hold the ship steady. This time a few British soldiers went ashore, taking rope pulleys and metal poles to secure in the rocks. Only when both teams were in place, and ropes holding the *Bordein* to the shore were secure through the pulleys and held by a dozen men on either bank, did Gibril order the anchor raised. The engine was going 'half ahead' to slow our stern-first approach to the gap, while the shore parties hurriedly took up the slack. As we reached the narrowest point, the engines went to 'full ahead' and orders were shouted over the raging torrent to keep us in the middle. It would only have taken a few bullets fired into those straining at the ropes to guarantee disaster. I stared apprehensively up at the rocks. While I could make out at least a hundred men scattered about, not one was aiming in our direction.

Gibril managed the entire affair, despite his wounded arm. It was a masterful display of rivermanship. Wilson had not interfered beyond yelling "Look out!" when he had been certain that our starboard wheel would be smashed to matchwood. The wily old cove had ignored him, waited a few more seconds until we were past another rock and then calmly raised a hand to have the shore party let out another yard or two of rope. Our starboard paddle wheel missed a pile of boulders by inches and then we were through. Those holding us to the western shore released their rope while on the opposite bank they hauled us tight round to miss the rock beyond the gap and then that rope too was gone and we were swept downstream and into a safer pool beyond. The anchor was dropped once more while ropes were recovered and fed back out to the heavily laden nuggar and then finally the felucca, which was still waiting upstream. They did not have engines to slow them down and came through the gap considerably faster. The packed humanity on the nuggar screamed in terror as they dipped down into the swirling current, yet the ropes kept them out of danger. Soon both craft were also safely anchored in the pool while we recovered the shore parties.

Getting everyone back on board took over an hour, as they had to scramble down the shore to a point where they could embark. A group of Mahdists came down the slope until they were barely fifty yards above the British soldiers. They stared at the foreign infidels, though more with curiosity than hostility. The sergeant in charge of the men wisely did not provoke them, for we were not out of trouble yet. Half a mile down the river and we had to repeat the whole process again, but by nightfall we were beyond the gorge. By some miracle both paddle wheels were still intact and the hull undamaged. The nuggar was back under tow with the felucca alongside. The shore parties were wet and exhausted. One man had been swept away, but had managed to grab a rock downstream and had been rescued. We had not lost a soul and our biggest obstacle was now behind us.

The river was much wider and calmer now. It was still strewn with islands, mudbanks and rocky outcrops, but there were no more cataracts between us and the British camp. We had the Mahdist artillery at Wad Habeshi to get past, but our own guns were still serviceable. Our soldiers would also be able to pin down their gunners to reduce their rate of fire. I remembered steaming past the then empty gun emplacements on the way upstream. We would be going faster downriver and if we could keep to the open channel then I fancied we had a good chance of making it through.

It turned out I was not alone in my optimism. Wilson had anchored the boat mid-stream to avoid any further desertions, but Leila told me that this was unnecessary. She had eavesdropped among the crew, who had also been amazed at our successful passage through the gorge. Now many were looking forward to re-joining their comrades on the remaining large steamer, the *Safia*, still moored at Matammeh, along with the smaller fourth vessel. For the first time since we had learned of the fall of Khartoum, there was an air of celebration in the vessel. A few began singing their strange chanting songs and some of the women hauled up buckets of water to do laundry, while others made bread to cook on the still hot sides of the boiler. Some of the British soldiers had tried to trade the bread for bully beef. Understandably, the Sudanese viewed the slimy pink mess in the tins with the greatest suspicion. I still had a tin of mutton for our dinner and that proved more acceptable for flatbread and some dried dates.

The enemy was still nearby; we could see pricks of light from campfires on the shore, mostly on the west bank. Around midnight one of those lights began to move towards us: a boat was approaching. Wilson had sent a messenger to wake me and instruct me to meet him in the small cabin below the wheelhouse. "It will be another messenger from the Mahdi," he predicted. "I want you to watch him like a hawk, especially if he goes anywhere near Khashm."

"Do you still not trust him?" I asked. "Without his help, I am sure we would not have got through the gorge."

"But what price is his help?" demanded Wilson. "Right now it would be foolish to trust anyone. Keep an eye on that courier and see if your woman can overhear any conversations between him and the colonel."

I went back to do as he asked, although Leila was still adamant that it was unnecessary. We had barely finished whispering among ourselves when a call went up as the boat came alongside. Another elderly emir stepped up onto the crowded deck, his eyes darting about as he took in the men, women and even a few children, as well as the damage from our approach to Khartoum. Wilson took him away to the small cabin with just Ibrahim, his interpreter, for company. He emerged, stony-faced, just five minutes later. His guest, however, was still smiling and *salaamed* Wortley and I as we stood nearby, before proceeding to the gap in the bulwark where his craft was tied up. Keeping close behind, I saw Khashm waiting beside the portal. The emir greeted him warmly too. They embraced, the Mahdist whispering something in the colonel's ear. There was no chance of Leila hearing what was said, but I noticed that as the emir dropped his hand from Khashm's shoulder, he slipped something into the colonel's pocket – a small packet wrapped in green ribbon. It was swiftly done. Leila caught my eye, for she had seen it too, but Khashm acted as though he did not know it was there. He stood at the rail, loudly talking to our visitor as he took his leave.

"He is wishing them a safe journey to the shore," whispered Leila beside me. "Did you see that packet being placed in his pocket?"

"Yes, but the emir still thinks that Khashm is playing us false, so he would have to hide any messages."

"*If* he is playing us false," came a new voice behind me. I turned to find Wilson staring suspiciously at his fellow colonel as the emir's boat pulled into the darkness. "A word with you in private please, Harrison." He looked up and added, "You too, Wortley."

A minute later we were sitting back in the small cabin with Ibrahim the interpreter, who had stayed from their earlier meeting. Wilson looked us each in the eye and then began. "The emir came to tell us that Gordon is barricaded in a church in Khartoum and that if we want to rescue him, we should turn back."

"I don't believe that," Wortley interjected. "Firstly, we have already had reports that Gordon is dead. But even if he were alive, he could not hold out for long in a church, they could simply blast it down."

"I agree," confirmed Wilson. "Even the emir did not seem convinced by his own message."

"It was probably just a pretext to get him aboard," I suggested, "so that he could deliver his message to Khashm."

"Did your guide overhear any conversation between them?" asked Wilson.

"No, but we both saw the emir drop a packet in Khashm's pocket when he left."

I suspect that the Sudanese officer was listening at the door, for barely were the words out of my mouth when there was a knock. Without waiting for a reply, the subject of our discussion walked in. Khashm looked around at our surprised expressions and grinned.

"Mr Harrison, I saw you watching me earlier." He reached into his pocket and pulled out the bundle of paper still wrapped in its green ribbon. "You probably knew that I had this before I did." He tossed the packet into the middle of the table. "Why don't we ask Ibrahim to read it for us, as I am sure we are all interested to find out what it contains."

"Please sit down, Colonel," said Wilson, gesturing to the remaining chair at the table. For a man who had remained icy calm as we had approached Khartoum, he was now embarrassed and flustered. He went decidedly pink as he cleared his throat and added, "I am sure none of us doubted your integrity."

Khashm simply grinned again and nodded an acknowledgement as the interpreter used a knife to cut through the ribbons. There were two letters. Ibrahim spread them out on the table and then picked up and opened the first. As soon as he had unfolded the parchment and glanced at the contents, he dropped it back on the table, as though reluctant to touch it further. "It is from the Mahdi himself," he whispered. "It carries his seal."

"So what does it say?" asked Wilson impatiently.

The interpreter gently spread the paper out again as though the document was a holy relic and began to read. "It is a pardon for the colonel, his family and any followers who help him deliver the British to the forces of the Mahdi."

"It is what I asked for when I spoke to the emir before we passed though the Sabaloka Gorge," Khashm reminded us, meeting Wortley's accusatory stare. "It shows that they took the offer seriously, which is why they held off attacking when they could."

Wilson nodded in agreement. "What is in the second letter?" he asked.

Ibrahim reached forward and unfolded the second despatch. This one he treated with less reverence and even smiled as he read, "It is from one of the emirs. It reminds the colonel of his promise to wreck the *Bordein* in front of Wad Habeshi and threatens an eternity in hell should he fail."

"You can burn both of those," instructed Khashm. "They are of no use to me."

"Are you sure?" asked Ibrahim, gazing down at the Mahdi's personal seal, as though wondering if this would be an act of sacrilege.

"Give it to me." Khashm stood and reached to pick up the pardon. Above the table a lantern hung illuminating the room. The glass had been shattered by a bullet on one side. He poked a corner of the paper in until it caught light and then held the document by the opposite corner, watching the flames consume it. His glinting eyes looked at us all in turn and then his gaze returned to Wilson. "I told you before that I have no intention of joining that devil. Perhaps you will see this as proof." With that he dropped the charred remains of the pardon on the table and walked out of the cabin.

It was convincing enough for me and even Wilson grudgingly admitted that he may have misjudged the man. The ruse had got us through the gorge and now all were sure that we could trust Khashm not to try and wreck the ship. We would have to stop in the morning to gather more fuel from the shore. Then we would make haste down the river that should take us past Wad Habeshi before dusk. If we made it, and I thought we had a good chance now, we would be back in the British camp by early the following day.

There was a new spring in my step as I left that cabin. What a report I would have to file when we returned! An exclusive from the only correspondent to set eyes on Khartoum. My imaginings had swiftly gone beyond Sudan and even Cairo. My thoughts went on to London, walking through the offices of the *Daily News*. The spontaneous applause I would receive for a series of exclusives that would have quadrupled sales. I was still smiling at the thought of the jealous envy of Burleigh when Leila pulled at my arm and guided me over to an empty patch of deck.

"Did you know that there is a plan to sink the ship tomorrow?" she asked.

I frowned, puzzled. "I told you about the plan, remember? But you need not worry, Colonel Khashm has promised he will do no such thing and has just burned his pardon to prove it."

220

"No, not Khashm, I knew he would not do it. It is some of the other Sudanese. They have heard from the emir's boat crew that the Mahdi will pardon anyone who delivers the British soldiers into his hands."

"But why on earth would they try to sink us now?" I exclaimed. "There is a very good chance that we will be safely back in the British camp in a day and a half."

"Because this is their land," she explained patiently. "The only home they have known, where their families have lived for many generations. The boat crew has told them that the Mahdi will personally lead a great host of fifty thousand to destroy the British. Many believe that with him at their head, the army will be invincible. So if they want to stay in their own country, the only way is to change sides."

My thoughts of glory began to crumble into dust. If the Mahdi did advance with tens of thousands of religious fanatics, they would probably destroy the British camp long before the river column came up to provide reinforcements. Then where would these Sudanese live if they survived the encounter? They could hardly stay in the Bayuda. The people living further north along the Nile were from a different tribe, who would not welcome intruders. This all now meant that there were perhaps a hundred potential saboteurs on board, and it would only take one to bring about our ruin.

Chapter 20

The next morning we steamed a few miles upriver and then stopped by another abandoned village to gather fuel. This time Wilson did not post sentries to deter deserters. "If they want to leave," he grumbled, "we are best off rid of them." Ever since I had passed on Leila's revelations he had been feeling increasingly bitter towards our former allies. Khashm had let it be known that he had been offered a pardon by the Mahdi, but had burned the document. Yet this made little difference. Leila reported that some did not believe him, while others thought that if a pardon had been given to Khashm, it would be given to others that carried out the deed.

There must have been some, perhaps a majority, of loyal Sudanese on the *Bordein*, but now the British aboard were getting increasingly paranoid. The Sudanese soldiers and crew would sit around in little huddles, while the women cooked and children played. They may well have been talking of harvests, camels or how they would avenge their families, yet to my imagination they were planning our destruction. If one glanced furtively in my direction or at the wheelhouse, then I took that as certain confirmation. Wortley was little better. "Treacherous swine," he muttered towards a junior Sudanese officer in a heated argument with several of his comrades. "They only have to stay loyal for one more day and we are safe."

"When will we pass Wad Habeshi?" I asked.

"If we get underway again by noon," he replied, "we should be there around three this afternoon." He paused and there hung a heavy stillness between us. I could not help but wonder if I would be dead, drowned or locked up in a cage by four, and I am sure he was thinking the same.

When we set off again, there was an air of tension on the ship that you could cut with a knife. The twenty-five British soldiers on board the *Bordein* were outnumbered four to one by the Sudanese soldiers, and there were many more of them in the nuggar and the felucca on tow behind. Even if they were not planning to participate, I was sure that every one of them had heard of the offer of a pardon to sink us in front of the guns. This time we did not attempt to hide our suspicion. Wortley

222

and two sentries were posted to the wheelhouse. They had orders to shoot anyone who tried to interfere with the helmsman or the man at the wheel himself should he steer towards an obstacle. The anxious crew member stood with the Bordein's captain to his left, Gibril to his right and Wortley with his revolver just behind him. Two more sentries guarded the entrance to the engine room, with a third inside to keep watch on the engineers. Unused to the extraordinary heat of the chamber, he was regularly rotated with his comrades outside to avoid him fainting. More British troops were stationed in the gun turrets, which became small fortresses from which to oversee the rest of the ship's complement. The Sudanese studied this new hostility with a wariness of their own. Khashm roamed the decks, assuring all who would listen that the British would be victorious. Then they would avenge family members killed or taken prisoner.

With the help of the current, we made good speed downriver. The banks either side, lined with abandoned fields, trees and the desert beyond, fell back behind us, marking every mile of progress. The Nile was broad now, dotted with islands and mud banks, but the water level was still getting lower. Rocks now protruded from the surface, their presence betrayed by ripples in the current. I had decided to place myself in the wheelhouse too, my own revolver safely in my pocket. If there was to be an attempt to take over the ship, I thought, it would happen there. I would do everything I could to make sure I got home. Wilson and Khashm were there too. It was so crowded that Leila had to sit outside, where she watched for any sudden moves among the rest of the crew. But they stayed as passive as the tethered goats kept for milk on the aft deck.

We had been steaming for an uneventful three hours when we rounded a broad, sweeping bend. The river ahead was ruler straight for several miles.

"Wad Habeshi is a couple of miles ahead on the left bank," called out Wilson consulting the chart. I stared ahead but could see nothing through the heat haze.

"I will walk around the deck," announced Khashm, "to ensure that everyone remains calm."

"I will come with you," said Wilson. I wondered if he was having last-minute fresh doubts about his fellow officer's loyalty. "It will be helpful for everyone to see that we are united." Standing to one side, I made room for them to leave the small wheelhouse.

It would take half an hour for us to get up to the guns. Whatever was about to happen would occur soon. Exchanging a glance with Wortley, I noticed him open the flap on his revolver holster for easy access to the weapon. Instinctively, I felt my own pistol through my jacket pocket.

For a quarter of an hour nothing happened at all. We steamed on right in the middle of the river. There was still no sign of Wad Habeshi, but remembering the gun emplacements and trenches we had seen on the way upriver, there would be little to see until we were right on top of it. I wondered if the *Bordein* would be more visible to the enemy. Would they be watching a smudge on the otherwise flat river and loading their pieces in readiness?

To this day I still do not know if what followed was by design or accident. It began when we spotted a rock in the river a quarter of a mile ahead. It was barely the size of a man's head protruding above the surface. The *Bordein*'s captain muttered something in Arabic to the helmsman and pointed to the left of the rock. There was a wide expanse of river there between the obstruction and the bank. As the man began to turn the wheel, Gibril stopped him and pointed to the right. On that side was a narrower channel between the rock and a mudbank, with an island full of vegetation between the mud bank and the eastern edge of the river. The two captains began to argue with increasing passion, while the helmsman stared from one to the other, without moving the wheel an inch.

"Quickly, make a decision!" I shouted to make myself heard.

The captain of the *Bordein* turned and pointed again to the left side. "There is clearly more space to manoeuvre over there."

"Nonsense," countered Gibril. "That water is wide and shallow. We would run aground for certain. To the right the island forces the river to run faster around it and the channel will be deeper."

I stared ahead; the rock was barely a few hundred yards away and we were still heading straight towards it. We had to steer away immediately

224

– there was no more time for argument. Wortley was ahead of me there, for he drew his revolver and pointed it at the helmsman. "Change course now!" he shouted. I doubt the crewman understood English, but the meaning was clear. His face was transfixed with terror as he glanced at the big barrel pointing at his head and turned to his front where both captains were still shouting different orders at him in his own language. In the end he just gave a wail, clutched his head and sank to his knees, leaving his superiors to resolve the situation. Gibril reacted first, hauling the wheel hard in his direction and growling when his rival tried to intervene. To this day I still don't think they were acting. Wortley's pistol swayed from one captain to the other, unsure who to trust. I had no idea who was right either and hung on to a rail as the ship heeled hard over. Gibril was swinging the wheel to starboard as fast as he could. I thought we would make it. Then everything happened at once. The deck jolted hard under my feet and I heard an agonising screech of metal.

The sound vibrated up from the bowels of the ship. The *Bordein*'s captain gave a howl of despair, as though it was his side that had been pierced. Men were shouting and screaming on the deck below. I glanced out of the port window. The boulder was still ten yards off, but there must have been a reef of rock below. I knew with horrible certainty that we were fatally damaged. My vainglorious hopes of journalistic fame were dashed. Never had my colleagues in Fleet Street felt so far away. I felt sick as the implications of that split second in time rushed in. What would we do now? Was death in a coming battle the best I could hope for? I had a sudden vision of myself cowering in a cage like a tortured dog, perhaps blinded or mutilated for their entertainment. Maybe they would drag me before a mob, before hacking off my head. All this flashed through my mind in less than a second, as with a sickening squeal, metal plates buckled beneath my feet.

I shook my head, bringing me back to the present. Gibril was still holding the wheel hard over and our bow was swinging across the channel towards the mud bank beyond.

"What are you doing?" shouted Wortley, raising his pistol again. "You are running us aground," he accused, answering his own question.

"We are sinking, the ship is holed," Gibril snapped, ignoring the gun. "Look behind you, the engine room is flooding." He was right. Clouds of steam were coming up out of the engine room hatch, as Nile water reached the hot boiler.

Wortley turned back to me, gaping for a moment as he tried to think of something sensible to say. "What the hell do we do now?" he came to at last.

It was a damn good question. Despite all our best endeavours, we were shipwrecked less than a mile upstream of the enemy battery. We were still forty miles south of the British camp and with a crew even more inclined to mutiny. They would see that there was no hope left and throw in their lot with the enemy to save themselves. I swore volubly, particularly when I heard some of the Sudanese on the deck cheering our disaster. They must have thought it was down to an act of sabotage. Who knows, perhaps it was. By the time Wilson rushed up the ladder to the wheelhouse, the bow of the vessel was just rising as it slid gently onto the mud.

"It was a hidden rock shelf," announced Gibril to the colonel, neglecting to mention the visible rock we had seen in advance. "On the mud we will not sink and we can inspect the damage."

"Quite so." Wilson's face was taught, only just containing his frustration and anger. His thoughts must have followed a similar journey to my own. Yet while I could easily have wept with despair, he remained outwardly calm and professional. "Although I very much doubt we will be given the opportunity to make repairs," he added before turning to his aide. "Wortley get everyone ashore. We can move from the mudbank across to that island. Set up work parties to remove the guns and ammunition – I have a feeling we will need them." Even through my own disappointment, I could not help but be impressed with Wilson then. There was no pointless recrimination or rage, just a calm assessment of what needed to be done.

When I got down on the main deck, I found Leila gathering our few possessions. Already people were lowering themselves over the side on ropes down onto the bank. Several had been knocked over and wounded in the collision. The soldier who had been in the boiler room was having

226

his scalded hands and face bandaged. One of the stokers had been less fortunate, his body was covered by a tarpaulin and Leila warned me not to look at him. "What happens now?" she asked anxiously.

"We will think of something," I replied. It was a bland assurance that carried no conviction whatsoever. "Let's get off this damn ship."

The vessel had heeled over on its undamaged side and in the end we lowered ourselves over the rail and dropped the few feet down into the soft mud. By the time I had extricated my boots from the stinking ooze, most were making their way across the bank and splashing through the shallow channel to the island beyond. The nuggar behind us was also disgorging its complement while the felucca had anchored in the channel. I wanted to look at the damage first, perhaps I still harboured the hope that the *Bordein* could be salvaged. I found Wilson there ahead of me and saw instantly that even this slim hope was futile. Three of the hull plates were bent, the middle one badly. There were gaps between them I could put my hand in.

Behind Wilson, several hundred yards across the river, a small group of Mahdist horsemen were reining up, evidently curious to see what had happened. I waited a few seconds but as Wilson did not seem aware of my presence, I splashed a foot noisily in the water and asked, "What are we going to do now?" horribly aware that I might not like the answer.

"Ah, Harrison," Wilson looked round and then frowned in irritation as a rifle fired behind us. Instinctively, I ducked but the bullet must have hit the mud somewhere. "I was just considering that myself," he continued. "Unless you have any other suggestions, I think we have two options."

I was astonished that he had come up with two ideas, never mind one. To me the situation was utterly hopeless. "No, I have no suggestions," I confirmed.

"Well, their guns and the main enemy force is on the western bank." He glanced at his watch. "It will be dusk in a couple of hours. We could use the cover of darkness to march north. We are just forty miles away from the British camp but there are a number of issues." He began to count them off on his fingers. "Firstly, I think that most of the Sudanese will abandon us and so we will be a pitifully small party. Secondly, we

227

will have to leave behind the larger guns and only take ammunition we can carry. There are also some wounded, which will slow us down." Several more rifles cracked behind us, but he took no notice. "Finally, the enemy will soon realise we have gone and will anticipate our direction of travel. I rather think they will do all they can to stop us escaping."

"We have seen some of their cavalry patrols on this side of the river," I offered. "Perhaps infantry too as all the villages we have passed have been abandoned."

"I dare say their horsemen will try to pin us down until reinforcements arrive," agreed Wilson. There was a clang as a Mahdist bullet finally managed to hit the metal hull of the *Bordein*. He gave a wry smile and added, "Although if it takes them this long to hit a ship, never mind a man, we might pull through after all."

It seemed to me that the Mahdi had set his sights on having us as prisoners, perhaps to deter the rest of the column from attacking. I did not see him letting us slip through his fingers so easily. "What is the other option?" I asked.

"We send a boat downriver tonight. With luck it will reach the British camp by nightfall tomorrow to let them know of our plight."

"Would they march a force up the eastern bank to support our retreat?" I asked as another bullet clanged into metal nearby.

"No. I was thinking that Lord Beresford might bring up the *Safia* to collect us. It would mean him steaming past the guns at Wad Habeshi twice, but I think that is our best chance."

"It would take him two days steaming against the current to get here. So we would need to hold out here for at least three days," I pointed out.

"Quite so," he agreed, then he noticed another figure standing respectfully beside the bow of the ship. "Ah, Jarvis, how is the unloading going?"

The sergeant saluted. "Mr Wortley's compliments, sir, but it will take at least another two hours." He glanced over his shoulder and added with barely contained rage, "Quite a few of the heathens have chosen this moment to desert us, sir. They are streaming across to the far shore as we speak."

"That may be for the best," Wilson smiled wearily. "We want men left we can rely on." There was another clang, this one alarmingly close. "Oh, and Jarvis," he continued, gesturing over his shoulder. "Get four of our best marksmen to see off those horsemen, will you?"

By the time I was back on the bank, two of the horsemen lay still on the ground and the rest were saddling up to ride off. However, with our riflemen lying prone, taking careful aim, I doubted that they would all get away.

By nightfall the two guns had been unloaded and much of the ammunition. Leila and I joined the procession of those carrying it to the new camp on the island. The land was covered in tall reeds, well over head height, and paths had been trampled to a newly made clearing in the centre. Throughout the evening more men had been slipping away; there were now little more than a hundred left. Some of the remaining Sudanese still looked undecided as to their loyalties. Khashm was still there along with Gibril and his fellow captain, who looked to be continuing their argument from earlier. Wortley had been detailed to pick the best of the lifeboats on the *Bordein* and six oarsmen to go downstream.

"I have found half a dozen crewmen who can handle an oar," he told Wilson later, "but I would not trust one of them now. The bastards are just as likely to rush me, then row up to the dock at Wad Habeshi and hand me over."

"You have your revolver," Wilson reminded him sternly. "I will need all the soldiers to defend our position here." We were standing at the edge of the island. The end of the lifeboat poked out of the reeds and beside it the suspect sailors sat in a circle on the ground. They were muttering to each other, and one shot a dark look in our direction. It certainly was not friendly. I was glad that I was not going with Wortley. Wilson must have seen it too, for he strolled to the edge of the water and stared downstream, where a glitter of distant torches marked out the location of Wad Habeshi. He looked back at the small rowing boat and must have reflected on the hopes of all of us that it would carry. Finally,

229

he reached a decision. "You can have four of the soldiers," he announced. Then he looked back at the oarsmen and added quietly, "Don't hesitate to shoot them if you have to. With four men you might have to take the oars yourselves."

They all set off half an hour later. At the front of the small cutter the six Sudanese pulled steadily at the oars, while Wortley sat in the stern with the tiller to steer. Near his legs four soldiers sat on the bottom of the boat, their rifles resting on the seat thwarts. The idea was that by sitting low they would be less likely to put a bullet through the craft should they have to fire. With the muzzles pointing at the oarsmen, the level of distrust within this critical group was clear.

We whispered messages of good luck as they pulled slowly away from the bank. There was not much of a moon, just enough to glint on the surface of the water. The boat was like a black hole in the ripples until it was too small to see. Wilson had gone off to try and improve the defences of the camp, but that was like trying to stop water leaving a sieve. The thick bank of reeds that surrounded it might stop the enemy from seeing us, but it also prevented us from seeing the enemy approach. Anyone could slip unseen in and out of the plants with ease. Already one soldier had been shot at by a nervous sentry after strolling out of the camp for a shit. The bullet had whistled inches past his head. New orders were issued that no one was to fire unless they were absolutely certain we were under enemy attack. The gunfire would give away our position and we wanted the Mahdists to assume we were marching down the eastern bank.

I had remained by the river enjoying a few minutes of cool solitude after the heat and drama of the day. The continuous rasp of crickets and frogs nearby was interspersed by distant hoarse whispers and shouts of men stumbling about in the reeds. The island was already a maze of narrow paths between the tall stems. Especially in the dark, it was easy to lose your way. Several cooking fires had been set up and the smell carried on the breeze. I doubted that we would fool the enemy for long. They would only have to send someone within a thousand yards of us to discover we were still here.

I had just heard a loud splash in the water and was wondering if there were crocodiles in this stretch, when I saw a distant flicker of light. It was a flurry of muzzle flashes from the direction of Wad Habeshi. Less than a second later the sound of gunfire reached me. I watched closely for any return of fire from the river but there was none. Did that mean that Wortley was not giving away his position as the oarsmen bent their backs to get them away from danger? Or did it mean that the fragile craft had been smashed, along with our hopes for rescue? I cursed the darkness, for there was no possible way of knowing.

Chapter 21

Dawn revealed that there had been another reduction in our number overnight. Surrounded by reeds and with the eastern bank within wading depth, it was ridiculously easy to slip away. Some had evidently taken the cover of night to do just that. There were less than eighty in the camp when the sun came up, including the reduced company of twenty British soldiers. Eighteen of those still in the camp were the wounded. Most, like the scalded British soldier, were able to walk and probably fight, but six were on stretchers. Khashm was still there and Gibril, but the other captain had vanished. It was a pathetic force with which to fight off a Mahdist army. Wilson had posted a lookout on the edge of the island that night, but the man had absconded by morning.

"Do you think we should move?" I asked Wilson. "There is no cover here. The reeds will not stop a bullet but will get in the way of us seeing the enemy. If they were to get on the island, they could drive us back until we are in the river."

"We will be spotted for certain on shore," he replied. "If we stay hidden, they may believe we have gone north along the eastern bank. It is what they would expect us to do."

"That is if some treacherous deserter has not sold us out," I grumbled. "It might buy them a pardon and some of them know about Wortley and the plans to bring the *Safia* to our rescue."

"If Wortley got past the guns last night, we only have to hold out here a couple more days." Wilson ran his fingers through his hair, which I would swear had gone greyer since we had embarked on this voyage. "Christ, I know the odds are slim, they are for every option, but we have made a plan and now we must stick to it. If they do bring that ship back, they will expect to find us here. We cannot be trapped away from the river."

I was feeling bitter at the prospect of a much more personal desertion: Leila was talking of leaving as well. She had come to me that morning to announce her intention to depart. Even though I had known that this was the purpose of her accompanying me, somehow I had never really accepted that it would happen. "You cannot be serious," I protested.

"You know that women cannot travel anywhere under the Mahdi's rule unless they are accompanied by their husband or male relative. You will be seized at the first settlement you come to, and heaven knows what would happen to you then."

"I must go. You British are retreating; every day takes me further from my brother."

"Your brother will never leave his beloved Mahdi while the man is victorious. Wait until we come back with the army, then the boot will be on the other foot. A few defeats inflicted on his precious prophet and he might see some sense."

"How do I know you British will come back now your General Gordon is dead? You told me that your Mister Gladstone did not want a war. Perhaps he will send his men home."

We continued in this vein for a while. Although I did not admit it, I was not sure what Gladstone would do when he discovered the fate of Gordon. All I cared about was not losing Leila. She was capable enough, but I was sure she would not survive on her own. Her mere existence as a single woman was cause for suspicion now. We could not trust any of the Sudanese to accompany her. Fond of her though I was, there was no way in hell that I would return to Khartoum as her companion. Even if I did, my pale skin and European ways would immediately arouse suspicion. No, she had to stay and so I continued to pile on the dangers, although in truth little creativity was required. She could see what a precarious business it was, but still felt obliged to try. In the end I persuaded her to delay for a day or two to see what transpired. Yet she swore that if the *Safia* did make it back, she would not go aboard.

The day was spent expanding the space of the central camp so that it was one clearing rather than a series of pockets. Reeds were then stacked over rudimentary shelters to provide some shade. Wilson had a party of men move the six-pounders across the island, so that they covered the approach from the eastern bank. It was tiring work with so few to help. Our leader also insisted that no fire could be lit until nightfall, to avoid giving away our position. Yet by late afternoon we discovered that at least some locals knew we were still there. Our deserters must have reached a nearby settlement and told them and now a deputation of village elders arrived on the eastern bank. Wilson did not want them to know how few we were and so sent Ibrahim to speak to them. He soon came back to say that they were asking to speak to Colonel Khashm, who they knew travelled on Gordon's steamers. Wilson nodded his assent; by now Khashm was probably the only Sudanese on the island that he entirely trusted. I decided to go along as well, but not just out of curiosity. I was hoping to learn some information that would deter Leila from leaving.

There were three of them, grizzled greybeards wearing the heavily patched nightshirts that signified their support for the Mahdi. They all *salaamed* profusely when they saw Khashm. I realised that he was a widely respected leader in the region. Through Ibrahim's whispered translation, I learned that they were apologising for having changed sides, explaining that they had been given very little choice in the matter. They were happy to answer Khashm's questions and confirmed that there was a large garrison at Wad Habeshi on the western bank, with a few boats that would allow troops to cross. There were also several bands of Mahdist cavalry patrolling the eastern shore, but none nearby. Khashm asked about Wortley's boat and was informed that it had been spotted and fired upon, but the soldiers had lost sight of it in the darkness. I asked if any bodies had been found the following morning, but was told that if there were any, they would have been carried miles downstream by the current.

I had been more than a little apprehensive about stepping onto the eastern bank of the Nile. The elders wore enemy dress and I feared they might have other soldiers nearby. It was soon clear, however, that their real loyalty was to Khashm rather than the prophet. They gave him all the information he wanted and made no enquiries about our strength. They even brought two sheep to feed us. As they prepared to leave, I asked how easy it would be for a woman to travel to Khartoum on her own. They all looked surprised at the question but were emphatic that such a thing was impossible. Any woman travelling such a distance would need an escort of heavily armed men and even then, might need permission from one of the Mahdi's emirs. I nodded in quiet satisfaction. Surely Leila would have to stay now.

As we waded back to the island, Khashm caught my arm. "Is your pretty companion planning on returning to Khartoum then, Mr Harrison?"

"She wants to, yes," I told him. "Her brother is one of the Mahdi's supporters and she has vowed to her father that she will try to get him back."

"Ah, the obligations of family," he replied. For a moment he said nothing more as we splashed our way on through the shallows and I imagined that he was thinking of his own. My thoughts were confirmed when he continued, "Those men promised to try and find out what has happened to my wife and children."

"Surely we will be long gone before they get news?" I asked.

"Yes, but I have many relatives here, this is my tribal land. One of them will get word to me. Now, would you like me to speak to your companion about reaching Khartoum?"

I thanked him for the offer, and readily accepted, thinking the information would carry far more weight coming from an impartial source.

That evening I lay staring up at the stars and wondering what the future held. If Wortley had got through, then the *Safia* should have started its return journey and would arrive the day after tomorrow. Surely the Mahdists would know where we were by now. Our deserters must have spread the word and cavalry patrols would have confirmed we were not marching north. I was surprised that they had left us alone this long and wondered if they were waiting for the cover of darkness to launch their attack. Something could be heard moving among the reeds, rustling or snapping the stems. Probably rats, although we had seen the marks of a crocodile in the mud too. Tired sentries sat around the perimeter. They would jerk awake from a doze at a noise and then stare glumly into the darkness, until their chins rested on their chests once more. Sleeping on the job was not ideal but they had been busy all day and we did not have enough men to rotate them. Wilson insisted that all rifles were kept unloaded to avoid an accidental discharge.

We had all enjoyed freshly cooked lamb that evening but the fat had dripped on to the burning reeds beneath the spits and the fires had blazed fiercely. Columns of burning cinders had risen into the sky above the glow of the flames. The Mahdists less than a mile downstream would have had to be blind not to see them. I felt certain we would have more visitors in the morning if not sooner.

That night the sky was crystal clear and compared to the day, bloody cold. As I tugged my blanket more tightly around me, I realised that I had got used to the desert nights. Leila lay beside me. We had talked little after her discussion with Khashm. I had hoped he had put her off her quest, but she could be stubborn.

"Do you have the same stars over London?" she asked me.

"Yes, but there are more lights in the city and smoke from chimneys, so often they are harder to see." There were thousands of stars above me, far more than I could see at home. If the scientists were right and they were all other suns like our own, with worlds like ours moving around them, then it made me feel pretty insignificant. I reached out and took Leila's hand and she gripped it tightly.

"I will think of you when I look up at the night sky," she whispered.

"Won't you be with me?" I asked, suddenly alarmed.

"Don't worry," she reassured me. "The colonel told me that I could not possibly travel to Khartoum on my own. I will need to find another way."

After the bustle of previous days, the following morning started with an indolent mood in camp. We had nowhere to go and little to do. I went and sat by the edge of the island where I could look downstream. I had expected to see a flotilla of craft bustling men across, but once more the river was empty. I maintained my vigil for several hours and then I heard voices talking of more visitors. Hurrying back, I learned that another party of local dignitaries had arrived and Khashm was already on his way to greet them. With nothing else to do, I decided to go across too. Now that there were no more desertions, another of the *Bordein*'s lifeboats was being used as a ferry. As it pulled into the far bank, I could hear voices on the other side of a clump of reeds. Pushing through I found over twenty heavily armed men all wearing the patched garb of the Mahdists, but I suspected that they were not true followers of the prophet. They stood grinning in a protective semi-circle around their leader, a woman who was laughing as she embraced Khashm.

"My God, is this your wife, has she escaped?" I blurted out, only to see from a sudden change in their expressions that I was wrong.

"This is one of my sisters," Khashm explained. "She has agreed to go to Khartoum to find out what has happened to my family." He paused for a moment, slightly embarrassed. "Might I ask my friend if you have any gold? It will be necessary to pay bribes and perhaps a ransom for their release. My wealth is lost in the city."

"Gold?" I repeated. "No, I was told to bring silver, but I have twenty large silver dollar coins you are welcome to. Wilson might have some gold."

"You are a good man, Harrison," Khashm beamed. "And if your companion still wants to go to Khartoum, she can accompany my sister. With her bodyguards, they should reach the city safely."

My jaw must have gaped as this was absolutely the last thing I wanted to hear. For a moment I wondered if I could keep this offer to myself, but I knew Leila would of course find out, and then she would never forgive me. If she had to go then this was the best way to reach the city, but at the forefront of my mind was the question: How the hell would she get back?

Later, back at the camp, Leila had jumped at the opportunity as I knew she would.

"My brother will help us return," she replied simply as she packed her possessions to join the shore party.

"But what if he does not want to leave?" I pressed. "You must admit that is a strong possibility."

"He is my brother. I protected him when he was little, he will protect me now. I am sure he will respect our father's wishes and return. When the waters of the Nile rise again there will be many boats taking goods north and we will travel on those." She sounded confident but then our eyes met and I saw her tears. She flung her arms about my neck, leaving my cheek wet as she whispered in my ear, "If Allah wills it, I will return. Tell my father what has happened when you get back to Cairo."

By the time we made it back to the eastern shore, the party of visitors had grown even larger. I was introduced to a man called Faqi Mustafa, who was the husband of one of Khashm's cousins. He was a garrulous fellow with a large red turban, and was delighted to meet one of the infidels. He was curious to know how many soldiers we had left and laughed when I told him it was over a hundred. He asked why we had not surrendered. "You must know that there is no escape," he boasted. "Our forces surround you and will soon drive all of the British out of Sudan. But for you there is a simple solution," he insisted. "If you lay down your arms and pledge loyalty to the prophet, he will be merciful." I told him we would bear that in mind.

Khashm came to my rescue by explaining that infidels took a while to accept when they are beaten. "Come back tomorrow," he advised, "and they may be willing to negotiate."

I thought no more about the man as I bid farewell to my companion and lover of many months. She had been far more than a guide and even though she wanted to go, I could not help but feel a sense of foreboding. Khashm's sister promised me that Leila would be protected until they reached the city and they had found her brother. That gave me little comfort, as by all accounts the brother was a religious fanatic. Heaven knew how he would treat his more worldly sibling. I gave her a final embrace and watched as she mounted a spare horse and trotted off down the track that ran parallel with the riverbank. As she disappeared behind the final bend, I confess that there was a tear in my eye too. I felt certain that I would never see her again.

Wilson was making tea when we returned to the camp. "Has your sister set off for Khartoum?" he asked Khashm, pulling forward two extra tin cups and starting to fill them.

"Yes, and thank you again for the gold. I pray it will see the release of any of my family that have survived," he replied, accepting one of the cups.

"Well, you certainly have enough family members around here," I told him before turning to Wilson. "I met the husband of a cousin earlier. A nosey blighter, who wanted to know how many soldiers we had."

"I trust you did not tell him," Wilson said, taking a sip of his brew.

"That 'nosey blighter' is the commander of the Mahdist forces at Wad Habeshi," Khashm informed me calmly. I could barely believe what I had just heard. The splash of tea being spat out on my left, indicated that Wilson felt the same.

"Are you telling me," he spluttered, "that you have been negotiating with the enemy?"

"He is my cousin's husband. What am I supposed to do when he visits but talk to him?" asked Khashm reasonably.

"Kill him or take him prisoner?" suggested Wilson in bewilderment.

"He would simply be replaced and he is far more useful alive," Khashm explained. "He is a boastful man and told me that a force to capture us has left Khartoum, marching down the eastern bank, but it will take another two days to get here. Faqi would like us to surrender to him, rather than a rival emir. He would earn much credit with the Mahdi if we did. I told him that you would need time to accept that you have no choice. He has few boats to cross the river and I think he will give us at least another day before he tries to force the situation." He turned to me and added, "Our deserters have already told him how many soldiers we have."

Wilson and I exchanged a glance. I was wondering now if we had been right to trust Khashm and I could see that he felt the same. The Sudanese man saw the look and laughed. "Do not worry, gentlemen, I have no intention of surrendering and neither should you. My sister tells me deserters have reported my treachery and I would be killed for certain. Your fate might be even worse."

"What on earth do you mean?" I asked, before regretting it. I had a horrible feeling that I did not want to know the answer.

"After their defeats to your army on the Nile, rumours have spread among the Mahdists that your men are *djinn*, demons who cannot be hurt by bullets. One of their leaders has vowed to flog some of your soldiers to death before their army, so that they can see you bleed and beg for mercy as they would."

"Christ," I muttered. "Just when you think the situation cannot get any worse it plumbs new depths." I could not help but imagine being triced up for the lash in front of a baying enemy. The searing pain and agony, knowing that there would be no pity. How it would get steadily worse as your back was flayed off your body until you expired. By contrast, being torn apart by a mob and beheaded, felt quite merciful.

"Well, I will not be taken alive," Wilson whispered while his fingers unconsciously brushed against his pistol holster. "We have at least another day and God willing Wortley got through with that message." He looked drawn as he added, "If the *Safia* does not come tomorrow, we will put the wounded in the felucca at night to take their chances sailing past the guns. The rest of us will march north along the eastern bank."

It was a grim prospect now that we knew enemies were gathering around us. I mouthed a silent prayer for Wortley and the *Safia*.

Chapter 22

You will not be surprised to learn that I did not sleep well that night. My imagination was filled with images of flesh turned into ragged offal. I thrashed about in my sleep and woke tangled in my blanket. As soon as it was light, I got up and made my way to the shore. I stared downriver more in hope than expectation, but the Nile was as empty as it had been the day before. Despondently, I returned to the camp where the others were stirring. The embers of the fire were re-kindled, we did not have to worry about smoke now, for everyone knew where we were. More reeds and sticks were piled on and soon a kettle was readied for tea. There was not much for breakfast as provisions were running low and Wilson was rationing what we had left in readiness for our march north. "We will leave at dusk," he was announcing, before he was rudely interrupted.

"Quiet, please sir, quiet." It was the youngest soldier with us, a lad who had barely started shaving. That he had so spoken to a colonel caused several to stare at him in astonishment. I saw the sergeant inhaling in indignation to deliver a reprimand, but Wilson held up a hand to quiet him. We were all listening now and then I heard what the boy's sharper hearing had detected. At first I thought it was coming from the kettle but that was some way from boiling. It came again and this time there was no mistake: it was a steam whistle.

"The *Safia*!" someone shouted but we were already on our feet and charging off towards the gap in the reeds that would give us a view of the river. My hopes, which had plunged the depths of despair the night before, were soaring again as we pushed aside the stems and saw a wonderous sight. A precious vessel, containing all our chances for deliverance, coming around the distant bend. Men were cheering, hats were thrown in the air. There was certainly a tear in my eye as I put my arm around Wilson's shoulder and declared, "Thank Christ, we are saved!"

Beresford was still sounding the whistle as though his life depended on it, which gave the Mahdists plenty of warning of his approach. Abruptly, there was a rumble of gunfire from the shore, with an immediate reply from the turrets of the *Safia*. We could hear the Gardner gun too, as it sprayed bullets over the enemy trenches and gun positions. Soon the western side of the vessel was wreathed in smoke but we could see its eastern wheel thrashing the water and a wave at its bow as it pushed towards us against the current.

"Do you think Wortley is aboard?" Wilson shouted to me above the cheering men. "He should be able to tell Beresford where we are."

"He need only look through his field-glasses," I replied, "and he can spot them himself." I gestured over my shoulder where half a dozen of our soldiers were waist deep in the river and waving their jackets over their heads. A proud naval officer, Beresford was not coming under the Egyptian flag, which had been replaced with a large white naval battle ensign. As I watched, it dipped slightly as though to acknowledge they had seen us.

"I say," Wilson pointed at the ship, "they have a second Gardner gun aboard – there is barely a pause between firing. We must have had some reinforcements to the camp at Matammeh."

"That will keep their heads dow— Oh no!" The soldiers' cheers immediately died in their throats. We all stared, stricken, as a plume of white steam rose from the centre of the vessel. It was exactly as we had seen when the *Bordein* struck the rock. "They have run aground!" I

241

gasped, stating the obvious, my mind numb with the awful horror. Our plight had been bleak before but to have our hopes raised and then dashed so quickly was a monumental cruelty. The paddlewheel we could see had stopped turning and the gunfire ceased. I could easily imagine the jubilant Mahdists cheering their latest triumph from the shore. Wilson was struggling to control his emotions and I felt my lip wobble with despair. I did not want anyone to see me weep and turned away for some privacy in the reeds.

"Wait... He has dropped his anchor," announced Gibril. Then, seeing that we had failed to realise the significance of the remark, he went on. "He would not do that if he was sinking, he would use the current to try and beach the ship." It seemed an irrelevant technicality to me – the ship was lost. But then the rattle of the Gardner restarted to signal it still had some fight left. "The ship is not listing," Gibril went on, giving his professional assessment, "I think a shell might have hit the engine."

"Can it be repaired?" Wilson almost whispered the enquiry, as though he knew that his own sanity would not survive another disappointment.

"If they have smashed the pistons, probably not," Gibril conceded. "But if it is the boiler then we have plenty of spare boiler plate. We have been using it to armour the ships."

"Those heathens will never give them the time to make repairs," grumbled one of the soldiers. "They are anchored right in front of the guns."

Wilson's back straightened and he cleared his throat. "Then we will have to go and give them some covering fire. Sergeant, we will break camp and march down the eastern bank until we are just south of the *Safia*. Bring the artillery we have taken from the *Bordein* and as much ammunition as we can carry."

I think we all knew that the task was *almost* hopeless, but when you are on the verge of losing your mind from disappointment, you grasp any slender chance like a drowning man clutching a rope. There was no argument. Men waded out of the river their faces now set in grim expressions of determination. We would do our best to give the *Safia* a chance of getting us away. If she was holed and sunk before she could

242

be repaired, well we would deal with that situation when it occurred. For now, I would not let my mind dwell on that.

I joined the advance party. If anyone did get away, I wanted to be among them. All we were taking were weapons, ammunition and some of the more lightly wounded. I grabbed my pistol and notebook and left everything else. Packs were emptied and filled with artillery shells, I had one with six of the brass cannisters on my back, clinking with every step. Even the wounded were not spared. Taking my turn with a stretcher I found the occupant with a shell in each arm and another two between his legs. Soldiers quickly separated the artillery barrels from their carriages and teams of them dragged or pushed them through the shallows and along the shore.

We had to travel just over a mile down the riverbank. Some tried to go at a half jogging run before the sun made the day too hot. We stuck to the trail through the abandoned fields and date groves, which meant we often lost sight of the *Safia* behind the reeds. Several times we heard bangs and clangs as the vessel was hit and each time my heart missed a beat. Yet those blessed Gardner guns kept up a steady fire to show that a defence was being maintained. I remember stumbling along over that rutted track, a stretcher handle in one hand, shell rims digging into my back, being shouted at by the man holding the handle behind to go faster. He was far fitter than me and I was exhausted, but I kept going. It was cathartic somehow. We ran because we had hope and while there was even the slimmest chance we might live, we would give it our all.

Halfway there we heard a new sound; metal on metal. I thought the first one was the sound of a shell striking the ship, but as the bangs settled into a regular rhythm, I realised it was the sound of a hammer. Someone was beating a metal plate with a hammer. It was the noise of someone making a repair. The ringing sound did more to summon us than any school bell did to a snottering brat. Not only was the *Safia* still fighting back, people aboard her clearly thought that she might once more get underway.

I was battered, bruised and cut from the sharp edges of the reed leaves when we finally pushed through to the riverbank again. The man on the stretcher was weeping from the pain we had inflicted on his broken leg

243

as we had stumbled along, but he was not complaining. Between his tears he thanked us for not leaving him behind, which must have been his terror. Then he stared with watery eyes at what might be our salvation. The *Safia* lay a little to our right, anchored no more than a hundred yards from the bank and over three hundred yards from the far shore. Beresford stood on deck. He was shouting something at us, but it was lost under the sound of gunfire.

Our arrival had not gone unnoticed by the Mahdists and soon bullets were buzzing into the trees above our heads. Their riflemen were well back from the river edge that had been exposed by the fall of the Nile. With no cover, that expanse of mud would have been fatal with the Gardner spraying fire on the shore. Instead, they were firing from the trees, perhaps five hundred yards away. It was a good distance for a marksman, which the Mahdists were certainly not. We had a few sharpshooters and Wilson set them to work picking off any of the fanatics they could find. He wanted our two cannon to open fire as quickly as they could on the enemy guns, as they were the biggest danger to the *Safia*. The barrels were soon being hauled onto the carriages, while I added the shells I had borne to a growing pile beside them.

Upstream, our felucca, carrying the worst of the wounded, and the nuggar were being sailed or hauled towards us. They carried the rest of our ammunition and food supplies, along with the few women and children from the crew still with us. There was barely any wind and they crept forward at a snail's pace.

We opened fire with our six-pounders barely fifteen minutes after we staggered onto the shore. Wilson made sure that every shell was carefully aimed to make the most of our dwindling supply. Several riflemen had climbed up into the fig trees above our heads for a better vantage point and the steady crack of Martini–Henrys showed they were finding their marks. As the only person in the advance party who was not a soldier, I suddenly felt redundant. Then I saw that Beresford was lowering a boat to bring us news.

"I have nothing to do here." I told Wilson. "I will go aboard the *Safia* to update Beresford on our position. Then I shall return to report on progress." The colonel nodded his agreement while privately I thought that once my feet were on a deck again, they would not leave until either the ship was sunk or in Matammeh. As the little boat pulled up on the mud a familiar face jumped out. It was Wortley.

"It is good to see you again, sir," he grinned at Wilson, shaking his offered hand before slapping me on the shoulder. "You too, Harrison. I hope we are giving you enough to write about."

"Enough to fill a book," I smiled back. "What on earth possessed you to return when you were safely away?"

"Someone had to show them where you were," he explained. That was a blatant lie as the listing wreck of the *Bordein* was clearly visible just next to the island. He saw me glance at it and grinned. "Well my men are here too and so this is where I belong."

Wilson cleared his throat gruffly and I wondered if he was feeling the emotion of the moment. "Let me tell you, Wortley," he insisted at last, "that the pleasure at our reacquaintance is all mine. I cannot tell you how much I have worried about whether you got through. But tell me, what is the damage on the *Safia*?"

"A shell has struck the boiler," he explained, "but there are no holes below the waterline. Lord Beresford told me to tell you that we should be underway again before sunset." He paused and looked a little embarrassed as he added, "Mr Benbow, the engineer, thinks that is a little optimistic. Yet he is confident that a repair can be affected, as long as there is no more damage."

"Thank God for that," I breathed, to a hearty "Amen" from several eavesdropping nearby.

A few minutes later and I was being rowed to the ship. Like its sister vessels, the decks were protected by high, thick wooden bulwarks or pieces of metal plate. Bullets thudded into them. Artillery shells were now less frequent as their gunners discovered that any movement around the guns attracted a five-round burst from the Gardners. Yet if I thought I would be able to shelter behind the ship's defences, I had not considered her redoubtable commander.

"Harrison, good to see you," Beresford shook my hand. "We heard you had smuggled yourself away in the convoy. Well everyone will be reading your account when you get back." He laughed and added, "I am pleased to play my part in keeping Fleet Street informed. Now, let me show you around." He showed no interest in Wilson or the rest ashore now helping to defend his vessel. Instead, he proudly introduced some of his gun crews pounding the shore, while boasting that he had had the foresight to bring extra ammunition. He told me that he had insisted on the second Gardner, that had just arrived in camp, being loaded onto the ship, and took me round to see where it was peppering the enemy trenches. "Damn fine weapons," he declared before clapping the gunner on the shoulder. "Travis, that bush to the left of the dead camel. I just saw a muzzle flash. Give it a burst, there's a good fellow."

The gunner traversed his weapon and five of the big rounds were duly despatched, but there was no fall of a body or a wounded man rolling away. I had taken a dislike to His Lordship on our journey up the Nile and was not about to change my opinion now. The man was an ambitious glory-hunter who was damned dangerous to be about. If he had not insisted on showing off his Gardner at Jakdul, pushing it out of the square, Burnaby would not have felt obliged to swing part of the rear face round to cover it. Beresford had lost many of the naval party there and if the square had stayed intact, most would have survived. His boastful tooting of his whistle that morning had cost us the element of surprise. Without it, he may have got past the guns and had everyone on deck blazing at the gunners for the return journey. I did not doubt that he was only showing interest in me to increase his profile in my reports. As things turned out when he published his own memoir, it was so misleading that one of my colleagues forced him to issue a correction.

I ducked as a Mahdist shell finally whistled overhead. Beresford stayed erect as he informed me that for the most part their standard of gunnery had been shocking. "A piece like that with a target less than a thousand yards away should hit us every time," he insisted.

"Well, I am grateful for their sloppiness," I muttered, standing upright again. "I suppose they have killed all the Egyptian gunners they captured along with the guns. They probably have no idea how to calculate the range using the sights."

"It is my gunners keeping their heads down," boasted Beresford. "They are firing blind."

"Well, they had one lucky hit," I reminded him. "How are the repairs coming along?"

"I have told Benbow I want to be underway again by four," replied Beresford. He glanced at his watch, noting that it was noon, then added, "That should give him more than enough time."

Taking my leave of His Lordship, I decided to look in the engine room myself. I saw instantly that Wortley was right; we would not be steaming anywhere that afternoon. There was a hole the size of a human head in one of the hull plates and, opposite it, a jagged opening the width of a fist in the side of the boiler. There was now a large funnel in this hole and a chain of crewmen were filling the boiler with river water. Next to them a fat, sweating man was swearing at them for getting in his way as he tried to drill a new hole near the breach. I waited for him to take a moment to catch his breath, noting that three more drill points were marked in chalk around the opening, before I stepped forward. "How long will it take to repair?" I asked.

The man wiped sweat from his brow and growled, "Tell His Lordship that it will be ready when it is ready." Then he turned to look at me and I saw his eyes widen in surprise, "You are new here?"

"Yes, I was with Wilson on the *Bordein*." I grinned sympathetically at the damage and added, "He was not sure about Beresford's estimate of an afternoon sailing and sent me to check."

"It is the heat that is the problem now," the engineer explained, putting down his drill. Even to someone used to the midday Sudanese sun, the little engine room had felt like a furnace as I had gone down the little ladder. He stepped out of the way of more men carrying buckets and held out a hand. "Henry Benbow," he introduced himself. "We already have a plate cut and bent for the repair," he pointed to a rectangle of steel with a hole in each corner. "But it needs to be fitted from inside the boiler and no one would survive going in there now." I held out my hand near the side of the great metal cylinder and knew that I would be scalded if I touched it. "We are filling it with water to draw out the heat. Then when it is bearable, we will send someone in. They will have to hold the plate to the hole and feed through the four bolts for us to tighten."

"But how can anyone get in?" I asked. The only opening I could see was the firebox and that was far too small for a man.

"We have a boy who will do it," Benbow explained. "We will cover him with grease and he should be all right." He must have seen my astonished expression and grinned. "Yes, all our lives hang on the courage of a Sudanese urchin. I doubt His Lordship will mention that in his report."

At four o'clock Beresford insisted an attempt was made to repair the boiler. "If we don't get it fixed now, then we won't have a chance of getting steam up and being underway by nightfall. In the dark we will not be able to keep the heads of their gunners down. They could do even more damage by dawn." He waved a large silver coin at the Sudanese boy and promised him another if he got the plate and bolts in place. The boy looked with avarice at the money and then in fear at the small black hole he would have to enter. We had filled and emptied the boiler twice by then with Nile water, but it was still hot to the touch. Putting my hand in, the space felt like an oven, but regardless, the lad was covered in grease and two stokers tried to insert him into the opening headfirst. He was screaming before he was halfway in, wriggling about and slipping from their grip.

"It is still too hot," Benbow announced, putting his own hand into the opening. Beresford looked set to object, but the engineer cut him off. "If the lad passes out and dies in there, we will all be dished too. There is no one else on board who will fit through the opening. We will just have to flush it again to cool it down." We could all see the sense in that argument and the naval commander gave a slow nod of acquiescence before climbing back up the ladder.

It took another two hours to cool down that boiler. We filled it twice more and poured gallons more water over the top to carry away some of the heat. As we worked the sun slowly crept down towards the western horizon, behind the Mahdist positions. The enemy knew that they were harder to spot now as our gunners squinted into the light and they became bolder. Rifle fire increased. Wooden planks had been hammered over the hole in the ship's side but they would not stop a shell. Indeed, one hitting that spot again would send a storm of splinters across the engine room that would probably kill us all as well as further damaging the boiler. But they were sufficient to stop a bullet, we could hear the slugs thumping into them. We had left a small gap to lower buckets into the Nile and twice we had to duck as bullets came through and ricocheted around the confined space. It was a miracle that none of us was hit. Then we heard the boom of one of their artillery pieces. Heaven knew where the shell went, for it did not strike the ship, but it served to remind us that time was limited.

"It is time to try again," Benbow announced after putting his bare arm deep into the boiler. I had done the same and while still warm it was no longer oven hot. The boy was shown his coin and reminded what had to be done. He had been greased again and this time had rags tied around his knees and feet to protect them. He said he wanted to climb in himself rather than be 'posted' by others and the engineer agreed. We watched anxiously as another shell whistled overhead while he slithered in. Finally, his little body disappeared and Benbow passed him the plate and a satchel with the four bolts and a couple of spares in case he dropped one. I moved to my station by the breach with orders to grab a bolt when it was fed through one of the drilled holes. I was to hold it, literally as though my life depended on it, until a nut was secured to its end.

We could hear the boy clanking around inside the chamber. He was still shouting that it was hot, but at least this time he stayed in. Then we finally saw his sweating face through the hole before our view was blocked by the plate. It was a struggle for someone so small to hold the heavy repair in place and insert the first bolt. We heard a wail and a clank as the first bolt fell onto the now darkened floor of the boiler but at last I saw a screw thread start to protrude through one of the holes. I grabbed it and pulled it out as far as it would go. With one corner secure it was easier to place the rest and soon I was holding two with another stoker doing the same as Benbow and his assistant started to wind on

249

the nuts. I breathed a sigh of relief as I stepped away and the repair was being secured in place. The boy scrambled out, panting like a dog, and the bolts were fully tightened. Benbow congratulated him on his courage and gave him the half crown. Rarely has a silver coin been so well earned.

We were still congratulating ourselves when Beresford came back down the ladder. "It is done, sir," Benbow reported. "I will have to put some caulking in the join to hold the pressure, but we could have steam up and be under way in a couple of hours."

"Well done, lad." His Lordship gave the urchin a smile of gratitude before tossing him a second coin. Then he turned back to us. "But it is too late now to see where we are going and we can't survive a night of shellfire. They are bound to hit us eventually."

"So what are we going to do?" I asked.

He looked surprisingly pleased with himself as he announced, "The enemy is watching us abandon ship right now."

Gasps of shock echoed around the engine room.

"We cannot abandon the ship now it is fixed," insisted Benbow.

"We will never make it back by land," I agreed. "They have cavalry on the eastern bank, which will slow us down and a big army is only a day away marching north from Khartoum."

"Don't worry, gentlemen," smiled Beresford, "we are not really abandoning the ship. We just want the enemy to *think* we are, so that they do not pepper us with fire all night. We cannot embark Colonel Wilson's party here under fire and so they are currently marching north, with plenty of burning torches so that the Mahdists can see they are leaving. Our own boats are rowing back and forth to the shore to give the impression we are going with them. The enemy will have seen the steam from their shell and think the damage cannot be repaired. We have held them off all day, but they will expect us to try and slip away under cover of darkness." He gestured at the engine, "Do whatever you need to with that, but you must maintain absolute silence. Then I want to be ready to weigh anchor at first light."

"What if they come across during the night to see if the ship really has been abandoned?" I pressed.

"I have had the Gardners destroy every boat we can see." Beresford shrugged, "We will just have to take that chance; it is the best plan I can think of."

None of us had a better idea. If they had their big Krupps artillery firing at us all night, they were bound to score more hits eventually. One shell near the waterline and we really would be sunk. Furthermore, we would be going quickly with the current and there were still rocks and sandbanks, which were near impossible to avoid in the darkness. We could not afford to run aground. I went up on deck to see that the felucca and nuggar had tried to make their way downriver. The smaller sailing craft with our wounded aboard had got away, but the nuggar was aground and in range of the Mahdist guns. Some of its occupants were already swimming or wading ashore.

The enemy was dividing its fire between the nuggar and us, but now that our guns were silent and abandoned, I could only hope Beresford's ruse would work and they would stop their attack on the *Safia*. The lifeboats were visible to our foes on the shore, near a conveniently burning torch. Some of the crew were hidden in bushes nearby and would row them back once the flames had sputtered out.

We all huddled out of sight on the eastern side of the ship. For a while, bullets continued to bounce like raindrops off the metal plates of the other side. Four times their Krupp guns boomed out, one shell creating a plume of water off the bow. A gunner on the deck beside me swore at their incompetence as though his professional pride was offended. I had no idea where the other shells landed, I was just grateful when they gave up. Perhaps their leader, Khashm's relative, wanted to take the ship as a prize in the morning.

It was too dark to see my watch, but it must have been around ten o'clock when they finally relented and the rifle fire slowly sputtered to a halt. It was replaced by the noise of drums and chanting as the Mahdists celebrated their victory, sure that their army would mop us up the following day. Our lookout on the western side, watching the enemy through a bullet hole, reported men dancing and celebrating in front of their fires, and there were no other boats to be seen. On the eastern bank flickering torches marked the progress of Wilson's party as they made their way north. I hoped to God that they did not find an enemy cavalry patrol before we were able to pick them up the following day. Even if they did make it unscathed, we were not out of the woods yet. When the Mahdists realised they had been tricked, they would pour an awful fire in our direction in the morning.

It was another chilly desert night. I lay with the rest of the crew on the deck and borrowed the edge of a blanket, for my own was back on the island. A few of those about me whispered enquiries about what I had seen at Khartoum. I was about to answer before Beresford ordered us all to silence, reminding us how easily sound travels over the water. I laid my head back and stared up at the stars. They reminded me of my conversations with Leila. I could not help but wonder what she was doing. Had Khashm's sister managed to negotiate her way past the Mahdist troops heading north on the eastern bank? If they had, then Leila was likely to reach Khartoum the following day, at which point I suspected her problems would only just begin. Assuming he had not been killed already, how would she find her brother and what reception would she get when she did?

I must eventually have fallen into a fitful sleep, for I was awoken by the sound of whispers. It was still dark. The edge of the blanket I had borrowed had been tugged off by its sleeping owner and I felt frozen. The sound was coming from the engine room. Wriggling my way across the deck, I peered down the hatch. Benbow was there with a couple of stokers and they had lit the boiler, carefully passing logs through the hatch the boy had used and heeding the engineer's instructions to shut the door slowly. "We don't want any sparks going up the funnel," he cautioned, "just a nice slow steady burn to raise pressure."

I swung my legs over the coaming and climbed down the ladder. It was not just for companionship; I was chilled to the bones and the flames of the fire drew me like a moth.

"We will have a brew on in a minute," Benbow whispered as he saw me crouch and hold my hands in front of the fire. "A cup of tea will soon sort you out."

I reached into my pocket for my watch and held it in the light to see the time. It had just gone five. "How long will it take to get underway?" I asked.

"At least an hour. His Lordship wants us moving as soon as there is light to see. Once the sun rises those devils will see smoke coming from the funnel and then the game will be up anyway."

A few minutes later I was comfortably ensconced in the engine room, a hot metal mug warming my hands and the heat from the fire thawing my bones. I had touched the far end of the boiler – the metal was no more than tepid. It would take a long time to produce steam. Benbow had shown me a grubby dial which pointed at the seven o'clock position. He told me it would need to be pointing vertically up before we had enough pressure to get underway. I had a nasty feeling that a tense morning lay ahead.

I kept checking my watch in the glow of the flames and by ten to six the engine room was packed with soldiers, as more had discovered the source of heat. Mugs of tea were passed round as we all watched the dial with almost hypnotic fascination. It had started to creep slowly round the face. There had been a murmur of approval from us spectators when Benbow gave it a tap when it had appeared stuck. It had leapt up to nine o'clock then and was now at half past ten. Yet in the world above us, I knew that the dawn glow of light would soon appear. Unless they were all asleep, the enemy would spot the smoke long before we were able to move.

The boiler was now far too hot to touch. It emanated heat like a massive radiator. Soldiers finished their tea and now quietly went about swapping places with those on deck. I watched a corporal come down the ladder, a blanket around his shoulders. He looked almost blue with cold. Seeing a gap in front of the firebox, he made straight for it and gave a sigh of satisfaction as he sat down on the warm metal plates of the deck. The door of the boiler was pushed to. Without thinking he reached forward with his bayonet and hooked its guard around the edge. Before any of us could shout a warning, he had yanked it swiftly open to stare at the flames.

"Careful with that door," whispered Benbow but before he could caution that it had to be moved slowly the chastened soldier had used his blade to slam it back. There was a clank of metal that sounded as loud as a church bell in the confined space, but it was not this that the engineer was worried about. He ran to the ladder and poked his head out to see that his worst fears were confirmed. "A plume of sparks has just come out of the funnel," he announced, before turning to the soldiers and adding, "You lot, out you go. I think you will be needed in a minute."

"Perhaps they won't see them," suggested a stoker hopefully, but the lie to that statement came immediately with the sudden beating of a drum. I too went up on the deck to check our situation. There was enough of a glow to the east to silhouette the ship, but our outline would be obscured by the dark trees behind us. To the west all I could see was a dark mass of land beyond the edge of the river. The drumming grew louder as the Mahdists' camp rapidly woke up. There were a handful of pinpricks of light as rifles were fired in our direction, but not many as they must have struggled to see us too. Beresford whispered for us to hold our fire and remain silent; he still hoped it might be put down to a false alarm. Men grimly went towards their guns, smelling the woodsmoke in the air above them. We all knew that in just a few minutes the truth would be revealed.

Chapter 23

Dawn comes quickly in the Sudan. Golden fingers spread across the sky and in a few short minutes, night becomes day. For Khashm's relative in charge of the garrison at Wad Habeshi, it was turning out to be a very bad morning. I suspect that he had reported to the Mahdi the night before that the steamer was abandoned. He would have added that our force had been seen heading north on the eastern bank. I remembered his smug features from our earlier meeting. He had probably boasted of the effectiveness of his guns in stopping us and the value of the ship as a prize. Now he was discovering that the ship was far from abandoned and making plans to slip out of his clutches. He rightly guessed that the Mahdi would not take such revelations well.

As soon as it was clear the deception was up, Beresford had our men open fire. We did not care about the rifles; it was their artillery that could stop us leaving. The two Gardners blazed away on the gun pits, while our six-pounders in their turrets also started dropping shells around them. The Mahdists too knew that the Krupps pieces were the only way that they could prevent our escape. The men rushing from their camp hesitated to charge into the maelstrom of fire, even as a familiar emir in a red turban was urging them on. They ran in groups of at least twenty in the hope that a handful would get through. Twice they were cut down almost to a man. Yet by either accident or design, the next attempt had two groups running only seconds apart. While the first suffered a similar fate to its predecessors, our guns were still reloading when the second charged into the pits. The emir was marshalling his men to make more attempts. Standing well away from the guns he was immune from our fire, or so he thought.

"That devil with the red turban on over there," I said, pointing him out to one of our own riflemen, "he is their leader. Can you take him down?" The soldier swung his barrel round and took aim. The rifle fired and I stepped around the muzzle smoke to the disappointing sight of Khashm's kinsman still on his feet. He was staring about him as he must have heard a bullet whip close by, yet he did not take cover – if we escaped he would probably be a dead man anyway. He simply started shouting at another group of men to run forward.

"It is a good distance, sir," said the soldier apologetically as he saw his target through the diminishing smoke. He inserted another cartridge into his Martini–Henry. This time he made a slight adjustment to the gun sight and took careful aim again. Once more the gun kicked into his shoulder, but this time the effort was not wasted. When I looked again, the emir was sprawled on the ground.

When I glanced back at the gun pits, it seemed that the villain might not have died in vain, for the barrel of one of the guns was moving. I watched in horror as the black dot of its muzzle turned to point directly at me. Beresford had seen it too and directed our own weapons to concentrate their fire, but their gunners had the protection of ditches and sandbags. Suddenly, there was the sound of tearing fabric just above my head, and a split second later I saw the muzzle smoke from the gun and then the sound of splintering wood. Turning to the eastern bank I saw the top of a tree tumbling to the ground. It was exactly in line with the ship. Whoever had survived to reach those trenches knew how to use the gun. If he was given the opportunity to reload, I was not sure we would survive. I turned away from the bulwark towards the engine room.

"How much longer?" I shouted to Benbow.

"Five minutes," he called back. "Tell Beresford five minutes."

I found His Lordship sheltering in the lee of the wheelhouse. Unopposed by our fire, the Mahdist riflemen were blazing away – even a poor marksman gets lucky occasionally. Bullets thudded rhythmically into the woodwork and every few seconds the sound of metal on metal would ring out as one hit the armour plate. "Benbow says he needs another five minutes," I gasped, having run up the ladder. "But that gunner seems to have his eye in."

The commander was staring at the shore with his glass. "We can't hit those in the trenches and they must have enough there to reload. We can't stay here like a sitting duck either." He turned to look at me. "Five minutes you say?" He pursed his lips and reached a decision. "We will weigh anchor and drift down on the current. That will upset their aim."

"But what if we run aground? We will be trapped."

"There is that mudbank the nuggar is on a few hundred yards behind us. I will anchor if we get close, but hopefully we will have engines again before that."

I stared aft at the water swirling around the sandbank. I wished Gibril was aboard instead of marching down the shore with Wilson. He would be far better at reading the river than a man used to the sea. Orders were shouted and three Sudanese sailors bravely exposed themselves to fire to haul up the anchor with the capstan. As soon as it was free of mud, I felt us start to move and not a second too soon, for we had barely gone twenty yards when the Mahdist gun fired again. A plume of water splashed up just beyond where the bow of the ship had been. They would not have risked putting their head up above the parapet to see we had moved, but they would now. I was sure this new wily gunner would be traversing his barrel in our direction.

As another bullet thudded into the woodwork just above my head, I decided to return to the engine room. As I dropped from the ladder, my gaze instantly turned to the dial. Even in the gloom I could see the pointer was close to vertical. "Surely we can go now?" I implored. "They have a new gunner on their artillery and the bastard knows his business. It will be too late in a minute; he only just missed with his last shot."

"It is not quite there, we have to wait a little longer," said Benbow, flinching as a bullet struck a metal hull plate behind him. repair. "Ideally we should be waiting for the dial to reach here," he pointed to the two o'clock position. "If we try too soon, we might not have enough power to start the wheels turning and we will just lose pressure for nothing." The door to the firebox was ajar, drawing in a jet of air to feed the flames that I glimpsed roaring away inside. There was nothing to do except stare impotently at the great engine as it built its strength. As two more bullets pinged off the plates outside, I decided to go back on deck. If we took a direct hit, the chances of survival were higher there than trapped in the bowels of the vessel below. Mind you, if we were sunk, those that drowned or who were killed by bursts of steam, might be the lucky ones.

Our two six-pounders were still banging away and I saw an explosion near the enemy guns, but who knew what damage they did to their opposing gunners. We were getting close to the sandbank now and Beresford had dropped the anchor again. He was playing out the chain, intending to pull it back in to reverse our direction and confuse their aim. "How much longer?" he asked tetchily as I returned.

"Just a few minutes more," I replied, deciding not to tell him that the power might not be sufficient even then. To his credit he did not fume or rage at the engineer. He knew that the man was doing his best and fully understood the danger we were in. Drifting downstream had increased the range by fifty yards and we had to hope that that was enough to put them off. The eastern side of the ship was now wreathed in smoke from our guns, but an explosion of mud nearby on the western shore showed that their artillery was still being manned. Clumps of earth fell into the water all around us, a few thudding onto the deck.

Perhaps that prompted Benbow to act, for we heard a clank of metal beneath our feet and a long extended 'chuff' sound. Instantly, the eyes of everyone aboard turned to the great paddle wheels. The movement was almost imperceptible, barely dipping a single bucket. There were groans from the machinery below deck as the power of steam wrestled with the force of the Nile. I am sure I heard the engineer shrieking some very colourful encouragement at his charge. Then there was another chuff and the wheel turned a little more, perhaps two buckets, still far too slow to fight the current. Then just as I thought he had thrown the lever too soon, another chuff, and the wheel moved some more. I think everyone aboard was now holding their breath and staring in fascination. The next chuff pushed the wheel on before it had stopped from its earlier effort and then came another and another as the engine finally settled into a rhythm and the great wheels began a continuous motion. Men all around the deck cheered as they felt the vessel move once more under its own power. Hats were waved, backs were slapped and at least one silent prayer was offered to the Almighty. Beresford shook my hand, his eyes gleaming and perhaps a little tearful in relief. But he knew we were not out of danger yet and yelled at his command to continue firing. The bow was still pointing up stream and there was no room to turn. We would have to go past the guns and turn around just north of the foundered *Bordein*. Then we would head past the guns a final time on our journey back

Fire from our decks was redoubled with everyone determined to keep the heads of our enemies down. The vulnerable paddle wheels were now churning the water with increasing pace and as they battled against the current, the Sudanese crewman hauled in on the anchor chain once more. Soon we were past the point we had spent the night and heading up to the broad expanse of the Nile beyond which we would be out of range of their guns. I stared at the island we had camped on, the place I had thought I might die and breathed a great sigh of relief. We just had to survive one more pass of the guns and then there would be no more gorges or cataracts between us and the British camp. We might be there by the end of the day.

Beresford skilfully used the current to help turn the vessel, while soldiers ran for more ammunition, cleaned gun barrels and readied themselves for the final run. A grinning Benbow stepped up on deck to more cheers and congratulations. Like a proud midwife, he announced to His Lordship that 'full ahead' was now available.

Our commander grinned wolfishly. "With that and the current behind us, we will fly past them. Their gunners will struggle to take aim. Wait for my word, and we will accelerate just as we come into range."

It was less than five minutes later when I felt the pace of the engines increase. Water foamed in the river behind us and we moved along at a cracking pace. If we hit an underwater rock now the bottom would have been torn out of the ship, but there was no time to worry about that. Beresford had a Sudanese helmsman but chose the course himself. He had sailed past the guns before and so knew the channel. Perhaps he distrusted the local pilots after hearing of the fate of the *Bordein* and the *Talahawiyeh*.

The Mahdists knew this was the last chance to stop us and avoid incurring the wrath of their prophet. Gunners showed themselves with reckless abandon as they tracked our progress and tried to align their weapons. They paid a heavy price as the two Gardners swept their trenches with a lethal fire, while our own six-pounders dropped shells in their midst. The soldiers aboard fired through loopholes to pick off their riflemen, who had charged to the riverbank on mass, blazing away with abandon. Dozens must have been shot down. Not having used it earlier, I found a loophole and let fly at them with my revolver, although at that range it would be a miracle if I hit what I aimed at.

Finally, we were past and Beresford changed course to throw a line at the nuggar and pull it off the mudbank. It was tugged off with ease and under tow as we rounded the next bend in the river. Half a mile further on Wilson's party, along with the wounded on board the felucca, was waiting to come aboard. As we rounded the bend and gave a blast on the steam whistle, men ran from the reeds waving and cheering. With a large enemy force marching quickly to catch them, we were their last hope.

Once more we anchored. After the injured men had been carefully unloaded, the felucca took a line back to shore and served as a ferry to bring the rest of the party aboard. Our Gardners pointed out over the reeds should any advance guard arrive to interfere. The decks were becoming too crowded so some men had to climb into the shot-peppered nuggar, but eventually all were rescued. Wortley and Wilson insisted on being the last to embark and shook my hand enthusiastically as they came aboard.

"I can't tell you how good it is to see you again," Wilson said. Then this usually stiffly formal man ignored my outstretched hand and embraced me instead. He held me tight for a moment and you could tell it was a heartfelt sentiment. Just one day earlier, he had been preparing to blow his brains out and now, with hope restored, there was little to stop us reaching the British camp.

His jubilant mood had quietened somewhat by late that afternoon. We had spent the rest of the day steaming steadily north down the Nile. Gibril was with Beresford at the helm and even though the level of the river continued to fall, they had comfortably avoided every obstacle. Each hour took us closer to safety, or at least the security of a thousand well-armed British troops. I spotted Wilson standing alone at the stern rail, staring back the way we had come and could guess what he was thinking. Now the euphoria of rescue had passed, he had to be considering the repercussions of our mission.

"Two days too late," he muttered as he sensed me standing beside him. "Do you think we will ever be forgiven?"

"We were not two days too late," I told him. "Our success in reaching the Nile forced the Mahdi to launch his attack. If we had arrived two days sooner, he would just have launched his attack earlier."

"But the Nile would have been higher then, and the assault might have failed."

"It would not have mattered, for I very much doubt that Gordon would have left with us anyway." I put my hand on his shoulder. "Have you met Gordon? Can you seriously imagine that he would just have jumped aboard the *Bordein* and sailed away with us, leaving all his loyal people behind? We would have been in Khartoum when it was overrun and then we would all have been dead."

"Are you saying that the whole venture was doomed to fail from the outset?"

"We would have needed to arrive in Khartoum in force to drive the Mahdi and his men off to save Gordon. Wolseley's plan was too complicated and too slow. We should have at least run a secondary force from the Red Sea to Berber, with garrisons protecting the wells and a telegraph line to the coast."

"I still feel responsible," sighed Wilson. "I am certain that General Wolseley will hold me accountable for Gordon's death."

He was right there, I thought. This campaign was supposed to be the pinnacle to Wolseley's glorious career. Instead, it had turned into an ignominious failure. The public clamour he had quietly encouraged against Gladstone would now be directed in his direction. I did not doubt that he would look for a scapegoat the minute he heard Khartoum had fallen. Wilson was the obvious candidate.

"You could not have done any more," I assured him. "It is a miracle we reached the Nile at all given the situation of the command you inherited. We certainly could not have got to Khartoum any sooner."

"That emir told us that Gordon was still alive and holding out in a church. You don't think that could have been true, do you?"

"It was bosh, simply an excuse to spread dissent amongst our crew. That other messenger told us that his head was on a pole outside the Mahdi's tent." I felt a pang of sadness as I thought back to my meeting with Gordon on that train. The piercing blue eyes and the way he saw instantly through my deception. Then I remembered the Bible quotation he gave me: *Many are the plans in a person's heart, but it is the Lord's purpose that prevails.*

"Gordon believed that all our futures are pre-ordained. I met him on his way out here…there was a strange calmness to him. It was as though he knew what was likely to happen to him once he reached Sudan. I think he may have decided he was staying with his people even then. He was willing to use his life as a bargaining chip to get Gladstone to do what he thought was the right thing."

"So many died," Wilson sighed. I was not sure if he was referring to the population of Khartoum or the soldiers we had lost on the march and so said nothing. "It is ironic," he went on, "that a man known around the world as 'Chinese Gordon', will now be famous as the martyr of Khartoum."

"A Christian martyr," I smiled sadly. "I rather think that if Gordon had to die, that is exactly how he would like to have been remembered."

Chapter 24

I felt a huge sense of relief as we finally laid eyes again on the British camp near Matammeh just before dusk. Beresford had sounded the whistle as we approached but there was no need, for almost everyone in the camp had lined the riverbank to witness our return. There was no air of celebration; the mood was more one of silent curiosity. Twelve days before they had seen two heavily laden steamers head off, fully expecting them to return with Gordon. After such a long and arduous journey, many had already turned their thoughts to the march back to Cairo, their mission complete. Now they saw just a quarter of those who had set out standing on the deck of a third ship and who only knew what would happen next.

I could see several of my press corps colleagues standing at the end of a rough rock jetty that the gangplank was lowered onto. One of the first ashore, I was soon surrounded by questions.

"What on earth happened to the rest of the rescue party?" demanded Burleigh. "Was there a massacre?"

"Did you see Gordon's body?" pressed MacDonald. "Are you sure he is dead?"

"What is Khartoum like?" asked another.

"Wait, wait…" I held up my hand to stop them. I was tired but pleased that they were not still angry with me after I had slipped away onto the ship on my own. "There was no massacre, and we only lost two Sudanese killed due to enemy action. There are some wounded – one British soldier has a broken leg and another has some steam burns – but they will both recover."

"So where are the rest?" persisted Burleigh.

"They deserted us after Khartoum fell," I explained. "The Mahdi had offered a pardon to anyone who helped sabotage the ships and deliver us to his hands. I dare say they are all now claiming that they had a hand in sinking our vessels. And no, we did not see a body, or get close to Khartoum. It had definitely fallen, though, we were fired on from guns just in front of the governor's residence. Now, what has happened here while I have been away?"

It transpired that I had missed very little. They had heard great celebrations in Matammeh but had not understood why until Wortley arrived the following morning. Beyond the appearance of a small party of reinforcements bringing the extra Gardner, they had just sat around waiting for us to return.

I was soon back in our part of the camp. Rafa had returned and was not surprised when I told him the news of his mistress. She had evidently forewarned him before she had embarked. The big man just quietly went off to fetch me some food, while my colleagues continued a debate they had been having since the news of Gordon's death had reached them: What would happen next?

There were two schools of thought. One group thought that with the relief no longer necessary, Gladstone would order his army home before it incurred more casualties. He had no interest in the Sudan and had only ordered the mission with the greatest reluctance.

Others believed that the murder of a national hero was an affront to our nation's honour that was too great to ignore. "The public will be in uproar," insisted Burleigh, "and they will demand that their government take revenge."

It was a question I had been pondering too, but it seemed to me that the answer was obvious. "We will have no choice but to retreat," I announced. "The boat column is probably only now at the northern end of the bend in the Nile. It will take them weeks more to fight their way past Berber and reach us. The Mahdi will know they are coming. He won't wait for them to arrive, just as he did not wait for us to reach Khartoum. They say he has fifty thousand men. I have seen their camp; it is vast and now even more have joined his ranks. He will want to give them another victory. We heard that he might personally lead his host north to destroy us here. His preaching will turn them all into murderous fanatics. We could not hope to destroy that number. We must pull back." It was a sombre assessment, yet no one could argue against it. Tired, I went to find my blanket, but sleep would not come. I found myself staring again at the stars and worrying about Leila.

All of the next day was spent writing an account of my voyage to rescue Gordon and our escape from capture. It was a tale every newspaper reader would want and it would be exclusive to the *Daily News*. Wilson was due to leave the following day to report personally to Wolseley. He had already told me that he would take my despatch with him. Perhaps he had guessed that he would need every favourable account of our endeavours to reach London to counter the recriminations from the general. As a precaution, I had written two copies: one to be transmitted from the army telegraph at the advance headquarters at Korti; the second went in a mail packet to Wadi Halfa on the border, to be sent by the Egyptian government telegraph.

Boscawen was to take command in the camp and await orders from Wolseley at Korti. No one knew how long we were likely to stay in the camp or in which direction we might march when we left. Supplies were running low and so rations were reduced to eke them out for as long as possible. Each day the smallest steamship with the shallowest draft was sent on patrol up or downriver from our position to look for enemy activity. It got close to Wad Habeshi, but there was no sign of an approaching army on either bank. There was no trace of a rumoured army marching from Berber to the north either. The little vessel would fire a few shells at Matammeh as it passed, but these didn't damage the great walls and usually the garrison did not even bother to reply.

I had been back in the camp a week when we awoke one morning to find hundreds of fresh soldiers marching towards us. They were the Royal Irish regiment and they had come on foot all the way from Korti. One hundred and seventy-six miles in eleven days. They had one camel for every four men to carry water and supplies and they had not lost a single man on the crossing. It certainly proved that Chambois was right – soldiers did not need to ride camels to cross the desert. One person, however, had brought plenty of camels with him: General Buller. Wolseley had sent his right-hand man to take command in the camp and as we had already learned, he did not travel lightly. His champagne supplies might have been diminished, but judging from the crates, not exhausted. He was soon established in a large tent pitched in the centre of the camp and summoning various officers to report. Boscawen emerged from his interview looking understandably crestfallen. It transpired that Wolseley and others at headquarters had been highly

265

critical of the column's inability to capture Matammeh. The colonel had been told to prepare a force to assault the town the following morning. Orders were hurriedly issued and weary men began once again to prepare their weapons.

Somehow Buller and Wilson had passed each other in the desert without one seeing the other. The general was keen to get a first-hand account of the journey to Khartoum and so Wortley was summarily ordered into the big tent. Buller had a formidable reputation, which must have made the young officer apprehensive. The lad was ashen-faced as he left. Burleigh and others had requested interviews with our new commander, but all had been refused. Yet I was not entirely surprised when, late that evening, a stiffly formal staff officer tapped me discreetly on the shoulder. Wortley must have told Buller that I had also been aboard the *Bordein*.

"Brandy?" the general barked at me as I entered his tent. Judging from the prominent red veins in his nose, he had been drinking for a while. I accepted the offer. As he poured the drink, Buller went on, "I understand from Wortley that there is some doubt that Gordon is dead at all. Some story about him being holed up in a church. I am astounded that Wilson did not make certain before he returned."

That, I thought, explained why Wortley had looked so anxious when he had left Buller. The general was searching for evidence to support Wolseley's scapegoating of Wilson. The young lieutenant might have been reluctant to contradict a general, but I had no such hesitation. Anyway, Buller struck me as one of those men who like to push people until they pushed back. "Gordon is definitely dead," I asserted firmly. "We saw that the city, including the governor's residence, had been overrun. Even if he had tried to hold out in a church, they could have blasted it down in a few hours. The most reliable account we had was that Gordon's head was on a pole outside the Mahdi's tent. The story about the church was merely a ruse to try and turn some of the Sudanese soldiers."

"But you did not land to be sure."

"We were being fired on from three sides. It would have been suicidal to attempt to land and it was something of a miracle that both ships managed to get away at all." I took a sip of my drink and looked him steadily in the eye.

Slightly bloodshot eyes returned my gaze. "Yet both ships were later sunk and I gather there were suggestions of sabotage."

I shrugged. "I was on the bridge of the *Bordein* when it struck. I am still not sure if one or both of the two captains colluded in the ship's destruction. One of them deserted with most of the crew, but Gibril stayed with us."

"What about their Colonel Khashm, can he be trusted?" He asked the question casually, perhaps too casually, as he stared at the amber liquid swirling around his glass. Yet there was a tension in his voice now and I sensed that this enquiry might be the reason behind my summons.

"Definitely." I paused as he frowned at the reply and then went on, "Without his ruse we would never have got through the gorge. The Mahdi will certainly know by now that he was deceived. It would be certain death for the colonel should he fall into their hands."

"That is…disappointing." The general was still staring at the contents of his glass and so did not see my eyebrows rise in surprise. Why would an officer's loyalty be disappointing? I sat quietly and waited for an explanation. After a long moment's pause he raised his gaze and continued. "Colonel Khashm came to see me earlier this evening. It seems he is quite well known among their people. One of the garrison of Matammeh crept out to give him information."

"It was probably a distant cousin – the fellow is related to half the country," I put in.

Buller frowned at the interruption and then went on. "He tells me that the Mahdi has just left Khartoum, leading fifty thousand men north up the riverbank on this side of the Nile. They should start to arrive here in little more than a week."

The press corps had speculated on such a move, yet it was still a shock to have it confirmed. Our days on the Nile now seemed to be numbered. "In which case, sir," I suggested carefully, "we should abandon our plans to assault Matammeh. We will need to preserve our fighting strength."

"Surely capturing the bastion is now more important than ever." Generals do not like their strategies challenged by mere correspondents and Buller was no different. "Fighting behind its walls is the only way we can withstand such a force and maintain a stronghold on the Nile for the boat column," he insisted.

"They have already tried an attack. The mud bricks absorb the explosive power of our shells. You would need to use most of the artillery ammunition we have left to create a single breach. Even then it would be defended robustly. Their own artillery is useless, but they can shoot their Remingtons all right. The assault force would lose hundreds dead and wounded simply covering the open ground." Buller stared at me petulantly, clearly unconvinced, and so I tried a softer tack. "We were both in South Africa, sir. I know a British soldier can beat several Zulus and our squares have done the same in Sudan. Some fight with spears here too, but they have far more guns than Cetshwayo's men and they are fired up with religious fervour. They still try to kill you even when they know they are dying, in fact especially when they know they are dying." I paused to let that sink in and then continued. "Even if we captured Matammeh, what would we do then? Do we have enough supplies to wait out until the boats get here? Even if we rebuffed an assault on the town, they would simply capture the wells at Abu Klea and Jakdul to cut our lines of retreat and communication. They could besiege us then as they did with Gordon."

"We could march north to meet the boats," Buller offered. It was a half-hearted suggestion as though he was already imagining the endless ambushes and skirmishes it would entail. With sudden vigour he slammed his glass down on the table and stood, holding out his hand. "Thank you, Harrison, you have given me much to consider. I wish you good night."

As I returned to my blanket I turned back to glance at the tent. The lantern inside revealed the silhouette of a man pacing up and down, lost in thought.

It cannot have been easy for Wolseley's trusted lieutenant to completely ignore the wishes of his chief. It was probably his blind obedience that had helped him reach his present rank and favour. Yet

General Redvers Buller was not slow to address the challenges that faced him. The following morning he announced that all wounded were to be evacuated to Korti that evening. Then he rode out with Boscawen and a small escort to view Matammeh for himself, before convening with the commissary officers to assess our remaining supplies. By noon more new orders were issued. Not only was the assault on Matammeh cancelled, but the whole desert column was to follow the wounded to Korti the following day. I was surprised at how quickly he had acted. He must have spent the previous night wrestling with alternatives. Once he had seen things for himself, however, there was really only one course of action he could take to preserve his command.

We watched as preparations for our departure began. Many of the camels would be carrying the wounded and the rest of us would have to march on foot. The Irish had proved it could be done and so now the Camel Corps was reduced to one camel for every four men. Correspondents had brought their own animals and while some had been killed by exhaustion or bullets, we had enough for one between two. I shared our best remaining beast with Rafa, but we had to abandon much of my equipment. The tent, its poles, folding table and chair were all piled to make bonfires that would warm us that evening. We had been eking out our food supplies, but now we could only take what we could carry. A great feast was prepared that evening. Goats were slaughtered and cooked over the piles of burning furniture and packing cases. We stuffed ourselves with the fresh meat, biscuits, tinned butter and jam until our beards were sticky with the stuff. Everyone took this last opportunity to get clean, washing ourselves and the best remaining clothes we had.

As we had splashed in the Nile, the long procession of wounded, together with a strong escort made their way over the embankment that the Mahdists had charged down weeks before and on into the Bayuda Desert. They left at dusk to march through the cool of the night; we were set to follow them the following evening. The population of Matammeh watched them depart, but beyond beating some drums showed no sign of interfering.

Perhaps it was indigestion, for that evening I did not sleep well. I held my watch to the flames of the fire to discover it was midnight and then sat on Burleigh's camp chair, which he had saved to destroy at the last minute. Suddenly I realised that the crackle I could hear was not coming from the flames in front of me, but the desert beyond. I got up again to be certain and sure enough, the sound was coming out of the dark desert. Shooting, a lot of shooting. I woke some of the others and together we listened. Was the column of wounded and their escort fighting their way through, or would they be forced back? Had the Mahdi's men anticipated our retreat and prepared an ambush on our line of march again? If the wounded were surrounded and forced to defend themselves in a *zariba*, at least they would know that the rest of us would soon be there too. The following night would be our turn; it did not promise to be a peaceful trip.

The next day was full of preparations. Most soldiers had either heard or been told about the nocturnal gunfire and there was an air of grim determination as we prepared for our own journey. Even after our feasting the night before and packing supplies to get us back to Korti, there was a ridiculously large stockpile to destroy. Hundreds of sacks of flour were thrown into the Nile, along with three thousand pounds of biscuit and many camel loads of tins of bully beef. Orders were given to spike the guns and then sink the two remaining steamers. Naturally, the captains of the vessels protested. The ships were their livelihood and they promised that they could reach our rowing boats coming up the Nile and give them support. Beresford refused to intervene and so the captain of the *Safia* came to me, asking if I could intercede with Buller on their behalf. I could see how some ships would be useful to the boat column and so went in search of the general.

I found him inspecting the camels. Those that had come with us were now well fed and rested, their sores healed and even scars from bullet wounds looked to be on the mend. Those that had come with Buller and the Royal Irish had only had a few days to recover their strength, but would at least make it back to the wells at Abu Klea. I joined a queue of officers waiting for orders or with questions of their own. When my turn came Buller listened patiently as I presented the case to save the ships.

Then he took me to one side, out of earshot of the others. "The boat column is taking longer to row around the bend than expected," he admitted. "The crews are also struggling with supplies; some of their food has gone rotten. They have just attacked a village on the northern tip of the bend, the one where your colleague Power of *The Times* and Gordon's aide were murdered. Unless things change, I doubt they will reach Berber, which means that the steamers are unlikely to be able to reach them. My orders stand: our steamers will have to be destroyed."

I was just thanking him for his time and explanation when another dust-covered officer arrived at his elbow. "Urgent despatch from General Wolseley, sir," he announced holding out a packet. I expected Buller to dismiss me and take it back to his tent, but to my surprise he opened the message in front of me. Unable to contain my curiosity, I stared at the paper but was unable to make out any words. There were several handwritten paragraphs and the first made Buller chuckle in wry amusement, while at the end he shook his head and gave a heavy sigh.

"Her Majesty's Government has changed its mind, Harrison," he announced at last. I made no reply, hoping he would continue. He did not disappoint. "Wolseley tells me that the Grand Old Man acronym for Gladstone has been reversed to MOG, standing for Murderer of Gordon. His government is teetering and needs to be seen to take action. The army has therefore been ordered to destroy the forces of the Mahdi. I am instructed to storm Matammeh without delay and then advance north to meet up with the river column, which will be receiving more supplies." He looked up again from his orders and stared at me in the eye. "Tell me, Harrison, given what you know now, is your opinion the same, that we should retreat?"

I held his gaze and did not hesitate in my response. "It is, sir, especially now I know about the boats. Even if they were resupplied, that would take time we don't have. If you stay here, I fear you will suffer the same fate as General Hicks. I don't want to end up like my colleague O'Donovan who was with him. You cannot hope to beat fifty thousand fanatical soldiers, who will know that we are running out of supplies." I gestured to where men were at that moment throwing sacks of flour into the river. "Even if we still had those stores, they would cut us off and whittle us down to nothing long before we could reach the boats."

"I agree," grunted Buller. "Just make sure you write that in your paper," he growled before turning on his heel. The remark took me by surprise. This was a man who had won the Victoria Cross; his courage was undoubted. I realised that he was perhaps shrewder than people gave him credit for. He knew his boss well. He had seen how Wilson was being blamed for failing to rescue Gordon. Perhaps he suspected that he would be framed for failing to avenge him.

We set off into the desert at six-thirty that evening. It was an army that had already fought its way through the desert once, winning two victories against overwhelming odds, but there was no air of triumph. We had failed to rescue Gordon and word of the great host marching towards us had spread quickly among the men. While no one was foolish enough to suggest that we stay to fight it out, they knew that we were running away. We had travelled thousands of miles, suffered months of hardship, lost friends, and all for nothing.

"It is a sad sight," said Burleigh as we watched them forming up in the fading evening light. "I doubt there will be British boots back here anytime soon."

"There are not that many intact British boots here now," I grumbled. "They look like tramps, but I'll wager that they will fight through anything the Mahdi has placed in our way." I patted the stock of my recovered Martini–Henry rifle, Burleigh had his too. If necessary, we would fight alongside the soldiers, for we had all wagered our lives on this venture. One thousand seven hundred men were gathered before us. Those who had proudly watched the elite of our regiments marching off to war would have been appalled at the view now. Most had thick beards for there had been no shaving soap for months and the hair did at least protect our faces from sunburn. Uniforms were tattered and torn, the cloth left bleached by the sun. Most men still had their cork helmets, some held together with strips of cloth, but the harsh sand and rocks had been ruinous for boots. I had holes in the soles of both of mine and I had ridden a camel nearly all of the way. Many of the Royal Irish Regiment that had come on foot had lost their boots entirely or had remnants

272

wrapped in pieces of grain sacks, of which there was now a plentiful supply after the dumping of flour.

Bugles sounded, proud men straightened their backs, irritable camels growled as they were forced off their knees and slowly the column began to move. The Gardner guns and some of our remaining artillery was at the front, while two of the seven-pounder cannon and around four hundred men, including two hundred Sudanese soldiers from the steamers, formed a guard to watch our rear. The few mounted hussars we had left would scout around the formation. Rafa took the reins of our remaining animal, and we headed off to join the middle of the line.

We were barely half an hour into the march when we came across the *zariba* where St Leger and Cameron were buried. We could smell the place before we could see it, as there were dozens of decomposing camels lying around its perimeter. A few men stepped out of line to search for possessions that had been left behind in our hurried departure. Burleigh and I went across too. I wanted to pay my respects to our colleagues, who had been buried after I had marched off in the square. The grave was undisturbed; there was plenty of carrion around for scavenging creatures without them having to dig. A bloodied bandage had been blown by the wind to wrap itself around the grave marker. Empty bully beef tins and spent cartridge cases glinted in the moonlight, littering the ground. It was a miserable place. I vividly remembered the time not long ago when I thought I might also perish there.

"Let's go," I whispered to Burleigh as though reluctant to disturb its ghosts. "This place gives me the creeps."

There were more spent cartridge cases a mile further on. It must have been where the column with the wounded had been ambushed. We shouted out for any survivors and made a sweep of the scrub on either side. We found no bodies, either our soldiers or the Mahdists. We kept going. By midnight we were finding our way through the acacia forest, searching for gaps that would avoid us being cut to pieces by the wickedly sharp thorns.

As the sun came up, we trudged on, an expanse of scrubby desert before us. There was no sign of the column of wounded who had left the day before, but we did catch the occasional glimpse of their ambushers – small groups of men on camels riding on the horizon on either side of us. They moved off when our hussars approached, but soon returned. Our movements were doubtless being reported back to the Mahdi and his generals.

At noon Buller called a halt to our progress. We were tired and hungry, but our first priority was to find protection from the sun burning down directly overhead. The press corps camels were couched down in two short rows and a groundsheet we had retained for the purpose had its corners tied to each of their saddles to provide a rectangle of shade. Gratefully, we all crawled underneath. Soon tea was brewed while biscuits smeared in jam were passed around for lunch. I was just starting to doze when I heard my name being called by someone outside the shelter. It was one of our hussar scouts leading a sweat-covered horse.

"Colonel Khashm asked me to find you, sir. I have come from the rearguard. He thought you would want to know that they have found your guide."

"Leila?" I gasped, astonished. "But she should be in Khartoum unless… My God she must have persuaded him to come after all. Is her brother with her?"

"No sir…she is in a bad way." The trooper's face creased with concern as he added, "I have seen her – she might not make it."

My brief moment of delight evaporated immediately. "What happened? How did you find her?"

"It was as we were about to enter the acacia forest," he started. "We saw some riders come over a hill about a mile off. As soon as they saw us, they pushed a bundle off the back of a camel onto the ground and rode away again. We thought it might be someone from the detachment with the wounded taken prisoner. A couple of Sudanese soldiers were sent out to look, while I scouted to make sure it was not an ambush. They recognised the woman. They had seen her with you on the *Bordein* so they carried her back."

"How badly is she wounded?" I asked, fearing the answer.

"She is barely conscious, sir. Battered, bruised and bloody. They are bringing her up now to see the surgeons." I ran past him then, back the way we had come, to see the rearguard no more than half a mile off, trudging steadily in our direction. There was a long line of camels in the middle of the group and I searched in vain for one carrying a woman. Most were burdened with bundles of supplies or parts of the seven-pounder cannon. I was on the point of asking when one of the soldiers, guessing my purpose, pointed to the second animal in the line. There was a tarpaulin over the bundle on its back and hanging from beneath it a slender, bloodstained human arm. Tentatively, I reached up, half expecting to feel the chill stiffness of a corpse. With relief I found her fingers warm and supple, but pulling back on the tarpaulin I exclaimed in horror. Draped now in a black robe she was lying face down over some boxes, secured by a rope around her waist. The cover was to protect her from the sun, for she was unconscious. She had clearly been badly beaten. One eye was purple and swollen and another vivid bruise was blossoming on her cheek.

"Leila, can you hear me?" I called, pulling gently on her arm. By way of reply, her good eye flickered briefly open as she uttered a soft groan.

"Are you Harrison?" I looked round to see the colonel of the Royal Irish Regiment striding towards me and nodded. "It is a grim business," he gestured towards Leila. "She has been unconscious since we found her, but that may be just as well. Her back is cut to ribbons – she has been flogged by the look of it. That is why we laid her on her front." He must have seen my stricken expression and gave a smile of sympathy. "I have seen men recover from worse. The surgeons will soon be able to look at her."

Most of the surgeons were in the group ahead with the wounded, but we had one with our column who was summoned as soon as Leila's camel knelt in the centre of the camp. A cursory glance saw her carried to his sickbay, where several other patients nursing cuts and blisters were chivvied off to give her some privacy. When her robe was cut away, I saw that her beautiful slender back was now a bloody ruin. The sawbones gave a grunt of disgust. "They are damned animals to do this to a woman. I will clean and stitch the worst of her wounds," he announced. "It might be easier now while she is insensible. But she will have to be carried flat on a stretcher tomorrow to stop the cuts re-

275

opening." I helped him with the cleaning; we only had a little water to spare and had to dab the gashes with cloth until the edges were clear to be sewn. It took two hours, during which time Leila did not make a sound. "It is a fever," the surgeon explained, "and it is more likely to kill her than her back injuries." When her wounds had been bandaged, I held her gently on her side while the surgeon tried to make her drink some water containing a dose of Warburg's Tincture. Most of it dribbled out of her swollen mouth, and so he resorted to a rubber tube and funnel to get some liquid and the medicine into her. "That is all I can do for now," he announced. "Tomorrow we should catch up with the wounded at Abu Klea. She can rest for a while there."

Leila's stretcher was carried to the press corps shelter where she was laid in the shade, Rafa keeping his mistress' brow cool with a damp cloth. Khashm came to see her too. He explained that she had only uttered one word when they found her, "Ishmael," the name of her brother. "Perhaps she was asking him to help her," he suggested. "We have no idea why she was attacked. I just pray that my sister was not similarly beaten – or worse."

We had covered twelve miles marching through the night on that first day. I was pleased that we delayed our departure until dawn on the second day. If we had to carry the stretcher, I did not want us stumbling over rocks in the dark. Rafa and I started to carry Leila while Burleigh's guide brought on our camel, but we soon found that the duty was shared. Khashm took a turn with the poles as did a number of his Sudanese soldiers; Leila had been popular with them too, chatting in their own tongue. Burleigh and MacDonald did a stint as did a British officer, who looked vaguely familiar. Embarrassed, he admitted that underneath the matted beard he was the same man who had only reluctantly taken her advice when the sandstorm had swept through his company of novice camel riders.

By late morning the oasis at Abu Klea was visible on the horizon and by noon we were enjoying its shade, if not its water. We had to hunt around for a well with any water in at all, for they re-filled slowly from the surrounding rock. Even then, it was the colour and consistency of muddy tea. Thank heavens I had not abandoned my filter, for the liquid was probably rife with pestilence. We strained off the worst, but the contents in the bottom can were still far from clear and so we boiled it too for good measure. Rafa managed to gently hold Leila so that she drank half a cupful, but she was still incoherent and delirious. We wrapped her in blankets and left her to rest. I longed to get back to Jakdul with its big tanks of clear, cool water, but that was a trek of some fifty miles. The surgeon insisted it was out of the question if Leila was to survive. He treated her with more of the tincture and asserted that she would have to rest for several days until the fever broke. Only then could she be moved. The words were barely out of his mouth before we heard the sound of gunfire to the south. Mahdists were closing in, using the scrub around us to snipe on the oasis.

That afternoon, the Royal Irish occupied what little high ground there was to provide some cover. They had missed the earlier battles and were keen to get stuck in. Yet the Mahdists were not fools and stayed at the extreme range for their Remingtons, which made them hard to spot amongst the squat little bushes and clumps of desert grass that dotted the surrounding landscape. The following day Buller announced that all but the rearguard and the wounded who could not travel would march on to Jakdul. The wells at Abu Klea clearly could not support a large number of men. The rearguard would buy time for the rest to make their escape. Buller himself would stay to command the rearguard, leaving Boscawen in charge of the rest of the column.

There was a part of me that felt a twinge of envy as I watched Burleigh and the others take their leave. We had made our farewells and promised each other drinks in Korti, but everyone knew that the Mahdi and his vast army was on our trail, fanatics driven by religious fervour and a thirst to destroy us. Perhaps even Korti would not be safe. They could follow us like some Mongol horde, all the way to Egypt. Yet for all that, there was no way I could abandon Leila. She had been my guide and lover for months. I had thought I had lost her once before when she headed south; I was not going to lose her again. Rafa and I tended to her that night, but while she thrashed about fitfully as though in troubled dreams, she did not say a word.

The following day the gunfire from the desert increased and the Royal Irish began to take casualties. Beresford and his naval party had stayed too, parochially guarding their pair of Gardners. They had a longer range than the rifles, but ammunition had to be used sparingly. His Lordship confided that they had fired nearly five thousand rounds from the *Safia*. Then in the afternoon we saw Mahdists bringing up a Krupps gun. It was slowly hauled across the desert and set up out of range of the Gardners. Buller held our gunners back from interfering and watched as it opened fire. We had heard distant cheering, which must have boosted the morale of those out in the scrub. The gunnery, however, was woeful, and the first shell landed a quarter of a mile away. Buller had scoffed. Now our general spoke to men who were among the finest gunners in the British army. "Show them our power," he encouraged. "Destroy that piece with your first shot." One of our seven-pounders was laid and sights checked and double checked. A single crack rang out and an instant later a burst of flame, smoke and dust appeared where the Krupps gun had been. It did not fire again. As the light faded, the Mahdists began to fall back, until the desert was once more as silent as the graves around us.

The next morning dawned quiet too, save for a croak from Leila. Her eyes opened and she smiled with pleasure at the sight of me. While Rafa gave her more to drink, I fetched a surgeon, who confirmed that her fever had broken. "Let her rest," he told us, "she will be ready to move in a few days."

That afternoon as I dozed beside her in the heat, I suddenly felt her hand tighten around mine. I sat up to find her awake and could contain my curiosity no longer. "Can you talk?" I asked. "What on earth happened to you?"

Her eyes welled with tears and for a moment I thought that speech was still beyond her. Then at last she whispered, "Ishmael". I gave her some more water and waited for her to gather some strength to say more. "He called me the whore of the infidels," she gasped at last. "His men wanted to stone me to death, but he, my own brother, ordered me whipped instead." Hot tears of anger ran down her cheeks. "He claimed it was a kindness and sent me back to your army."

278

I did not press her anymore. She was exhausted by her revelations and fell asleep. I went off to find Khashm. I wanted to tell him that his sister was probably safe. We sat together afterwards staring out into the empty desert. "What will you do when we get back to Korti?" I asked.

"There is nothing for me in Egypt," he replied. "While there are only a few routes to cross the desert for an army, there are many more for small groups of men. I will go back in disguise to Khartoum to find any of my family who survive. Then we will find a place where we can live in peace. This Mahdi is too strict – the people will not suffer his rule for long. There will be a rebellion and I will join it."

"Will you do something for me?" I asked.

Khashm grinned. "I know what you will ask, and I will do it gladly."

"What do you think I will ask?"

"You want me to find their leader called Ishmael from Egypt. Then you want me to slide a blade into his ribs while whispering in his ear that it is a gift from the 'whore of the infidels'." It turned out he had understood me exactly.

We had all expected the Mahdists to return in strength the following day, but they did not, nor did they the next day or the one after that. In fact, six days passed before scouts reported a large host of the enemy approaching. They estimated six thousand, but clouds of dust on the horizon beyond indicated yet more were not far behind. Fortunately, by then our situation was much improved. Leila had been well enough to walk a few steps. Restored to her habitual white robes, she looked more her old self. She was eating well and the swellings, while still colourful, were going down. Wolseley had sent Buller six hundred camels and orders that must have crossed with his subordinates advising of our retreat. He was still expecting Matammeh to have been attacked. At least the animals were useful as were the supply dumps that Boscawen established between Abu Klea and Jakdul.

We left the oasis eight days after we arrived, this time with camels to ride, although some of the Royal Irish preferred to stay on foot. Our route was clearly marked by the bleached bones of animals that had died on our advance two months before. Soon we were approaching the black hills of Jakdul and their cool pools of water, but we could not stay there for long. We knew that there was not enough water at Abu Klea to support the large host of the enemy – it had barely been enough for our much smaller column. They would press on to Jakdul without delay.

We spent the day in the cool shady clefts of the rocks, drinking and filling every water bottle to the brim. That evening officers spotted dust clouds to the east and a proposal was put to General Buller. For once he prevaricated; it was against the gentlemanly principles of warfare, even though the enemy had used the same tactic to annihilate the force of General Hicks. In the end he turned a blind eye as his officers organised the poisoning and contamination of the pools. Mouldering animal corpses, the contents of latrine ditches and anything else that would make the water unusable was thrown in. When they had finished, no army would be able to use Jakdul until the winter rains flushed the pools clear. The Mahdi's men would be forced to retreat to Abu Klea and the Nile, suffering a terrible thirst on the way.

I felt no sympathy for them as we set off again in the cool of the night. The devils would have shown us no quarter had we fallen into their hands. Now at least Korti and the route back to Egypt would be safe from their predations. They would come north eventually, though; I did not doubt that. They would follow the Nile, wreaking revenge on any who had helped their enemies – local leaders and villages who had been keen to assist us on our way south, certain the mighty British army would be victorious. Now our once proud soldiers looked weak and beaten in their tattered uniforms. Our retreat north felt like a betrayal, abandoning them to a tyrannical rule.

I was not surprised that I was summoned to see Wolseley within hours of arriving back in Korti. His aide showed me into his tent and then left. It was the first time we had been alone together since my interview with him in Ashanti territory. He did not waste any time on pleasantries but got straight down to business.

"Ah, Harrison, I understand that you have persistently broken military orders while on this campaign. You were told that no correspondents were to board the steamer to Khartoum, yet you disregarded this instruction. Now you have the audacity to submit an account of the journey for transmission." He reached among the papers on his desk and held up the opened envelope with my handwriting on it. I swear his neatly trimmed moustache bristled with pompous pride as he announced, "I hope you will appreciate that in the circumstances I cannot countenance its transmission."

I felt a cold fury build in me, but stayed calm as, unbidden, I sat down in a canvas chair opposite his desk. His eyebrows rose in surprise as I took a deep breath and brushed some of the desert dust off my trousers. "You don't understand, do you?" I started. "When generals are victorious, we have no choice but to paint you as heroes." Now I looked him in the eye and smiled with absolutely no warmth at all. "But when generals fail, the public, our readers, will want to apportion blame. We correspondents will decide who are the heroes and the villains. We are united that Colonel Wilson will not be blamed for this catastrophe. You will send that despatch, or we will heap such ordure on your head that you will not be given the command of a Hackney Omnibus, never mind an army."

"How dare you threaten me," he began. Puffing himself up he jabbed a finger across the desk. "You are a nobody, while I have a string of successful campaigns to my name. My officers will back me up. If you speak one word against me, I will see you ruined."

"A string of successes *until now*," I stressed. "Anyone who studies this venture will see that it was doomed to fail from the outset. Your precious boats would never have reached Khartoum in time to have saved Gordon. Even if the desert column had arrived en masse at the city, it would not have been enough to drive off fifty thousand fanatics. As for your officers," I concluded, "I think you will find that they are far more interested in protecting their own reputations than yours."

His mouth opened and closed twice without emitting a sound. Then he deflated slightly as he stared down at the papers on his desk, where I suspected there was evidence of my final point. "You would not dare—" he started, but I cut him off.

"It won't just be the press," I warned him. "Thousands of the best men in the army have toiled the last six months rowing in a futile mission up the Nile. They have barely had sight of the enemy and were still hundreds of miles away when Gordon was butchered. What do you

281

think their officers will say to their influential friends when they finally return to civilisation?"

Wolseley sat back in his chair as the realisation dawned that he could not keep the press silent for ever. For years he had treated us with contempt, going out of his way to make life difficult by excluding us from supplies and banning us from transport. Now these chickens were coming home to roost.

"But why?" he whispered the words, almost in an appeal.

I thought back to Burnaby, St Leger, Cameron and the men whose names I did not know. There was the Sudanese soldier securing the funnel on the *Bordein,* the sergeant shot several times while lying wounded on his cacolet, not to mention the hundreds who had succumbed to disease on the journey. They had all died in vain, due to the vanity of this man who had refused to adapt his plans for the seasons or the circumstances. I also recalled my last interview with Wolseley when we had been fighting the Ashanti. "It is in the national interest, old boy," I told him, getting up and leaving the tent.

Historical Notes

Many of the historical characters below would merit a book in their own right, indeed several already have autobiographies and biographies, some more than one. I have therefore included on the following pages abridged details on the leading players to enhance the content of the book. We are now in an era where most have stood in front of a camera. The exception is the Mahdi. As he believed that the use of the train merited execution as an apostate, it is unlikely anyone was brave enough to suggest that he sat for a photographer.

For a more detailed account of the efforts to rescue General Gordon I can recommend *Khartoum: The Ultimate Imperial Adventure* by Michael Asher and *Beyond the Reach of Empire* by Mike Snook. Both include a large amount of first-hand material from the books mentioned above. The authors have also visited the Sudan to view battlefields for themselves – something not recommended even today without a large, heavily armed escort.

Wolseley

General Garnet Wolseley did not command a campaign again after the Gordon Relief Expedition. However, most of the blame for this disaster was apportioned to Gladstone, who had delayed the start of the venture. Many considered that by the time Wolseley was given the go ahead, it was already far too late for it to succeed. While Harrison is critical, had Wolseley sent the whole ten thousand relief force through the Bayuda, it is likely that water supplies would have been insufficient, particularly at Abu Klea. After all, there was not enough water for the much smaller returning force to stay there for more than a day. Some historians believe he would have done much better to use the Red Sea route and capture the water holes on the way to Berber. While not without risk, this would have taken months off the time to reach Khartoum.

There are accounts of Wolseley purposefully misleading journalists. He does recommend doing so in his published guide for officers. He also excluded correspondents from official military transport and military supplies on the journey up the Nile.

Wolseley was born in Ireland to minor Anglo–Irish nobility. His father died when he was just seven, leaving his mother with seven children to support on an army pension. Unable to afford a commission or Sandhurst, he appealed to a fellow Dubliner, Lord Wellington, for assistance. After some delay, Wellington delivered and he was given an ensign's commission. With no family money, he was forced to seek advancement by demonstrating courage and efficiency. He sought action in Burma, where he was badly wounded and fought bravely throughout the Crimean War, Indian Rebellion and advance to Peking, by which time he was a major. He took leave to investigate the American Civil War, meeting Generals Lee, Longstreet and Jackson. Then he served in Canada, where he first came to national attention by the efficient way that he put down a rebellion in a remote area of the country, leading to a knighthood. This was followed by an exemplary campaign against the Ashanti in West Africa, timed between the fever seasons. This made him a household name in Britain as well as earning him the thanks of Parliament, a grant of £25,000 and promotion to general.

He earned more honours for putting down the revolt of the Egyptian army in Egypt, and perhaps surprisingly, another vote of thanks for leading the Gordon expedition. This was in August 1885, under the new Tory administration, which in opposition had been pressing Gladstone to act sooner. He later replaced the Duke of Cambridge as Commander in Chief of the army. He died in 1913.

Gladstone

Shortly after confirmation of Khartoum's fall reached London, news came of a Russian advance towards Afghanistan. The danger was probably exaggerated as it provided an excuse to withdraw British forces from the Sudan and Egypt. Despite this, Gladstone's popularity did not recover from the death of Gordon. A rebuke from the queen on the failure of the rescue mission was leaked to the press. Gladstone was forced to resign as prime minister in June 1885. He regained the premiership, albeit briefly, the following year. He was soon in opposition once more, but led Britain again from 1892–94.

In all, Gladstone was prime minister for twelve years, spread over four non-consecutive terms, as well as serving a similar spell as chancellor of the exchequer. He had a political career of over sixty years and was one of the great statesmen of the nineteenth century.

Gordon

The son of an army officer, Charles George Gordon entered the Royal Military Academy at fifteen, training to be an engineer. His first posting was to Wales, which would have been uneventful, but for the fact that he experienced a profound conversion to Christianity, having previously been disinterested in religious matters. From this point on, his faith was to govern much of his life.

He served in the Crimean War, gaining a reputation for calmness under fire. He was not slow to protest against orders he disagreed with and railed against the use of Russian women as slaves by Britain's Turkish allies. Like Wolseley he then went on to serve in China on the march to Peking. He remained in China where he was given the command of the Ever Victorious Army, intended to protect Shanghai. Under Gordon's leadership it did achieve a string of successes, with its general often leading from the front, armed only with a cane. His achievements were lauded in the press at Shanghai and subsequently in London, where Queen Victoria viewed him as an outstanding example of one of her officers with high moral standards. As well as Chinese honours, he was promoted to colonel and given a knighthood on completing his assignment.

Frustrated with peacetime activities, he visited Constantinople where he was offered the governorship of Kordofan province in Sudan. This would give him the opportunity to quell the slave trade in the region, a goal that was close to his heart. Having been given leave from the British army, he took the post and served with vigour and some success. He was frustrated with the corruption and obstacles put in his way by many, including the governor general of Sudan, and resigned his post after three years. Instead of accepting the resignation, the Egyptians offered Gordon the chance to rule the whole of Sudan as the new governor general, which he accepted. He thought this would give him the power to quell the slave trade and he did have much more success, capturing the leading slaver Zubair. He finally left the Sudan in July 1879, exhausted after five and a half years' service. The lapse back into corrupt ways under his replacement created resentment which helped the Mahdi attract followers when he declared himself a prophet in 1881.

The dilemma the Mahdi presented Britain and Gordon's final involvement in the Sudan was largely as described in this book. There is a famous painting of Gordon's death, *General Gordon's Last Stand* by George William Joy, and a film, *Khartoum*, starring Charlton Heston as Gordon; both depict him unarmed and putting up no resistance at his death. However, the only one of his officers who fought alongside him at the end and survived describes a different scene. In his account Gordon went down fighting. He was firing his revolver into the enemy when he was stabbed in the back with a spear. His head was presented to the Mahdi, while his body was probably tipped into the Nile.

A number of his contemporaries talk about his piercing blue eyes and religious manner. One commentator described him as a prophet pretending to be a general, while the Mahdi was a general pretending to be a prophet.

Wilson

There is no record of any war correspondent travelling on the *Bordein*, although Melton Prior did try to smuggle himself aboard and was discovered before departure. The main source for what happened on the voyage is the detailed account written by Sir Charles Wilson himself called *From Korti to Khartoum*. Harrison's account ties in closely with this work including the trials through the cataracts, how Colonel Khashm al-Mus Bey deceived the Mahdists into allowing them back through the Sabaloka Gorge and how both vessels foundered. It even includes incidental details such as the unknown Sudanese soldier bravely securing the funnel and Khashm's various relatives, including the local Mahdist commander, visiting them while marooned on the island.

There were attempts by Wolseley and others, such as Beresford, to pin the blame for the failure to rescue Gordon on Wilson. They claimed that he had delayed too long at Matammeh before embarking for Khartoum. However, this ignored reports from prisoners of Mahdist armies marching on his command from the north and south, when he arrived on the shores of the Nile. The ships also needed refuelling for the journey. When the full facts were known, his conduct in fighting the square to the Nile was considered exemplary and his return from Khartoum little short of a miracle. He too was given a vote of thanks from parliament for his contribution to the campaign.

The Bordein

Astonishingly, the *Bordein* can still be seen in Khartoum. This is not due to any fond recollection by the Sudanese of Wilson's exploits, but instead because it is the oldest surviving paddle steamer on the Nile. She is pictured here in a less armoured state than Wilson's time and in her current condition. She had been abandoned as a wreck but has now been restored. (Hopefully the vessel has survived the more recent bout of shelling and civil war in the region.)

Beresford

Lord Charles Beresford was a well-connected naval officer, personal friend of the Prince of Wales and something of a self-publicist. He first won fame at the bombardment of Alexandria, where he had ensured that he had two war correspondents aboard his vessel to report on his heroics. He certainly did not lack confidence; his determination to prove the value of his Gardner gun at Abu Klea nearly resulted in the breaking of the square and did cost the lives of Burnaby and most of the naval party manning the gun.

He was a staunch critic of Wilson, claiming in his memoirs that he had been ready to sail the *Bordein* to Khartoum as soon as it had arrived. In reality he was incapacitated by the boil on his rump and knew that the vessels needed refuelling. One of the war correspondents, MacDonald, forced him to publish a correction. Aboard the *Safia*, Beresford did conduct the rescue of Wilson's party, despite the damage to the boiler. A small boy really was used to make the repair and Beresford did organise the apparent abandonment of the vessel to deter the Mahdists from firing at it all night. He too was commended by parliament for his contribution to the campaign.

Buller

Redvers Buller was a man of undoubted courage, carrying out several heroic rescues during the Zulu Wars that earned him the Victoria Cross. He was one of Wolseley's inner circle, known as the Ashanti Ring, but showed that he was capable of swift independent action when he arrived at Matammeh. He quickly assessed the situation and saw that his orders from Wolseley were impractical. His retreat from the Nile saved his command. As Harrison suggests, Buller was probably an alcoholic at this time, and certainly travelled in style. He had forty-six camels for his personal supplies, including prodigious quantities of champagne.

He was given command of British forces during the Second Boer War and while slow to adapt to Boer tactics, he was to some extent scapegoated for a series of military failures. He was later dismissed from the army.

Cochrane

Those who have read my earlier series of books, in which Cochrane's ancestor features heavily, may think I have taken a flight of fancy to include a Cochrane in this account. However, Lord Archibald Cochrane was there, and as described by Harrison, spent much of his time in charge of the baggage train. He published a memoir of his adventures in the Sudan, which can still be bought today. While he was on campaign, he received news that his father had died and he had become the twelfth Earl of Dundonald.

Burleigh

Bennet Burleigh's extraordinary career is as mentioned by Harrison. He did flee to the United States to escape responsibilities at home and took part in the Civil War. He fought for the Confederates, twice escaping from prison. He was a tenacious gatherer of news and with his fighting experience, was one of the leaders amongst the group of correspondents who travelled to Sudan. He fought in the squares as described by Harrison and was the first war journalist to be mentioned in despatches for running boxes to help fortify the areas around the Matammeh *zariba*. He did try to flee the square when he thought all was lost, but was forced to return by enemy cavalry. Perhaps he had lost some of his nerve as a result, for otherwise he would have been almost certain to try and travel onboard the *Bordein*.

Burnaby

Frederick (Fred) Burnaby was another Victorian hero, a colonel in the Household Cavalry and a man of undoubted strength and courage, yet the fighting in the Sudan was to be the first and last military action he was to experience. He was a tall man, six foot four inches, and had immense strength. There are accounts of him carrying two small ponies down a flight of stairs, one under each arm. He had made his name as an explorer, using his long periods of leave to go on expeditions. This had taken him to Khartoum during Gordon's earlier tenure but his most famous adventures had been through Central Asia. Much of this region was closed to travellers, but Burnaby planned to travel from St Petersburg all the way to Afghanistan. The trip took four months during the winter of 1875–6. He did not reach his destination but visited many unknown kingdoms that were soon to be crushed by an invasion from Russia. The published account of his travels that freezing winter, *A Ride to Khiva*, was immediately popular and brought him fame, which only increased with his other exploits, such as crossing the English Channel in a hot air balloon.

Initially, he had travelled to the Sudan on leave at the request of the wife of his friend, Valentine Baker. She had wanted an officer with her husband who could be relied upon. He had thus gone to war for the first time in a tweed hunting jacket, armed with a shotgun. He was one of the few survivors of the first battle of El Teb and also managed to rescue his valet, who had gone to war with him. Accounts of precisely how the square was opened at Abu Klea are not aligned, but it seems likely that Burnaby swung part of the rear face round to help protect the crew of the Gardner. He had not realised that Mahdists were hidden in a dip behind the square and when they charged into the breach, he was quick to try and close it again. To give his soldiers time to reform, he engaged the enemy outside the square. He fought ferociously, rescuing several other soldiers that had been cut off in the melee before taking a spearpoint to the throat.

Baker

Every newspaper subscriber in Britain knew of the name Valentine Baker, but not for his many military accomplishments. He had enjoyed an outstanding career, showing courage in the Crimean War, becoming colonel of a fashionable cavalry regiment, the 10th Hussars. The unit was also known as the Prince of Wales' Own; the queen's eldest son was its honorary colonel and became a close friend of Baker. He had also travelled with Burnaby on one of his adventures and been an observer in the Franco–Prussian war. All seemed set for greater glory, until he shared a train carriage with a Miss Dickinson on a journey to Dover. This pretty young woman was later found hanging on to the outside of the train, accusing Baker of indecently assaulting her. (The incident led to the introduction of corridor coaches.) There was a great scandal, a trial with Baker found guilty and sent to prison for a year. To add to his disgrace, the queen cashiered him from the army as a dissolute influence on her already wayward heir. Forced to leave the country after his release, Baker had found employment in the Ottoman Empire, but was now desperate to restore his reputation by some martial valour.

The British controlled Egyptian army appointments, but the Khedive had the power to appoint his own head of the police force, which had been trained with rifles to deal with any civil insurrection. Baker was appointed its chief. When war broke out in the Sudan, the Khedive wanted to rescue some of his garrisons by the Red Sea, but the British government was reluctant to release Egyptian army units. They had British officers among them and after the Hicks disaster, Gladstone did not want any more British casualties. The Khedive decided to use the only other unit available to him: his police force under Baker. The Mahdist warriors had already developed a fearsome reputation amongst Egyptians, who were aware of the annihilation of the much larger force under Hicks. As Leila described, many policemen were horrified at the prospect of fighting in the Sudan and some took extreme measures to avoid the posting.

On arrival in Sudan, Baker completely underestimated the fighting ability of the Beja, who were armed with just spears and swords. He probably also did not fully appreciate how low the morale of his own force was. He had three and a half thousand men, nearly all armed with modern breach-loading rifles and some artillery, while the enemy in the region were less than a thousand. When he marched inland, the Beja showed themselves on some high ground near a place called El Teb, at the end of a trail. Baker led his men straight towards them down the track, unaware that most of the Beja force was hidden in the desert on either side. At a signal they attacked, rising up out of the ground and taking the Egyptians completely by surprise. There was immediate panic-stricken confusion amongst Baker's force and it was impossible to organise any defence. Most of those who were mounted, like Baker and Burnaby, were able to cut their way out and get away, but only around seven hundred of the three and a half thousand men made it back to the shore.

Baker remained to ensure that the British force, which arrived just weeks later, did not make the same mistakes he had. He fought bravely at the second battle of El Teb, where he was wounded. He never did restore his reputation and died, still head of the Egyptian police, four years later.

Mahdi

Born Muhammad Ahmad, the Mahdi came from a family of boat builders, but he followed a career of religious study. He eventually built his own mosque and developed a reputation as a powerful speaker and mystic. In 1881 he was persuaded by one of his followers called Abdullahi (who succeeded him) to declare himself the Mahdi, the chosen prophet, to unite the people of Islam. Initially, he got little recognition, but as he gradually defeated or evaded forces sent by the Khedive to arrest him, he attracted attention. He acquired both Muslim and non-Muslim followers, who joined his cause for both religious and political reasons – seeing his movement as a means to liberate them from the corrupt Egyptian regime. To attract followers, and in breach of traditional Islamic injunctions, the Mahdi allowed the enslavement of free Muslims if they did not support him and forbade the enslavement of traditional slaves, such as the black tribes to the south, if they did support him. The defeat of the army under Hicks greatly increased his reputation and he controlled a territory stretching from the Red Sea to Central Africa. The capture of Khartoum was the high point in his rule. Perhaps there was a curse on him if Gordon was killed, for the Mahdi himself was dead six months later. He probably died of typhus although there were more colourful rumours that he had been murdered by a concubine.

The movement and nation he created was to survive his death, under the rule of his successor, for another thirteen years.

Kitchener

Colonel Herbert Kitchener led the scouts for the Gordon Relief Expedition, often ranging ahead of the army disguised in Arab dress. Born in Ireland, he had been brought up in Switzerland and had volunteered in a French ambulance during the Franco–Prussian War. He caught pneumonia when he had ascended in a hot air balloon to see the Army of the Loire in action. He was commissioned into the British Royal Engineers in 1871 and had various postings, mostly in the Middle East where he surveyed what was then Palestine. He was fluent in Arabic and could master its dialects. This may have been appreciated by the Arabs he worked with, but he was less popular amongst his British colleagues. Kitchener was a loner, socially awkward, brusque and intimidating to junior ranks. There was no doubting his efficiency, though and he did an excellent job of scouting for Wolseley. By 1892 he was a brigadier and in command of the Egyptian army.

In 1896 Kitchener was given orders to invade Northern Sudan and capture Khartoum. It was something that he must have been considering since the Gordon Relief Expedition as he already had settled in his mind how it would be done. He had learned from Wolseley's experience; instead of using the Nile, he would build a railroad. The rail line the old Khedive had built was already being extended to Wadi Halfa on the Egyptian/Sudanese border. Now Kitchener planned to build two new lines. The first would go from Wadi Halfa to Dongola, supporting his army as he drove the enemy back from the northern part of Sudan. The second would go from Wadi Halfa to Abu Hamed, at the top of the northern bend in the Nile. This would take out five hundred miles of the twisting river and leave a relatively straight stretch of water south to Khartoum. This railway line would then be extended as they advanced to maintain supplies, until it reached the Sudanese capital. An extraordinary feat of engineering would be required to build this second track over two hundred miles of the hostile Nubian desert and then over three hundred miles following the river. Every rail, sleeper, nut and bolt, not to mention the locomotives, carriages, coal and tools had to be sent down the existing lines, as well as food and water for the workforce. An engineer himself, Kitchener could appreciate the difficulties and appointed Percy Girouard, one of the very best railway engineers, to lead the project.

Girouard got to work. Few if any of the workers had any railway building experience and more had to be trained to run the railway as signallers, station masters, engineers etc when it was complete. A workforce of nearly a thousand men was recruited. While they could be protected from thirst, hunger and Mahdists, sadly little could be done about disease and several hundred died in a typhus epidemic.

Dongola was captured in late 1896 and the second line begun the following year. Progress was slow and steady. By 1898 Kitchener's army had reached the stretch of Nile north of Khartoum with the railway following in its wake. The Mahdists were driven out of Berber and a battle was fought at Atbara in April. By September 1898 the army had reached Omdurman. The battle there saw a British and Egyptian force of twenty thousand face a Mahdist army of around fifty thousand. While outnumbered, Kitchener's force had vastly better artillery, machine guns and armed gunboats in support. Despite fighting bravely, the Mahdists suffered an overwhelming defeat, with twelve thousand killed, a similar number wounded and five thousand taken prisoner. Kitchener's force lost less than fifty men killed and fewer than four hundred wounded. Bennet Burleigh was present at this battle too.

In the eyes of many, Gordon had been avenged. The Mahdi's tomb was desecrated and his remains thrown into the Nile. It was alleged that Kitchener kept the skull, but after an outcry this was buried at Wadi Halfa. The tomb has since been restored.

Kitchener went on to command British forces during the Boer War in South Africa and in India. At the outset of the First World War, Kitchener was appointed as Secretary of State for War. His face and pointing finger were famously used in recruitment posters and he was instrumental in organising a massive recruitment campaign for the army. In 1916 he was killed when the ship he was travelling on to Russia, struck a mine and sank in a storm. He was the most senior British officer lost in the war.

War Correspondents Killed

In most campaigns war correspondents stay safely at the rear to do their reporting and survive unscathed. The war in the Sudan, however, produced a particularly heavy butcher's bill for British newspapers. **Edmund O'Donovan** of the *Daily News* and **Frank Vizetelly** of the *Illustrated London News* were both with General Hicks when he was attacked and never heard from again.

Frank Power of the *Times*, aged just twenty-six, was murdered with Gordon's aide and others when their steamer was wrecked on the northern tip of the great bend of the Nile.

The *Manchester Guardian* correspondent, **Captain William Henry Gordon**, was lost in the desert between Korti and Jakdul. He was never seen again and presumed died of thirst.

At the battle near Matammeh **St Leger Herbert** and **John Alexander Cameron** were killed while Bennet Burleigh, Harry Pearse and Frederic Villiers were wounded.

Also by this author

Assignment Paris

In addition to the eleven volume Thomas Flashman series, Robert Brightwell is writing the 'Assignment' series featuring fledgling war correspondent, Thomas Harrison. Readers of Robert's Flashman books may find descriptions of his grandfather familiar and certainly this Thomas has similar personality traits.

Harrison's first assignment sees him sent to Paris. After an idyllic start, things go downhill fast when he joins the French army on its march to Berlin in the Franco–Prussian war of 1870. He soon learns that despite advantages in weaponry, he has joined a force that can turn snatching defeat from the jaws of victory into an art form. Suffice to say that the citizens of Berlin evade trouble and Paris soon finds itself under threat.

Thomas is at the heart of a crucial period in French history that would later lead to two World Wars. He risks death by shelling, is sentenced to death in a bizarre kangaroo court and nearly freezes in a winter attack. Having fought with the French army, he later finds himself attacked by it, as he is drawn by a vision of beauty into a world of rebellion and revolution.

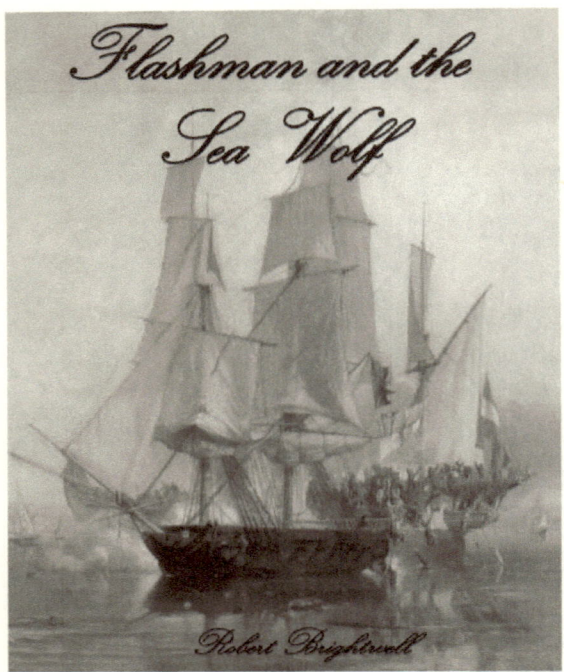

Flashman and the Seawolf

This first book in the Thomas Flashman series covers his adventures with Thomas Cochrane, one of the most extraordinary naval commanders of all time.

From the brothels and gambling dens of London, through political intrigues and espionage, the action moves to the Mediterranean and the real life character of Thomas Cochrane. This book covers the start of Cochrane's career including the most astounding single ship action of the Napoleonic war.

Thomas Flashman provides a unique insight as danger stalks him like a persistent bailiff through a series of adventures that prove history really is stranger than fiction.

Flashman and the Cobra

This book takes Thomas to territory familiar to readers of his nephew's adventures, India, during the second Mahratta war. It also includes an illuminating visit to Paris during the Peace of Amiens in 1802.

As you might expect Flashman is embroiled in treachery and scandal from the outset and, despite his very best endeavours, is often in the thick of the action. He intrigues with generals, warlords, fearless warriors, nomadic bandit tribes, highland soldiers and not least a four-foot-tall former nautch dancer, who led the only Mahratta troops to leave the battlefield of Assaye in good order.

Flashman gives an illuminating account with a unique perspective. It details feats of incredible courage (not his, obviously) reckless folly and sheer good luck that were to change the future of India and the career of a general who would later win a war in Europe.

Flashman in the Peninsula

While many people have written books and novels on the Peninsular War, Flashman's memoirs offer a unique perspective. They include new accounts of famous battles, but also incredible incidents and characters almost forgotten by history.

Flashman is revealed as the catalyst to one of the greatest royal scandals of the nineteenth century which disgraced a prince and ultimately produced one of our greatest novelists. In Spain and Portugal he witnesses catastrophic incompetence and incredible courage in equal measure. He is present at an extraordinary action where a small group of men stopped the army of a French marshal in its tracks. His flatulent horse may well have routed a Spanish regiment, while his cowardice and poltroonery certainly saved the British army from a French trap.

Accompanied by Lord Byron's dog, Flashman faces death from Polish lancers and a vengeful Spanish midget, not to mention finding time to perform a blasphemous act with the famous Maid of Zaragoza. This is an account made more astonishing as the key facts are confirmed by various historical sources.

Flashman's Escape

This book covers the second half of Thomas Flashman's experiences in the Peninsular War and follows on from *Flashman in the Peninsula*. Having lost his role as a staff officer, Flashman finds himself commanding a company in an infantry battalion. In between cuckolding his soldiers and annoying his superiors, he finds himself at the heart of the two bloodiest actions of the war. With drama and disaster in equal measure, he provides a first-hand account of not only the horror of battle but also the bloody aftermath.

Hopes for a quieter life backfire horribly when he is sent behind enemy lines to help recover an important British prisoner, who also happens to be a hated rival. His adventures take him the length of Spain and all the way to Paris on one of the most audacious wartime journeys ever undertaken.

With the future of the French empire briefly placed in his quaking hands, Flashman dodges lovers, angry fathers, conspirators and ministers of state in a desperate effort to keep his cowardly carcass in one piece. It is a historical roller-coaster ride that brings together various extraordinary events, while also giving a disturbing insight into the creation of a French literary classic!

Flashman and Madison's War

This book finds Thomas, a British army officer, landing on the shores of the United States at the worst possible moment – just when the United States has declared war with Britain! Having already endured enough with his earlier adventures, he desperately wants to go home but finds himself drawn inexorably into this new conflict. He is soon dodging musket balls, arrows and tomahawks as he desperately tries to keep his scalp intact and on his head.

It is an extraordinary tale of an almost forgotten war, with inspiring leaders, incompetent commanders, a future American president, terrifying warriors (and their equally intimidating women), brave sailors, trigger-happy madams and a girl in a wet dress who could have brought a city to a standstill. Flashman plays a central role and reveals that he was responsible for the disgrace of one British general, the capture of another and for one of the biggest debacles in British military history.

Flashman's Waterloo

The first six months of 1815 were a pivotal time in European history. As a result, countless books have been written by men who were there and by those who studied it afterwards. But despite this wealth of material there are still many unanswered questions including:

-Why did the man who promised to bring Napoleon back in an iron cage, instead join his old commander?

-Why was Wellington so convinced that the French would not attack when they did?

-Why was the French emperor ill during the height of the battle, leaving its management to the hot-headed Marshal Ney?

-What possessed Ney to launch a huge and disastrous cavalry charge in the middle of the battle?

-Why did the British Head of Intelligence always walk with a limp after the conflict?

The answer to all these questions in full or in part can be summed up in one word: Flashman.

This extraordinary tale is aligned with other historical accounts of the Waterloo campaign and reveals how Flashman's attempt to embrace the quiet diplomatic life backfires spectacularly. It includes the return of old friends and enemies from both sides of the conflict and is a fitting climax to Thomas Flashman's Napoleonic adventures.

Flashman and the Emperor

This seventh instalment in the memoirs of the Georgian rogue Thomas
Flashman reveals that, despite his suffering through the Napoleonic
Wars, he did not get to enjoy a quiet retirement. Indeed, middle age
finds him acting just as disgracefully as in his youth, as old friends pull
him unwittingly back into the fray.

He re-joins his former comrade in arms, Thomas Cochrane, in what is
intended to be a peaceful and profitable sojourn in South America.
Instead, he finds himself enjoying drug-fuelled orgies in Rio, trying his
hand at silver smuggling and escaping earthquakes in Chile before
being reluctantly shanghaied into the Brazilian navy.

Sailing with Cochrane again, he joins the admiral in what must be one
of the most extraordinary periods of his already legendary career. With
a crew more interested in fighting each other than the enemy, they use
Cochrane's courage, Flashman's cunning and an outrageous bluff to
carve out nothing less than an empire which will stand the test of time.

Flashman and the Golden Sword

Of all the enemies that our hero has shrunk away from, there was one he feared above them all. By his own admission they gave him nightmares into his dotage. It was not the French, the Spanish, the Americans or the Mexicans. It was not even the more exotic adversaries such as the Iroquois, Mahratta or Zulus. While they could all make his guts churn anxiously, the foe that really put him off his lunch were the Ashanti.

"You could not see them coming," he complained. "They were well armed, fought with cunning and above all, there were bloody thousands of the bastards."

This eighth packet in the Thomas Flashman memoirs details his misadventures on the Gold Coast in Africa. It was a time when the British lion discovered that instead of being the king of the jungle, it was in fact a crumb on the lip of a far more ferocious beast. Our 'hero' is at the heart of this revelation after he is shipwrecked on that hostile shore. While waiting for passage home, he is soon embroiled in the plans of a naïve British governor who has hopelessly underestimated his foe. When he is not impersonating a missionary or chasing the local women, Flashman finds himself being trapped by enemy armies, risking execution and the worst kind of 'dismemberment,' not to mention escaping prisons, spies, snakes, water horses (hippopotamus) and crocodiles.

Flashman at the Alamo

When other men might be looking forward to a well-earned retirement to enjoy their ill-gotten gains, Flashman finds himself once more facing overwhelming odds and ruthless enemies, while standing (reluctantly) shoulder to shoulder with some of America's greatest heroes.

A trip abroad to avoid a scandal at home leaves him bored and restless. They say 'the devil makes work for idle hands' and Lucifer surpassed himself this time as Thomas is persuaded to visit the newly independent country of Texas. Little does he realise that this fledgling state is about to face its biggest challenge – one that will threaten its very existence.

Flashman joins the desperate fight of a new nation against a pitiless tyrant, who gives no quarter to those who stand against him. Drunkards, hunters, farmers, lawyers, adventurers and one English coward all come together to fight and win their liberty.

Flashman and the Zulus

While many people have heard of the battle at Rorke's Drift, (featured in the film *Zulu*) and the one at Isandlwana that preceded it, few outside of South Africa know of an earlier and equally bloody conflict. Under a tyrannical king, the Zulu nation defended its territory with ruthless efficiency against white settlers. Only a naïve English vicar, with his family and some translators are permitted to live in the king's capital. It is into this cleric's household that Thomas Flashman finds himself, as a most reluctant guest.

Listening to sermons of peace and tolerance against a background of executions and slaughter, Thomas is soon fleeing for his life, barely a spearpoint ahead of regiments of fearsome warriors. He is soon to learn that there is a fate even worse than his own death. He is pitched in with Boers and British settlers as they fight a cunning and relentless foe. Thomas strives for his own salvation, before discovering that chance has not finished with him yet.

Flashman's Winter

This book fills in two gaps in Flashman's career, hitherto uncovered by his memoirs. The bulk of this volume is taken up with Flashman's adventures in what was then Prussia, but which now comprises Poland, Russia and the Baltic states. In 1806 Prussia declared war on France and in a disastrous campaign lost most of its territory. Russia was forced to come to its aid and Britain too sent observers to assess how to help. Flashman joins this mission in what should have been a safe diplomatic visit – but of course was anything but.

From bloody, frozen retreats to battles in blizzards, he is soon in the thick of the action as a country fights for its very survival. Diplomatic intrigues follow and, with the aid of a Russian countess, our hero uncovers the enemy's plans – and works to frustrate them.

Also included is the short story Flashman's Christmas, set in Paris a few months after the battle of Waterloo. As royalists conduct vindictive purges on former Bonapartists, Flashman is embroiled in a notorious eve of execution jail-break as he is reunited with old friends to outwit old enemies.